# MARY, A FICTION

## and

# THE WRONGS OF WOMAN, OR MARIA

broadview editions
series editor: L.W. Conolly

# MARY, A FICTION

## and

# THE WRONGS OF WOMAN, OR MARIA

## Mary Wollstonecraft

*edited by Michelle Faubert*

**b**

broadview editions

**Library and Archives Canada Cataloguing in Publication**

Wollstonecraft, Mary, 1759-1797
  Mary, a fiction and The wrongs of woman, or, Maria / Mary Wollstonecraft ; edited by Michelle Faubert.

(Broadview editions)
Includes bibliographical references.
ISBN 978-1-55481-022-2

  I. Faubert, Michelle, 1973- II. Title. III. Title: Wrongs of woman. IV. Title: Maria. V. Series: Broadview editions

PR5841.W8M3 2012            823'.6            C2012-900212-7

**Broadview Editions**

The Broadview Editions series represents the ever-changing canon of literature in English by bringing together texts long regarded as classics with valuable lesser-known works.

Advisory editor for this volume: Michel Pharand

Broadview Press is an independent, international publishing house, incorporated in 1985.

We welcome comments and suggestions regarding any aspect of our publications—please feel free to contact us at the addresses below or at broadview@broadviewpress.com.

*North America*
Post Office Box 1243, Peterborough, Ontario, Canada K9J 7H5
2215 Kenmore Avenue, Buffalo, NY, USA 14207
Tel: (705) 743-8990; Fax: (705) 743-8353
email: customerservice@broadviewpress.com

*UK, Europe, Central Asia, Middle East, Africa, India, and Southeast Asia*
Eurospan Group, 3 Henrietta St., London WC2E 8LU, United Kingdom
Tel: 44 (0) 1767 604972; Fax: 44 (0) 1767 601640
email: eurospan@turpin-distribution.com

*Australia and New Zealand*
NewSouth Books
c/o TL Distribution, 15-23 Helles Ave., Moorebank, NSW, Australia 2170
Tel: (02) 8778 9999; Fax: (02) 8778 9944
email: orders@tldistribution.com.au

www.broadviewpress.com

Broadview Press acknowledges the financial support of the Government of Canada through the Canada Book Fund for our publishing activities.

This book is printed on paper containing 100% post-consumer fibre.

Typesetting and assembly: True to Type Inc., Claremont, Canada.

PRINTED IN CANADA

"[A] mother, labouring under a portion of the misery, which the constitution of society seems to have entailed on all her kind ... will dare to break through all restraint to provide for your happiness — ... will voluntarily brave censure herself, to ward off sorrow from your bosom."
*The Wrongs of Woman,* Chapter VII

This book is dedicated to my mother, Yvonne Faubert, and the mother of feminism, Mary Wollstonecraft.

# Contents

# Acknowledgements

I am profoundly grateful to the many individuals and organizations without whose help I could not have completed this edition. I performed a large part of the research and writing of this text during a half-year sabbatical leave from teaching duties at the University of Manitoba Department of English, Film, and Theatre; I owe thanks to my department and the Faculty of Arts at the University of Manitoba for supporting my leave temporally—as well as financially where the Faculty of Arts is concerned, since they provided me with sabbatical funding. I am also thankful to the Social Sciences and Humanities Research Council of Canada for supporting this endeavour financially. The final stages of this edition were completed with the help of an Association of Commonwealth Universities Titular Fellowship, which enabled me to complete it while serving as a Visiting Fellow at Northumbria University, where I printed off the manuscript. Thanks go to Gillian Drinkald and the IT team at Northumbria University for their technical help in the final printing stages of the manuscript, and to Northumbria University for footing the printing costs. I would also like to recognize my students' contributions to this edition. These students are the 2009 graduate class at the University of Manitoba, Romantic Medicine; Bryn Jones-Square, my MA student; and Patricia Cooper and Barbara May. Their enthusiasm for Wollstonecraft's work and insights into her fiction inspired me and helped me to gain a fresh perspective on it.

I also owe a debt of thanks to several individuals who have contributed their time and ideas to the creation of this text. At Broadview Press, Marjorie Mather and the readers of the proposal and manuscript were hugely helpful; Leonard Conolly and Michel Pharand suggested excellent opportunities for additional notes and edited the manuscript with generous care. Pamela Perkins, of the University of Manitoba, also read the proposal and suggested several changes, while David Smith at the Media Lab at the University of Manitoba offered technical and printing support for the sources of this project. Thanks are also due to Flavio Gregori of the University of Venice for directing me to excellent translations of Petrarch's work; Julie Murray of Carlton University for her informative paper on female memoirs at the 2011 ICR conference; and Auste Mickunaite at the British

Library for completing the necessary forms for permissions of Wollstonecraft's texts. The employees in the main Humanities Reading Room at the British Library made my time researching there efficient and most enjoyable; I offer thanks to them for their efforts.

In closing, I want to thank my husband, Javier Uribe, for his tireless support of and interest in my work, especially by accompanying me to research this project in England during the winter of 2010. Finally, I owe a debt of gratitude to Allan Ingram of Northumbria University for reading and commenting on every part of this project, including the proposal. Allan offered me detailed and invaluable advice and information, without which this edition would be poor, indeed. He read carefully every page of it and offered constructive criticism about many passages; several important annotations to the texts would not exist without his keen eye and wealth of knowledge. I am fortunate that Allan was working on the Broadview edition of Jonathan Swift's *Gulliver's Travels* while I was creating this text, and that he so generously shared his experiences of the editorial process and his manuscript with me, which served as a model for many parts of my own manuscript. I am deeply grateful for Allan's mentorship.

# Introduction

Writing was then the only alternative, and she wrote some
rhapsodies descriptive of the state of her mind; but the events
of her past life pressing on her, she resolved circumstantially
to relate them, with the sentiments that experience, and
more matured reason, would naturally suggest. They might
perhaps instruct her daughter, and shield her from the
misery, the tyranny, her mother knew not how to avoid. (*The
Wrongs of Woman*, Chapter II)

Imprisoned in an insane asylum, the protagonist of Mary Wollstonecraft's (1759-97) *The Wrongs of Woman, or Maria* (1798)
writes her memoirs to educate her absent child. The above
description of Maria's instructive story may also function as an
apt summary of both of Wollstonecraft's novellas, the other entitled *Mary, A Fiction* (1788) (hereafter *Maria* and *Mary*). Indeed,
her two sustained works of fiction contain all of the elements
present in the above passage: they are both strongly autobiographical, contain plenty of "sentiment" derived from "reason,"
and aim to show her largely female audience—for women were,
traditionally, the greatest consumers of novels of sensibility and
the Gothic, the genres in which she wrote—how to elude "the
tyranny" that Wollstonecraft, the mother of feminism, "knew not
how to avoid" until, perhaps, her final months. Wollstonecraft's
novellas explore some of the major issues that Romantic-era
culture presented to women, such as the crippling ideals of femininity celebrated in the cult of sensibility or sentiment,[1] unequal

---

1 I use the terms "sentiment" and "sensibility" interchangeably, as Wollstonecraft does in *The Female Reader*: under the heading "False Sensibility," she writes, "There is nothing in which self-deception is more notorious than in what regards sentiment and feeling" (86). I recognize,
however, that she sometimes uses the latter term as indicative of a genuine
and noble characteristic, as in *Mary*, whereas she uses the former term
with aversion as signifying a false sensation and givenness to celebrate
weakness, as in the *Rights of Woman*. For more information on the critical
use of these terms, see Claire Knowles's *Sensibility and Female Poetic
Tradition, 1780-1860* (2009), Jerome McGann's *The Poetics of Sensibility*
(1996), and Chris Jones's *Radical Sensibility* (1993). Other notable critical
works on the novel of sensibility are Helen Small's *Love's Madness:
Medicine, the Novel, and Female Insanity 1800-1865* (1998), R.F. Brissenden's *Virtue in Distress: Studies in the Novel of Sentiment from (continued)*

education, and domestic subjugation. Throughout her work, we may trace her equivocal and sometimes contradictory treatment of these themes and her exploration of how women are formed—and may be reformed—by culture.

Wollstonecraft's novellas bookend her years of writing and political activism. Better known for her polemical prose, such as *A Vindication of the Rights of Men* (1790) and *A Vindication of the Rights of Woman* (1792), Wollstonecraft used her fiction to explore many of the same ideas that appear in these works, such as the question of essentialism in human character: she queries whether people have innate qualities, intelligence, or, indeed, rights (the final element being a product of the first two in many ways). In *Rights of Men*, she denies that the class system reflects a natural hierarchy of people that justly establishes some people as leaders of others. In *Rights of Woman*, she applies these principles to a discussion of women's social situation, arguing that they are not born intellectually weaker, vainer, and more conniving than are men, but that culture makes them so. And in her fiction, she surmises that the forces of culture—such as education, class, occupation, and literature—form female character and identity, but she goes further than merely to describe her gender through these terms. Rather, in Wollstonecraft's hands, fiction becomes a tool that women may use to escape these cultural bonds. Through novellas that attack and attempt to displace the pernicious influence of sentimental literature, Wollstonecraft provides a literary antidote for them.

Despite her admirably bold agenda, these short works of fiction have been given short shrift in Romanticist and even Wollstonecraftian criticism. *Mary* has long been relegated to the critical category of "juvenilia" and *Maria*, which was unfinished at Wollstonecraft's premature death and published by William

---

Richardson to Sade* (1974), and John Mullan's *Sentiment and Sociability: The Language of Feeling in the Eighteenth Century* (1988). I focus on the female novel of sensibility, as Wollstonecraft did for the most part, but there also existed male novels of sensibility in the period, such as Henry Mackenzie's *The Man of Feeling* (1771), Laurence Sterne's *A Sentimental Journey through France and Italy and Continuation of the Bramine's Journal* (1768), and Robert Sadler's *Wanley Penson; or, The Melancholy Man: A Miscellaneous History, in Three Volumes* (1792). Wollstonecraft may draw upon these depictions of male sentiment in *Rights of Men*, where she casts Edmund Burke's writing persona in *Reflections on the Revolution in France* as a disingenuous, sissified man of sentiment. Moreover, Diane Long Hoeveler points out that, in *Mary*, the title-character's love-interest, Henry, is a man of feeling ("Gothic" n.p.).

Godwin in *Posthumous Works of the Author of A Vindication of the Rights of Woman*, is sometimes dismissed as a fragment. At best, the novellas have been treated as the creative expressions of her more famous polemical prose. I wish to suggest, however, that they should not be regarded solely as part of the contextual framework that highlights her more developed prose works, early or unfinished as the novellas may be. Viewed in light of eighteenth-century feminist theories of education, 1790s radicalism, and various medical theories about the development of the mind and gender differences, *Mary* and *Maria* stand as Wollstonecraft's efforts to manifest her complex ideas in terms of plot and character. Moreover, by using fiction to convince her female readers of her claims about the negative influence of sentimental literature upon the female character, Wollstonecraft attempts to counteract its influence and change her readers' characters—an objective that would have seemed unattainable in *Rights of Woman*, given that so few women read polemical prose. In this way, her fiction not only dramatizes her theories in its pages, but it also seeks to replicate Wollstonecraft's principles in the minds of her readers and thereby effect social change.

### Female Friends and Male Tyrants: The Early Years

Any discussion of Wollstonecraft's novellas must begin with an account of her life, as both are strongly autobiographical. One might argue that her fiction is so by necessity. After all, the great theme of almost all of her writing is female education and development, and Wollstonecraft had dedicated her adult life to the education of girls and to her own education; she taught herself German, Italian, and French, for example (Godwin *Memoirs* 64), and read the works of history, philosophy, and medicine that were denied her as a girl. However, to say that Wollstonecraft's childhood education was inadequate to prepare her for a life of intellectual endeavour and political activism is not to say that her childhood was extraordinarily deficient. In fact, her family was middle-class and, at least for a while, rather well off.

Mary Wollstonecraft was born in Spitalfields, London, in 1759, the second of seven children of an Irish mother, Elizabeth Dickson Wollstonecraft, and English father, Edward John Wollstonecraft, the son of a successful weaver.[1] For half a decade

---

1 My main guide for the dates of Wollstonecraft's biography is the chronology in the *Cambridge Companion to Mary Wollstonecraft*, edited by Claudia L. Johnson (xv-xix).

(1763-68), Wollstonecraft's father moved his family from place to place in an effort to set himself up as a gentleman farmer. They eventually settled in Yorkshire, but they were financially and emotionally unstable, as Edward had become a violent alcoholic. This circumstance, coupled with Elizabeth's fearful submission to her husband, and both parents' clear preference for their eldest son, Edward (or "Ned," born in 1757), made domestic life a torment for their eldest daughter.[1]

Perhaps as an escape from her family life, Wollstonecraft formed intense friendships with other girls. The first was Jane Arden, to whom she wrote in late 1773, "I have formed romantic notions of friendship. — I have been once disappointed: — I am a little singular in my thoughts of love and friendship; I must have the first place or none" (*Letters* 13).[2] A few years later, upon moving to Hoxton on the outskirts of London, Wollstonecraft formed a relationship with a neighbouring clergyman and his wife; Mr. Clare undertook to educate Wollstonecraft and the couple thereby earned her love. Through this nurturing relationship, Wollstonecraft met Francis (Fanny) Blood, the object of her life-long devotion and, as Godwin describes the episode in the *Memoirs of the Author of A Vindication of the Rights of Woman* (1798), her first love: "a connection ... originated about this time, between Mary and a person of her own sex, for whom she contracted a friendship so fervent, as for years to have constituted the ruling passion of her mind. The name of this person was Frances Blood; she was two years older than Mary" (19).[3] Wollstonecraft wrote to Jane Arden during these heady first years of friendship that she loved Fanny "better than all the world beside.... To live with this friend is the height of my ambition," adding that "She

---

1  Wollstonecraft wrote to Jane Arden from Bath in early 1780, "my father's violent temper and extravagant turn of mind, was the principal cause of my unhappiness" (*Letters* 23).

2  All citations in this introduction to *Letters* are to *The Collected Letters of Mary Wollstonecraft* (2003), edited by Janet Todd.

3  Unless otherwise stated, all references to Godwin's *Memoirs* in this introduction are to the first edition (*Memoirs of the Author of A Vindication of the Rights of Woman*. London: Johnson, 1798), but I use the second edition in the appendices. I use the first edition here because Godwin edited out some fascinating comments for the second edition, such as his reference to Johann von Goethe's *The Sorrows of Young Werther* (1774) in this passage about Wollstonecraft's first meeting with Fanny, in which, as Godwin depicts it, Fanny played Charlotte to Wollstonecraft's Werther (20).

has a masculine understanding, and sound judgment, yet she has every feminine virtue" (*Letters* 25).[1] To be sure, Wollstonecraft loved Fanny so dearly that she would name her first daughter after her and cast her as Ann, the best friend of the protagonist in her first novella, *Mary*. Wollstonecraft's female friendships showed her a realm of love and appreciation that was not sullied by the gender disparity apparent in her family, such as in her mother's meek submission to her father and both parents' preference for Ned.

Wollstonecraft's relationships with the members of her immediate family would give her first-hand experience with several feminist issues about which she would later write: the dearth of good jobs for middle-class women; their lack of respect within the family and, yet, their unequal share of responsibility for its ailing members; and the trap for women that is marriage. After moving his family to Wales and back to the outskirts of London in 1776-78, Edward Wollstonecraft's dire financial woes continued to plague the family, forcing Wollstonecraft to find work as a paid companion to Mrs. Dawson, of Bath, a situation on which she would later comment in *Thoughts on the Education of Daughters* (1787): for women, she declares,

> Few are the modes of earning a subsistence, and those very humiliating. Perhaps to be an humble companion to some rich old cousin, or what is still worse, to live with strangers, who are so intolerably tyrannical, that none of their own relations can bear to live with them, though they should even expect a fortune in reversion. It is impossible to enumerate the many hours of anguish such a person must spend. (69-70)

Wollstonecraft left this daily lesson in "anguish" in 1781 to care for her dying mother in London. After Elizabeth Wollstonecraft died in 1782, Edward Wollstonecraft remarried and moved to Wales, leaving the remaining children to fend for themselves.

---

1 Such comments have led recent critics to speculate on Wollstonecraft's possible lesbian tendencies. For a discussion of the homosocial and queer aspects of Wollstonecraft's writing and reception, see, for example, Claudia Johnson's *Equivocal Beings* (1995), Katherine Binhammer's "The 'Singular Propensity' of Sensibility's Extremities: Female Same-Sex Desire and the Eroticization of Pain in Late-Eighteenth-Century British Culture" (2003), and Ashley Tauchert's "Escaping Discussion: Liminality and the Female-Embodied Couple in Mary Wollstonecraft's *Mary, A Fiction*" (2000).

Older brother Ned refused his familial responsibilities, too, despite his financial advantages as a London-based lawyer, and Wollstonecraft carried the full weight of responsibility for her younger siblings—in addition to Fanny Blood's family, with whom she lived at this time. To add to her concerns, Wollstonecraft's sister Eliza married Meredith Bishop in 1782, gave birth to a daughter the following year, and then plummeted into an acute postpartum depression. Believing that Bishop was the source of Eliza's troubles, Wollstonecraft helped her sister to flee in secret from her husband and daughter, the latter of whom died in 1784. A letter that Wollstonecraft wrote to another sister, Everina, about their escape describes a scene that expresses the episode poignantly: "to make my trial still more dreadful I was afraid in the coach she was going to have one of her flights [of mania] for she bit her *wedding ring* to pieces" (*Letters* 43). To Wollstonecraft, marriage was the tie that would lead to a woman's downfall, as her experience with her beloved friend, Fanny Blood, would seem to confirm the following year.

Wollstonecraft's first attempt to gain economic independence from the world of men was by opening a school for girls in 1784 at Islington, which failed in immediate terms. However, the endeavour planted the seed of future success for her intellectual life since her entire *oeuvre* may be said to develop her ideas about female education. So dedicated to this endeavour was she that she attempted a second time to establish a school, this time at Newington Green, with Fanny Blood and sister Eliza; sister Everina joined them later that year. Perhaps as important to her intellectual life were the people she met at Newington Green: a famous, dissenting preacher named Richard Price, his circle of radical friends, and Samuel Johnson. Godwin describes the meeting with Dr. Johnson in tantalizing terms:

> It was during her residence at Newington Green, that she was introduced to the acquaintance of Dr. Johnson, who was at that time considered as in some sort the father of English literature. The doctor treated her with particular kindness and attention, had a long conversation with her, and desired her to repeat her visit often. This she firmly purposed to do; but the news of his last illness, and then of his death, inter- vened to prevent her making a second visit. (*Memoirs* 45)

Wollstonecraft enthusiasts cannot but feel frustrated by the prospect of what such a friendship could have produced had it flourished. Despite the positive developments that occurred at Newington Green, Wollstonecraft was not to remain long there, and for a reason that must have confirmed her distrust of marriage. Fanny Blood left the school in 1785 to marry her beloved, Hugh Skeys, in Lisbon, whence Wollstonecraft soon travelled to assist Fanny in the birth of her first child. Fanny died of tuberculosis in Wollstonecraft's arms not long after the baby was born. Godwin reports in the *Memoirs*, "She arrived but a short time before her friend was prematurely delivered, and the event was fatal to both mother and child. Frances Blood, hitherto the chosen object of Mary's attachment, died on the twenty-ninth of November 1785" (46). This momentous event would have confirmed Wollstonecraft's early misgivings about marriage: she believed that Fanny had died because of her submission to her husband's wishes to have children (Fanny was weak and consumptive before she became pregnant). She had written to Jane Arden as early as 1781, "I am averse to any matrimonial tie" (*Letters* 30) and in a later commentary about the marriage of Jane Arden's sister, she wrote to Jane: after the "joy, and all that, is ... over ..., and all the raptures have subsided, and the dear hurry of visiting and figuring away as a bride, and all the rest of the delights of matrimony are past and gone," they will "have left no traces behind them, except disgust" (*Letters* 38).[1] Wollstonecraft's attitude toward marriage and men is unsurprising. After all, she came from a family with an abusive father, and a mother who had submitted meekly to her husband, perhaps like Fanny. In a commentary about Wollstonecraft's relationship with her father, Godwin states memorably, "Mary was what Dr. Johnson would have called, 'a very good hater'" (*Memoirs* 10). She would transform this rage against male tyranny into the most significant early feminist texts in the western world, for she believed female education was the route to increased independence for women.

## Wollstonecraft's Formation as a Radical Feminist Writer

The topic of female education would define Wollstonecraft's literary output and career path, but the "first-mover" for these

---

1 Nor did Wollstonecraft hesitate to express her views of marriage to men. Indeed, in a letter from 1790, written to a mysterious suitor who seems to have offered to marry her in order to keep her financially secure, Wollstonecraft writes: it is "an insult ... the bare supposition that I could for a moment think of *prostituting* my person for a maintenance; for in that point of view does such a marriage appear to me" (*Letters* 174).

crucial biographical developments was prosaic: she needed money. Upon her return from Lisbon, Wollstonecraft was forced to close the school at Newington Green because it had fallen into financial difficulties in her absence. She combined her knowledge about female education and her desperation for money in 1786 when she began writing her first text, "a duodecimo pamphlet of one hundred and sixty pages, entitled, *Thoughts on the Education of Daughters*" (*Memoirs* 51), as Godwin describes it. To pay off her debts, she became a governess in Ireland for the Viscount Kingsborough's family in the same year and was still with them in 1787 when *Thoughts* was published. This work, which was influenced by Wollstonecraft's own experience as a teacher and her reading of such works as *Letters on the Improvement of the Mind, Addressed to a Young Lady* (1777) by Hester Chapone, helped to form her literary fate in another way, too. Seeking publication, she forced herself to overcome her reticence and write to an acquaintance she had acquired at Newington Green, Joseph Johnson. He would go on to publish all of her works and become one of her closest friends and business partners. In her fateful first letter to Joseph Johnson, dated 5 December 1786, she mentions the governing theme of her future writing and, it seems, her inspiration to publish on it quickly: "When I had the pleasure of seeing you, if I mistake not, you mentioned to me, that Mrs. Barbauld intended undertaking a new plan of education" (*Letters* 94-95). She had met Anna Lætitia Barbauld at Johnson's famous supper-parties, at which he also introduced her to such literary notables as the radical writers William Blake, Thomas Holcroft, Thomas Paine, and—most significantly for Wollstonecraft's personal life—William Godwin, her future husband and father of their daughter, Mary, who went on to write *Frankenstein* and marry Percy Bysshe Shelley. Although Wollstonecraft earned only 10 guineas from the publication of *Thoughts* and gave the remuneration to the Bloods, this publishing endeavour shaped her personal and professional destiny.[1]

---

1  The motivation behind her transformation into a writer—the need for money—would also become a major theme in her prose works. Indeed, Wollstonecraft highlights the issue of eighteenth-century women's unequal access to decent jobs in her most famous prose work, *A Vindication of the Rights of Woman*. In Chapter IX, entitled "Of the Pernicious Effects which Arise from the Unnatural Distinctions Established in Society," she writes extensively about how middle-class women's inability to support themselves financially—because of a dearth of good careers for them (undereducated as they are)—forces women to marry for money, which she terms "legal prostitution" (338), a phrase that still shocks and resonates today.

Wollstonecraft's career as an author had begun in earnest by this time and she continued to develop her craft. While in Bristol with the Kingsboroughs, she composed her first works of fiction, *Mary, A Fiction* and the fragmentary "Cave of Fancy." The latter work is modelled after Johnson's *Rasselas* and delineates a physiognomical thesis that was surely inspired by her reading for her unpublished abridgement of *Essays on Physiognomy* by Johann Caspar Lavater. As for *Mary*, Godwin describes the biographical elements, potential reception, and major virtues in *Memoirs*:

> A considerable part of this story consists, with certain modifications, of the incidents of her own friendship with Fanny. All the events that do not relate to that subject are fictitious. This little work, if Mary had never produced any thing else, would serve, with persons of true taste and sensibility, to establish the eminence of her genius. The story is nothing. He that looks into the book only for incident, will probably lay it down with disgust. But the feelings are of the truest and most exquisite class; every circumstance is adorned with that species of imagination, which enlists itself under the banners of delicacy and sentiment. A work of sentiment, as it is called, is too often another name for a work of affectation. He that should imagine that the sentiments of this book are affected, would indeed be entitled to our profoundest commiseration. (59-60)

Godwin touches on one of Wollstonecraft's main objectives for the novellas that bookend her career as a writer: to define and illustrate "true ... sensibility" and obliterate the pernicious influence of false sensibility. As I will show, this aim is bound up with her goal of reforming the female character, the possibilities of which she dramatized in her life by becoming a writer—hardly an appropriate job for a woman, according to most people in the early Romantic period. Wollstonecraft was forced into total devotion to this career path when she was dismissed from her duties as a governess in 1787, perhaps because Lady Kingsborough objected to her bond with her daughter, Margaret.[1] Immediately

---

1 Wollstonecraft describes Margaret, the future Lady Mount Cashell, as "so much attached to me I govern her completely" (*Letters* 124). In the *Letters*, Todd attributes Margaret King's abandonment of her husband in later life to her devotion to Wollstonecraft's teachings, adding, as more proof of her attachment to her former governess, that she *(continued)*

thereafter, Wollstonecraft returned to London to work with Joseph Johnson as a reader and translator. She took great pleasure in her new independence and livelihood. She wrote to her sister Everina on 7 November 1787, "if I exert my talents in writing I may support myself in a comfortable way. I am then going to be the first of a new genus — I tremble at the attempt yet if I fail" (*Letters* 139). The "new genus" that she believed herself to embody was that of the intellectual woman writer. As such, she exemplified the independent, intellectual woman that she hoped her writings would help to create.

Crucially, Wollstonecraft developed her professional identity as a writer through many avenues. At the same time that she began to publish her original writing with Joseph Johnson, she also began reviewing for the *Analytical Review*, a monthly journal that he and Thomas Christie had just launched. Critic Anne Chandler points out that Johnson and Christie established the periodical on a scientific paradigm; as the title suggests, it aimed to study texts in the Enlightenment spirit of objective analysis and the search for truth (3). The philosophy behind the journal helped to form Wollstonecraft's approach to writing at this crucial early stage of her writing career. Although her work for the *Analytical Review* has not been studied by many scholars,[1] its impor-

---

"called herself Mrs. Mason, the name of the governess in Wollstonecraft's *Original Stories*," and that she "became a friend of Percy Bysshe and Mary Shelley" (124). The circumstances surrounding Wollstonecraft's dismissal from her duties as a governess are equally interesting. According to Todd in *Mary Wollstonecraft: A Revolutionary Life* (2000), "Years later, when the third King girl had grown up to become as scandalous as her teacher, and Lord Kingsborough was accused of murdering his nephew, now his daughter's lover, the gossip was repeated that Wollstonecraft and his Lordship had been intimate" (104). For more information about this scandal, see N.F. Lowe's "Mary Wollstonecraft and the Kingsborough Scandal" (1994), pages 294-96 of Claire Tomalin's biography, *The Life and Death of Mary Wollstonecraft* (1974, 1992), and pages 68-76 of Edward C. McAleer's *The Sensitive Plant: A Life of Lady Mount Cashell* (1958); see also Janet Todd's *Daughters of Ireland: The Rebellious Kingsborough Sisters and the Making of a Modern Nation* (2004) and Clarissa Campbell Orr's volume, *Wollstonecraft's Daughters: Womanhood in England and France 1780-1920* (1996).

1  Work on this aspect of Wollstonecraft's writing includes Ralph M. Wardle's "Mary Wollstonecraft, Analytical Reviewer" (1947), the very similarly titled "Mary Imlay, Analytical Reviewer" (1982) by Walter de Brouwer, and Sally Stewart's "Mary Wollstonecraft's Contributions to the *Analytical Review*" (1984).

tance is considerable because it is closely related to her fiction and provides valuable insight into her writing goals in general. While some of her reviews for the periodical illustrate her early conventionality—for example, critic Ralph M. Wardle notes that some of her reviews for female conduct literature "reflect her utter satisfaction" with the conservative texts (1005)—even this writing sometimes shows her increasingly unconventional ideas about female education, which would soon be confirmed unmistakeably in her glowing and detailed review of Catharine Macaulay's *Letters on Education* (November, 1790) (Wardle 1007), in which Macaulay outlines her radical feminist view of female education.[1] Also revealing are Wollstonecraft's reviews of scientific works, such as Reverend Samuel S. Smith's *Essays on the Causes of the Variety of Complexion and Figure in the Human Species* in December 1788. This early experience with scientific literature confirmed her involvement with the radical goal of the *Analytical Review* to foster a cultural interest in science alongside conduct books and fiction. Wollstonecraft's critical prose for the periodical provided her with knowledge of a broad range of subjects and writing in a polemical, argumentative style that would have been thought "masculine"—as opposed to the creative and emotional demands of domestic fiction thought more appropriate for female writers, if they dared to write at all.

As if testing the extent of her abilities, Wollstonecraft continued to publish in a wide variety of forms over the next few years. As in *Mary*, she combined her interest in female education and fiction in *Original Stories*, which was published by Johnson in 1788 and reissued with illustrations by William Blake in 1791. While Wollstonecraft does not state explicitly in her preface that the tales conveyed by the fictional Mrs. Mason—a rather stern and unsympathetic educator—are for girls' ears alone, she has only two pupils, Mary and Caroline. Wollstonecraft would delimit her intended audience more explicitly in 1789 with the publication of *The Female Reader*, an edited volume containing, as the subtitle states, "miscellaneous pieces in prose and verse; selected from the best writers, and disposed under proper heads; for the improvement of young women" and "To which is prefixed A Preface, Containing Some Hints on Female Education." Oddly, though, just as Wollstonecraft was defining her role as a writer of works on female education, she simultaneously negated her identity in another way: she used the male pseudonym "Mr.

---

1 See Appendix B1 for more information on Macaulay.

Cresswick, Teacher of Elocution" in *The Female Reader*. As Godwin comments in the *Memoirs*, "At the commencement of her literary carreer [sic], she is said to have conceived a vehement aversion to the being regarded, by her ordinary acquaintance, in the character of an author, and to have employed some precautions to prevent its occurrence" (64). In the following year she published *A Vindication of the Rights of Men* anonymously, maybe for the same reason. Much more than her other works of 1790, both of which are translations—*Young Grandison*, Maria van de Werken de Cambon's adaptation of Samuel Richardson's novel, and Christian Gotthilf Salzmann's *Elements of Morality*, illustrated by Blake—*Rights of Men* established Wollstonecraft as a major force among English radicals, in part because it was the first response to Edmund Burke's *Reflections on the Revolution in France* (1790), coming out before even Thomas Paine's famous response to Burke, *Rights of Man* (1791). The spirited, often favourable (and, when negative, still serious) reception of Wollstonecraft's first *Vindication* seems to have convinced her to take the final leap in establishing her identity as a radical writer and, by the end of 1790, she published a second edition of the work under her name. Buoyed by the success of her first *Vindication*, Wollstonecraft began to write the second in 1791, *Rights of Woman*, which Johnson would publish in 1792 to largely positive reviews.[1]

## The Thorny Path of Love

At the same time that these significant developments in Wollstonecraft's professional life were underway, her romantic life also became more eventful. She first met William Godwin in 1791 when Joseph Johnson invited both of them to a dinner he gave to honour Thomas Paine, but this encounter did not augur their later success as a couple. As Godwin recounts in the *Memoirs*,

---

1 R.M. Janes notes that all but one of the reviews of the work were positive, partly because the conservative journals ignored it completely. Janes adds that the commonality between all of the positive reviews (in *Analytical Review* [Johnson's periodical], *Literary Magazine*, *General Magazine*, *New York Magazine*, *Monthly Review*, *New Annual Register*) was the recognition of its central focus on education: "Most reviewers took it to be a sensible treatise on female education and ignored those recommendations in the work that might unsettle the relations between the sexes" (293, 294).

The interview was not fortunate. Mary and myself parted, mutually displeased with each other. I had not read her *Rights of Woman*.... I had therefore little curiosity to see Mrs. Wollstonecraft, and a very great curiosity to see Thomas Paine. Paine, in his general habits, is no great talker ...; the conversation lay principally between me and Mary. I, of consequence, heard her, very frequently when I wished to hear Paine. (94)

As Godwin would attest later in the *Memoirs*, though, he would find her character changed for the better in response to the painful events of the following years (129). In 1792, the same year that she was revising *Rights of Woman* for republication, she fell violently in love with the painter Henry Fuseli, whom she had met through Johnson, but she was disappointed in his rejection of her extraordinary proposal to live with him and his wife. In an attempt to escape the pain of seeing Fuseli, Wollstonecraft fled to France, where she renewed her acquaintance with Paine, became close friends with English radicals such as Helen Maria Williams, and met leading Girondins (Godwin, *Memoirs* 98-100, 102). It was not until 1793 that her most significant relationship in France was to develop, though. She began an affair with the American merchant Gilbert Imlay, became pregnant, and, although they were unmarried, registered as his wife at the American Embassy so that she could claim the protection of American citizenship when France declared war on England, putting English ex-patriots in danger of being arrested. Calling herself "Mrs. Imlay" now in her letters and to acquaintances, Wollstonecraft must have felt that she had found a new personal identity that, like her new professional identity as a female reformist, divided her from her painful history as an unhappy, oppressed, and powerless daughter.

Godwin's *Memoirs* and Wollstonecraft's letters suggest that she had very little previous romantic experience up until this time. Finally, at age 34, she was in love. Godwin writes, quoting some of her letters to Imlay,

Mary now reposed herself upon a person, of whose honour and principles she had the most exalted idea. She nourished an individual affection, which she saw no necessity of subjecting to restraint; and a heart like her's was not formed to nourish affection by halves. Her conception of Mr. Imlay's "tenderness and worth, had twisted him closely round her heart;" and she "indulged the thought, that she had thrown out some tendrils, to cling to the elm by which she wished to be supported." This was "talking a new language to her;" but, "conscious that she was not a parasite-plant," she was willing to encourage and foster the luxuriancies of affection. Her confidence was entire; her love was unbounded. Now, for the first time in her life she gave a loose to all the sensibilities of her nature. (113-14)[1]

Godwin singles out Wollstonecraft's words from her letters that show not only the depth of her love for Imlay, but also a critical stage in her thinking about relationships between men and women and her attitude toward the language of sensibility. Oddly, Wollstonecraft had excoriated such language in *Rights of Woman*, labelling "ignoble" Anna Lætitia Barbauld's identical comparison of women to flowers and men to the "sheltering oak" or "tougher yew" in her poem, "To a Lady, With Some Painted Flowers." She denounces

> this sensual error, ... the false system of female manners ..., which robs the whole sex of its dignity, and classes the brown and fair with the smiling flowers that only adorns [sic] the land. This has ever been the language of men, and the fear of departing from a supposed sexual character, has made even women of superiour sense [i.e., Barbauld] adopt the same sentiments. (112-13)

How true would she prove her final statement to be through her own example. However much Wollstonecraft censured this kind of sensibility in the *Rights of Woman* (as the passages I have chosen for Appendix A4 of this volume illustrate), she clearly continued to struggle with its attractions, which is why *Mary*, for example, appears to celebrate some traditional characteristics of sensibility as much as it redefines it. Critics have long debated whether the novella is critical or representative of sensibility.[2] I submit that the

---

1 Godwin quotes from Wollstonecraft's letter to Imlay dated 14 January 1794 (*Letters* 245).

2 To summarize the most influential expressions of this debate, Anne K. Mellor claims that Wollstonecraft wrote *Mary* when she was still fully devoted to the ideals of sensibility ("Introduction" xii). By contrast, Gary Kelly asserts that "*Mary* condemns systemic sexism in society and especially the contribution to it of a culture of false sensibility as em-

conflicting evidence from Wollstonecraft's writing—including her letters—regarding her attitude towards sensibility reveals the impossibility of resolving the matter and proves only her ambivalence. She was working through her confusion as she wrote and lived. As an author, she does indeed cast herself as an educator, but, by giving several of her protagonists (who are pupils in some way) her own name, she also suggests that she is also a student who is still working through the themes about which she writes. As she notes in her preface to *Mary*, the volume is about the education of a female "genius" of the same name; *Maria* describes the brutal lessons a woman of sensibility must learn in the world outside of books; and, although it does not deal so explicitly with sensibility, one of Mrs. Mason's students in *Original Stories* is named "Mary." Wollstonecraft's fiction is unified by its focus on education: hers and ours. And, to be sure, her romantic involvement with Imlay, which called up her latent affection for the ideals of sensibility, left her in no doubt as to her status as an *ingénue*.

For Wollstonecraft, the course of love was to be as turbulent as were the politics in her new home of France, but both would provide fodder for more publications. Having followed Imlay to Le Havre while pregnant with their child and inspired by her first-hand experience of the events of the French Revolution, she wrote and published (in London) *An Historical and Moral View of the French Revolution* in 1794. The same year, Imlay left for London, abandoning Wollstonecraft and their baby—whom Wollstonecraft named "Frances" (or "Fanny," as she always termed her), after Fanny Blood—in Le Havre. She moved back to London in 1795 to live with Imlay, only to discover that he had been unfaithful to her, whereupon she tried to commit suicide. As Godwin reports in the *Memoirs*,

> She formed a desperate purpose to die.... Mr. Imlay became acquainted with her purpose, at a moment when he was uncertain whether or no it were already executed, and ... his feelings were roused by the intelligence. It was perhaps owing to his activity and representations, that her life was, at this time, saved. She determined to continue to exist. (127)

---

bodied in a particular kind of 'sentimental' novel, or novel of manners" (xv), arguing that it manifests Wollstonecraft's attempt to redefine the form. Thus, Kelly seeks to christen the novel as a representative of a new form: "*Mary* is, then, a feminist Sentimental Bildungsroman, or novel of 'education'" (xvi).

Nor was this her only suicide attempt provoked by her despair over her failing relationship with Imlay. In Godwin's words, "she was twice, with an interval of four months, from the end of May to the beginning of October [of 1795], prompted ... to purposes of suicide. Yet in this period she wrote her *Letters from Norway*. Shortly after its expiration she prepared them for the press, and they were published in the close of that year" (146). Desperate to illustrate her devotion to Imlay, Wollstonecraft undertook a harrowing trip to Scandinavia, whence she travelled with baby Fanny and her (amazingly loyal) maid, Marguerite, to represent Imlay to some of his business partners. The volume Godwin mentions above, *Letters Written during a Short Residence in Sweden, Norway, and Denmark* (1796), is Wollstonecraft's memoir of the trip, written in the form of a series of letters to Imlay. It is a highly personal and emotional account of her experiences, and one in which she continued to explore the meanings and value of sensibility and sentiment for women. In Letter VI, she writes of baby Fanny,

> You know that, as a female, I am particularly attached to her
> — I feel more than a mother's fondness and anxiety, when I
> reflect on the dependent and oppressed state of her sex. I
> dread lest she should be forced to sacrifice her heart to her
> principles, or principles to her heart. With trembling hand I
> shall cultivate sensibility, and cherish delicacy of sentiment,
> lest, whilst I lend fresh blushes to the rose, I sharpen the
> thorns that will wound the breast I would fain guard — I
> dread to unfold her mind, lest it should render her unfit for
> the world she is to inhabit — Hapless woman! what a fate is
> thine! (66)

If such effusions were intended to act upon Imlay's sense of guilt and persuade him not to make Wollstonecraft's own "fate" so hard, they failed. However, they reached other ears with great success.

Improbably, these memoirs about her heartbreak and disappointment in love generated her next love affair. Godwin confesses that *Letters Written ... [in] Denmark* made him in love with Wollstonecraft's "imagination and sensibility" even before he met her for the second time:

> The narrative of this voyage is before the world, and perhaps
> a book of travels that so irresistibly seizes on the heart, never,

in any other instance, found its way from the press. The occasional harshness and ruggedness of character, that diversify her *Vindication of the Rights of Woman*, here totally disappear. If ever there was a book calculated to make a man in love with its author, this appears to me to be the book. She speaks of her sorrows, in a way that fills us with melancholy, and dissolves us in tenderness, at the same time that she displays a genius which commands all our admiration. Affliction had tempered her heart to a softness almost more than human. (129)

Evidently, what attracted Godwin to Wollstonecraft was her "softness," born of "affliction," as it appeared in *Letters Written ... [in] Denmark*. These traditional feminine ideal characteristics seemed to him to replace the unattractive "harshness and ruggedness of character" that he discerned in her more radical and feminist writings. In short, like Wollstonecraft, Godwin, too, was prey to the allure of feminine ideals outlined by the culture of sensibility. From another perspective, though, this publication illustrates Wollstonecraft's growing opposition to sensibility's ideal of women as helpless, weak, and unassertive. Urged by a desire to preserve independence and financial security for herself and Fanny—indeed, Wollstonecraft refused Imlay's offers to maintain them financially more than once (e.g., *Letters* 328, 334)—Wollstonecraft turned her chaotic experiences into successful publications and thereby asserted her economic and cultural power.

That both Wollstonecraft and Godwin remained attached to the ideals of sensibility to a degree, even when these ideals undermined their devotion to equality between the sexes, does not suggest that they were not powerful representatives of radical politics, or that we must reconsider our evaluation of their philosophical positions. The inconsistencies between what they expressed in their polemical works and their letters, memoirs, and fiction only show that they were human, rather than walking manifestoes. Beset by the powerful cultural forces that tempt each of us to succumb, at times, to the lure of popular notions of beauty and perfection, both writers occasionally submitted to the ideals of sensibility, perhaps without considering that they were doing so. On the whole, however, and compared with their contemporaries, each was, indeed, a radical egalitarian. So much is clear from Godwin's assessment of his burgeoning love affair with Wollstonecraft in 1796: "It grew with equal advances in the mind of each. It would have been impossible for the most minute observer to have said who was before, and who was after. One sex did not take the priority which long-established custom has awarded it" (*Memoirs* 150). Godwin seems at pains in this passage to assert that their relationship was unconventional and reflected their radical politics, perhaps to ward off criticism of their marriage in 1797 when Wollstonecraft was pregnant with their baby; after all, both Godwin and Wollstonecraft had denounced marriage in their polemical works.[1] No one could accuse them of conventionality in their living arrangements, though: Godwin reveals, "influenced by the ideas I had long entertained upon the subject of cohabitation, I engaged an apartment, about twenty doors from our house in the Polygon, Somers Town, which I designed for the purpose of my study and literary occupations" (168). A single room may have been enough for Virginia Woolf in which to write, but Wollstonecraft demonstrated the need for a house of one's own. In the eyes of their contemporaries, the couple's liberal lifestyle was more disturbing than any hints of their traditionalism. Many friends rejected Wollstonecraft when she married Godwin because the union proved that she had never been married to Imlay and that Fanny had been born out of wedlock.

Having struggled all her life to find a romantic partner who would return her deep and passionate love, and who would also respect her need to retain her autonomy and identity as a radical writer, Wollstonecraft seems to have found an ideal mate in Godwin. The *Memoirs* are full of his encomiums about her writing, and he is especially warm in his praise of her radical feminist works. For example, his description of her attitude towards her task in writing the *Rights of Woman* is rousing and presents her in a heroic light:

> Never did any author enter into a cause, with a more ardent desire to be found, not a flourishing and empty declaimer, but an effectual champion. She considered herself as standing forth in defence of one half of the human species, labour-

---

1   As I mention in note 1 of Chapter V of *Maria* (196), Wollstonecraft calls marriage "legal prostitution" in *Rights of Woman* (338). In *An Enquiry Concerning Political Justice* (1793), Godwin calls marriage "an affair of property, and the worst of all properties" and advocates for its "abolition" (Vol. 2: 381, 382). Godwin's fear of being accused of inconsistency was not unfounded; in a letter from Robert Southey to William Taylor from 1 July 1804, Southey writes of Godwin's "weathercock instability of opinion" (Robberds 507).

ing under a yoke which, through all the records of time, had degraded them from the station of rational beings, and almost sunk them to the level of the brutes. She saw indeed, that they were often attempted to be held in silken fetters, and bribed into the love of slavery; but the disguise and the treachery served only the more fully to confirm her opposition. (79-80)

He cherished her tenderly as a lover, too, writing, "The loss of the world in this admirable woman, I leave other men to collect; my own I well know" (194). Readers familiar with the cold rationality of Godwin's *Enquiry* and the formal language of *Caleb Williams* (1794) must find his confession of his feelings during Wollstonecraft's last days profoundly touching. For example, he writes, "Sunday, the third of September, I now regard as the day, that finally decided on the fate of the object dearest to my heart that the universe contained" (180). Wollstonecraft had given birth to their baby on 30 August 1797, and died on 10 September because the placenta was not fully removed, resulting in an agonizing and fatal infection. Wollstonecraft was buried in the churchyard at old St. Pancras, the same church where she and Godwin were married only half a year before.[1]

## Wollstonecraft's Reception and Legacy

Wollstonecraft died with several significant projects unpublished, unfinished, or in the early planning stages, and with no thorough memoir or biography about her. Godwin attempted to consolidate her status as a writer by producing a couple of posthumous publications by and on her. He carefully preserved and edited her unpublished writings as *Posthumous Works of the Author of A Vindication of the Rights of Woman*, a four-volume work that he published with Joseph Johnson in 1798. Besides *Maria*, which

---

1 Wollstonecraft's body is no longer at old St. Pancras, however. As Miriam Brody notes in *Mary Wollstonecraft: Mother of Women's Rights* (2000), "The founding mother now lies buried in Bournemouth, a seaside resort in southern England. The site of the original grave was destroyed when the great Victorian railroad stations at St. Pancras and King's Cross were erected in London in the mid 19th century. Mary Shelley's son, Sir Percy Shelley, moved his grandmother's grave to the town where he lived. She and William Godwin lie there together. But the original gravestone Godwin designed still stands in the small churchyard of St. Pancras Parish Church in north London" (150).

comprises the first two volumes of this collection, it contains *Letters to Imlay* and other miscellaneous pieces. Another work that Godwin published in that year, the *Memoirs of the Author of A Vindication of the Rights of Woman*, which is the first biography of Wollstonecraft, established her posthumous literary and personal reputation for many years to come, but not in a positive way.[1] In this work, Godwin describes various aspects of Wollstonecraft's life—such as her multiple suicide attempts, her sexual relationship with Imlay, her pursuit of Fuseli, and her two pregnancies while unmarried—that were hitherto unknown to the wider public or had only been rumoured. As a result of the *Memoirs*, Wollstonecraft was publicly branded not just as a fallen woman, but also as a dangerous adulteress who had attempted to bully other members of her sex into her vicious ways. Godwin seems to have been too blinded by love and grief to anticipate the firestorm that would erupt upon the publication of these aspects of her life—or perhaps he overrated too highly the public's liberality and regard for Wollstonecraft. Robert Southey famously derided Godwin for "the want of all feeling in stripping his dead wife naked" (Robberds 507) in a letter to William Taylor, 1 July 1804, but Godwin's motives for writing the *Memoirs* were the best, judging by what he writes of the matter to Hugh Skeys, the widower of Wollstonecraft's beloved friend, Fanny, a month after Wollstonecraft's death: "I think the world is entitled to some information respecting persons that have enlightened & improved it. I believe that it is a tribute due to the memory of such persons, as I [am] strongly of opinion that the more intimately we are acquainted with their hearts, the more we shall be taught to respect & love them" (*Letters of William Godwin* 251; inserted word Clemit's addition). His expectations were woefully erroneous. Far from common was the reaction of a Silesian count named Christoph Georg Gustav von Schlabrendorf (1750-1824), a devoted admirer; he wrote in the margins of his edition of Godwin's *Memoirs*,

The authoress of the right of woman [sic] believed, loved and lived, according to what she wrote. This was the cause of her

---

1  In her "Chronology" of Mary Wollstonecraft in the *Cambridge Companion to Mary Wollstonecraft*, Claudia Johnson states that Godwin's *Memoirs* were "also included" as part of the *Posthumous Works* ("Chronology" xix); this is only true of the Dublin edition. The *Memoirs*, as first published by Johnson in London, appeared separate from the *Posthumous Works*.

unhappiness, why she was scorned by her own sex. She wanted to restore women's human rights in a bourgeois world; rights which had been denied to women, in all countries, by men's power, despotism, and legislation. And even when she could not restore these injured, withheld rights through her persuasive writings, at least she would not have them taken from herself. And in doing so she overstepped the boundaries of social prejudices and superstition, and the opinion of the world turned against this unhappy woman. And still Mary was the most noble, virtuous, sensuous female creature, that I ever met. (quoted in *Letters* 207, 229-30)

Her status as the mother of feminism and a courageous radical who lived according to her hard-won beliefs was only recognized widely more than a century later.

After being branded as damaging to the cause of feminism or, worse, virtually ignored throughout the nineteenth century, Wollstonecraft's contributions to the fight for women's equality were recognized over the course of the twentieth century. However, the perception of her life and work was far from consistent. As Cora Kaplan notes in "Mary Wollstonecraft's Reception and Legacies"—a thorough primer on the topic that covers almost a century of Wollstonecraft criticism and biography—modern readers turned their attention to the mother of feminism when Virginia Woolf mused on her "experiments in living" (e.g., 248). This narrow focus on Wollstonecraft's biography was to characterize commentary about her for decades to come (249), which is unfortunate, but not only because it is insufficiently scholarly or often disparages her; such purely biographical commentary is nefarious because, as Kaplan rightly observes, the notoriety of Wollstonecraft's "emotional and sexual history ... has inhibited access to the writing" (247). Critics' own personal and cultural agendas distort the image of Wollstonecraft as, alternately, a "foremother and sometime heroine" of second-wave feminism, a Hollywood leading lady in "soft focus," a chaotic teenager with wayward desires (253), an uneducated naïf, a hack-writer, "a successful autodidact" (256), a savvy radical, and an intellectual contributing and responding to the great issues of education and equality in her day (257). Wollstonecraft became part of the cultural conversation again in the modern period and after, but she was not always portrayed accurately or fruitfully.

The reception of Wollstonecraft's novellas has been inconsistent, too. They were completely eclipsed by the *Vindications* in early- to mid-twentieth-century work on Wollstonecraft, but they began to appear in such texts as the 1973 American Penguin edition of *Mary Wollstonecraft*, by Eleanor Flexner, who wrote of her subject, "she had no talent whatever for writing fiction" (quoted in Kaplan 253). In her own day, Wollstonecraft's *Maria* was hardly acknowledged, perhaps because it was inaccessible or invisible as part of the *Posthumous Works*, or perhaps because the notoriety of the *Memoirs* overshadowed Wollstonecraft's original fiction and destroyed her potential audience. *Mary* fared little better in the Romantic period and was almost disowned by Wollstonecraft herself. In a note that likely accompanied the author's delivery of her first novella to her sister Everina in 1797, Wollstonecraft writes, "As for my *Mary*, I consider it as a crude production, and do not very willingly put it in the way of people whose good opinion, as a writer, I wish for; but you may have it to make up the sum of laughter" (*Letters* 404). As for readers' reception of it, the fact that Wollstonecraft had to introduce it to her own sister nine years after it was published suggests that the novella was far from a best-seller. Contemporary critics are sometimes equally dismissive. While recent historicist criticism on Wollstonecraft's fiction acknowledges its value as part of the broader cultural conversation of her day, Kaplan notes that "the supposed poor quality of her fiction demotes her" in many of these works (257). Even critics who take the novellas seriously enough to devote entire articles to their interpretation sometimes judge them harshly; for instance, in a fascinating exploration of *Mary*'s contribution to the female Gothic literary form, Diane Long Hoeveler intensifies Wollstonecraft's epistolary judgement of her work thus: "Let me begin by examining Wollstonecraft's *Mary*, as crude a piece of fiction as one is likely to read" ("Gothic" n.p.; Wollstonecraft *Letters* 404). Nevertheless, *Mary* had its admirers in the Romantic period, and they were not all named "Godwin." As Todd notes, parts of it were "anthologized (together with Sterne's *A Sentimental Journey*) in *The Young Gentleman & Lady's Instructor* (1809)" (*Sensibility* 122). Works from the 1990s and later by such scholars as Harriet Guest, Mary Poovey, Claudia L. Johnson, Richard Holmes, and Cora Kaplan herself that seek to understand the broader cultural—including political and economic—ramifications of Wollstonecraft's contribution to the culture of sentiment (263-67) have begun to frame her fiction as performing a serious social function, much like her educational texts. I applaud this new understanding of Wollstonecraft's novellas and agree that these aspects of her output function identically: for Wollstonecraft, sensibility is at once the greatest contributor to women's miseducation and, at least in *Mary*, the greatest hope for their re-education as the intellectual equals of men.

## Sensibility, Education, and the Nature/Nurture Debate of the 1790s

If *Maria* and *Mary* have garnered too little critical attention, the likely cause is that they have not been considered sufficiently through intertextual examinations that are essential to a full appreciation of the cultural work they accomplish. This Broadview edition of the novellas seeks to remedy this problem. By examining them in light of such texts as Wollstonecraft's letters, her polemical and educational prose, similar works by other authors such as feminists and political reformists, the literature of sentiment, and contemporary medical texts, we can appreciate the complexity and sophistication of her writing goals as a radical feminist in the 1790s. Gary Kelly's influential study, *The English Jacobin Novel, 1780-1805* (1976), encourages readers to consider Jacobin novelists' fiction in the context of their polemical writing and includes some of Wollstonecraft's closest friends and allies as representatives of this school of writers. Just as Godwin's *Caleb Williams* (1794) fictionalizes his polemical text, *Enquiry Concerning Political Justice* (1793), we may see Wollstonecraft's fiction—especially *Maria*—as illustrative of the philosophical and political messages that she had expressed in her non-fiction prose. It may have been the goal of every English Jacobin writer to challenge and educate by presenting, in the accessible form of fiction, ideas with which readers might not be inclined to engage if they were presented only as polemical and political texts, but this rhetorical strategy was particularly well suited to Wollstonecraft's purposes for several reasons. In late eighteenth-century England, women were the dominant consumers of novels, particularly novels of sensibility—the form with which both of these novellas engage to varying degrees—and they comprised her target audience with respect to her feminist message. Moreover, this former governess of girls began her writing career producing educational works for females, making Wollstonecraft's fiction appear to be calculated extensions of her didactic *oeuvre*.[1] Nor are her engagements with sensibility and education unconnected. As I will show, they constitute a sophisticated inquiry into contemporary notions, including medical, of the basis of the female character.

The educational aims of these novellas must be considered in the context of Wollstonecraft's overall goal for female education and its relationship to 1790s radicalism in general, in which she attempted to include women as beneficiaries of the wider fight for human rights, which, to that point, blazed mostly on behalf of the lower classes in France and slaves in the colonies.[2] Building on the argument of the French Revolutionaries, who claimed that all humans are equal, Wollstonecraft added that women must be equal to men, an obvious logical extension of the Revolutionaries' position that they, nevertheless, refused to recognize: women were not considered to be full *citoyennes* in the new French Republic. As Wollstonecraft presents the argument in *Rights of Woman*, if women are fully human and equal to men, then their minds must be innately equal, as well—or, as she summarizes the argument for her largely Christian audience, "if woman be allowed to have an immortal soul, she must have as the employment of life, an understanding to improve" (135). Moreover, if late eighteenth-century women did not demonstrate their intellectual equality with men, Wollstonecraft continued, it was because they were not given an education equal to that of men. This situation was born, in a classic Catch-22, of the bigoted assumption that women are not born with the same intellectual capacity as men, rendering a male's education wasted on or frustrating to them.[3]

Not only were women given a less rigorous education than were men, Wollstonecraft argues, but what and how they were taught, such as through novels of sensibility, also convinced

---

1 Had she lived, Wollstonecraft would have continued producing educational works, according to Godwin in the *Memoirs*. He claims that she intended to publish "a series of Letters on the Management of Infants," adding, "Another project, of longer standing, was of a series of books for the instruction of children" (170).

2 Slavery had been outlawed in England since 1772 but remained legal and prevalent in the English colonies.

3 To demonstrate her focus on education and human equality, Wollstonecraft addresses the *Rights of Woman* to M. Talleyrand-Périgord, an influential architect of the new educational curriculum in the French Republic. He based the new curriculum on Jean-Jacques Rousseau's notion that females should be educated to be charming mates to males.

them to cherish their weakness. Novels of sensibility were traditionally associated with women both as readers and producers of such works, and Wollstonecraft's novellas, *Mary* and *Maria*, explore how this form—in which she writes, in the first case, and with which she engages thematically in the case of *Maria*—was essential to the construction of femininity. She thereby reiterates a claim she establishes in Section II of *Rights of Woman*:

> Women, subjected by ignorance to their sensations, and only taught to look for happiness in love, refine on sensual feelings.... [These] women ... are amused by the reveries of the stupid novelists, who, knowing little of human nature, work up stale tales, and describe meretricious scenes, all retailed in a sentimental jargon, which equally tend to corrupt the taste, and draw the heart aside from its daily duties. I do not mention the understanding, because never having been exercised, its slumbering energies rest inactive, like the lurking particles of fire which are supposed universally to pervade matter. (425-26)

Instead of promoting the development of their rational abilities and knowledge, women's reading encouraged them to be intellectually lazy, according to Wollstonecraft. She blames the culture of sensibility—created by sentimental authors and the women who buy their novels—for the situation she describes. To exacerbate the problem, novels of sensibility present female weakness of body and mind as sexually attractive and feminine. These novels are insidiously educational: they teach women how to behave by presenting, as the height of beauty, an example of debased femininity. Early in *Rights of Woman*, Wollstonecraft establishes that her goal to educate and improve women is one with her attack on novels of sensibility:

> anxious to render my sex more respectable members of society, I shall try to avoid that flowery diction which has glided from essays into novels, and from novels into familiar letters and conversation.
> These pretty nothings — these caricatures of the real beauty of sensibility ... create a kind of sickly delicacy ... and a deluge of false sentiments and over-stretched feelings, stifling the natural emotions of the heart, render the domestic pleasures insipid, that ought to sweeten the exercise of those

severe duties, which educate a rational and immortal being
for a nobler field of action.

The education of women has, of late, been more attended
to than formerly; yet they are still reckoned a frivolous sex.
(8)

In her declaration that the language of sensibility slips "from
novels into familiar letters and conversation," and that this language, in turn, changes the very character and experience of
women (they "render the domestic pleasures insipid," for
example), Wollstonecraft asserts that the frivolous character of
women in her time is acculturated. Herein lies the motivation
behind all of her feminist writings, polemical and fictional: she
believed that women's character was not innate, but that they
could be educated to be more intellectual and rational, and less
emotional and frivolous. In other words, Wollstonecraft was at the
centre of what we call the "nature/nurture" debate today, and she
comes down firmly on the "nurture" side of the discussion.

This contention—that female character is acquired and not
"natural" or innate—was hotly debated in the 1790s, but this
intellectual battle had begun years earlier, as Rousseau's comments on sexual difference in *Émile* (1762) show. As the most
influential proponent of the "nature" side of the nature/nurture
debate, Rousseau writes that the physical differences between the
sexes

> must necessarily have an influence over their moral charac-
> ter: such an influence is, indeed, obvious, and perfectly
> agreeable to experience; clearly demonstrating the vanity of
> the disputes that have been held concerning the superiority
> or equality of the sexes;.... In those particulars which are
> common to both, they are equal; and as to those wherein
> they differ, no comparison is to be made between them. A
> perfect man and a complete woman should no more resem-
> ble each other in mind than in feature. (3)

By the end of the century, such writers as Richard Polwhele
argued that woman's weaker mind was an intrinsic and therefore
unchangeable corollary of her (undeniably) weaker body. In his
scathing poem "The Unsex'd Females" (1798), he identifies the
natural female body and mind in the lines that follow his description of the abnormal women who indulge their interest in science
through the study of botany:

Far other is the female shape and mind
By modest luxury heighten'd and refin'd;
Those limbs, that figure, tho' by Fashion grac'd,
By Beauty polish'd, and adorn'd by Taste. (ll. 39-42)

Moreover, he presents Wollstonecraft as the chief of such "unsex'd" intellectual females—an unnatural monster if ever there was one, for what is a "female" without a sex? Polwhele claims that Wollstonecraft commands women away from their innate softness and interest in sentimental literature:

'Go, go (she cries) ye tribes of melting maids,
Go, screen your softness in sequester'd shades';
. . . . . . . . . . . . . . . . . . . . . . . . . . . . . . . . . .
What tho' the fine Romances of Rousseau
Bid the flame flutter, and the bosom glow. (ll. 67-68; 71-72)

Polwhele suggests that women's love for sentimental literature is natural, and that other forms of reading and therefore education, such as the scientific, is à rebours for women. This patriarchal view of formalized female education was supported by some women writers, too. Anna Lætitia Barbauld thought a more rigorous education for girls would only produce female savants—again, useless, freakish creatures—instead of "good wives and agreeable companions," as women should be, she argued (quoted in Brackett 31). She believed that "a father or brother [would] ... be the best teacher for girls, whose high passions at age 15 would prohibit learning" (30-31). In short, Barbauld agreed that women's bodies ineluctably formed their minds, for her suggestion that teenage girls' "high passions" would prohibit the development of their intellects is akin to saying that they "think with their hormones." Clearly, then, Wollstonecraft's position on female education was radical and showed her own indulgence in scientific knowledge that was traditionally off-limits to proper females, since it demonstrates her comprehension of such medical questions as the link between mind and body, and innate versus learned characteristics.

The stakes in this debate about the basis of the female character were high: if the Wollstonecraftian argument were to be accepted as correct, then it would follow that women could be educated out of their silliness. More to the point, if women were to be found innately equal to men intellectually, then society would have an obligation to eradicate women's folly through education in the interest of equality, humanity, and Christian access to salvation, as Wollstonecraft presents the argument in *Rights of Woman* (135). Wollstonecraft herself attempted to accomplish this educative task, Trojan-horse-style, by attacking from behind enemy lines and creating a new kind of novel of sensibility in *Mary*. Notably, she does not try to displace the form entirely, since, after all, she shows her continued attachment to the ideal of sensibility in the above passage from *Rights of Woman* when she claims that there exists a "real beauty of sensibility," a genuine sensibility. Defining it and exploring its relationship to female education and development is her goal in *Mary*.

The epigraph of her first novella—which can be translated from the French original (by Jean-Jacques Rousseau) as "The exercise of the most sublime virtues raises and nourishes genius"—confirms that her protagonist, Mary, was not created in the mould of the usual sentimental heroine, as Wollstonecraft informs the reader in the first paragraph of *Mary*'s "advertisement." These heroines' weak bodies and fainting, sobbing behaviour—indicative of their weak character—signify their adherence to the cult of sensibility. Rather, Wollstonecraft's novella of true sensibility, as she viewed it, focusses on the "genius," or the original and creative *mind*, of Mary and how it develops through a course of self-education, or "nourish[ment]," guided by her virtuous disposition. Yet, several aspects of *Mary* also confirm the novella as an offering to the annals of traditional sensibility, such as the emphasis on Mary's benevolence, apparent in her treatment of her dying friend Ann and beloved Henry, and her charity, revealed in her care for Ann's family and the poor of London near the novella's end. Sometimes Wollstonecraft lays on the sensibility so thickly that she appears to be writing a manifesto of the form, as in the following passage of Mary's meditations, written after she has recovered from a grief-and-charity-induced illness and witnessed the success of her aid to yet another starving family:

> Mary's tears flowed not only from sympathy, but a complication of feelings and recollections; the affections which bound her to her fellow creatures began again to play, and reanimated nature. She ... wrote with her pencil a rhapsody on sensibility.
> "Sensibility is the most exquisite feeling of which the human soul is susceptible: when it pervades us, we feel

happy.... It is this quickness, this delicacy of feeling, which
enables us to relish the sublime touches of the poet, and the
painter; it is this, which expands the soul, gives an enthusiastic greatness, mixed with tenderness, when we view the magnificent objects of nature; or hear of a good action.... Softened by tenderness; the soul is disposed to be virtuous. Is
any sensual gratification to be compared to that of feeling the
eyes moistened after having comforted the unfortunate?"
(135)

Besides the focus on Mary's tears, sympathy, and "good
action[s]" in this passage, that she is here recovering from a near-
fatal disappointment in love also reveals Wollstonecraft's attachment to the traditional representation of the woman of sensibility
as weak and defined by romantic interests. Elsewhere in the
novella, Wollstonecraft goes so far as to present Mary as a proto-
Patmorian "angel in the house" who is so morally above debasing sensual needs that she is almost bodiless: in Chapter IV, the
author asserts that Mary possesses "such power over her
appetites and whims, that without any great effort she conquered
them so entirely, that when her understanding or affections had
an object, she almost forgot she had a body which required nourishment" (92). Just as tellingly, though, other depictions of
Mary's physical presence and power diverge sharply from the one
above. Wollstonecraft writes of Mary, "As to herself, she did not
fear bodily pain; and, when her mind was agitated, she could
endure the greatest fatigue without appearing sensible of it"
(114). By presenting Mary as superior to her physical limitations
because she has strengthened her "genius" or mind through self-
education, Wollstonecraft offers the same opportunity to her
female readers, who may learn a new feminine ideal of physical
and mental strength through this novella. At least, Wollstonecraft's contemporary readers may have recognized the
inconsistencies in her delineation of a woman of sensibility, and
they may have been inspired to question, with the author, "What
ideals of sensibility are worth keeping?" and "Can a woman's
character be altered through education?"

Wollstonecraft would later change tactics by changing literary
forms in *Maria*, but her goal of challenging sensibility remained
the same: in her final work of sustained fiction, she uses the
Gothic form to show the horrors of a life built on the lies of conventional sensibility. The madhouse setting of the novella is a representation of the "mind-forg'd manacles," to borrow a phrase

from Blake, the mental confinement that sentiment imposes upon women. Wollstonecraft establishes, in no uncertain terms, that the title-character, Maria, fell in love with George Venables— her husband- and gaoler-to-be—because of her sentimental character. Her interest in him was first inspired by her desire to "see new characters ... such as fancy had pourtrayed" (215), and Maria's good opinion of him was also formed by her imaginative life, rather than reality: she confesses, "I began to imagine him superior to the rest of mankind" (215). Moreover, it was as a result of a scene distinctively sentimental in character that Maria fell in love with Venables. In the same chapter, Maria recounts that she was gathering financial and other support for the unfortunate sister of her maid, an employment that sent her into "rapture[s]" of pleasure, as it would for any woman of sensibility. But nothing was so pleasurable to her as the moment when Venables secretly "slid a guinea into ... [her] hand" for the cause: Maria notes,

> What a revolution took place, not only in my train of thoughts, but feelings! I trembled with emotion — now, indeed, I was in love. Such delicacy, too, to enhance his benevolence! I felt in my pocket every five minutes, only to feel the guinea; and its magic touch invested my hero with more than mortal beauty. My fancy had found a basis to erect its model of perfection on. (220)

The references to sentimental literature are unmistakable: the benevolent scheme, the quiver of emotion, Venables as a "hero," and the involvement of her "fancy." All of these details serve to show that the madhouse in which Maria later finds herself is the confinement of sentiment, for the sentimental "hero," Venables, is responsible for Maria's incarceration there. In *Maria*, Wollstonecraft dramatizes her contention in *A Vindication of the Rights of Woman* that traditional novels of sentiment pervert women's character by encouraging them to be obsessed with love, weak or even ill, and silent, among other problematic ideals. By reading *The Wrongs of Woman, or Maria* in conjunction with passages from *Rights of Woman*, to which the novella's full title responds diametrically, one sees Wollstonecraft's message clearly: the traditional ideals of literary sensibility are responsible for perverting feminine character.

Equally clear is the didactic function of this novella, in which half of the complete chapters are comprised of Maria's memoirs, written for her (possibly dead) baby daughter. Chapter VII begins, "ADDRESSING these memoirs to you, my child, uncertain whether I shall ever have an opportunity of instructing you, many observations will probably flow from my heart, which only a mother — a mother schooled in misery, could make." Just as Wollstonecraft's titular heroines share the root-name "Mary" in a way that establish them as early Romantic-era Everywomen—representative of every female reader, as well as Mary Wollstonecraft herself—Maria's daughter is also archetypal and representative of all of Wollstonecraft's female readers. This interpretation is supported by the title of one of Wollstonecraft's earliest educational works, *Thoughts on the Education of Daughters*, in which "daughters" may be understood to signify young women in general. Serendipitously, too, history has anointed Wollstonecraft the "mother of feminism," again confirming us all as her "daughters." In both of her novellas, Wollstonecraft attempts to educate her (largely female) audience, but her methods differ. Wollstonecraft's educational approach is of the carrot variety in *Mary*: she tries to attract her female readers to a new type of sensibility and alternate ideal of femininity that centres on the development of the female intellect, and to replace traditional notions of female weakness of body and emotions—although Wollstonecraft intimates her doubt about having achieved this goal through the dispiriting ending of *Mary*. However, her didactic method in *Maria* more closely resembles the stick variety: in her last fictionalization of her philosophy about the female character, Wollstonecraft attempts to frighten her female readers into an awareness of the dangers of blindly accepting and replicating feminine ideals from the cult of sensibility.

### Nervous Bodies, Associationist Education, and the Female Character

Scholars have long recognized that Wollstonecraft's novellas explore the nature of sensibility, engage with English literary form, and teach her readers about gender ideals, but what has been largely overlooked is the subtle way in which she participates in contemporary psycho-medical debates about the formation of human character through these means. Simply arguing that female education should be equal to men's presupposes her radical belief that women are innately equal to men in intellectual capacity and, thus, that the mental differences between Romantic-era men and women—to which Wollstonecraft freely admitted in *Rights of Woman*—were acculturated, acquired, learned. Her disavowal of ideas about women as espoused in the culture of sensibility was also a denial that women's weak character reflected their physical difference from men. Respectively, these ideas may be traced roughly to associationist and nervous medical models of human character, both popular eighteenth-century psycho-medical approaches.

Wollstonecraft's involvement with the *Analytical Review*, with its scientific edge, suggests that her thinking was influenced by current medical and psychological theories, but she also declares her belief that other women should attain scientific knowledge in *Rights of Woman*: "Women might study the art of healing, and be physicians as well as nurses," she declares (337). She goes on to assert that if women would "not waste their time in following the fashionable vagaries of dress, the management of their household and children need not shut them out from literature, nor prevent their attaching themselves to a science, with that steady eye which strengthens the mind" (443). A few pages before, she states a similar sentiment, but with a more psychological focus that hints closely at her interest in nerve-theory and associationism:

> the bills of mortality are swelled by the blunders of self-willed old women, who give nostrums of their own without knowing any thing of the human frame. It is likewise proper, only in a domestic view, to make women acquainted with the anatomy of the mind, by allowing the sexes to associate together in every pursuit; and by leading them to observe the progress of the human understanding in the improvement of the sciences and arts. (411)[1]

Such passages—as well as her physiognomical focus in "Cave of Fancy"[2] and her work on an abridgment of "J.C. Lavater's *Physiognomy*, from the French, which has never been published"

---

1  I do not imply, however, that Wollstonecraft was blindly devoted to the whole system of medicine in her time. In fact, she was very critical of medical practitioners, as her following words about doctors from *Rights of Woman* reveal: "Do you then believe that these magnetisers [sic], who, by hocus pocus tricks, pretend to work a miracle, are delegated by God.... They do not cure for the love of God, but money. These are the priests of quackery" (420-21).

2  See Appendix A2, containing passages from "Cave of Fancy," for more information about Wollstonecraft's exploration of physiognomy in this fiction.

(65-66), as Godwin describes one of her projects from 1788—show Wollstonecraft's medical interest in the development of the mind and character. Most illustrative of her knowledge about these matters, though, are the many comments in *Rights of Woman* about women's "nervous complaints" (note 272) and the "tone of nerves" (76) of men of science, or the entire chapter entitled "The Effect which an Early Association of Ideas has upon the Character" (259), the first sentence of which demonstrates her familiarity with both nerve theory and associationism:

> Educated in the enervating style recommended by the writers on whom I have been animadverting; and not having a chance, from their subordinate state in society, to recover their lost ground, is it surprising that women every where appear a defect [sic] in nature? Is it surprising, when we consider what a determinate effect an early association of ideas has on the character, that they neglect their understandings, and turn all their attention to their persons? (259)[1]

If nervous fainting fits are the hallmark of the real-life woman of sensibility, then it is because irresponsible writers have "educated" their female reader with their "enervating style" and made her that way. Such is the associationist view of "the character," to recall Wollstonecraft's title, and herein lies her unique view of the deplorable circumstance "that women every where appear a defect in nature." Crucially, they only "appear" to be naturally defective. As Wollstonecraft goes on to illustrate in this chapter, and, more subtly, throughout her fiction, womankind can be educated to appear, as they innately are, equal to men.

Wollstonecraft's devotion to the craft of fiction and her comments on the ways in which literature forms female character prepare us to recognize the conflation of these topics with her medical interests. As G.S. Rousseau argues in his seminal essay, "Nerves, Spirits, and Fibres: Towards Defining the Origins of Sensibility," notions about human character as portrayed in novels of sensibility owed much to eighteenth-century nerve theory.[2] Nerve theory presented the body as having a

---

1   See Appendix A4, containing selections from *Rights of Woman*, for more information about Wollstonecraft's familiarity with associationism.
2   In addition to C.M. Ranger's "'Finely Fashioned Nerves' in Mary Wollstonecraft's *The Wrongs of Woman*" (1999), some recent publi-   (*continued*)

particular physical structure that was, for the most part, intrinsic, but was always difficult to alter once settled on the human frame. According to nerve theory, there exists in the human body physical, though invisible, fluids that flow through superfine tubes, or nerves—and, the theory went, the finer or more delicate the nerve, the more sensitive the person (and in the literature of sensibility, the more admirable and feminine the heroine). Nerve theory proposed that certain bodies were more predisposed to being nervous, especially the bodies of women and aristocrats, but it also accounted for the influence of lived experience in the formation of one's nerves. For instance, many nerve theorists, such as George Cheyne in the 1730s and Thomas Trotter later in the century, worried that English indulgence in luxuries and lack of exercise would weaken the nerves and debilitate the nation. Trotter is best known for *A View of the Nervous Temperament* (1808), which resumed the in-depth study of nerves that had previously been accomplished by his mentor, William Cullen. Trotter argues that England had become decadent, too luxurious, and recommended "recurring to simplicity of living and manners, so as to check the increasing prevalence of nervous disorders; which, if not restrained soon, must inevitably sap our physical strength of constitution; make us an easy conquest to our invader; and ultimately convert us into a nation of slaves and idiots" (vii). In short, the physical nature of nervous debility gave it a kind of permanence, such that entire generations could be "con-

---

cations on the intersection of the literature of sensibility and nerve-theory are: G.J. Barker-Benfield's *The Culture of Sensibility: Sex and Society in Eighteenth-Century Britain* (1992); Geoffrey M. Sill's "Neurology and the Novel: Alexander Monro Primus and Secundus, *Robinson Crusoe*, and the Problem of Sensibility" (1997); Raymond Stephanson's "Richardson's 'Nerves': The Physiology of Sensibility in *Clarissa*" (1988); Peter Melville Logan's *Nerves and Narratives: A Cultural History of Hysteria in Nineteenth-Century British Prose* (1997); and Janet Oppenheim's *"Shattered Nerves": Doctors, Patients, and Depression in Victorian England* (1991), which is a study of the Victorian response to these topics. Recent explorations of nerve theory and Romantic literature in general include Judith Stanton's and Harriet Guest's "'A Smart Strike on the Nerves': Two Letters from Charlotte Smith to Thomas Cadell, with a Title Page" (2009); Christopher Gabbard's "From Idiot Beast to Idiot Sublime: Mental Disability in John Cleland's *Fanny Hill*" (2008); and Peter Melville Logan's "Narrating Hysteria: *Caleb Williams* and the Cultural History of Nerves (1996).

vert[ed]" into degenerate beings.[1] In particular, the aristocratic female body as presented in novels of sensibility had innately finer, more sensitive nerves that made it more susceptible to surrounding stimuli, usually pitiable and emotional. This state of extreme sensitivity made her more likely to be overcome by affect, which was manifested in fainting fits and trembling— and because the heroine of sensibility was aristocratic, sympathetic, and lovely, she embodied a popular and desirable ideal, even though she was scarcely more than a puddle of tears.

Nor, indeed, was Wollstonecraft always condemnatory of the ideal of feminine weakness as espoused in the cult of sensibility. In at least one of her letters, she describes her own delicately nervous state with some relish to her sister, Everina: "so my eyes roll in the wild way you have *seen* them. A deadly paleness overspreads my countenance — and yet so weak am I a sudden thought or any recollect emotion of tenderness will" disturb her, she claims (*Letters* 148, 151). Yet, this epistolary performance of her fragility demonstrates the very attitude that Wollstonecraft so roundly condemns in *Education of Daughters* when she writes, "Many ladies are delicately miserable, and ... are full of self-applause, and reflections on their own superior refinement. Painful feelings are prolonged beyond their natural course, to gratify our desire of appearing heroines, and we deceive ourselves as well as others" (86). In this identification of the danger of sensibility as residing in how women learn to define themselves through literary representations of the best kind of females—aristocratic, sympathetic, and beautiful heroines—Wollstonecraft also confirms that feminine character is acquired and not innate. This alteration of her perspective provided her with the impetus to question these very ideals.

Wollstonecraft's attempt to revise the ideals of femininity as expressed in the cult of sensibility reveals subtle changes in her thinking about the formation of the female character from broadly nervous to associationist models. While the former located character in the body—such that the fragile body of the

---

1   Similarly, and from a lay perspective, Catharine Macaulay clarifies how pernicious the culture of nerves was for women, in particular, when she writes in *Letters on Education* (1790) that, "From a false notion of beauty and delicacy, their system of nerves is depraved before they come out of their nursery; and this kind of depravity has more influence over the mind, and consequently over morals, than is commonly apprehended" (129-30). In the same text, though, she confirms that change, through education, is still possible, as I discuss below.

woman manifests her emotional weakness, while the sturdy male body expresses his stronger intellect and emotional temperament—the latter posited character as obtained through education. In "Mary Wollstonecraft on Education," Alan Richardson writes, "associationist psychology, influentially applied to schooling and pedagogy in Locke's *Some Thoughts Concerning Education* (1693) ... [was] subscribed to by nearly every important writer on education in Wollstonecraft's time" (24). Elsewhere he argues that Wollstonecraft's *Rights of Woman* is strongly influenced by Catharine Macaulay's associationist view of human character: "Arguing (as does Macaulay) from associationist principles [in *Rights of Woman*] ..., Wollstonecraft holds that sexual differences in mind and character are largely if not wholly produced by education" (*Social Practice* 175). Indeed, Macaulay asserts (to her fictional addressee),

> The great difference that is observable in the characters of the sexes, Hortensia, as they display themselves in the scenes of social life, has given rise to much false speculation on the natural qualities of the female mind.... [even] though the doctrine of innate ideas, and innate affections, are in a great measure exploded by the learned. (*Letters* 127)

In other words, women are innately equal to men intellectually, but their life experiences and formal education make them appear to be less than equals. Macaulay claims that a new method of education based on the principles of associationism would change this disparity; however, she adds, "without adequate knowledge of the power of association, by which a single impression calls up a host of ideas, which, arising in imperceptible succession, form a close and almost inseparable combination, it will be impracticable for a tutor to fashion the mind of his pupil according to any particular idea he may frame of excellence" (*Letters* v-vi). Doubtlessly, Wollstonecraft's ideas about associationism were also formed through her reading of original texts of the theory. David Hartley's associationist theory, as presented in *Observations on Man, his Frame, his Duty, and his Expectations* (1749), was popularized late in eighteenth-century England by Joseph Priestley's text, *Hartley's Theory of the Human Mind, on the Principle of the Association of Ideas; With Essays relating to the Subject of It* (1775; 2nd edition), which was published in 1790 by none other than Joseph Johnson. Given that Wollstonecraft had already been contributing to Johnson's *Analytical Review* for a couple of years by the time of Priestley's publication, and in consideration of its scientific focus, we can assume that she was familiar with the work. In *Hartley's Theory of the Human Mind*, Priestley explains that the theory posits

> the human mind to have acquired a stock of ideas, by means of the external senses, and that these ideas have been variously associated together; so that when one of them is present, it will introduce such others as it has the nearest connection with, and relation to, nothing more seems to be necessary to explain the phenomena of *memory*. For we have no power of calling up any idea at pleasure, but only recollect such as have a connection, by means of former associations, with those that are at any time present to the mind. (xxix; Priestley's emphasis)

He later confirms Hartley's contention that our associations are the basis of human character, or, as he puts it, "make any man whatever he is":

> all our *intellectual pleasures and pains*, ... [and] all the phenomena of *memory, imagination, volition, reasoning*, and every other mental affection and operation, are only different modes, or cases, of the association of ideas: so that nothing is requisite to make any man whatever he is, but a sentient principle [mind]. (xxiv; Priestley's emphasis)

Wollstonecraft seized on this principle of associationism as the key to her feminism: to those who claimed that her reformist texts needlessly stirred contention—since women were intrinsically weak in character and mind, both reflections of her body, and thus would ever be so—she answered that women were educated to be as they presently were and could therefore be taught to acquire more intellectual strength. To be sure, associationism presented human character as far more than biological destiny: Priestley notes that his explanation will not satisfy the pure materialist, who is "accustomed to consider all matter in the most gross and general manner, as if it was subject to no laws but those of the five mechanical powers" (xxi).[1] By attempting to define a

---

1 Although early associationism as outlined by Hartley had a strong component of emphasis on the body in its description of memory as the after-effect of vibrations in the the medullary substance *(continued)*

new female character through education, Wollstonecraft repudiates ideal femininity as it is defined by sensibility and nerve theory, and she echoes the most current developments in the medical theory of her time. Indeed, by the 1790s, nerve theory was beginning to pass out of fashion, and associationism has long been linked with high-Romantic concepts of mind.[1]

---

in the nerves, which he called "vibratiuncles," this aspect of the theory was widely mocked as unsubstantiated and unempirical. Priestley was eager to de-emphasize this aspect of associationism in his influential publication of Hartley's theory and focussed, instead, on its relevance to education.

1   Studies on the associationist knowledge of the canonical Romantic poets are numerous and began to appear as early as the 1930s, while later critics researched how Shelley's, Coleridge's, Wordsworth's, and other famous Romantic writers' reading of associationism—mostly that of Hartley, as popularized by Priestley's text—might have impacted their literary works. Most of these critics outline evidence of associationist thinking in canonical Romantic writers' work, while a few, such as Cairns Craig in *Associationism and the Literary Imagination* (2007), go further to explain how associationism is integrally linked with the stated ideals of Romantic literature. Besides Isabelle Bour's notable article, "Epistemological Ambiguities: Reason, Sensibility and Association of Ideas in Mary Wollstonecraft's *Vindication of the Rights of Woman*" (1999), I refer here to Alan Richardson's "Of Heartache and Head Injury: Reading Minds in *Persuasion*" (2002), and Leon Howard's "Thomas Odiorne: An American Predecessor of Wordsworth" (1939), in which the critic explores the two writers' interests in associationism. Other more recent works of this nature include: J.C. Sallé's article "Hazlitt the Associationist" (1964); Robert Brainard Pearsall's article "Wordsworth Reworks His Hartley" (1970); Jonathan Lamb's articles "Language and Hartleian Associationism in *A Sentimental Journey*" (1980) and "Hartley and Wordsworth: Philosophical Language and Figures of the Sublime" (1982); Bryan Keith Shelley's "The Synthetic Imagination: Shelley and Associationism" (1983); Joseph E. Reihl's "Keats's 'Ode on a Grecian Urn' and Eighteenth-Century Associationism" (1983); Beth Lau's "Keats, Associationism, and 'Ode to a Nightingale'" (1983); John Hayden's "Wordsworth, Hartley, and the Revisionists" (1984); Jerome Christensen's "Philosophy/Literature: The Associationist Precedent for Coleridge's Late Poems" (1984); W.H. Christie's "Francis Jeffrey's Associationist Aesthetics" (1993); Marjorie Garson's "Associationism and the Dialogue in *Emma*" (1997); William Hatherell's "'Words and Things': Locke, Hartley and the Associationist Context for the Preface to *Lyrical Ballads*" (2006); and Malcolm Andrew's "The English Cottage as Cultural Critique and Associationist Paradigm" (2006). While the greatest number of critical studies on the links between literature and associationism are Romantic in focus, Romanticists by no means inaugurated research into the topic. They may have

By questioning the ideals of femininity presented in the literature of sensibility in both of her educational novellas, Wollstonecraft challenges the fictional form and educates women by
encouraging them to accept a different type of feminine ideal.
Tracing Wollstonecraft's thinking about these psycho-medical
models of human character in such diverse contexts as her
letters, reviews, and polemical prose prepares her readers to recognize these topics in her fiction. With a focus on female education, Wollstonecraft filters some of the most salient concerns of
her culture into novellas aimed at a female audience. The complexity of her educational plan—one in which she endeavoured to
weave together, in the entertaining and therefore attractive form
of fiction, her well-developed theories about education, femininity, human character, medicine and literary culture—helps to
explain why she found writing her final novella such a challenge.
Of Wollstonecraft's feelings about *Maria*, Godwin writes in
*Memoirs*,

> impressed, as she could not fail to be, with the consciousness
> of her talents, she was desirous, in this instance, that they
> should effect what they were capable of effecting. She was
> sensible how arduous a task it is to produce a truly excellent
> novel; and she roused her faculties to grapple with it. All her
> other works were produced with a rapidity, that did not give
> her powers time fully to expand. But this was written slowly
> and with mature consideration. She began it in several forms,
> which she successively rejected, after they were considerably
> advanced. She wrote many parts of the work again and
> again, and, when she had finished what she intended for the
> first part, she felt herself more urgently stimulated to revise
> and improve what she had written, than to proceed, with
> constancy of application, in the parts that were to follow.
> (171-72)

Almost as though she had a presentiment of her early death, Wollstonecraft attempted to combine her great talents and diverse
knowledge into a single text that would, as Godwin puts it,

taken their cue from critics of eighteenth-century literature, who began
publishing articles on the topic decades earlier with such works as
Howard Anderson's "Associationism and Wit in *Tristram Shandy*"
(1969) and Martin Kallich's "The Association of Ideas and Akenside's
*Pleasures of Imagination*" (1947), to mention only two of several.

produce a particular "effect" on her audience and answer her hope for womankind. In so doing, she created an appropriate bookend for the literary conversation that she began a decade earlier in *Mary*. Viewed in light of eighteenth-century feminist and medical theories of education, the development of the human mind, and gender differences, *Mary* and *Maria* stand as Wollstonecraft's efforts to put her complex ideas into practice and create the new state of womanhood about which she had only declaimed in her polemical prose.

# Works Cited and Consulted

Note: The following is a list of works that I consulted in writing the Introduction, textual footnotes, and appendices.

"Accommodation bill." *The Oxford English Dictionary Online.* 2nd ed. 2008. Web. 12 August 2010.

"Adelphi." *The Oxford English Dictionary Online.* 2nd ed. 2008. Web. 20 July 2010.

Anderson, Howard. "Associationism and Wit in *Tristram Shandy.*" *Philological Quarterly* 48 (1969): 27-41.

Andrew, Malcolm. "The English Cottage as Cultural Critique and Associationist Paradigm." *Literature and Place 1800-2000.* Ed. and intro. P. Brown and M. Irwin. Oxford: Peter Lang, 2006. 49-68.

Anon. *Jamie's Complaint, or, The Answer to Auld Robin Gray.* [London?], [1795?]. *Eighteenth-Century Collections Online.* Web. 19 April 2010.

——. *The Book of Common Prayer, and Administration of the Sacrament, According to the Use of the Church of England: Together with the Psalter or Psalms of David, Pointed as They are to be Sung or Said in Churches.* London: T. Davison, 1792.

——. *The History of Eliza Warwick.* 2 vols. Dublin: S. Price, W. Whitestone, et al., 1778.

——. *Emma; or, The Unfortunate Attachment. A Sentimental Novel.* 3 vols. London: T. Hookham, 1773. Vol. 3.

Ariosto, Ludovico. *Orlando Furioso.* 1532. Trans. and intro. Guido Waldman. Oxford: Oxford UP, 1974, 1998.

Aristotle. *De Anima* (On the Soul). Ed. and intro. Hugh Lawson-Tancred. London: Penguin, 1986.

Arnold, Thomas. *Observations on the Nature, Kinds, Causes, and Prevention of Insanity, Lunacy, or Madness.* Leicester: G. Robinson, 1782-86. 2 vols.

Barker-Benfield, G.J. *The Culture of Sensibility: Sex and Society in Eighteenth-Century Britain.* Chicago: U of Chicago P, 1992.

"Bastille." *The Oxford English Dictionary Online.* 2nd ed. 2008. Web. 19 July 2010.

Batteux, Charles. *Les Beaux Arts Réduits à un Même Principe.* Paris: Durand, 1746.

Beckford, William. *Modern Novel Writing, or The Elegant Enthusiast; and Interesting Emotions of Arabella Bloomville. A Rhapsodical Romance; Interspersed with Poetry. By the Right Hon. Lady*

*Harriet Marlow*. 2 vols. London: G.G. and J. Robinson, 1796.

Beddoes, Thomas. *Extract of a Letter on Early Instruction, Particularly that of the Poor* ([no publishing information given]: 1792). *Eighteenth-Century Collections Online*. Web. 22 May 2008.

Blackstone, William. *The Commentaries of Sir William Blackstone, Knt. on the Laws and Constitution of England; Carefully Abridged*. Ed. William Curry. London: W. Clarke and Son, 1796.

Blair, Hugh. *Lectures on Rhetoric and Belles Lettres*. 3 vols. Dublin: Whitestone, Colles, et al., 1783.

"Borough." *The Oxford English Dictionary Online*. 2nd ed. 2008. Web. 27 October 2011.

Bour, Isabelle. "Epistemological Ambiguities: Reason, Sensibility and Association of Ideas in Mary Wollstonecraft's *Vindication of the Rights of Woman*." *Bulletin de la Société d'études Anglo-Américaines des XVIIe et XVIIIe Siècles* 49 (1999): 299-310.

"Bowel." *The Oxford English Dictionary Online*. 2nd ed. 2008. Web. 30 April 2010.

Brackett, Virginia. *The Facts on File Companion to British Poetry: 17th and 18th Centuries*. 2 vols. New York: Facts on File, 2008. Vol. 2.

Brainard Pearsall, Robert. "Wordsworth Reworks His Hartley." *Bulletin of the Rocky Mountain Modern Language Association* 24.2 (1970): 75-83.

Brissenden, R.F. *Virtue in Distress: Studies in the Novel of Sentiment from Richardson to Sade*. London: Macmillan, 1974.

Brody, Miriam. *Mary Wollstonecraft: Mother of Women's Rights*. Oxford: Oxford UP, 2000.

Brown, Thomas. *Lectures on the Philosophy of the Human Mind*. 1820. Edinburgh: William Tait, 1828.

Burke, Edmund. *Reflections on the Revolution in France, and On the Proceedings in Certain Societies in London Relative to that Event. In a Letter Intended to have been Sent to a Gentleman in Paris*. London: J. Dodsley, 1790. *Eighteenth-Century Collections Online*. Web. 10 April 2011.

———. *A Philosophical Enquiry into the Origin of our Ideas of the Sublime and Beautiful*. London: R. and J. Dodsley, 1757. *Eighteenth-Century Collections Online*. Web. 25 April 2011.

———. *A Vindication of Natural Society: or, A View of the Miseries and Evils Arising to Mankind from Every Species of Artificial*

*Society*. 1756. *Eighteenth-Century Collections Online*. Web. 25 April 2011.

Burnet, James, Lord Monboddo. *Of the Origin and Progress of Language*. 6 vols. Edinburgh: A. Kincaid & W. Creech, Edinburgh, 1792.

Burton, Frances. *Family Law*. London: Routledge Cavendish, 2003.

Burwick, Frederick. *Poetic Madness and the Romantic Imagination*. University Park: Pennsylvania State UP, 1996.

Butler, Joseph. *The Analogy of Religion*. London: James, John and Paul Knapton, 1736.

Carkesse, James. "Lucida Intervella: Containing Divers Miscellaneous Poems." 1679. *Patterns of Madness in the Eighteenth Century: A Reader*. Ed. Allan Ingram. Liverpool: Liverpool UP, 1998.

Cartwright, Mrs. H. *The Platonic Marriage: A Novel, In a Series of Letters*. 3 vols. London: Logographic, 1786.

Cervantes Saavedra, Miguel de. *The History and Adventures of the Renowned Don Quixote. Translated from the Spanish of Miguel de Cervantes Saavedra, To which is Prefixed, Some Account of the Author's Life*. 1755. By T. Smollett, M.D. 2 vols. London: A. Millar et al., 1755. *Eighteenth-Century Collections Online*. Web. 25 April 2011.

"Chancery." *The Oxford English Dictionary Online*. 2nd ed. 2008. Web. 12 August 2010.

Chandler, Anne. "The 'Seeds of Order and Taste': Wollstonecraft, the Analytical Review, and Critical Idiom." *European Romantic Review* 16.1 (2005): 1-21.

Chesterfield, Philip Dormer Stanhope, Earl of. *Lord Chesterfield's Advice to his Son, on Men and Manners: or, a New System of Education, in which the Principles of Politeness, the Art of Acquiring a Knowledge of the World, with Every Instruction Necessary to Form a Man of Honour, Virtue, Taste, and Fashion, are Laid Down In a Plain, Easy, & Familiar Manner*. 2nd ed. 1775. *Eighteenth-Century Collections Online*. Web. 21 April 2011.

Cheyne, G. *The English Malady: or, A Treatise of Nervous Diseases of All Kinds, as Spleen, Vapours, Lowness of Spirits, Hypochondriacal, and Hysterical Distempers &c*. London: G. Strahan and J. Leake, 1733.

Christensen, Jerome. "Philosophy/Literature: The Associationist Precedent for Coleridge's Late Poems." *Philosophical Approaches to Literature: New Essays on Nineteenth- and Twentieth-*

*Century Texts.* Ed. W.E. Cain. Lewisburg: Bucknell UP, 1984. 27-50.

Christie, W.H. "Francis Jeffrey's Associationist Aesthetics." *British Journal of Aesthetics* 33.3 (1993): 257-70.

Coxon, Roger. *Chesterfield and his Critics.* Norwood, PA: Norwood Editions, 1977.

Craig, C. *Associationism and the Literary Imagination: From the Phantasmal Chaos.* Edinburgh: Edinburgh UP, 2007.

Crawford, Rachel. *Poetry, Enclosure, and the Vernacular Landscape, 1700-1830.* Cambridge: Cambridge UP, 2002.

"Custom-house." *The Oxford English Dictionary Online.* 2nd ed. 2008. Web. 22 July 2010.

Darwin, Robert Waring. *Principia Botanica: or, A Concise and Easy Introduction to the Sexual Botany of Linnæus. With the Genera; Their Mode of Growth, (as Tree, Shrub, or Herb;) The Number of Species to Each Genus.* Newark: Allin and Co., 1787.

Defoe, Daniel. *Roxana: The Fortunate Mistress.* 1724. Ed. John Mullan. Oxford: Oxford UP, 1998.

DeMaria, Robert Jr. Notes to Thomas Paine's *Common Sense* (1776). *British Literature: 1640-1789. An Anthology.* 2nd ed. Oxford: Blackwell, 1996, 2001. 848-50.

"Desideratum." *The Oxford English Dictionary Online.* 2nd ed. 2008. Web. 21 April 2011.

Donnelly, Michael. *Managing the Mind: A Study of Medical Psychology in Early Nineteenth-Century Britain.* London: Tavistock, 1983.

Dryden, John. *Fables, Ancient and Modern; Translated into Verse, from Homer, Ovid, Boccace, and Chaucer: With Original Poems.* 1700. Edinburgh: A. Kincaid and W. Creech, and J. Balfour, 1773.

——. *Alexander's Feast: or, The Power of Musick. An Ode, Written by Mr. Dryden. Set to Musick by Mr. Handel.* [London?]: [n.p.], 1739.

——. "Absalom and Achitophel." *The Broadview Anthology of British Literature: The Restoration and the Eighteenth Century.* Ed. Joseph Laurence Black, et al. Peterborough: Broadview, 2006. 71-86.

Duff, William. *An Essay on Original Genius; and Its Various Modes of Exertion in Philosophy and the Fine Arts, Particularly in Poetry.* London: Edward and Charles Dilly, 1767.

Duncan, Andrew, ed. "Physiognomical Fragments." *Medical and Philosophical Commentaries.* 20 vols. London: J. Murray, 1776. Vol. 4. 11-34.

Eger, Elizabeth. *Bluestockings: Women of Reason from Enlightenment to Romanticism*. Houndmills: Palgrave Macmillan, 2010.

"Excite." *The Oxford English Dictionary Online*. 2nd ed. 2008. Web. 20 July 2010.

"Fetid [gum]." *The Oxford English Dictionary Online*. 2nd ed. 2008. Web. 14 May 2011.

Forster, E.M. *Aspects of the Novel*. 1927. Harmondsworth: Penguin, 1968.

Gabbard, D. Christopher. "From Idiot Beast to Idiot Sublime: Mental Disability in John Cleland's *Fanny Hill*." *PMLA: Publications of the Modern Language Association of America* 123.2 (2008): 375-89, 534-35.

"Gall." *The Oxford English Dictionary Online*. 2nd ed. 2008. Web. 10 May 2010.

Garson, Marjorie. "Associationism and the Dialogue in *Emma*." *Eighteenth-Century Fiction* 10.1 (1997): 79-100.

"Genius." *The Oxford English Dictionary Online*. 2nd ed. 2008. Web. 22 March 2010.

Godwin, William. *The Letters of William Godwin. Vol. I: 1778-1797*. Ed. Pamela Clemit. Oxford: Oxford UP, 2011. 3 vols.

———. *Things as They Are; or, The Adventures of Caleb Williams*. 1794. Ed. and intro. David M. McCracken. Oxford: Oxford UP, 1970, 1982.

———. *Memoirs of the Author of* A Vindication of the Rights of Woman. London: J. Johnson; and G.G. and J. Robinson, 1798.

———, ed. *Posthumous Works of the Author of A Vindication of the Rights of Woman*. 4 vols. London: J. Johnson, 1798.

———. Preface to the Letters. *Posthumous Works of the Author of A Vindication of the Rights of Woman*. 4 vols. London: J. Johnson, 1798. Vol. 3. unpag. 3 pages.

———. *Things as They Are; or, The Adventures of Caleb Williams*. 3 vols. London: B. Crosby, 1794. Vol. 3. 267-70.

———. *Enquiry Concerning Political Justice, and its Influence on General Virtue and Happiness*. 2 vols. Dublin: Luke White, 1793. *Eighteenth-Century Collections Online*. Web. 27 April 2011.

Goethe, Johann Wolfgang von. *The Sorrows of Werter: A German Story*. 2 vols. Dublin: C. Jackson, 1780.

Gray, Thomas. "Elegy Written in a Country Churchyard." London: R. Dodsley, 1751.

Green, Thomas. *A Dissertation on Enthusiasm; Shewing the Danger of its Late Increase, and the Great Mischiefs It has Occasioned, Both in Ancient and Modern Times*. London: J. Oliver, 1755.

Gregory, John. *A Father's Legacy to his Daughters.* 2nd ed. London: W. Strahan and T. Cadell, 1774. *Eighteenth-Century Collections Online.* Web. 19 March 2010.

"Groat." *The Oxford English Dictionary Online.* 2nd ed. 2008. Web. 12 August 2010.

Hammond, James. "Elegy XIII." *Love Elegies. Written in the Year 1732.* London: G. Hawkins, 1743. 15-18. *Eighteenth-Century Collections Online.* Web. 11 May 2011.

Hartley, D. *Observations on Man, his Frame, his Duty, and his Expectations.* 2 vols. London: James Leake and Wm. Frederick, 1749. Vol. 1. *Eighteenth-Century Collections Online.* Web. 4 July 2008.

Hatherell, William. "'Words and Things': Locke, Hartley and the Associationist Context for the Preface to *Lyrical Ballads.*" *Romanticism: The Journal of Romantic Culture and Criticism* 12.3 (2006): 223-35.

Hayden, John. "Wordsworth, Hartley, and the Revisionists." *Studies in Philology* 81.1 (1984): 94-118.

Hays, Mary. *Female Biography: or, Memoirs of Illustrious and Celebrated Women, of All Ages and Countries.* 6 vols. London: Richard Phillips, 1803. Vol. 1. *Google eBook.* Web. 8 November 2011.

Haywood, Eliza. *Love in Excess; Or, The Fatal Enquiry.* 1719-20. Ed. David Oakleaf. 2nd ed. Peterborough: Broadview, 2000.

Hill, Robert Gardiner. *Total Abolition of Personal Restraint in the Treatment of the Insane.* 1838. New York: Arno, 1976.

Hoeveler, Diane Long. "The Construction of the Female Gothic Posture: Wollstonecraft's *Mary* and Gothic Feminism." *Gothic Studies* 6.1 (2004): 30-44. *Literature Online.* Web. 7 April 2011.

Holy Bible, The. *Containing the Old and New Testaments Translated Out of the Original Tongues and with the Former Translations Diligently Compared and Revised by his Majesty's Special Command. Appointed to be Read in Churches. Authorized King James Version.* 1611. Iowa Falls: World Bible Publishers, [n.d.].

Horace. *Satires, Epistles, Ars Poetica.* Ed. and trans. H.R. Fairclough. Cambridge: Harvard UP, 1978.

Howard, Leon. "Thomas Odiorne: An American Predecessor of Wordsworth." *American Literature: A Journal of Literary History, Criticism, and Bibliography* 10.4 (1939): 417-36.

Hunter, Ian and Ida Macalpine, eds. Introduction to Philippe Pinel. *Three Hundred Years of Psychiatry 1535-1860.* London: Oxford UP, 1963. 602-06.

Ingram, Allan. Introduction. *Patterns of Madness in the Eighteenth Century*. Liverpool: Liverpool UP, 1998. 1-10.

Israel, Saul and Norma H. Roemer. *World Geography Today*. New York: Loyal Durand, 1962.

Janes, R.M. "On the Reception of Mary Wollstonecraft's *A Vindication of the Rights of Woman*." *Journal of the History of Ideas* 39.2 (1978): 293-302.

Johnson, Samuel. "Reflections upon the State of Portugal, From the Foundation of that Monarchy to the Present Time." *The Works of Samuel Johnson, LL.D.* 14 vols. London: John Stockdale, 1788. Vol. 14. 190-98.

———. "No. 60. Saturday, June 9." *The Idler*. 2 vols. London: J. Newbery, 1761. Vol. 2. 39-46.

———. *The Prince of Abissinia* [sic]. *A tale*. [*Rasselas*] 2 vols. London: R. and J. Dodsley, 1759.

———. *A Dictionary of the English Language: In Which the Words are Deduced from Their Originals, and Illustrated in Their Different Significations by Examples from the Best Writers*. 1755. 2 vols. 4th ed. Dublin: Thomas Ewing, 1775. *Eighteenth-Century Collections Online*. Web. 8 April 2011.

Jones, Chris. *Radical Sensibility: Literature and Ideas in the 1790s*. London and New York: Routledge, 1993.

Kallich, Martin. "The Association of Ideas and Akenside's *Pleasures of Imagination*." *Modern Language Notes* 62.3 (1947): 166-73.

Kaplan, Cora. "Mary Wollstonecraft's Reception and Legacies." *The Cambridge Companion to Mary Wollstonecraft*. Ed. Claudia Johnson. Cambridge: Cambridge UP, 2002. 246-70.

Kelly, Gary. Endnotes and Introduction to *Mary* and *The Wrongs of Woman*. *Mary* and *The Wrongs of Woman*. By Mary Wollstonecraft. Ed. and intro. Gary Kelly. Oxford: Oxford UP, 2007.

———. *The English Jacobin Novel, 1780-1805*. Oxford: Oxford UP, 1976.

Knowles, Claire. *Sensibility and Female Poetic Tradition, 1780-1860: The Legacy of Charlotte Smith*. Farnham, UK: Ashgate, 2009.

Lamb, Jonathan. "Hartley and Wordsworth: Philosophical Language and Figures of the Sublime." *Modern Language Notes* 97.5 (1982): 1064-85.

———. "Language and Hartleian Associationism in *A Sentimental Journey*." *Eighteenth-Century Studies* 13 (1980): 285-312.

Lau, Beth. "Keats, Associationism, and 'Ode to a Nightingale.'"

Keats-Shelley Journal: Keats, Shelley, Byron, Hunt, and Their Circles 32 (1983): 46-62.

Lavater, Johann Caspar. *Essays on Physiognomy; For the Promotion of the Knowledge and the Love of Mankind.* Trans. Thomas Holcroft. London: G.G.J. and J. Robinson, 1789. Vol. 1. *Eighteenth-Century Collections Online.* Web. 11 April 2011.

Lawlor, Clark. *Consumption and Literature: The Making of the Romantic Disease.* Basingstoke: Palgrave, 2006.

Lindsay, Anne. "Auld Robin Gray." *The Oxford Book of English Verse, 1250-1900.* Vol. 2. Ed. Arthur Thomas Quiller-Couch. Oxford: Oxford UP, 2008. Vol. 2. 552-53.

Locke, John. *An Essay Concerning Human Understanding.* 1690. 3 vols. Glasgow: Robert Urie, 1759. Vol. 1.

Logan, P.M. *Nerves and Narratives: A Cultural History of Hysteria in Nineteenth-Century British Prose.* London: U of California P, 1997.

Logan, Peter Melville. "Narrating Hysteria: Caleb Williams and the Cultural History of Nerves." *Novel: A Forum on Fiction* 29.2 (1996): 206-22.

Macaulay, Catharine. *History of England from the Accession of James I to that of the Brunswick Line.* London: J. Nourse, R. and J. Dodsley, and W. Johnston, 1763-83. 8 vols.

Macaulay Graham, Catharine. *Letters on Education. With Observations on Religious and Metaphysical Subjects.* Dublin: H. Chamberlaine and Rice, 1790.

Mackenzie, Henry. *The Man of Feeling.* 1771. Ed. and intro. Brian Vickers. London: Oxford UP, 1967.

McCracken, David. Introduction. *Things as They Are; or, The Adventures of Caleb Williams.* 1794. By William Godwin. Ed. and intro. David M. McCracken. Oxford: Oxford UP, 1970, 1982. vii-xxii.

McGann, Jerome. *The Poetics of Sensibility: A Revolution in Literary Style.* Oxford: Clarendon, 1996.

Mellor, A.K. "Physiognomy, Phrenology, and Blake's Visionary Heads." *Blake in His Time.* Ed. R.N. Essick and D.R. Pearce. Bloomington: Indiana UP, 1978.

"Mephitic" and "mephitical." *The Oxford English Dictionary Online.* 2nd ed. 2008. Web. 12 August 2010.

"Methodism." *The Oxford English Dictionary Online.* 2nd ed. 2008. Web. 12 August 2010.

"Milk fever." *The Oxford English Dictionary Online.* 2nd ed. 2008. Web. 12 August 2010.

"Milky." *The Oxford English Dictionary Online.* 2nd ed. 2008.

Web. 10 May 2010.

Milton, John. *Paradise Lost.* 1667. *John Milton.* Ed. Stephen Orgel and Jonathan Goldberg. Oxford: Oxford UP, 1991. 355-618.

——. *L'Allegro.* 1645. *John Milton.* Ed. Stephen Orgel and Jonathan Goldberg. Oxford: Oxford UP, 1991. 22-25.

——. *A Masque of the Same Author Presented at Ludlow Castle, 1634 Before the Earl of Bridgewater Then President of Wales* ['Comus']. 1634. John Milton. Ed. Stephen Orgel and Jonathan Goldberg. Oxford: Oxford UP, 1991. 44-71.

More, Hannah. "Sensibility: A Poetical Epistle to the Hon. Mrs. Boscawen." *Sacred Dramas: Chiefly Intended for Young Persons: The Subjects taken from the Bible. To Which is Added, Sensibility, A Poem.* London: T. Cadell, 1782. 269-90.

Morell, Thomas. *Judas Maccabæus. A Sacred Drama. As it is Perform'd at the Theatre-Royal in Covent-Garden. The Musick by Mr. Handel.* Dublin: James Hoey, 1748.

Mullan, John. *Sentiment and Sociability: The Language of Feeling in the Eighteenth Century.* Oxford: Clarendon, 1988.

Newton, Isaac, Sir. *Opticks: Or, A Treatise of the Reflections, Refractions, Inflections and Colours of Light.* 2nd ed. London: W. and J. Innys, 1718. *Eighteenth-Century Collections Online.* Web. 16 May 2011.

"Occiput." *The Oxford English Dictionary Online.* 2nd ed. 2008. Web. 14 May 2011.

O'Halloran, Sylvester. *A Complete Treatise on Gangrene and Sphacelus; With a New Method of Amputation.* London: Paul Vaillant, 1765.

Oppenheim, J. *"Shattered Nerves": Doctors, Patients, and Depression in Victorian England.* New York: Oxford UP, 1991.

Pagano, Frank N. "Burke's View of the Evils of Political Theory: or, A Vindication of Natural Society." *Polity* 17.3 (1985): 446-62. *JSTOR.* Web. 24 April 2011.

Paine, Thomas. *Rights of Man. Being an Answer to Mr. Burke's Attack on the French Revolution.* 4th ed. London: J.S. Jordan, 1791.

"Peace." *The Oxford English Dictionary Online.* 2nd ed. 2008. Web. 11 August 2010.

Perfect, William. *Cases of Insanity, the Epilepsy, Hypochondriacal Affection, Hysteric Passion, and Nervous Disorders, Successfully Treated.* Rochester: T. Fisher, [1785?]. *Eighteenth-Century Collections Online.* Web. 14 May 2011.

Petrarca, Francesco (Petrarch). Sonnet 173. *Petrarch: The Can-*

zoniere, or Rerum Vulgarium Fragmenta. 1327(?). Ed. Mark
Musa and Barbara Manfredi. Bloomington: Indiana UP,
1996. 265.

Philp, Mark. Introduction. *Rights of Man, Common Sense, and
Other Political Writings*. By Thomas Paine. Ed. Mark Philp.
Oxford: Oxford UP, 1998. vi-xxvii.

Pinel, Philippe. *A Treatise on Insanity*. Trans. D.D. Davis.
Sheffield: Cadell & Davies, 1806.

Polwhele, Richard. "The Unsex'd Females." *The Longman
Anthology of British Literature: The Romantics and Their Contemporaries*. Vol. 2A. Ed. Susan Wolfson and Peter Manning. 4th
ed. New York: Pearson Longman, 2010. 323-27.

Pope, Alexander. "Epistle II. — Of the Characters of Women."
1735. *An Essay on Man, and Other Poems*. London: John
Sharpe, 1829. 63-72.

———. "An Essay on Criticism." 1711. *Norton Anthology of
English Literature, The Major Authors*. Ed. M.H. Abram and
Stephen Greenblatt. 8th ed. New York: Norton, 2006. 1123-
36.

Preece, R. *Animals and Nature: Cultural Myths, Cultural Realities*.
Vancouver: U of British Columbia P, 1999.

Priestley, Joseph. *Experiments on the Generation of Air from Water;
To Which are Prefixed, Experiments Relating to the Decomposition
of Dephlogisticated and Inflammable Air*. London: J. Johnson,
1793.

———. *Hartley's Theory of the Human Mind, on the Principle of the
Association of Ideas; With Essays Relating to the Subject of It*.
1775. 2nd ed. London: J. Johnson, 1790. *Eighteenth-Century
Collections Online*. Web. 2 July 2008.

"Putrid" and "putrid fever." *The Oxford English Dictionary
Online*. 2nd ed. 2008. Web. 3 April 2010.

Ranger, C.M. "'Finely Fashioned Nerves' in Mary Wollstonecraft's *The Wrongs of Woman*." *Notes and Queries* 46.1
(1999): 27-28.

Reid, Thomas. *An Inquiry into the Human Mind, on the Principles
of Common Sense*. Dublin: Alexander Ewing, 1764. *Eighteenth-
Century Collections Online*. Web. 19 March 2010.

Reihl, Joseph E. "Keats's "Ode on a Grecian Urn" and Eighteenth-Century Associationism." *Publications of the Arkansas
Philological Association* 9.1 (1983): 85-96.

"Rhapsody." *The Oxford English Dictionary Online*. 2nd ed.
2008. Web. 19 July 2010.

Richardson, Alan. "Mary Wollstonecraft on Education." *The

*Cambridge Companion to Mary Wollstonecraft.* Ed. Claudia L. Johnson. Cambridge: Cambridge UP, 2002. 24-41.

———. "Of Heartache and Head Injury: Reading Minds in *Persuasion.*" *Poetics Today* 23.1 (2002): 141-60.

———. *Literature, Education, and Romanticism: Reading as Social Practice, 1780-1832.* Cambridge: Cambridge UP, 1994.

Richardson, Samuel. *The History of Sir Charles Grandison.* 1753-54. Ed. and intro. Jocelyn Harris. Oxford: Oxford UP, 1986.

———. *Clarissa, or The History of a Young Lady.* 1747-48. Ed. and intro. Angus Ross. London: Penguin, 1985.

Robberds, J.W. ed. *A Memoir of the Life and Writings of the Late William Taylor of Norwich ... Containing his Correspondence of Many Years with the late Robert Southey.* 2 vols. London: John Murray, 1843. Vol. 1. *Google eBook.* Web. 8 November 2011.

Robinson, Daniel. "Theodicy versus Feminist Strategy in Mary Wollstonecraft's Fiction." *Eighteenth-Century Fiction* 9.2 (1997): 183-202.

Rousseau, G.S. "Science." *The Context of English Literature. The Eighteenth Century.* Ed. Pat Rogers. London: Methuen, 1978. 153-207.

———. "Nerves, Spirits, and Fibres: Towards Defining the Origins of Sensibility." *Studies in the Eighteenth Century III: Papers Presented at the Third David Nichol Smith Memorial Seminar.* Ed. R.F. Brissenden. Toronto: U of Toronto P, 1976. 137-57.

Rousseau, Jean-Jacques. *Emilius and Sophia: or, A New System of Education.* [*Émile, ou, de l'Éducation.*] 2nd ed. 4 vols. London: T. Becket and P.A. De Hondt, 1763.

———. *Julie, ou, La Nouvelle Héloïse: Lettres de Deux Amants Habitants d'Une Petite Ville au Pied des Alpes.* 1761. Paris: Éditions Garnier Frères, 1960.

Rowe, Thomas. *The Fair Penitent, a Tragedy.* Edinburgh: G. Hamilton and J. Balfour, 1755.

Sadler, Robert. *Wanley Penson; or, The Melancholy Man: a Miscellaneous History, in Three Volumes.* London: C. and G. Kearsley, 1792.

Sallé, J.C. "Hazlitt the Associationist." *Review of English Studies: A Quarterly Journal of English Literature and the English Language* 15.57 (1964): 38-51.

"Seton." *The Oxford English Dictionary Online.* 2nd ed. 2008. Web. 14 May 2011.

Sha, Richard C. *Perverse Romanticism: Aesthetics and Sexuality in Britain, 1750-1832.* Baltimore: Johns Hopkins UP, 2009.

Shakespeare, William. *The Tragedy of Julius Caesar.* 1599. *The RSC (Royal Shakespeare Company) William Shakespeare Complete Works.* Ed. Jonathan Bate and Eric Rasmussen. New York: The Modern Library, 2007. 1801-58.

——. *The Tragedy of Hamlet, Prince of Denmark.* 1600? *The RSC (Royal Shakespeare Company) William Shakespeare Complete Works.* Ed. Jonathan Bate and Eric Rasmussen. New York: The Modern Library, 2007. 1918-2003.

——. *A Midsummer Night's Dream.* 1600? *The RSC (Royal Shakespeare Company) William Shakespeare Complete Works.* Ed. Jonathan Bate and Eric Rasmussen. New York: The Modern Library, 2007. 365-412.

——. *Twelfth Night, or, What You Will.* 1601. *The RSC (Royal Shakespeare Company) William Shakespeare Complete Works.* Ed. Jonathan Bate and Eric Rasmussen. New York: The Modern Library, 2007. 645-97.

——. *The Tragedy of King Lear.* 1605-06. *The RSC (Royal Shakespeare Company) William Shakespeare Complete Works.* Ed. Jonathan Bate and Eric Rasmussen. New York: The Modern Library, 2007. 2004-80.

——. "Sonnet 130: My Mistress' Eyes are Nothing like the Sun." 1609. *The RSC (Royal Shakespeare Company) William Shakespeare Complete Works.* Ed. Jonathan Bate and Eric Rasmussen. New York: The Modern Library, 2007. 2458.

——. *The Tempest.* 1611. *The RSC (Royal Shakespeare Company) William Shakespeare Complete Works.* Ed. Jonathan Bate and Eric Rasmussen. New York: The Modern Library, 2007. 1-51.

——. *The Famous History of the Life of King Henry the Eighth.* 1613. *The RSC (Royal Shakespeare Company) William Shakespeare Complete Works.* Ed. Jonathan Bate and Eric Rasmussen. New York: The Modern Library, 2007. 1382-1455.

——. *The Tragedy of Othello, the Moor of Venice.* 1622. *The RSC (Royal Shakespeare Company) William Shakespeare Complete Works.* Ed. Jonathan Bate and Eric Rasmussen. New York: The Modern Library, 2007. 2086-2157.

——. *Twelfth Night: or, What You Will. As it is Acted at the Theatres-Royal in Drury-Lane and Covent-Garden.* London: J. Rivington, W. Strahan, J. Hinton, etc, 1775[?].

Shelley, Bryan Keith. "The Synthetic Imagination: Shelley and Associationism." *The Wordsworth Circle* 14.1 (1983): 68-73.

Shelley, Mary. *Frankenstein.* Ed. M.K. Joseph. Oxford: Oxford UP, 1969.

Sill, Geoffrey M. "Neurology and the Novel: Alexander Monro

Primus and Secundus, *Robinson Crusoe*, and the Problem of Sensibility." *Literature and Medicine* 16.2 (1997): 250-65.

"Slop" and "slop-shop." *The Oxford English Dictionary Online*. 2nd ed. 2008. Web. 30 April 2010.

Small, Helen. *Love's Madness: Medicine, the Novel, and Female Insanity, 1800-1865*. Oxford: Oxford UP, 1998.

Smart, Christopher. *A Translation of the Psalms of David, Attempted in the Spirit of Christianity, and Adapted to the Divine Service*. London: Dryden Leach, for the author, 1765.

Smith, Adam. *The Theory of Moral Sentiments*. London: A. Millar, 1759. *Eighteenth-Century Collections Online*. Web. 19 March 2010.

Smith, Charlotte Turner. "Sonnet VI: To Hope." *Elegiac Sonnets*. 1784. 3rd ed. London: J. Dodsley, H. Gardner, and J. Bew, 1786.

Stanton, Judith and Harriet Guest. "'A Smart Strike on the Nerves': Two Letters from Charlotte Smith to Thomas Cadell, with a Title Page." *Women's Writing* 16.1 (2009): 6-19.

Stephanson, Raymond. "Richardson's 'Nerves': The Physiology of Sensibility in *Clarissa*." *Journal of the History of Ideas* 49.2 (1988): 267-85.

Sterne, Laurence. *A Sentimental Journey through France and Italy and Continuation of the Bramine's Journal*. 1768. Ed. Melvyn New and W.G. Day. Gainesville: UP of Florida, 2002.

"Summum bonum." *The Oxford English Dictionary Online*. 2nd ed. 2008. Web. 21 April 2011.

Sunstein, Emily. *A Different Face: The Life of Mary Wollstonecraft*. New York: Harper and Row, 1975.

Sydenham, Thomas. *The Whole Works of That Excellent Practical Physician, Dr. Thomas Sydenham*. 9th ed. London: J. Darby, 1729. *Google eBook*. Web. 14 May 2011.

Tasso, Torquato. *Rinaldo, A Poem; In XII. Books: Translated from the Italian of Torquato Tasso*. Trans. John Hoole. London: J. Dodsley, Pall-Mall, 1792.

"Terrific." *The Oxford English Dictionary Online*. 2nd ed. 2008. Web. 21 April 2010.

Thomson, James. "Song: For Ever Fortune, Wilt Thou Prove." *Poems on Several Occasions*. London: A. Millar, 1750. 16.

——. *The Seasons, A Hymn, A Poem to the Memory of Sir Isaac Newton, and Britannia, A Poem*. London: J. Millan, 1730.

"Thousandweight." *The Oxford English Dictionary Online*. 2nd ed. 2008. Web. 20 July 2010.

Todd, Janet, ed. Endnotes to *Mary* and *Maria*. *Mary* and *Maria* by Mary Wollstonecraft. *Matilda* by Mary Shelley. London: Penguin, 2004.

——. Introduction. *The Collected Letters of Mary Wollstonecraft*. By Mary Wollstonecraft. Ed. and intro. Janet Todd. London: Penguin, 2003. ix-xxix.

——. *Mary Wollstonecraft: A Revolutionary Life*. London: Weidenfeld and Nicolson, 2000.

——. *Sensibility: An Introduction*. London: Methuen, 1986.

Trotter, Thomas. *A View of the Nervous Temperament; Being a Practical Inquiry into the Increasing Prevalence, Prevention, and Treatment of Those Diseases Commonly Called Nervous, Bilious, Stomach, Liver Complaints, Indigestion, Low Spirits, Gout, &c.* Troy: Wright, Goodenow, & Stockwell, 1808.

Tuke, Samuel. *A Description of the Retreat, an Institution near York, for Insane Persons of the Society of Friends.* York: W. Alexander, 1813.

"Typhus." *The Oxford English Dictionary Online.* 2nd ed. 2008. Web. 3 April 2010.

"Vellicate." *The Oxford English Dictionary Online.* 2nd ed. 2008. Web. 14 May 2011.

Voltaire (François-Marie Arouet). *The Philosophical Dictionary.* 1752. Glasgow: Robert Urie, 1766.

"Vulgar." *The Oxford English Dictionary Online.* 2nd ed. 2008. Web. 26 March 2010.

Wakefield, Priscilla. *Reflections on the Present Condition of the Female Sex; With Suggestions for its Improvement.* London: J. Johnson, 1798.

Walrond, Sallie. *Looking at Carriages.* London: J.A. Allen, 1992.

Wardle, Ralph. "Mary Wollstonecraft, Analytical Reviewer." *PMLA. Publications of the Modern Language Association of America* 62.4 (1947): 1000-09.

Whytt, Robert. *Observations on the Nature, Causes, and Cure of those Disorders which have been Commonly called Nervous, Hypochondriac, or Hysteric: To Which are Prefixed Some Remarks on the Sympathy of the Nerves.* Edinburgh: T. Becket, 1765. *Google eBook.* Web. 14 May 2011.

Wolfson, Susan and Peter Manning. "Catherine Macaulay." *The Longman Anthology of British Literature: The Romantics and Their Contemporaries.* Vol. 2A. 4th ed. Ed. Susan Wolfson and Peter Manning. New York: Pearson Longman, 2010. 319-20.

Wolfson, Susan J. "Mary Wollstonecraft and the Poets." *The*

*Cambridge Companion to Mary Wollstonecraft*. Ed. Claudia
Johnson. Cambridge: Cambridge UP, 2002. 160-88.

Wollstonecraft, Mary. *The Collected Letters of Mary Wollstonecraft*.
Ed. and intro. Janet Todd. New York: Penguin, 2003.

——, and Mary Shelley. *Mary; Maria; Matilda*. Ed. and intro.
Janet Todd. New York: Penguin, 1992.

——. *Collected Letters of Mary Wollstonecraft*. Ed. Ralph M.
Wardle. Ithaca: Cornell UP, 1979.

——. "The Wrongs of Woman, or Maria." *Posthumous Works of
the Author of A Vindication of the Rights of Woman*. 4 vols. Ed.
William Godwin. London: J. Johnson, 1798. Vols. 1 and 2.

——. "Cave of Fancy. A Tale." *Posthumous Works of the Author of
A Vindication of the Rights of Woman*. 4 vols. London: J.
Johnson, 1798. Vol. 4. 99-155.

——. *Letters Written During a Short Residence in Sweden, Norway,
and Denmark*. London: J. Johnson, 1796.

——. *A Vindication of the Rights of Woman: With Strictures on Political and Moral Subjects*. London: J. Johnson, 1792.

——. *The Female Reader; or Miscellaneous Pieces in Prose and
Verse; Selected from the Best Writers, and Disposed under Proper
Heads; for the Improvement of Young Women. By Mr. Cresswick,
Teacher of Elocution* [Mary Wollstonecraft]. *To Which is Prefixed
A Preface, Containing Some Hints on Female Education*.
London: J. Johnson, 1789.

——. *Mary, A Fiction*. London: J. Johnson, 1788.

——. *Thoughts on the Education of Daughters: With Reflections on
Female Conduct, in the More Important Duties of Life*. London:
J. Johnson, 1787.

Wordsworth, W. "Preface" to *Lyrical Ballads*. 1800, 1850. *The
Prose Works of William Wordsworth*. Ed. W.J.B. Owen and J.W.
Smyser. Oxford: Clarendon, 1974. Vol. 1. 119-59.

"Writ." *The Oxford English Dictionary Online*. 2nd ed. 2008.
Web. 12 May 2010.

Wyatt, Sir Thomas. "Avising the Bright Beams of Those Fair
Eyes." 1557. *The Poetical Works of Sir Thomas Wyatt. With a
Memoir*. Boston: Little, Brown and Company, 1854. 10.

Yearsley, Ann. *Stanzas of Woe, Addressed from the Heart on a Bed
of Illness, to Levi Eames, Esq. Late Mayor of the City of Bristol*.
London: G.G.J. and J. Robinson, 1790.

Young, Edward. *The Complaint; or, Night-thoughts on Life, Death,
& Immortality*. 1742. 5th ed. London: R. Dodsley, 1743.

# Mary Wollstonecraft: A Brief Chronology

1759       Born the second of seven children on 27 April in
           London to Edward John and Elizabeth Dickson Woll-
           stonecraft.

1763-74    Determined to become a gentleman farmer, Edward
           moves the family around England, from Epping to
           Barking, then to Beverley, where Wollstonecraft devel-
           ops a close friendship with Jane Arden, and finally to
           Hoxton; father becomes a violent alcoholic and
           squanders family funds; Wollstonecraft meets neigh-
           bouring clergyman, Mr. Clare, and his wife, who
           welcome her into their family and help to educate her.

1775       Meets Fanny Blood through the Clares and develops
           a deep and lasting affection for her; Fanny is the
           model for Ann in *Mary, A Fiction*, and the namesake
           of Wollstonecraft's first child.

1776-77    Wollstonecraft family moves to Wales, then back to
           London.

1778       Becomes a paid companion to Mrs. Dawson in
           Bath.

1781-82    Moves to London to nurse sick mother, who dies in
           1782; takes on responsibility for settling the financial
           futures of her younger siblings when older brother
           Ned neglects his duties; father remarries and moves to
           Wales; sister Eliza marries Meredith Bishop.

1783       After giving birth to daughter, sister Eliza suffers from
           serious postpartum depression; Wollstonecraft attrib-
           utes the illness to Meredith's supposed poor treat-
           ment of Eliza.

1784       Assists Eliza in leaving husband and baby, the latter of
           whom dies later that year.

1784       Starts a short-lived school in Islington, then a more
           successful one at Newington Green to support
           herself, her sisters, and Fanny Blood, who leaves in
           1785 to marry Hugh Skeys in Lisbon; Wollstonecraft
           meets Reverend Richard Price and his non-conformist
           friends, as well as Samuel Johnson.

| 1785 | Sails to Lisbon to help Fanny with childbirth; Fanny dies and Wollstonecraft returns to London the same year. |
|------|---|
| 1786 | Newington Green school closes; Wollstonecraft becomes governess to Kingsboroughs in Ireland. |
| 1787 | Publishes *Thoughts on the Education of Daughters* with Joseph Johnson, as she would all of her works thereafter; composes "Cave of Fancy"; is dismissed by the Kingsboroughs; goes to London to review for Joseph Johnson and Thomas Christie's *Analytical Review*; intensifies foreign language self-education to prepare for career in translating and publishing. |
| 1788 | Publishes *Mary, A Fiction* and *Original Stories from Real Life*. |
| 1789 | Publishes *The Female Reader*. |
| 1790 | Publishes *A Vindication of the Rights of Men*. |
| 1791 | Publishes a second edition of *Original Stories*; starts writing *A Vindication of the Rights of Woman*; meets William Godwin, but they are mutually unimpressed with each other and do not develop their acquaintance further at this time. |
| 1792 | Publishes *A Vindication of the Rights of Woman*; through friendship with Johnson, meets circle of writers and artists, some of them radical, such as Thomas Holcroft, William Blake, Anna Lætitia Barbauld, and Henry Fuseli; falls madly in love with Fuseli and proposes to live with him and his wife in a threesome, but is refused; to escape the torments of her passion, she moves to Paris. |
| 1793 | Meets and begins romance with Gilbert Imlay; becomes pregnant with his child. |
| 1794 | Follows Imlay to Le Havre; gives birth to Fanny in May; publishes *An Historical and Moral View of the French Revolution*. |
| 1795 | Follows Imlay to London; attempts suicide upon learning of his infidelity; travels to Scandinavia with Fanny and maid to conduct business for Imlay, returning to England in September; attempts suicide again out of despondence over failing relationship with Imlay. |
| 1796 | Publishes *Letters Written during a Short Residence in Sweden, Norway, and Denmark*; ends relationship with |

Imlay; begins romance with Godwin; begins *The Wrongs of Woman.*

1797    Becomes pregnant with Godwin's child; marries Godwin at St. Pancras church in London; Mary is born on 30 August; Wollstonecraft dies on 10 September of complications resulting from childbirth and is buried at St. Pancras Churchyard.

1798    Godwin publishes *Posthumous Works of the Author of A Vindication of the Rights of Woman,* which contains *The Wrongs of Woman, or Maria,* "Cave of Fancy," her letters to Imlay, and other short works; also publishes the controversial *Memoirs of the Author of A Vindication of the Rights of Woman.*

# A Note on the Text

In almost every case, I have consulted eighteenth-century editions of the physical source text in the British Library to create my transcriptions in this volume. For the primary source texts, I used the British Library's editions of Mary Wollstonecraft's *Mary, A Fiction*, published by J. Johnson in 1788 (shelfmark C.39.f.32) and "The Wrongs of Woman, or Maria; a Fragment" from volume four of *Posthumous Works of the Author of A Vindication of the Rights of Woman: In Four Volumes*, edited by William Godwin, published in London and printed for J. Johnson and G.G. & J. Robinson in 1798 (shelfmark 629.d.11). The only texts that I consulted electronically (in every case through *Eighteenth-Century Collections Online*, accessed through the University of Manitoba Libraries website) are Burke's, Lavater's, Perfect's, and Priestley's, as well as Godwin's *Enquiry*.

I have endeavoured to maintain the integrity of the source text in all of my transcriptions in this edition, including in the appendices. I have duplicated almost every oddity of the source text — including antiquated or erroneous punctuation and spelling — in order to maintain the authenticity of the eighteenth-century text, and so that this edition may serve as a reliable scholarly source. Some of the changes I have made include differences in font size and spacing (but not capitalization) in the front and back matter of the texts, as well as in the headers and footers. I have also inserted my own quotation marks or italics when titles of other works appear in the source text, such as in Godwin's *Posthumous Works* title, since it refers to the title of Wollstonecraft's book. When I have inserted my own words for clarity, I enclose them in square brackets; when, in a few instances, the square brackets appear in the source text, I write that this is the case in a note. I have added none of my own emphases through italics; all that appear in these transcriptions appear in the source text. Where the text is confusing because of errors in the original, I have pointed out the changes I have made in a note, or I have duplicated the oddities, but appended a note to recognize it, when necessary.

# MARY,

# A

# FICTION.

*L'exercice des plus sublimes vertus éleve et nourrit le génie.*[1]
ROUSSEAU.

LONDON:
PRINTED FOR J. JOHNSON, ST. PAUL'S CHURCH-
YARD.
MDCCLXXXVIII.[2]

---

1 "The exercise of the most sublime virtues raises and nourishes genius."
This epigraph, from Genevan-*philosophe* Jean-Jacques Rousseau's (1712-78) *Julie, ou, La Nouvelle Héloïse* (1761), gestures to three of the main themes of *Mary*: female natural genius, education—indeed, this novella is a kind of early *bildungsroman*—and sensibility, to which the phrase "sublime virtues" refers. Wollstonecraft responds to Rousseau again in *A Vindication of the Rights of Woman* (1792) (hereafter *Rights of Woman*), but in this text she focuses on his contention in *Émile, ou, de l'Éducation* (1762) that girls—in particular, the eponymous character's mate, Sophie—should be educated to be the charming supporters of more rational males. She notes in Chapter II, "Rousseau, and most of the male writers who have followed his steps, have warmly inculcated that the whole tendency of female education ought to be directed to one point: — to render them pleasing" (*Rights of Woman* 51).

2 Early though it is, this publication of 1788 was not the first that Wollstonecraft produced with radical publisher Joseph Johnson (1738-1809). Johnson published Wollstonecraft's first text, *Thoughts on the Education of Daughters: With Reflections on Female Conduct, in the More Important Duties of Life* in 1787. The two became good friends and co-edited the *Analytical Review*.

# ADVERTISEMENT.

IN delineating the Heroine of this Fiction,[1] the Author attempts to develop a character different from those generally portrayed. This woman is neither a Clarissa, a Lady G---, nor a[2] Sophie. — It would be vain to mention the various modifications of these models, as it would to remark, how widely artists wander from nature, when they copy the originals of great masters. They catch the gross parts; but the subtile spirit evaporates; and not having the just ties, affectation disgusts, when grace was expected to charm.

Those compositions only have power to delight, and carry us willing captives, where the soul of the author is exhibited, and animates the hidden springs. Lost in a pleasing enthusiasm, they live in the scenes they represent; and do not measure their steps in a beaten track, solicitous to gather expected flowers, and bind them in a wreath, according to the prescribed rules of art.

These chosen few, wish to speak for themselves, and not to be an echo — even of the sweetest sounds — or the reflector of the

---

1 By calling Mary a "Heroine" here and reiterating the word "Fiction" to describe this novella, as she does in the subtitle, Wollstonecraft draws attention to the generic category of her text. While the common descriptor "history" implies a claim to reality (to be sure, this novella has a strongly autobiographical element) and "romance" speaks to a text's fantastic qualities, "fiction" suggests an invented situation. As such, Wollstonecraft seems to express the desirability of cultivating female genius at the same time that she casts doubt over the achievement of this goal. She defines her word "fiction" in the final paragraph of the "Advertisement."

2 Rousseau. [Wollstonecraft's note] Although the textual marker for Wollstonecraft's note comes before—not, as is more common, after—the relevant word in the text, the author certainly means to point out that the name "Sophie" comes from Rousseau's writing, specifically *Émile* (cf. p. 73, note 1). In this sentence, Wollstonecraft also mentions "Clarissa," the eponymous character of Samuel Richardson's (1689-1761) *Clarissa, or The History of a Young Lady* (1747-48) and "Lady G—," a thinly veiled reference to Lady Grandison, formerly Harriet Byron, later wife of Sir Charles Grandison in Samuel Richardson's *The History of Sir Charles Grandison* (1753-54). Like Sophie, these idealized female characters are defined through contact with more powerful male characters.

most sublime beams. The[1] paradise they ramble in, must be of their own creating — or the prospect soon grows insipid, and not varied by a vivifying principle, fades and dies.

In an artless tale, without episodes, the mind of a woman, who has thinking powers is displayed. The female organs have been thought too weak for this arduous employment; and experience seems to justify the assertion. Without arguing physically about *possibilities* — in a fiction, such a being may be allowed to exist; whose grandeur is derived from the operations of its own faculties, not subjugated to opinion; but drawn by the individual from the original source.[2]

---

1  I here give the Reviewers an opportunity of being very witty about the Paradise of Fools, &c. [Wollstonecraft's note] Again, the note marker comes, oddly, before the phrase to which it refers. Wollstonecraft invokes Book III, lines 431-97, of John Milton's *Paradise Lost* (1667), in which Milton describes a "Paradise of Fools" (l. 496) in a strongly anti-Catholic segment of the epic. Wollstonecraft's point seems to have more to do with the self-created nature of Miltonian heavens and hells, however, as in Satan's famous line in Book I of *Paradise Lost*, "The mind is its own place, and in itself / Can make a heaven of hell, a hell of heaven" (ll. 254-55).

2  In a letter to Reverend Henry Dyson Gabell on 13 September 1787, Wollstonecraft expands on her intention in this narrative to display the results of self-directed education from her own example: "I have lately written, a fiction which I intend to give to the world; it is a tale, to illustrate an opinion of mine, that a genius will educate itself" (*Letters* 136).

# MARY.

--------------------------

## CHAP. I.

MARY, the heroine of this fiction, was the daughter of Edward, who married Eliza, a gentle, fashionable girl, with a kind of indolence in her temper, which might be termed negative good-nature: her virtues, indeed, were all of that stamp. She carefully attended to the *shews* of things, and her opinions, I should have said prejudices, were such as the generality approved of. She was educated with the expectation of a large fortune, of course became a mere machine: the homage of her attendants made a great part of her puerile amusements, and she never imagined there were any relative duties for her to fulfil: notions of her own consequence, by these means, were interwoven in her mind, and the years of youth spent in acquiring a few superficial accomplishments, without having any taste for them.[1] When she was first introduced into the polite circle, she danced with an officer, whom she faintly wished to be united to; but her father soon after recommending another in a more distinguished rank of life, she

---

1 Eliza's education—and, for that matter, Mary's, which Wollstonecraft describes hereafter—illustrates the author's belief that upper-class girls and young women are cheated out of a serious education because of the social attitude that their goal in life is to be married. In short, their financial future depends on their marital status, not on their intellect or training, and even their personal fulfillment lies in their relationships with men, rather than the discovery of their talents and development of their individual characters. When Wollstonecraft mentions Eliza's "superficial accomplishments," she refers to the typical education of an upper-class woman of her time, which occurred almost entirely in the home and aimed at making her an ideal wife and hostess: she learned French, drawing, dancing, music, and the use of globes; she might also learn some practical skills, such as embroidery, plain sewing, and accounts. In *Rights of Woman*, Wollstonecraft asserts that genuine knowledge consists in acquiring philosophical and logical abilities and that a woman's autonomy—her claim to an individual, even spiritual, identity apart from any man's—is identical with her ability to attain them:

> The power of generalizing ideas, of drawing comprehensive conclusions from individual observations, is the only acquirement, for an immortal being, that really deserves the name of knowledge.... This power has not only been denied to women; but writers have insisted that it is inconsistent, with a few exceptions, with their sexual character. Let men prove this, and I shall grant that woman only exists for man. (114)

readily submitted to his will, and promised to love, honour, and obey, (a vicious fool,) as in duty bound.

While they resided in London, they lived in the usual fashionable style, and seldom saw each other; nor were they much more sociable when they wooed rural felicity for more than half the year, in a delightful country, where Nature, with lavish hand, had scattered beauties around; for the master, with brute,[1] unconscious gaze, passed them by unobserved, and sought amusement in country sports. He hunted in the morning, and after eating an immoderate dinner, generally fell asleep: this seasonable rest enabled him to digest the cumbrous load; he would then visit some of his pretty tenants; and when he compared their ruddy glow of health with his wife's countenance, which even rouge could not enliven, it is not necessary to say which a *gourmand* would give the preference to.[2] Their vulgar dance of spirits were

---

1 The word "brute" is important in Wollstonecraft's lexicon. It appears twenty-four times in *Rights of Woman*, the very premise of which depends upon the notion that humans are, by definition, not "brutes," which acquires the meaning of base instinct in the absence of reason throughout the text. Wollstonecraft argues that, as humans, women must be recognized as having reason. On the first page of Chapter I, she queries,

In what does man's pre-eminence over the brute creation consist? The answer is as clear as that a half is less than the whole; in Reason.

What acquirement exalts one being above another? Virtue; we spontaneously reply.

For what purpose were the passions implanted? That man by struggling with them might attain a degree of knowledge denied to the brutes; whispers Experience. (15-16)

2 Wollstonecraft warns of the death of passion in marriage in *Rights of Woman*, Chapter II: "The woman who has only been taught to please will soon find that her charms are oblique sun-beams, and that they cannot have much effect on her husband's heart when they are seen every day, when the summer is past and gone.... When the husband ceases to be a lover — and the time will inevitably come, her desire of pleasing will then grow languid, or become a spring of bitterness" (51-52). Partly for this reason, she argued against marriage—even though she was to revise her position on it and convinced William Godwin to marry her when she became pregnant with her second illegitimate child (the future Mary Shelley [1797-1851], author of *Frankenstein* [1818]). Yet, her use of the word "*gourmand*" to describe the lust of Mary's father for his female tenants also points to the opposite problem plaguing marriage that Wollstonecraft outlines in *Rights of Woman*: "Women then having necessarily some duty to fulfil, more noble than to adorn their

infinitely more agreeable to his fancy than her sickly, die-away languor. Her voice was but the shadow of a sound, and she had, to complete her delicacy, so relaxed her nerves, that she became a mere nothing.[1]

Many such noughts are there in the female world! Yet she had a good opinion of her own merit, — truly, she said long prayers, — and sometimes read her Week's Preparation:[2] she dreaded that horrid place vulgarly called *hell*, the regions below; but whether her's was a mounting spirit, I cannot pretend to determine; or what sort of a planet would have been proper for her, when she left her *material* part in this world, let metaphysicians settle; I[3] have nothing to say to her unclothed spirit.

---

persons, would not contentedly be the slaves of casual appetite, which is now the situation of a very considerable number who are, literally speaking, standing dishes to which every glutton may have access" (314). By calling lustful men "*gourmands*" and "gluttons," Wollstonecraft implies that women who exist to be attractive are passive objects, or consumable beings like cattle—the very "brutes" that she is at pains to argue women are not in this tract.

1  Wollstonecraft's description of a nervous woman who is "a mere nothing" inaugurates her development of the figure of the ideal woman of sensibility, who appears throughout *Rights of Woman*. For example, she writes of women of sensibility whose "uncultivated understandings make them entirely dependent on their senses for employment and amusement" and who are thus unable "to curb the wild emotions that agitate a reed over which every passing breeze has power," so insubstantial are they; she goes on to lament that women are positively advised against developing physical strength:

> Nature has given woman a weaker frame than man; but, to ensure her husband's affections, must a wife, who, by the exercise of her mind and body, whilst she was discharging the duties of a daughter, wife, and mother, has allowed her constitution to retain its natural strength, and her nerves a healthy tone, is she, I say, to condescend, to use art, and feign a sickly delicacy, in order to secure her husband's affection? (54-55)

2  The "Week's Preparation" is religious catechism to prepare the Christian devotee for holy communion. Wollstonecraft's mockery of Mary's mother on the point of religion should not be understood as disrespect for religion as a whole, since she was devout during this period (see p. 84, note 1). Rather, she mocks the empty show of faith that is not matched by spiritual fervour.

3  This instance of self-referentiality from an otherwise third-person omniscient narrator should be considered in combination with Mary's dialogue later in the work, in which she speaks and ap-  *(continued)*

As she was sometimes obliged to be alone, or only with her French waiting-maid, she sent to the metropolis for all the new publications, and while she was dressing her hair, and she could turn her eyes from the glass, she ran over those most delightful substitutes for bodily dissipation, novels. I say bodily, or the animal soul, for a rational one[1] can find no employment in polite circles. The glare of lights, the studied inelegancies of dress, and the compliments offered up at the shrine of false beauty, are all equally addressed to the senses.[2]

When she could not any longer indulge the caprices of fancy one way, she tried another. *The Platonic Marriage, Eliza Warwick*, and some other interesting tales were perused with eagerness.[3] Nothing could be more natural than the developement of the passions, nor more striking than the views of the human heart. What delicate struggles! and uncommonly pretty turns of thought! The picture that was found on a bramble-bush, the new sensitive-plant, or tree, which caught the swain by the upper-garment, and presented to his ravished eyes a portrait. — Fatal image! — It planted a thorn in a till then insensible heart, and sent a new kind of a knight-errant into the world. But even this was nothing to the catastrophe, and the circumstance on which it hung, the hornet settling on the sleeping lover's face. What a *heart-rending* accident! She planted, in imitation of those suscep-tible souls, a rose bush; but there was not a lover to weep in

---

parently holds ideals suspiciously like those of the narrator, making this narrative an early instance of free-indirect discourse, a point of view that is more often associated with Jane Austen's (1775-1817) most popular novels.

1 A reference to Aristotelian (c. 350 BCE) definitions of the soul (vegeta-tive, sensitive, and rational) as outlined in *De Anima*.

2 These references to romantic situations suggest that Wollstonecraft aims her barbs not at novels in general, but specifically novels of sensibility, which revolve around love-plots. She thus begins to develop a daring idea that would become the core of her argument in *Rights of Woman*: that novels of sensibility hypocritically advanced the ideal of a woman who is so chaste that she is almost bodiless (see p. 79, note 1), but, in reality, they foster sexual lust in their female readers (e.g., *Rights* 431).

3 *The Platonic Marriage: A Novel, In a Series of Letters* (1786), by Mrs. H. Cartwright, and the anonymously published novel *The History of Eliza Warwick* (1778). In the endnotes to his edition of *Mary*, Gary Kelly points out that the incidents described at the end of this paragraph are from *The Platonic Marriage*.

concert with her, when she watered it with her tears. — Alas! Alas!

If my readers would excuse the sportiveness of fancy, and give me credit for genius, I would go on and tell them such tales as would force the sweet tears of sensibility to flow in copious showers down beautiful cheeks, to the discomposure of rouge, &c. &c. Nay, I would make it so interesting, that the fair peruser should beg the hair-dresser to settle the curls himself, and not interrupt her.

She had besides another resource, two most beautiful dogs, who shared her bed, and reclined on cushions near her all the day. These she watched with the most assiduous care, and bestowed on them the warmest caresses.[1] This fondness for animals was not that kind of *attendrissement*[2] which makes a person take pleasure in providing for the subsistence and comfort of a living creature; but it proceeded from vanity, it gave her an opportunity of lisping out the prettiest French expressions of ecstatic fondness, in accents that had never been attuned by tenderness.

She was chaste, according to the vulgar acceptation of the word, that is, she did not make any actual *faux pas*; she feared the world, and was indolent; but then, to make amends for this seeming self-denial, she read all the sentimental novels, dwelt on the love-scenes, and, had she thought while she read, her mind would have been contaminated; as she accompanied the lovers to the lonely arbors, and would walk with them by the clear light of the moon. She wondered her husband did not stay at home. She was jealous — why did he not love her, sit by her side, squeeze her hand, and look unutterable things? Gentle reader, I will tell thee; they neither of them felt what they could not utter. I will not pretend to say that they always annexed an idea to a word; but they had none of those feelings which are not easily analyzed.

---

1 This aspect of Mary's mother seems to be based on Lady Kingsborough, for whom Wollstonecraft worked as a governess for an unhappy year (1786-87) in Ireland. In a letter to her sister, Everina, Wollstonecraft writes of her employer, "To see a woman without any softness in her manners caressing animals, and using infantine expression — is you may conceive very absurd and ludicrous — but a fine Lady is new species to me of animals" (85).

2 French for "tenderness" or "sentiment."

# CHAP. II.

IN due time she brought forth a son, a feeble babe; and the following year a daughter. After the mother's throes she felt very few sentiments of maternal tenderness: the children were given to nurses, and she played with her dogs. Want of exercise prevented the least chance of her recovering strength; and two or three milk-fevers brought on a consumption, to which her constitution tended.[1] Her children all died in their infancy, except the two first, and she began to grow fond of the son, as he was remarkably handsome. For years she divided her time between the sofa, and the card-table. She thought not of death, though on the borders of the grave; nor did any of the duties of her station occur to her as necessary. Her children were left in the nursery; and when Mary, the little blushing girl, appeared, she would send the awkward thing away. To own the truth, she was awkward enough, in a house without any play-mates; for her brother had been sent to school, and she scarcely knew how to employ herself; she would ramble about the garden, admire the flowers, and play with the dogs. An old house-keeper told her stories, read to her, and, at last, taught her to read. Her mother talked of enquiring for a governess when her health would permit; and, in the interim desired her own maid to teach her French. As she had learned to read, she perused with avidity every book that came in her way. Neglected in every respect, and left to the operations of her own mind, she considered every thing that came under her inspection, and learned to think. She had heard of a separate state, and that angels sometimes visited this earth. She would sit in a thick wood in the park, and talk to them; make little songs addressed to

---

1   The *Oxford English Dictionary* (hereafter *OED*) defines "milk fever" as "occurring in a woman shortly after childbirth (formerly supposed to be caused by the beginning of lactation)." That this "mere nothing" should contract tuberculosis completes the portrait of her as an ideal woman of sensibility. As Clark Lawlor observes in *Consumption and Literature: The Making of the Romantic Disease* (2006), Romantic-era ideas about consumption presented it as a spiritualizing, even beautifying, wasting disease, all characteristics of the ideal woman of sensibility. Mary's mother takes no exercise in part because she has been pregnant—doctors commonly recommended absolute rest for pregnant women until the late eighteenth century—but she also fosters physical fragility as a sign of her superiority as a woman of sensibility, against which Wollstonecraft rails throughout *Rights of Woman*.

them, and sing them to tunes of her own composing; and her native wood notes wild were sweet and touching.[1]

Her father always exclaimed against female acquirements, and was glad that his wife's indolence and ill health made her not trouble herself about them. She had besides another reason, she did not wish to have a fine tall girl brought forward into notice as her daughter; she still expected to recover, and figure away in the gay world.[2] Her husband was very tyrannical and passionate; indeed so very easily irritated when inebriated, that Mary was continually in dread lest he should frighten her mother to death;[3] her sickness called forth all Mary's tenderness, and exercised her compassion so continually, that it became more than a match for

---

1  The phraseology in this sentence is from John Milton's *L'Allegro* (1645) ("Or sweetest Shakespeare Fancy's child, / Warble his native wood-notes wild" [ll. 133-34]), but it is used to confirm another literary link: with Rousseau's writings on the child of nature and the development of genius outside of the confines of standard education. In April 1791, Wollstonecraft would use the phrase again in a review of Ann Yearsley's (1756-1806) *Stanzas of Woe* (1790) for Johnson's *Analytical Review*. Yearsley was commonly called "the milkmaid poet," and, like Stephen Duck (1705-56, "the thresher poet") and John Clare (1793-1864, "the peasant poet"), she rose to popularity when English readers were fascinated by the notion of "natural" or "rural"—untaught—geniuses.

2  This idea of competition between women Wollstonecraft would develop more fully in *The Wrongs of Woman*, most memorably in the episode in which Jemima drives the pregnant girlfriend of her lover from his home and to suicide, one of the many episodes that gives the title its power as a *double-entendre*.

3  This passage strongly recalls a scene from Wollstonecraft's own life, as reported by Godwin in *Memoirs of the Author of A Vindication of the Rights of Woman* (1798) (hereafter *Memoirs*):

    her father's temper, led him sometimes to threaten ... violence towards his wife. When that was the case, Mary would throw herself between the despot and his victim, with the purpose to receive upon her own person the blows that might be directed against her mother. She has even laid whole nights upon the landing-place near their chamber-door, when, mistakenly, or with reason, she apprehended that her father might break out into paroxysms of violence. (9-10)

    Meanwhile, a biographical instance that Godwin details in a passage that follows shortly thereafter ("In some instance of passion exercised by her father to one of his dogs, she was accustomed to speak of her emotions of abhorrence, as having risen to agony" [10]) seems to be the inspiration for a phrase that Wollstonecraft uses a few paragraphs from this point in the text: "her father had a dog hung in a passion."

self-love, and was the governing propensity of her heart through life. She was violent in her temper; but she saw her father's faults, and would weep when obliged to compare his temper with her own. — She did more; artless prayers rose to Heaven for pardon, when she was conscious of having erred; and her contrition was so exceedingly painful, that she watched diligently the first movements of anger and impatience, to save herself this cruel remorse.

Sublime ideas filled her young mind — always connected with devotional sentiments; extemporary effusions of gratitude, and rhapsodies of praise would burst often from her, when she listened to the birds, or pursued the deer. She would gaze on the moon, and ramble through the gloomy path, observing the various shapes the clouds assumed, and listen to the sea that was not far distant. The wandering spirits, which she imagined inhabited every part of nature, were her constant friends and confidants. She began to consider the Great First Cause, formed just notions of his attributes, and, in particular, dwelt on his wisdom and goodness. Could she have loved her father or mother, had they returned her affection, she would not so soon, perhaps, have sought out a new world.[1]

Her sensibility prompted her to search for an object to love; on earth it was not to be found: her mother had often disappointed her, and the apparent partiality she shewed to her brother gave her exquisite pain — produced a kind of habitual melancholy, led her into a fondness for reading tales of woe, and made her almost realize the fictitious distress.

She had not any notion of death till a little chicken expired at her feet; and her father had a dog hung in a passion. She then

---

1 The implication here that Mary's reliance on God and heaven is the result of childhood neglect, and that religion is, therefore, merely dressing for psychological wounds should not be understood as reflective of Wollstonecraft's flippant or contemptuous attitude toward religion, despite the similarities between the speaker and Wollstonecraft in other respects—not to mention those between Wollstonecraft and her namesake, the "Heroine" of this tale. Indeed, her letters show that, particularly at this time in her life, Wollstonecraft was quite religious: for example, in a letter to her sister, Eliza Bishop, of June 1787, Wollstonecraft writes, "I do not forget that Gracious Being who has delivered me out of so many troubles, and allowed me to receive his mercies through the medium of my fellow-creatures" (129). However, by the end of her life, her religiosity had waned. Godwin reports in *Memoirs*, "during her whole illness, not one word of a religious cast fell from her lips" (190).

concluded animals had souls, or they would not have been subjected to the caprice of man; but what was the soul of man or beast? In this style year after year rolled on, her mother still vegetating.

A little girl who attended in the nursery fell sick. Mary paid her great attention; contrary to her wish, she was sent out of the house to her mother, a poor woman, whom necessity obliged to leave her sick child while she earned her daily bread. The poor wretch, in a fit of delirium stabbed herself, and Mary saw her dead body, and heard the dismal account; and so strongly did it impress her imagination, that every night of her life the bleeding corpse presented itself to her when she first began to slumber.[1] Tortured by it, she at last made a vow, that if she was ever mistress of a family she would herself watch over every part of it. The impression that this accident made was indelible.

As her mother grew imperceptibly worse and worse, her father, who did not understand such a lingering complaint, imagined his wife was only grown still more whimsical, and that if she could be prevailed on to exert herself, her health would soon be re-established. In general he treated her with indifference; but when her illness at all interfered with his pleasures, he expostulated in the most cruel manner, and visibly harassed the invalid. Mary would then assiduously try to turn his attention to something else; and when sent out of the room, would watch at the door, until the storm was over, for unless it was, she could not rest. Other causes also contributed to disturb her repose: her mother's luke-warm manner of performing her religious duties, filled her with anguish; and when she observed her father's vices, the unbidden tears would flow. She was miserable when beggars were driven from the gate without being relieved; if she could do it unperceived, she would give them her own breakfast, and feel gratified, when, in consequence of it, she was pinched by hunger.

She had once, or twice, told her little secrets to her mother; they were laughed at, and she determined never to do it again. In this manner was she left to reflect on her own feelings; and so strengthened were they by being meditated on, that her character early became singular and permanent. Her understanding was

---

1  Wollstonecraft would attempt suicide twice in her life. According to
   Godwin's *Memoirs*, "she was twice, with an interval of four months,
   from the end of May to the beginning of October, prompted ... to purposes of suicide" (146).

strong and clear, when not clouded by her feelings; but she was too much the creature of impulse, and the slave of compassion.

## CHAP. III.

NEAR her father's house[1] lived a poor widow, who had been brought up in affluence, but reduced to great distress by the extravagance of her husband;[2] he had destroyed his constitution while he spent his fortune; and dying, left his wife, and five small children, to live on a very scanty pittance. The eldest daughter was for some years educated by a distant relation, a Clergyman. While she was with him a young gentleman, son to a man of property in the neighbourhood, took particular notice of her. It is true, he never talked of love; but then they played and sung in concert; drew landscapes together, and while she worked he read to her, cultivated her taste, and stole imperceptibly her heart. Just at this juncture, when smiling, unanalyzed hope made every prospect bright, and gay expectation danced in her eyes, her benefactor died. She returned to her mother — the companion of her youth forgot her, they took no more sweet counsel together. This disappointment spread a sadness over her countenance, and made it interesting. She grew fond of solitude, and her character appeared similar to Mary's, though her natural disposition was very different.

She was several years older than Mary, yet her refinement, her taste, caught her eye, and she eagerly sought her friendship: before her return she had assisted the family, which was almost reduced to the last ebb; and now she had another motive to actuate her.

As she had often occasion to send messages to Ann, her new friend, mistakes were frequently made; Ann proposed that in future they should be written ones, to obviate this difficulty, and render their intercourse more agreeable. Young people are mostly fond of scribbling; Mary had had very little instruction; but by copying her friend's letters, whose hand she admired, she soon

---

1  The phrase "Near her father's house," which Wollstonecraft repeats almost exactly as the first words of the next chapter, reminds us that in the Romantic period men—not daughters, wives, or sisters—owned property and other major assets.

2  Edward Wollstonecraft, Mary Wollstonecraft's father, also spent the family fortune that he had inherited from his father in unsuccessful attempts to establish himself as a gentleman farmer (Godwin *Memoirs* 15).

became a proficient; a little practice made her write with tolerable correctness, and her genius gave force to it. In conversation, and in writing, when she felt, she was pathetic, tender and persuasive; and she expressed contempt with such energy, that few could stand the flash of her eyes.[1]

As she grew more intimate with Ann, her manners were softened, and she acquired a degree of equality in her behaviour: yet still her spirits were fluctuating, and her movements rapid. She felt less pain on account of her mother's partiality to her brother, as she hoped now to experience the pleasure of being beloved; but this hope led her into new sorrows, and, as usual, paved the way for disappointment. Ann only felt gratitude; her heart was entirely engrossed by one object, and friendship could not serve as a substitute; memory officiously retraced past scenes, and unavailing wishes made time loiter.

Mary was often hurt by the involuntary indifference which these consequences produced. When her friend was all the world to her, she found she was not as necessary to her happiness; and her delicate mind could not bear to obtrude her affection, or receive love as an alms, the offspring of pity. Very frequently has she ran to her with delight, and not perceiving any thing of the same kind in Ann's countenance, she has shrunk back; and, falling from one extreme into the other, instead of a warm greeting that was just slipping from her tongue, her expressions seemed to be dictated by the most chilling insensibility.

She would then imagine that she looked sickly or unhappy, and then all her tenderness would return like a torrent, and bear away all reflection. In this manner was her sensibility called forth, and exercised, by her mother's illness, her friend's misfortunes, and her own unsettled mind.

## CHAP. IV.

NEAR to her father's house was a range of mountains; some of them were, literally speaking, cloud-capt, for on them clouds continually rested, and gave grandeur to the prospect; and down

---

1   Godwin wrote about Wollstonecraft in *Memoirs*, "Mary was what Dr. Johnson would have called, 'a very good hater'" (10). The friendship between Mary and Ann is modelled after Wollstonecraft's youthful relationship with Fanny Blood (1757-85), whose married surname was Skeys. Wollstonecraft named her first baby, fathered by the American Gilbert Imlay (1754-1828), after her first love, Fanny.

many of their sides the little bubbling cascades ran till they swelled a beautiful river. Through the straggling trees and bushes the wind whistled, and on them the birds sung, particularly the robins; they also found shelter in the ivy of an old castle, a haunted one, as the story went; it was situated on the brow of one of the mountains, and commanded a view of the sea.[1] This castle had been inhabited by some of her ancestors; and many tales had the old house-keeper told her of the worthies who had resided there.

When her mother frowned, and her friend looked cool, she would steal to this retirement, where human foot seldom trod — gaze on the sea, observe the grey clouds, or listen to the wind which struggled to free itself from the only thing that impeded its course. When more cheerful, she admired the various dispositions of light and shade, the beautiful tints the gleams of sunshine gave to the distant hills; then she rejoiced in existence, and darted into futurity.

One way home was through the cavity of a rock covered with a thin layer of earth, just sufficient to afford nourishment to a few stunted shrubs and wild plants, which grew on its sides, and nodded over the summit. A clear stream broke out of it, and ran amongst the pieces of rocks fallen into it. Here twilight always reigned — it seemed the Temple of Solitude; yet, paradoxical as

---

1   This detailed description of landscape illustrates the Romantic obses-
    sion not only with the natural world, but also, in particular, with
    sublime environments of mountains, oceans, and any large and awe-
    inspiring sight that fills the observer with a sense of admiration and fear.
    Edmund Burke's (1729-97) aesthetic treatise, *A Philosophical Enquiry
    into the Origin of our Ideas of the Sublime and Beautiful* (1757), inspired
    the fascination for the coming generations of literary and travel writers,
    of which Wollstonecraft was both. In *Letters Written During a Short Resi-
    dence in Sweden, Norway, and Denmark* (1796), she reveals her debt to
    Burke when she writes, "what misery, as well as rapture, is produced by
    a quick perception of the beautiful and sublime when it is exercised in
    observing animated nature, when every beauteous feeling and emotion
    excites responsive sympathy, and the harmonised soul sinks into melan-
    choly or rises to ecstasy, just as the chords are touched, like the Æolian
    harp agitated by the changing wind" (72). In this novella, her attention
    to the cottage and the robins that visit it anticipate the increasing inter-
    est in contained, localized beauty—or the picturesque—which, accord-
    ing to Rachel Crawford in *Poetry, Enclosure, and the Vernacular Landscape,
    1700-1830* (2002), caught the imagination of early nineteenth-century
    writers more than their forebears.

the assertion may appear, when the foot sounded on the rock, it terrified the intruder, and inspired a strange feeling, as if the rightful sovereign was dislodged. In this retreat she read Thomson's *Seasons*, Young's *Night-Thoughts*, and *Paradise Lost*.[1]

At a little distance from it were the huts of a few poor fishermen, who supported their numerous children by their precarious labour. In these little huts she frequently rested, and denied herself every childish gratification, in order to relieve the necessities of the inhabitants. Her heart yearned for them, and would dance with joy when she had relieved their wants, or afforded them pleasure.

In these pursuits she learned the luxury of doing good; and the sweet tears of benevolence frequently moistened her eyes, and gave them a sparkle which, exclusive of that, they had not; on the contrary, they were rather fixed, and would never have been observed if her soul had not animated them. They were not at all like those brilliant ones which look like polished diamonds, and dart from every superfice, giving more light to the beholders than they receive themselves.[2]

---

1   James Thomson's (1700-48) *The Seasons* (1727-30); Edward Young's (1683-1765) *The Complaint; or, Night-thoughts on Life, Death, & Immortality* (1742); and Milton's *Paradise Lost* (1667). Mary's reading list constitutes a kind of proto-Romantic primer, with the first two works illustrating the importance of eighteenth-century "graveyard poetry," particularly in the formation of Romantic-era notions of sensibility (of which Mary is a representative), and Milton's epic gesturing to the heroine's appreciation of the weighty and sublime.

2   A reference to the Petrarchan sonnet tradition that idealized women as heavenly, faultlessly beautiful, and (as the last phrase here indicates) whose importance and very existence derives from their relation to men. The reference to the poetic figure involving the light in a woman's eyes may be from Petrarch's (1304-74) sonnet 173, "*Mirando 'l sol de' begli occhi sereno*" (c. 1327?) (translated as "While gazing at the clear sun of fair eyes" by Mark Musa [265] or Sir Thomas Wyatt's (1503-42) English re-working of it, "Avising the Bright Beams" (1557). (I am indebted to Flavio Gregori for directing me to the Musa translation.) In denying that her heroine lives up to these idealizing standards, though, Wollstonecraft follows more closely the poetic rebellion made famous by William Shakespeare (1564?-1616) in "Sonnet 130: My Mistress' Eyes are Nothing like the Sun" (1609). Notably, however much she protests that this woman of sensibility should live for others, Mary repeatedly devotes her life to caring for the ill.

Her benevolence, indeed, knew no bounds; the distress of others carried her out of herself; and she rested not till she had relieved or comforted them.[1] The warmth of her compassion often made her so diligent, that many things occurred to her, which might have escaped a less interested observer.

In like manner, she entered with such spirit into whatever she read, and the emotions thereby raised were so strong, that it soon became a part of her mind.

Enthusiastic sentiments of devotion at this period actuated her; her Creator was almost apparent to her senses in his works; but they were mostly the grand or solemn features of Nature which she delighted to contemplate. She would stand and behold the waves rolling, and think of the voice that could still the tumultuous deep.

These propensities gave the colour to her mind, before the passions began to exercise their tyrannic sway, and particularly pointed out those which the soil would have a tendency to nurse.

Years after, when wandering through the same scenes, her imagination has strayed back, to trace the first placid sentiments they inspired, and she would earnestly desire to regain the same peaceful tranquillity.

Many nights she sat up, if I may be allowed the expression, *conversing* with the Author of Nature, making verses, and singing hymns of her own composing. She considered also, and tried to discern what end her various faculties were destined to pursue; and had a glimpse of a truth, which afterwards more fully unfolded itself.

She thought that only an infinite being could fill the human soul, and that when other objects were followed as a means of happiness, the delusion led to misery, the consequence of disappointment. Under the influence of ardent affections, how often has she forgot this conviction, and as often returned to it again,

---

1 Scottish philosopher Adam Smith's (1723-90) *The Theory of Moral Sentiments* (1759) established the importance of sympathy as a social adherent and motivator and influenced late eighteenth-century notions of sensibility, as Wollstonecraft's words indicate here. In the suggestion that Mary's sympathy for others creates an almost palpable bond between herself and the objects of her pity ("the distress of others carried her out of herself"), Wollstonecraft may refer specifically to Section I, Part I of Smith's book, entitled "Of Sympathy," in which he develops the idea that "The passions ... may seem to be transfused from one man to another, instantaneously" (6).

when it struck her with redoubled force. Often did she taste unmixed delight; her joys, her ecstacies arose from genius.[1]

She was now fifteen, and she wished to receive the holy sacrament; and perusing the scriptures, and discussing some points of doctrine which puzzled her, she would sit up half the night, her favourite time for employing her mind; she too plainly perceived that she saw through a glass darkly;[2] and that the bounds set to stop our intellectual researches, is one of the trials of a probationary state.

But her affections were roused by the display of divine mercy; and she eagerly desired to commemorate the dying love of her great benefactor. The night before the important day, when she was to take on herself her baptismal vow, she could not go to bed; the sun broke in on her meditations, and found her not exhausted by her watching.

The orient pearls were strewed around — she hailed the morn, and sung with wild delight, Glory to God on high, good will towards men.[3] She was indeed so much affected when she joined in the prayer for her eternal preservation, that she could hardly conceal her violent emotions; and the recollection never failed to wake her dormant piety when earthly passions made it grow languid.

These various movements of her mind were not commented on, nor were the luxuriant shoots restrained by culture. The servants and the poor adored her.

---

1 As the subtitle of *Mary* suggests, one of the major themes of this novella is genius, specifically how it develops according to the natural inclination of the subject and what may result from such an experiment for the female genius. Wollstonecraft uses the word "genius" as it appears in the third definition of today's *OED* and, indeed, as it was used throughout the eighteenth century: "Of persons: Characteristic disposition; inclination; bent, turn or temper of mind." In his influential *Dictionary of the English Language* (1755), Samuel Johnson (1709-84) gives a similar definition as his fourth ("Disposition of nature by which any one is qualified for some peculiar employment") and fifth ("Nature; disposition"). The other relevant meaning of "genius" for this period Johnson gives as his second definition: "A man endowed with superiour faculties." Similarly, the *OED* gives, as the fifth definition, "Native intellectual power of an exalted type."

2 From St. Paul's letter to the Corinthians: "For now we see through a glass, darkly; but then face to face: now I know in part; but then shall I know even as also I am known" (1 Corinthians 13:12).

3 These phrases are from the Communion portion of the Anglican mass in the *Book of Common Prayer*: "GLORY be to God on high, and in earth peace, good will toward men" (282).

In order to be enabled to gratify herself in the highest degree, she practiced the most rigid œconomy, and had such power over her appetites and whims, that without any great effort she conquered them so entirely, that when her understanding or affections had an object, she almost forgot she had a body which required nourishment.

This habit of thinking, this kind of absorption, gave strength to the passions.

We will now enter on the more active field of life.

## CHAP. V.

A FEW months after Mary was turned of seventeen, her brother was attacked by a violent fever, and died before his father could reach the school.

She was now an heiress, and her mother began to think her of consequence, and did not call her *the child*.[1] Proper masters were sent for; she was taught to dance, and an extraordinary master procured to perfect her in that most necessary of all accomplishments.

A part of the estate she was to inherit had been litigated, and the heir of the person who still carried on a Chancery suit,[2] was only two years younger than our heroine. The fathers, spite of the

---

1   This abrupt end to the fictional eldest brother's life and Mary's inheritance of the family wealth (and respect) may be viewed as Wollstonecraft's revenge fantasy. Janet Todd describes "her envy for her eldest brother Ned, who had been singled out by their mother's favour and by their grandfather's excluding will, which left a third of his estate to this one child" (*Letters* xxi) of seven, of which Wollstonecraft was the eldest girl. The issue of primogenitureship, the passing of family wealth to the eldest son, would become a flashpoint in the English debate about the French Revolution, with Thomas Paine (1737-1809) responding to Edmund Burke's defence of the class system in *Reflections on the Revolution in France* (1790) with the following reply in *The Rights of Man* (1791):

> By the aristocratical law of primogenitureship, in a family of six children, five are exposed. Aristocracy has never more than one child. The rest are begotten to be devoured. They are thrown to the cannibal for its prey, and the natural parent prepares the unnatural repast. (82; Paine's emphasis)

2   The second definition of "chancery" in the *OED* is as follows: "The court of the Lord Chancellor of England, the highest court of judicature next to the House of Lords; but, since the Judicature Act of 1873, a division of the High Court of Justice."

dispute, frequently met, and, in order to settle it amicably, they one day, over a bottle, determined to quash it by a marriage, and, by uniting the two estates, to preclude all farther enquiries into the merits of their different claims.

While this important matter was settling, Mary was otherwise employed. Ann's mother's resources were failing; and the ghastly phantom, poverty, made hasty strides to catch them in his clutches. Ann had not fortitude enough to brave such accumulated misery; besides, the canker-worm was lodged in her heart, and preyed on her health. She denied herself every little comfort; things that would be no sacrifice when a person is well, are absolutely necessary to alleviate bodily pain, and support the animal functions.

There were many elegant amusements, that she had acquired a relish for, which might have taken her mind off from its most destructive bent; but these her indigence would not allow her to enjoy: forced then, by way of relaxation, to play the tunes her lover admired, and handle the pencil he taught her to hold, no wonder his image floated on her imagination, and that taste invigorated love.

Poverty, and all its inelegant attendants, were in her mother's abode; and she, though a good sort of a woman, was not calculated to banish, by her trivial, uninteresting chat, the delirium in which her daughter was lost.

This ill-fated love had given a bewitching softness to her manners, a delicacy so truly feminine, that a man of any feeling could not behold her without wishing to chase her sorrows away. She was timid and irresolute, and rather fond of dissipation; grief only had power to make her reflect.

In every thing it was not the great, but the beautiful, or the pretty, that caught her attention. And in composition, the polish of style, and harmony of numbers, interested her much more than the flights of genius, or abstracted speculations.

She often wondered at the books Mary chose, who, though she had a lively imagination, would frequently study authors whose works were addressed to the understanding.[1] This liking taught

---

1 Wollstonecraft would make the subject of female education a pillar of her argument in *Rights of Woman*, declaring at several points that the range of women's reading should be expanded. For instance, she writes, "Gardening, experimental philosophy, and literature, would afford them subjects to think of and matter for conversation, that in some degree would exercise their understandings" (165).

her to arrange her thoughts, and argue with herself, even when under the influence of the most violent passions.

Ann's misfortunes and ill health were strong ties to bind Mary to her; she wished so continually to have a home to receive her in, that it drove every other desire out of her mind; and, dwelling on the tender schemes which compassion and friendship dictated, she longed most ardently to put them in practice.

Fondly as she loved her friend, she did not forget her mother, whose decline was so imperceptible, that they were not aware of her approaching dissolution. The physician, however, observing the most alarming symptoms; her husband was apprised of her immediate danger; and then first mentioned to her his designs with respect to his daughter.

She approved of them; Mary was sent for; she was not at home; she had rambled to visit Ann, and found her in an hysteric fit. The landlord of her little farm had sent his agent for the rent, which had long been due to him; and he threatened to seize the stock that still remained, and turn them out, if they did not very shortly discharge the arrears.

As this man made a private fortune by harassing the tenants of the person to whom he was deputy, little was to be expected from his forbearance.

All this was told to Mary — and the mother added, she had many other creditors who would, in all probability, take the alarm, and snatch from them all that had been saved out of the wreck. "I could bear all," she cried; "but what will become of my children? Of this child," pointing to the fainting Ann, "whose constitution is already undermined by care and grief — where will she go?" — Mary's heart ceased to beat while she asked the question — She attempted to speak; but the inarticulate sounds died away. Before she had recovered herself, her father called himself to enquire for her; and desired her instantly to accompany him home.

Engrossed by the scene of misery she had been witness to, she walked silently by his side, when he roused her out of her reverie by telling her that in all likelihood her mother had not many hours to live; and before she could return him any answer, informed her that they had both determined to marry her to Charles, his friend's son; he added, the ceremony was to be performed directly, that her mother might be witness of it; for such a desire she had expressed with childish eagerness.

Overwhelmed by this intelligence, Mary rolled her eyes about, then, with a vacant stare, fixed them on her father's face; but they were no longer a sense; they conveyed no ideas to the brain. As she drew near the house, her wonted presence of mind returned: after this suspension of thought, a thousand darted into her mind, — her dying mother, — her friend's miserable situation, — and an extreme horror at taking — at being forced to take, such a hasty step; but she did not feel the disgust, the reluctance, which arises from a prior attachment.

She loved Ann better than any one in the world — to snatch her from the very jaws of destruction — she would have encountered a lion. To have this friend constantly with her; to make her mind easy with respect to her family, would it not be superlative bliss?

Full of these thoughts she entered her mother's chamber, but they then fled at the sight of a dying parent. She went to her, took her hand; it feebly pressed her's. "My child," said the languid mother: the words reached her heart; she had seldom heard them pronounced with accents denoting affection; "My child, I have not always treated you with kindness — God forgive me! do you?" — Mary's tears strayed in a disregarded stream; on her bosom the big drops fell, but did not relieve the fluttering tenant. "I forgive you!" said she, in a tone of astonishment.

The clergyman came in to read the service for the sick, and afterwards the marriage ceremony was performed. Mary stood like a statue of Despair, and pronounced the awful vow without thinking of it; and then ran to support her mother, who expired the same night in her arms.

Her husband set off for the continent the same day, with a tutor, to finish his studies at one of the foreign universities.

Ann was sent for to console her, not on account of the departure of her new relation, a boy she seldom took any notice of, but to reconcile her to her fate; besides, it was necessary she should have a female companion, and there was not any maiden aunt in the family, or cousin of the same class.

## CHAP. VI.

MARY was allowed to pay the rent which gave her so much uneasiness, and she exerted every nerve to prevail on her father effectually to succour the family; but the utmost she could obtain was a small sum very inadequate to the purpose, to enable the poor woman to carry into execution a little scheme of industry near the metropolis. Her intention of leaving that part of the country, had much more weight with him, than Mary's arguments, drawn from motives of philanthropy and friendship; this was a language he did not understand; expressive of occult qualities he never thought of, as they could not be seen or felt.

After the departure of her mother, Ann still continued to languish, though she had a nurse who was entirely engrossed by the desire of amusing her. Had her health been re-established, the time would have passed in a tranquil, improving manner.

During the year of mourning they lived in retirement; music, drawing, and reading, filled up the time; and Mary's taste and judgment were both improved by contracting a habit of observation, and permitting the simple beauties of Nature to occupy her thoughts.

She had a wonderful quickness in discerning distinctions and combining ideas, that at the first glance did not appear to be similar. But these various pursuits did not banish all her cares, or carry off all her constitutional black bile.[1] Before she enjoyed Ann's society, she imagined it would have made her completely happy: she was disappointed, and yet knew not what to complain of.

As her friend could not accompany her in her walks, and wished to be alone, for a very obvious reason, she would return to her old haunts, retrace her anticipated pleasures — and wonder how they changed their colour in possession, and proved so futile.

She had not yet found the companion she looked for. Ann and she were not congenial minds, nor did she contribute to her comfort in the degree she expected. She shielded her

---

1 The phrase "black bile" is a reference to the ancient and medieval theory that the health of the human body and mind relies on the balance of the four humours within it. If one has an excess of black bile (or choler—blood, yellow bile, and phlegm are the three other humours), then one would be prone to melancholy. Common medical treatment attempted to reduce the excess of a humour, or increase an insufficient humour, through measures such as purges and bleeding. In the foregoing sentence, the description of Mary's talent for "discerning distinctions and combining ideas" is a reference to John Locke's (1632-1704) hugely influential work, *An Essay Concerning Human Understanding* (1690), in which he defines "wit" and "judgment" thus: "*Wit* ... [lies] most in the assemblage of ideas, and putting those together with quickness and variety, wherein can be found any resemblance or congruity ... [but] *judgment*, on the contrary, lies quite on the other side, in separating carefully, one from another, ideas where can be found the least difference, thereby to avoid being mis-led by similitude" (219).

from poverty; but this was only a negative blessing; when under the pressure it was very grievous, and still more so were the apprehensions; but when exempt from them, she was not contented.

Such is human nature, its laws were not to be inverted to gratify our heroine, and stop the progress of her understanding, happiness only flourished in paradise — we cannot taste and live.

Another year passed away with increasing apprehensions. Ann had a hectic cough,[1] and many unfavourable prognostics: Mary then forgot every thing but the fear of losing her, and even imagined that her recovery would have made her happy.

Her anxiety led her to study physic, and for some time she only read books of that cast;[2] and this knowledge, literally speaking, ended in vanity and vexation of spirit, as it enabled her to foresee what she could not prevent.

As her mind expanded, her marriage appeared a dreadful misfortune; she was sometimes reminded of the heavy yoke, and bitter was the recollection!

In one thing there seemed to be a sympathy between them, for she wrote formal answers to his as formal letters. An extreme dislike took root in her mind; the sound of his name made her turn sick; but she forgot all, listening to Ann's cough, and supporting her languid frame. She would then catch her to her bosom with convulsive eagerness, as if to save her from sinking into an opening grave.

---

1  Ann's "hectic cough" is a common sign of tuberculosis, or consumption. The original for Ann, Fanny Skeys (née Blood), died of consumption.
2  Wollstonecraft was a strong advocate of basic medical education for women (which was thought improper at the time) partly because she worried about the dangers of traditional medicine as practiced by women without proper academic training:
    In public schools women, to guard against the errors of ignorance, should be taught the elements of anatomy and medicine, not only to enable them to take proper care of their own health, but to make them rational nurses of their infants, parents, and husbands; for the bills of mortality are swelled by the blunders of self-willed old women, who give nostrums of their own without knowing any thing of the human frame. (410-11)
    She shows herself here to be a promoter of modern scientific knowledge, not just a blind advocate for all women.

# CHAP. VII.

IT was the will of Providence that Mary should experience almost every species of sorrow. Her father was thrown from his horse, when his blood was in a very inflammatory state, and the bruises were very dangerous; his recovery was not expected by the physical tribe.[1]

Terrified at seeing him so near death, and yet so ill prepared for it, his daughter sat by his bed, oppressed by the keenest anguish, which her piety increased.

Her grief had nothing selfish in it; he was not a friend or protector; but he was her father, an unhappy wretch, going into eternity, depraved and thoughtless. Could a life of sensuality be a preparation for a peaceful death? Thus meditating, she passed the still midnight hour by his bedside.

The nurse fell asleep, nor did a violent thunder storm interrupt her repose, though it made the night appear still more terrific to Mary. Her father's unequal breathing alarmed her, when she heard a long drawn breath, she feared it was his last, and watching for another, a dreadful peal of thunder struck her ears. Considering the separation of the soul and body, this night seemed sadly solemn, and the hours long.

Death is indeed a king of terrors when he attacks the vicious man![2] The compassionate heart finds not any comfort; but dreads an eternal separation. No transporting greetings are anticipated, when the survivors also shall have finished their course; but all is black! — The grave may truly be said to receive the departed — this is the sting of death!

Night after night Mary watched, and this excessive fatigue impaired her own health, but had a worse effect on Ann; though

---

1  Wollstonecraft's use of the odd phrase "physical tribe" to describe physicians may indicate a degree of disdain, as it seems to present them as members of a primitive club—although it was not uncommon for authors to use the word "tribe" in this (now uncommon) sense, such as in calling birds members of the "feathered tribe." The phrase "inflammatory state" to describe blood denoted that it was infected. For example, in *A Complete Treatise on Gangrene and Sphacelus; With a New Method of Amputation* (1765), Sylvester O'Halloran (1728-1807) states, "The next state of blood which may produce a gangrene, is an hot, bilious, and highly inflammatory one. The parts are endued with a great degree of sensibility; and a slight hurt will often bring on the most alarming symptoms" (5).

2  Job 18:14: "His confidence shall be rooted out of his tabernacle, and it shall bring him to the king of terrors."

she constantly went to bed, she could not rest; a number of uneasy thoughts obtruded themselves; and apprehensions about Mary, whom she loved as well as her exhausted heart could love, harassed her mind. After a sleepless, feverish night she had a violent fit of coughing, and burst a blood-vessel. The physician, who was in the house, was sent for, and when he left the patient, Mary, with an authoritative voice, insisted on knowing his real opinion. Reluctantly he gave it, that her friend was in a critical state; and if she passed the approaching winter in England, he imagined she would die in the spring; a season fatal to consumptive disorders. The spring! — Her husband was then expected. — Gracious Heaven, could she bear all this.

In a few days her father breathed his last. The horrid sensations his death occasioned were too poignant to be durable: and Ann's danger, and her own situation, made Mary deliberate what mode of conduct she should pursue. She feared this event might hasten the return of her husband, and prevent her putting into execution a plan she had determined on. It was to accompany Ann to a more salubrious climate.

## CHAP. VIII.

I MENTIONED before, that Mary had never had any particular attachment, to give rise to the disgust that daily gained ground. Her friendship for Ann occupied her heart, and resembled a passion. She had had, indeed, several transient likings; but they did not amount to love. The society of men of genius delighted her, and improved her faculties. With beings of this class she did not often meet; it is a rare genus;[1] her first favourites were men past the meridian of life, and of a philosophic turn.

---

1 Wollstonecraft's use of the terms "class" and "genus" in this sentence suggests the influence of botanical studies on her thinking, particularly Carl Linnaeus's (1707-78) 1732 theory of the sexual System of Plants. Richard Sha argues in *Perverse Romanticism: Aesthetics and Sexuality in Britain, 1750-1832* (2009) that Wollstonecraft, along with several other Romantic-era radicals, adopted Linnaeus' frank approach to plant sexuality as the basis for their revolutionary discourse on human sexuality. Wollstonecraft may have read *Principia Botanica: or, A Concise and Easy Introduction to the Sexual Botany of Linnæus. With the Genera; Their Mode of Growth, (as Tree, Shrub, or Herb;) The Number of Species to Each Genus* ... (1787), published only a year before *Mary*, which sought to popularize Linnaean botany; it was written by Robert Waring Darwin (1724-1816), older brother of Erasmus Darwin (1731-1802) and uncle to Charles Darwin (1809-82).

Determined on going to the South of France, or Lisbon; she wrote to the man she had promised to obey. The physicians had said change of air was necessary for her as well as her friend. She mentioned this, and added, "Her comfort, almost her existence, depended on the recovery of the invalid she wished to attend; and that should she neglect to follow the medical advice she had received, she should never forgive herself, or those who endeavoured to prevent her." Full of her design, she wrote with more than usual freedom; and this letter was like most of her others, a transcript of her heart.

"This dear friend," she exclaimed, "I love for her agreeable qualities, and substantial virtues. Continual attention to her health, and the tender office of a nurse, have created an affection very like a maternal one — I am her only support, she leans on me — could I forsake the forsaken, and break the bruised reed — No — I would die first! I must — I will go."

She would have added, "you would very much oblige me by consenting;" but her heart revolted — and irresolutely she wrote something about wishing him happy. — "Do I not wish all the world well?" she cried, as she subscribed her name — It was blotted, the letter sealed in a hurry, and sent out of her sight; and she began to prepare for her journey.

By the return of the post she received an answer; it contained some common-place remarks on her romantic friendship, as he termed it; "But as the physicians advised change of air, he had no objection."

## CHAP. IX.

THERE was nothing now to retard their journey; and Mary chose Lisbon[1] rather than France, on account of its being

---

1 Romantic-era treatments for tuberculosis often included travel to warmer climates (which is why, for example, John Keats went to Rome, where he died). Wollstonecraft travelled to Lisbon to be with her friend Fanny Skeys (*née* Blood), who had tuberculosis and died in Portugal only half a year after giving birth. As Wollstonecraft reports in a letter to her sister, Eliza, "when I arrived here [in Lisbon] Fanny was in labour and ... four hours after she was delivered of a boy" (63). In *Memoirs*, Godwin adds that Wollstonecraft's "residence in Lisbon was not long. She arrived but a short time before her friend was prematurely delivered, and the event was fatal to both mother and child. Frances Blood, hitherto the chosen object of Mary's attachment, died on the twenty-ninth of November 1785" (47).

further removed from the only person she wished not to see.

They set off accordingly for Falmouth,[1] in their way to that city. The journey was of use to Ann, and Mary's spirits were raised by her recovered looks — She had been in despair — now she gave way to hope, and was intoxicated with it. On ship-board Ann always remained in the cabin; the sight of the water terrified her: on the contrary, Mary, after she was gone to bed, or when she fell asleep in the day, went on deck, conversed with the sailors, and surveyed the boundless expanse before her with delight. One instant she would regard the ocean, the next the beings who braved its fury. Their insensibility and want of fear, she could not name courage; their thoughtless mirth was quite of an animal kind, and their feelings as impetuous and uncertain as the element they plowed.

They had only been a week at sea when they hailed the rock of Lisbon, and the next morning anchored at the castle.[2] After the customary visits, they were permitted to go on shore, about three miles from the city; and while one of the crew, who understood the language, went to procure them one of the ugly carriages peculiar to the country, they waited in the Irish convent, which is situated close to the Tagus.[3]

Some of the people offered to conduct them into the church, where there was a fine organ playing; Mary followed them, but Ann preferred staying with a nun she had entered into conversation with.

---

1 Falmouth is a town and port on the River Fal on the south coast of Cornwall, England.

2 The "rock of Lisbon," also known as Cape Roca (or *Cabo da Roca*) in the Sintra area of Portugal, is the most westward point of mainland Europe. The Castle of São Jorge (or *Castelo de São Jorge*) overlooks the city of Lisbon and the Tagus River (*Rio Tejo*). The distance between the two points is roughly 60 kilometres by sea.

3 Probably a reference to the convent of Bom Sucesso in Belém, Lisbon, which was founded by Irish Dominican nuns in 1639. Situated near the banks of the Tagus, it is about 7.5 kilometres from Lisbon. Wollstonecraft's reference to Portugal's "ugly carriages" is curious. The National Coach Museum, also in Belém, Lisbon, houses a fine collection of Portuguese carriages from as early as the seventeenth century that are stunning. However, historian Sallie Walrond describes the "Portuguese Cabriolet," "built between 1767 and 1790" as differing "considerably from an English Cabriolet" (97); this difference may have given rise to Wollstonecraft's condemnation.

One of the nuns, who had a sweet voice, was singing; Mary was struck with awe; her heart joined in the devotion; and tears of gratitude and tenderness flowed from her eyes. My Father, I thank thee! burst from her — words were inadequate to express her feelings. Silently, she surveyed the lofty dome; heard unaccustomed sounds; and saw faces, strange ones, that she could not yet greet with fraternal love.

In an unknown land, she considered that the Being she adored inhabited eternity, was ever present in unnumbered worlds. When she had not any one she loved near her, she was particularly sensible of the presence of her Almighty Friend.

The arrival of the carriage put a stop to her speculations; it was to conduct them to an hotel, fitted up for the reception of invalids. Unfortunately, before they could reach it there was a violent shower of rain; and as the wind was very high, it beat against the leather curtains, which they drew along the front of the vehicle, to shelter themselves from it; but it availed not, some of the rain forced its way, and Ann felt the effects of it, for she caught cold, spite of Mary's precautions.

As is the custom, the rest of the invalids, or lodgers, sent to enquire after their health; and as soon as Ann left her chamber, in which her complaints seldom confined her the whole day, they came in person to pay their compliments. Three fashionable females, and two gentlemen; the one a brother of the eldest of the young ladies, and the other an invalid, who came, like themselves, for the benefit of the air. They entered into conversation immediately.

People who meet in a strange country, and are all together in a house, soon get acquainted, without the formalities which attend visiting in separate houses, where they are surrounded by domestic friends. Ann was particularly delighted at meeting with agreeable society; a little hectic fever generally made her low-spirited in the morning, and lively in the evening, when she wished for company. Mary, who only thought of her, determined to cultivate their acquaintance, as she knew, that if her mind could be diverted, her body might gain strength.

They were all musical, and proposed having little concerts. One of the gentlemen played on the violin, and the other on the german-flute.[1] The instruments were brought in, with all the eagerness that attends putting a new scheme in execution.

---

1 A "german-flute" is a transverse flute, so called to distinguish it from the recorder, which is held in front of the flautist, as opposed to the side. The word "german" is not capitalized in the source text.

Mary had not said much, for she was diffident; she seldom joined in general conversations; though her quickness of penetration enabled her soon to enter into the characters of those she conversed with; and her sensibility made her desirous of pleasing every human creature. Besides, if her mind was not occupied by any particular sorrow, or study, she caught reflected pleasure, and was glad to see others happy, though their mirth did not interest her.

This day she was continually thinking of Ann's recovery, and encouraging the cheerful hopes, which though they dissipated the spirits that had been condensed by melancholy, yet made her wish to be silent. The music, more than the conversation, disturbed her reflections; but not at first. The gentleman who played on the german-flute, was a handsome, well-bred, sensible man; and his observations, if not original, were pertinent.

The other, who had not said much, began to touch the violin, and played a little Scotch ballad; he brought such a thrilling sound out of the instrument, that Mary started, and looking at him with more attention than she had done before, and saw, in a face rather ugly, strong lines of genius.[1] His manners were awkward, that kind of awkwardness which is often found in literary men: he seemed a thinker, and delivered his opinions in elegant expressions, and musical tones of voice.

When the concert was over, they all retired to their apartments. Mary always slept with Ann, as she was subject to terrifying dreams; and frequently in the night was obliged to be supported, to avoid suffocation.[2] They chatted about their new acquaintance in their own apartment, and, with respect to the gentlemen, differed in opinion.

## CHAP. X.

EVERY day almost they saw their new acquaintance; and civility produced intimacy. Mary sometimes left her friend with them;

---

1 A passing reference to Johann Caspar Lavater's (1741-1801) theory of physiognomy. See *The Wrongs of Woman* (p. 165, note 1) for more information on this topic, as well as Appendix D2 for passages from Lavater's text, and Appendix A2 for passages from Wollstonecraft's physiognomical fiction, "Cave of Fancy."

2 Ann's tuberculosis, a fatal lung disease, is the probable cause of her symptoms of suffocation at night; tuberculosis also causes night-sweats, which may be connected to her nightmares (that is, she may perceive that the nightmares are produced by or cause her night-sweats).

while she indulged herself in viewing new modes of life, and searching out the causes which produced them. She had a metaphysical turn, which inclined her to reflect on every object that passed by her; and her mind was not like a mirror, which receives every floating image, but does not retain them:[1] she had not any prejudices, for every opinion was examined before it was adopted.

The Roman Catholic ceremonies attracted her attention, and gave rise to conversations when they all met; and one of the gentlemen continually introduced deistical notions, when he ridiculed the pageantry they all were surprised at observing. Mary thought of both the subjects, the Romish tenets, and the deistical doubts; and though not a sceptic, thought it right to examine the evidence on which her faith was built. She read Butler's *Analogy*, and some other authors: and these researches made her a christian from conviction, and she learned charity, particularly with respect to sectaries;[2] saw that apparently good and solid arguments might take their rise from different points of view; and she rejoiced to find that those she should not concur with had some reason on their side.

---

1   A reference to the "common sense" school of philosophy, founded by Scottish philosopher Thomas Reid (1710-96), who established an epistemology of sensation in his seminal work, *An Inquiry into the Human Mind, on the Principles of Common Sense* (1764), where he argues "that the mind, like a mirror, receives the images of things from without, by means of the senses" (120).

2   The phrases "deistical doubts" and "sceptic[ism]" are linked in this passage; both deism and the eighteenth-century philosophy of scepticism offered a challenge to conventional English religion on the basis of empirical reality. Deism includes belief in a divine creator as the source of material reality, but it rejects the Christian belief in supernatural events and the Bible. Religious scepticism was expressed most forcefully in eighteenth-century England by the Scottish empiricist philosopher David Hume (1711-76), who argued that all of our ideas are formed by our sensory perceptions of the world and, therefore, we can have no idea of God because we can never imagine that about which we have never had a previous idea. Joseph Butler (1692-1752) attempted to defend orthodox religion from such attacks in *The Analogy of Religion* (1736), in which he argues that the similarity between the Biblical account of divine rule and natural law proves that there must be one Divine source for both. Finally, "sectaries" refers to adherents to religious sects; they were frequently maligned as zealous and "enthusiastic," or mad.

# CHAP. XI.

WHEN I mentioned the three ladies, I said they were fashionable women; and it was all the praise, as a faithful historian, I could bestow on them; the only thing in which they were consistent. I forgot to mention that they were all of one family, a mother, her daughter, and niece. The daughter was sent by her physician, to avoid a northerly winter; the mother, her niece, and nephew, accompanied her.

They were people of rank; but unfortunately, though of an ancient family, the title had descended to a very remote branch — a branch they took care to be intimate with; and servilely copied the Countess's airs. Their minds were shackled with a set of notions concerning propriety, the fitness of things for the world's eye, trammels which always hamper weak people. What will the world say? was the first thing that was thought of, when they intended doing any thing they had not done before. Or what would the Countess do on such an occasion? And when this question was answered, the right or wrong was discovered without the trouble of their having any idea of the matter in their own heads. This same Countess was a fine planet, and the satellites observed a most harmonic dance around her.[1]

After this account it is scarcely necessary to add, that their minds had received very little cultivation. They were taught French, Italian, and Spanish; English was their vulgar tongue. And what did they learn? Hamlet will tell you — words — words.[2] But let me not forget that they squalled Italian songs in the true *gusto*. Without having any seeds sown in their understanding, or the affections of the heart set to work, they were brought out of their nursery, or the place they were secluded in, to prevent their faces being common; like blazing stars, to captivate Lords.

---

1 A reference to the Pythagorean theory of the harmony of the spheres, in which the earth and other planets are said to "dance" or move around a central point in a numerically predictable and beautiful way correspondent to the chords of musical instruments, thereby producing a symphony.

2 From Act II, Scene ii of William Shakespeare's *The Tragedy of Hamlet, Prince of Denmark* (1600?):
Polonius: "... What / do you read, my lord?"
Hamlet:      "Words, words, words." (ll. 195-97)

They were pretty, and hurrying from one party of pleasure to another, occasioned the disorder which required change of air. The mother, if we except her being near twenty years older, was just the same creature; and these additional years only served to make her more tenaciously adhere to her habits of folly, and decide with stupid gravity, some trivial points of ceremony, as a matter of the last importance; of which she was a competent judge, from having lived in the fashionable world so long: that world to which the ignorant look up as we do to the sun.

It appears to me that every creature has some notion — or rather relish, of the sublime. Riches, and the consequent state, are the sublime of weak minds: — These images fill, nay, are too big for their narrow souls.

One afternoon, which they had engaged to spend together, Ann was so ill, that Mary was obliged to send an apology for not attending the tea-table. The apology brought them on the carpet; and the mother, with a look of solemn importance, turned to the sick man, whose name was Henry, and said; "Though people of the first fashion are frequently at places of this kind, intimate with they know not who; yet I do not choose that my daughter, whose family is so respectable, should be intimate with any one she would blush to know elsewhere. It is only on that account, for I never suffer her to be with any one but in my company," added she, sitting more erect; and a smile of self-complacency dressed her countenance.

"I have enquired concerning these strangers, and find that the one who has the most dignity in her manners, is really a woman of fortune." "Lord, mamma, how ill she dresses": mamma went on; "She is a romantic creature, you must not copy her, miss; yet she is an heiress of the large fortune in ---shire, of which you may remember to have heard the Countess speak the night you had on the dancing-dress that was so much admired; but she is married."

She then told them the whole story as she heard it from her maid, who picked it out of Mary's servant. "She is a foolish creature, and this friend that she pays as much attention to as if she was a lady of quality, is a beggar." "Well, how strange!" cried the girls.

"She is, however, a charming creature," said her nephew. Henry sighed, and strode across the room once or twice; then took up his violin, and played the air which first struck Mary; he had often heard her praise it.

The music was uncommonly melodious, "And came stealing on the senses like the sweet south."[1] The well-known sounds reached Mary as she sat by her friend — she listened without knowing that she did — and shed tears almost without being conscious of it. Ann soon fell asleep, as she had taken an opiate. Mary, then brooding over her fears, began to imagine she had deceived herself — Ann was still very ill; hope had beguiled many heavy hours; yet she was displeased with herself for admitting this welcome guest. — And she worked up her mind to such a degree of anxiety, that she determined, once more, to seek medical aid.

No sooner did she determine, than she ran down with a discomposed look, to enquire of the ladies who she should send for. When she entered the room she could not articulate her fears — it appeared like pronouncing Ann's sentence of death;[2] her faultering tongue dropped some broken words, and she remained silent. The ladies wondered that a person of her sense should be so little mistress of herself; and began to administer some common-place comfort, as, that it was our duty to submit to the will of Heaven, and the like trite consolations, which Mary did not answer; but waving her hand, with an air of impatience, she exclaimed, "I cannot live without her! — I have no other friend; if I lose her, what a desart will the world be to me." "No other friend," re-echoed they, "have you not a husband?"

Mary shrunk back, and was alternately pale and red. A delicate sense of propriety prevented her replying; and recalled her bewildered reason. — Assuming, in consequence of her recollec-

---

1 Misquoted from William Shakespeare's *Twelfth Night, or What You Will* (1601). An edition of the play published around 1775 gives the following lines for Act I, Scene i:

> If music be the food of love, play on
> Give me excess of it ...
> That strain again, it had a dying fall:
> O, it came o'er my ear, like the sweet south,
> That breathes upon a bank of violets. (ll. 1-2; 4-6)

"South" began to be transcribed as "sound" sometime during the Victorian period and most modern editions, including the Royal Shakespeare Company edition (2007), provide the latter reading.

2 In 1785, Wollstonecraft wrote to her sister, Eliza Bishop, from Lisbon, "Fanny has been so exceedingly ill since I wrote ... [that] I intirely gave her up — and yet I *could not* write and tell you so, it seemed like signing her death warrant" (63; Wollstonecraft's emphasis).

tion, a more composed manner, she made the intended enquiry, and left the room. Henry's eyes followed her while the females very freely animadverted on her strange behaviour.

## CHAP. XII.

THE physician was sent for; his prescription afforded Ann a little temporary relief; and they again joined the circle. Unfortunately, the weather happened to be constantly wet for more than a week, and confined them to the house. Ann then found the ladies not so agreeable; when they sat whole hours together, the thread-bare topics were exhausted; and, but for cards or music, the long evenings would have been yawned away in listless indolence.

The bad weather had had as ill an effect on Henry as on Ann. He was frequently very thoughtful, or rather melancholy; this melancholy would of itself have attracted Mary's notice, if she had not found his conversation so infinitely superior to the rest of the group. When she conversed with him, all the faculties of her soul unfolded themselves; genius animated her expressive countenance and the most graceful, unaffected gestures gave energy to her discourse.

They frequently discussed very important subjects, while the rest were singing or playing cards, nor were they observed for doing so, as Henry, whom they all were pleased with, in the way of gallantry shewed them all more attention than her. Besides, as there was nothing alluring in her dress or manner, they never dreamt of her being preferred to them.

Henry was a man of learning; he had also studied mankind, and knew many of the intricacies of the human heart, from having felt the infirmities of his own. His taste was just, as it had a standard — Nature, which he observed with a critical eye.[1] Mary could not help thinking that in his company her mind

---

1 This statement anticipates one Wollstonecraft would later write in *Letters Written During a Short Residence in Sweden, Norway, and Denmark* (1796): "Nature is the nurse of sentiment, — the true source of taste" (72). Viewed as a specific reference to eighteenth-century aesthetic theory, Wollstonecraft's comment on nature as the standard for just taste seems to respond to the debate made famous by Charles Batteux (1713-80) in *Les Beaux Arts Réduits à un Même Principe* (or "the fine arts reduced to a single principle") (1746), in which the author argues, firstly, that the arts are mimetic in character and aim to please the taste, and, secondly, that nature is the highest form of beauty and art must therefore imitate nature in order to please the audience. Viewed more broadly, this comment reminds us that Wollstonecraft writes at the start

expanded, as he always went below the surface. She increased her
stock of ideas, and her taste was improved.

He was also a pious man; his rational religious sentiments
received warmth from his sensibility; and, except on very particular occasions, kept it in proper bounds;[1] these sentiments had
likewise formed his temper; he was gentle, and easily to be
intreated. The ridiculous ceremonies they were every day witness
to, led them into what are termed grave subjects, and made him
explain his opinions, which, at other times, he was neither
ashamed of, nor unnecessarily brought forward to notice.

## CHAP. XIII.

WHEN the weather began to clear up, Mary sometimes rode out
alone, purposely to view the ruins that still remained of the earthquake: or she would ride to the banks of the Tagus, to feast her
eyes with the sight of that magnificent river.[2] At other times she

---

of the Romantic era. While a major feature of Romantic-era thought is,
undoubtedly, subjectivity—the idea that we create the world by observing
it, as opposed to being passive recipients of the external world—this perspective may be viewed as a response to Enlightenment-era empirical
philosophy, such as that of John Locke (1632-1704), which posited that
truth and reality could be ascertained through observation of and experimentation on the environment, including the natural. Thus, throughout
the mid- to late-eighteenth century, the natural environment was viewed
as the standard that could concretize and finalize disputed facts, open
questions, and abstract judgments—like matters of taste. By denying subjectivity somewhat, Wollstonecraft's view might be characterized as pre-
Romantic, but, by celebrating nature and, in fact, personifying it by capi-
talizing the word "Nature," it fits firmly into high Romantic-era thought.

1 Wollstonecraft takes pains here to save her religious character from
imputations of what would have been termed "enthusiasm," or the religious zeal that was identifiable with insanity. A rise in the number of
religious sects in Britain, and conservative distrust of their style of religious observance, was accompanied by an inundation of texts warning
of the perils of "enthusiasm," such as Thomas Green's (fl. 1750-58) *A
Dissertation on Enthusiasm; Shewing the Danger of its Late Increase, and the
Great Mischiefs It has Occasioned* (1755), in which he delineates the
many kinds of madness that are mistaken for piety (e.g., 79).

2 The Great Lisbon Earthquake of 1 November 1755 caused a tsunami
and fires, almost totally destroying the city; it became a major point of
discussion for Enlightenment philosophers. The "magnificent" "Tagus
River is the longest river on the Iberian Peninsula. It rises in eastern
Spain ... 100 miles [or 160.9 kilometres] from the Mediterranean Sea"
(Israel 103, 101).

would visit the churches, as she was particularly fond of seeing historical paintings.

One of these visits gave rise to the subject, and the whole party descanted on it; but as the ladies could not handle it well, they soon adverted to portraits; and talked of the attitudes and characters in which they should wish to be drawn. Mary did not fix on one — when Henry, with more apparent warmth than usual, said, "I would give the world for your picture, with the expression I have seen in your face, when you have been supporting your friend."

This delicate compliment did not gratify her vanity, but it reached her heart. She then recollected that she had once sat for her picture — for whom was it designed? For a boy! Her cheeks flushed with indignation, so strongly did she feel an emotion of contempt at having been thrown away — given in with an estate.

As Mary again gave way to hope, her mind was more disengaged; and her thoughts were employed about the objects around her.

She visited several convents, and found that solitude only eradicates some passions, to give strength to others; the most baneful ones. She saw that religion does not consist in ceremonies; and that many prayers may fall from the lips without purifying the heart.

They who imagine they can be religious without governing their tempers, or exercising benevolence in its most extensive sense, must certainly allow, that their religious duties are only practiced from selfish principles; how then can they be called good? The pattern of all goodness went about *doing* good.[1] Wrapped up in themselves, the nuns only thought of inferior gratifications. And a number of intrigues were carried on to accelerate certain points on which their hearts were fixed:

---

1 Wollstonecraft's early religiosity, which stressed charity and her life-long dedication to moral responsibility, is in evidence in this passage; it also echoes part of her argument from *Rights of Woman*, in which she delineates moral action, as opposed to empty platitudes, as the rule by which women should live: "morality is very insidiously undermined, in the female world, by the attention being turned to the shew instead of the substance.... We should rather endeavour to view ourselves as we suppose that Being views us who seeth each thought ripen into action, and whose judgment never swerves from the eternal rule of right" (308-09). For more information on Wollstonecraft's religiosity and her novellas, see Daniel Robinson's "Theodicy versus Feminist Strategy in Mary Wollstonecraft's Fiction."

Such as obtaining offices of trust or authority; or avoiding those that were servile or laborious. In short, when they could be neither wives nor mothers, they aimed at being superiors, and became the most selfish creatures in the world: the passions that were curbed gave strength to the appetites, or to those mean passions which only tend to provide for the gratification of them. Was this seclusion from the world? or did they conquer its vanities or avoid its vexations?

In these abodes the unhappy individual, who, in the first paroxysm of grief, flies to them for refuge, finds too late she took a wrong step. The same warmth which determined her will make her repent; and sorrow, the rust of the mind, will never have a chance of being rubbed off by sensible conversation, or new-born affections of the heart.

She will find that those affections that have once been called forth and strengthened by exercise, are only smothered, not killed, by disappointment; and that in one form or other discontent will corrode the heart, and produce those maladies of the imagination, for which there is no specific.[1]

The community at large Mary disliked; but pitied many of them whose private distresses she was informed of; and to pity and relieve were the same things with her.

The exercise of her various virtues gave vigor to her genius, and dignity to her mind; she was sometimes inconsiderate, and violent; but never mean or cunning.

## CHAP. XIV.

THE Portuguese are certainly the most uncivilized nation in Europe. Dr. Johnson would have said, "They have the least mind."[2] And can such serve their Creator in spirit and in truth?

---

1 Here "specific" refers to a prescription or cure for a sickness. By applying this concept from the world of physical medicine to the realm of psychological illness ("maladies of the imagination"), Wollstonecraft reveals her interest in the nascent field of psychological medicine.

2 Wollstonecraft is quite mistaken about what Johnson "would have said" about Portugal, since his essay "Reflections on the State of Portugal" praises the nation highly and emphasizes the close relationship between the British and the Portuguese, who, he claims, were saved from the enslavement and destitution wrought by their reliance on Spain through British aid (197). (I am indebted to Allan Ingram for pointing me to this essay.) It seems likely that Wollstonecraft is thinking *(continued)*

No, the gross ritual of Romish ceremonies is all they can comprehend: they can do penance, but not conquer their revenge, or lust. Religion, or love, has never humanized their hearts; they want the vital part; the mere body worships. Taste is unknown; Gothic finery, and unnatural decorations, which they term ornaments, are conspicuous in their churches and dress. Reverence for mental excellence is only to be found in a polished nation.

Could the contemplation of such a people gratify Mary's heart? No: she turned disgusted from the prospects — turned to a man of refinement. Henry had been some time ill and low-spirited; Mary would have been attentive to any one in that situation; but to him she was particularly so; she thought herself bound in gratitude, on account of his constant endeavours to amuse Ann, and prevent her dwelling on the dreary prospect before her, which sometimes she could not help anticipating with a kind of quiet despair.

She found some excuse for going more frequently into the room they all met in; nay, she avowed her desire to amuse him: offered to read to him, and tried to draw him into amusing conversations; and when she was full of these little schemes, she looked at him with a degree of tenderness that she was not conscious of. This divided attention was of use to her, and prevented her continually thinking of Ann, whose fluctuating disorder often gave rise to false hopes.

A trifling thing occurred now which occasioned Mary some uneasiness. Her maid, a well-looking girl, had captivated the clerk of a neighbouring compting-house.[1] As the match was an advantageous one, Mary could not raise any objection to it, though at this juncture it was very disagreeable to her to have a stranger about her person. However, the girl consented to delay the marriage, as she had some affection for her mistress; and, besides, looked forward to Ann's death as a time of harvest.[2]

---

of a Johnsonian maxim (or "beauty," as the many eighteenth-century publications providing his maxims call them) about how the civilization of a nation is a just measure of its intelligence. In the endnote from her edition of *Mary*, Janet Todd suggests that this passage refers to a Johnsonian quip in which he opposes the concept of "more mind" to capacities of "judgment" and "imagination" (212, endnote 22). Shocking as this scathing anti-Catholic passage may be to readers today, Wollstonecraft's views were not unique; such screeds were far from uncommon in English works from the period.

1   A "compting-house" is an accounting or book-keeping office.
2   Traditionally, servants received their deceased masters' or mistresses' minor belongings, such as clothes and trinkets.

Henry's illness was not alarming, it was rather pleasing, as it gave Mary an excuse to herself for shewing him how much she was interested about him; and giving little artless proofs of affection, which the purity of her heart made her never wish to restrain. The only visible return he made was not obvious to common observers. He would sometimes fix his eyes on her, and take them off with a sigh that was coughed away; or when he was leisurely walking into the room, and did not expect to see her, he would quicken his steps, and come up to her with eagerness to ask some trivial question. In the same style, he would try to detain her when he had nothing to say — or said nothing.

Ann did not take notice of either his or Mary's behaviour, nor did she suspect that he was a favourite, on any other account than his appearing neither well nor happy. She had often seen that when a person was unfortunate, Mary's pity might easily be mistaken for love, and, indeed, it was a temporary sensation of that kind. Such it was — why it was so, let others define, I cannot argue against instincts. As reason is cultivated in man, they are supposed to grow weaker, and this may have given rise to the assertion, "That as judgment improves, genius evaporates."[1]

## CHAP. XV.

ONE morning they set out to visit the aqueduct;[2] though the day was very fine when they left home, a very heavy shower fell before they reached it; they lengthened their ride, the clouds dispersed, and the sun came from behind them uncommonly bright.

---

1 Many major philosophers, such as Hugh Blair (1718-1800) and James Beattie (1735-1803), wrote extensively on the nature of genius in the eighteenth century. As Wollstonecraft's comment here indicates, genius was opposed to judgment because it was thought to be innate and allied with the unfettered imagination, while judgment is learned and associated with reason. The phrase "original genius" denoted these ideas, as in William Duff's (1732-1815) *An Essay on Original Genius; and Its Various Modes of Exertion in Philosophy and the Fine Arts, Particularly in Poetry* (1767). Wollstonecraft echoes this phrase in "Hints. (Chiefly to have been incorporated in the second part of the *Rights of Woman*)": "'Genius decays as judgement increases.' Of course, those who have the least genius, have the earliest appearance of wisdom" (*Posthumous* 185). Wollstonecraft echoes Samuel Johnson's words in *The Idler*, 9 June 1759: "genius decays as judgment increases" (41).

2 The Lisbon Aqueduct (*Aqueduto das Águas Livres* in Portuguese), built in 1746 to bring clean drinking water to Lisbon, was a feat of incredible engineering: its soaring stone arches (the tallest is 65 *(continued)*

Mary would fain have persuaded Ann not to have left the carriage; but she was in spirits, and obviated all her objections, and insisted on walking, tho' the ground was damp. But her strength was not equal to her spirits; she was soon obliged to return to the carriage so much fatigued, that she fainted, and remained insensible a long time.

Henry would have supported her; but Mary would not permit him; her recollection was instantaneous, and she feared sitting on the damp ground might do him a material injury: she was on that account positive, though the company did not guess the cause of her being so. As to herself, she did not fear bodily pain; and, when her mind was agitated, she could endure the greatest fatigue without appearing sensible of it. When Ann recovered, they returned slowly home; she was carried to bed, and the next morning Mary thought she observed a visible change for the worse. The physician was sent for, who pronounced her to be in the most imminent danger.

All Mary's former fears now returned like a torrent, and carried every other care away; she even added to her present anguish by upbraiding herself for her late tranquillity — it haunted her in the form of a crime.

The disorder made the most rapid advances — there was no hope! — Bereft of it, Mary again was tranquil; but it was a very different kind of tranquillity. She stood to brave the approaching storm, conscious she only could be overwhelmed by it.

She did not think of Henry, or if her thoughts glanced towards him, it was only to find fault with herself for suffering a thought to have strayed from Ann. — Ann! — this dear friend was soon torn from her — she died suddenly as Mary was assisting her to walk across the room. — The first string was severed from her heart — and this "slow, sudden death"[1] disturbed her reasoning

---

metres) were the tallest stone arches in the world when it was built, and, amazingly, it survived the Lisbon earthquake that occurred only nine years after it was completed.

1  From Young's *The Complaint: or, Night Thoughts on Life, Death, & Immortality* (1743):

How Many fall as sudden, not as safe?
As sudden, tho' for Years admonisht home:
Of human Ills the last Extreme beware,
Beware, Lorenzo! a slow-sudden Death.
How dreadful that deliberate Surprize? (ll. 385-89)

"Lorenzo" certainly refers to Lorenzo de Medici (1449-92), the ruler of Florence and great patron of the arts, who died prematurely from a sudden illness at age forty-three.

faculties; she seemed stunned by it; unable to reflect, or even to feel her misery.

The body was stolen out of the house[1] the second night, and Mary refused to see her former companions. She desired her maid to conclude her marriage, and request her intended husband to inform her when the first merchantman was to leave the port, as the packet had just sailed, and she determined not to stay in that hated place any longer than was absolutely necessary.

She then sent to request the ladies to visit her; she wished to avoid a parade of grief — her sorrows were her own, and appeared to her not to admit of increase or softening. She was right; the sight of them did not affect her, or turn the stream of her sullen sorrow; the black wave rolled along in the same course; it was equal to her where she cast her eyes; all was impenetrable gloom.

## CHAP. XVI.

SOON after the ladies left her, she received a message from Henry, requesting, as she saw company, to be permitted to visit her: she consented, and he entered immediately, with an unassured pace. She ran eagerly up to him — saw the tear trembling in his eye, and his countenance softened by the tenderest compassion; the hand which pressed hers seemed that of a fellow-creature. She burst into tears; and, unable to restrain them, she hid her face with both her hands: these tears relieved her, (she had before had a difficulty in breathing,) and she sat down by him more composed than she had appeared since Ann's death; but her conversation was incoherent.

She called herself "a poor disconsolate creature!" — "Mine is a selfish grief," she exclaimed — "Yet, Heaven is my witness, I do not wish her back now she has reached those peaceful mansions, where the weary rest. Her pure spirit is happy; but what a wretch am I!"

Henry forgot his cautious reserve. "Would you allow me to call you friend?" said he in a hesitating voice. "I feel, dear girl, the tenderest interest in whatever concerns thee." His eyes spoke the

1  In their editions of *Mary*, both Kelly and Todd point out that Ann's body must be removed from the house surreptitiously because she was a Protestant. To expand on this point, we may extrapolate that Mary gave it a Protestant burial in this Catholic country.

rest. They were both silent a few moments; then Henry resumed the conversation. "I have also been acquainted with grief! I mourn the loss of a woman who was not worthy of my regard. Let me give thee some account of the man who now solicits thy friendship; and who, from motives of the purest benevolence, wishes to give comfort to thy wounded heart.

"I have myself," said he, mournfully, "shaken hands with happiness, and am dead to the world; I wait patiently for my dissolution; but, for thee, Mary, there may be many bright days in store."

"Impossible," replied she, in a peevish tone, as if he had insulted her by the supposition; her feelings were so much in unison with his, that she was in love with misery.

He smiled at her impatience, and went on. "My father died before I knew him, and my mother was so attached to my eldest brother, that she took very little pains to fit me for the profession to which I was destined: and, may I tell thee, I left my family, and, in many different stations, rambled about the world; saw mankind in every rank of life; and, in order to be independent, exerted those talents Nature has given me: these exertions improved my understanding; and the miseries I was witness to, gave a keener edge to my sensibility. My constitution is naturally weak; and, perhaps, two or three lingering disorders in my youth, first gave me a habit of reflecting, and enabled me to obtain some dominion over my passions. At least," added he, stifling a sigh, "over the violent ones, though I fear, refinement and reflection only renders the tender ones more tyrannic.

"I have told you already I have been in love, and disappointed — the object is now no more; let her faults sleep with her! Yet this passion has pervaded my whole soul, and mixed itself with all my affections and pursuits. — I am not peacefully indifferent; yet it is only to my violin I tell the sorrows I now confide with thee. The object I loved forfeited my esteem; yet, true to the sentiment, my fancy has too frequently delighted to form a creature that I could love, that could convey to my soul sensations which the gross part of mankind have not any conception of."

He stopped, as Mary seemed lost in thought; but as she was still in a listening attitude, continued his little narrative. "I kept up an irregular correspondence with my mother; my brother's extravagance and ingratitude had almost broken her heart, and made her feel something like a pang of remorse, on account of her behaviour to me. I hastened to comfort her — and was a comfort to her.

"My declining health prevented my taking orders, as I had intended; but I with warmth entered into literary pursuits; perhaps my heart, not having an object, made me embrace the substitute with more eagerness. But, do not imagine I have always been a die-away swain. No: I have frequented the cheerful haunts of men, and wit! — enchanting wit! has made many moments fly free from care. I am too fond of the elegant arts; and woman — lovely woman! thou hast charmed me, though, perhaps, it would not be easy to find one to whom my reason would allow me to be constant.

"I have now only to tell you, that my mother insisted on my spending this winter in a warmer climate; and I fixed on Lisbon, as I had before visited the Continent." He then looked Mary full in the face; and, with the most insinuating accents, asked "if he might hope for her friendship? If she would rely on him as if he was her father; and that the tenderest father could not more anxiously interest himself in the fate of a darling child, than he did in her's."

Such a crowd of thoughts all at once rushed into Mary's mind, that she in vain attempted to express the sentiments which were most predominant. Her heart longed to receive a new guest; there was a void in it: accustomed to have some one to love, she was alone, and comfortless, if not engrossed by a particular affection.

Henry saw her distress, and not to increase it, left the room. He had exerted himself to turn her thoughts into a new channel, and had succeeded; she thought of him till she began to chide herself for defrauding the dead, and, determining to grieve for Ann, she dwelt on Henry's misfortunes and ill health; and the interest he took in her fate was a balm to her sick mind. She did not reason on the subject; but she felt he was attached to her: lost in this delirium, she never asked herself what kind of an affection she had for him, or what it tended to; nor did she know that love and friendship are very distinct; she thought with rapture, that there was one person in the world who had an affection for her, and that person she admired — had a friendship for.

He had called her his dear girl; the words might have fallen from him by accident; but they did not fall to the ground. My child! His child, what an association of ideas! If I had had a father, such a father! — She could not dwell on the thoughts, the wishes which obtruded themselves. Her mind was unhinged, and passion unperceived filled her whole soul. Lost, in waking dreams, she considered and reconsidered Henry's account of himself; till she actually thought she would tell Ann — a bitter recollection then roused her out of her reverie; and aloud she begged forgiveness of her.

By these kind of conflicts the day was lengthened; and when she went to bed, the night passed away in feverish slumbers; though they did not refresh her, she was spared the labour of thinking, of restraining her imagination; it sported uncontrouled; but took its colour from her waking train of thoughts. One instant she was supporting her dying mother; then Ann was breathing her last, and Henry was comforting her.

The unwelcome light visited her languid eyes; yet, I must tell the truth, she thought she should see Henry, and this hope set her spirits in motion: but they were quickly depressed by her maid, who came to tell her that she had heard of a vessel on board of which she could be accommodated, and that there was to be another female passenger on board, a vulgar one;[1] but perhaps she would be more useful on that account — Mary did not want a companion.

As she had given orders for her passage to be engaged in the first vessel that sailed, she could not now retract; and must prepare for the lonely voyage, as the Captain intended taking advantage of the first fair wind. She had too much strength of mind to waver in her determination; but to determine wrung her very heart, opened all her old wounds, and made them bleed afresh. What was she to do? where go? Could she set a seal to a hasty vow, and tell a deliberate lie; promise to love one man, when the image of another was ever present to her — her soul revolted. "I might gain the applause of the world by such mock heroism; but should I not forfeit my own? forfeit thine, my father!"

There is a solemnity in the shortest ejaculation, which, for a while, stills the tumult of passion. Mary's mind had been thrown off its poise; her devotion had been, perhaps, more fervent for

---

1 In this sense, the word "vulgar" signifies "Belonging to the ordinary or common class in the community; not distinguished or marked off from this in any way; plebeian" (*OED*), not, as we more commonly use it today, "Having a common and offensively mean character; coarsely commonplace; lacking in refinement or good taste; uncultured, ill-bred" (*OED*). Even so, the narrator's use of the word is surprising, since an ideal of sensibility is to forge bonds across class boundaries—and one would expect that the (eventually) pro-French Revolutionary Wollstonecraft would uphold this ideal, even if she does attempt to rewrite the ideals of sensibility in other ways in this fiction.

some time past; but less regular. She forgot that happiness was not to be found on earth, and built a terrestrial paradise liable to be destroyed by the first serious thought: when she reasoned she became inexpressibly sad, to render life bearable she gave way to fancy — this was madness.

In a few days she must again go to sea; the weather was very tempestuous — what of that, the tempest in her soul rendered every other trifling — it was not the contending elements, but *herself* she feared!

## CHAP. XVII.

IN order to gain strength to support the expected interview, she went out in a carriage. The day was fine; but all nature was to her a universal blank; she could neither enjoy it, nor weep that she could not. She passed by the ruins of an old monastery on a very high hill; she got out to walk amongst the ruins;[1] the wind blew violently, she did not avoid its fury, on the contrary, wildly bid it blow on, and seemed glad to contend with it, or rather walk against it. Exhausted, she returned to the carriage was soon at home, and in the old room.

Henry started at the sight of her altered appearance; the day before her complexion had been of the most pallid hue; but now her cheeks were flushed, and her eyes enlivened with a false vivacity, an unusual fire. He was not well, his illness was apparent in his countenance, and he owned he had not closed his eyes all night; this roused her dormant tenderness, she forgot they were so soon to part — engrossed by the present happiness of seeing, of hearing him.

Once or twice she essayed to tell him that she was, in a few days, to depart; but she could not; she was irresolute; it will do to-morrow; should the wind change they could not sail in such a hurry; thus she thought, and insensibly grew more calm. The Ladies prevailed on her to spend the evening with them; but she retired very early to rest, and sat on the side of her bed several hours, then threw herself on it, and waited for the dreaded to-morrow.

---

1 Probably the ruins of the Carmo Monastery (*el Convento da Ordem do Carmo*), formerly a medieval monastery in the Chiado neighbourhood of Lisbon that was destroyed in the 1755 earthquake; the ruins remain today as the main trace of the disaster.

# CHAP. XVIII.

THE ladies heard that her servant was to be married that day, and that she was to sail in the vessel which was then clearing out at the Custom-house.[1] Henry heard, but did not make any remarks; and Mary called up all her fortitude to support her, and enable her to hide from the females her internal struggles. She durst not encounter Henry's glances when she found he had been informed of her intention; and, trying to draw a veil over her wretched state of mind, she talked incessantly, she knew not what; flashes of wit burst from her, and when she began to laugh she could not stop herself.

Henry smiled at some of her sallies, and looked at her with such benignity and compassion, that he recalled her scattered thoughts; and, the ladies going to dress for dinner, they were left alone; and remained silent a few moments: after the noisy conversation it appeared solemn. Henry began. "You are going, Mary, and going by yourself; your mind is not in a state to be left to its own operations — yet I cannot, dissuade you; if I attempted to do it, I should ill deserve the title I wish to merit. I only think of your happiness; could I obey the strongest impulse of my heart, I should accompany thee to England; but such a step might endanger your future peace."

Mary, then, with all the frankness which marked her character, explained her situation to him, and mentioned her fatal tie with such disgust that he trembled for her. "I cannot see him; he is not the man formed for me to love!" Her delicacy did not restrain her, for her dislike to her husband had taken root in her mind long before she knew Henry. Did she not fix on Lisbon rather than France on purpose to avoid him? and if Ann had been in tolerable health she would have flown with her to some remote corner to have escaped from him.

"I intend," said Henry, "to follow you in the next packet; where shall I hear of your health?" "Oh! let me hear of thine," replied Mary. "I am well, very well; but thou art very ill — thy health is in the most precarious state." She then mentioned her intention of going to Ann's relations. "I am her representative, I have duties to fulfil for her: during my voyage I shall

---

1 The *OED* defines "custom-house" as "A house or office at which custom is collected; esp. a government office situated at a place of import or export, as a seaport, at which customs are levied on goods imported or exported."

have time enough for reflection; though I think I have already determined."

"Be not too hasty, my child," interrupted Henry; "far be it from me to persuade thee to do violence to thy feelings — but consider that all thy future life may probably take its colour from thy present mode of conduct. Our affections as well as our sentiments are fluctuating; you will not perhaps always either think or feel as you do at present: the object you now shun may appear in a different light." He paused. "In advising thee in this style, I have only thy good at heart, Mary."

She only answered to expostulate. "My affections are involuntary — yet they can only be fixed by reflection, and when they are they make quite a part of my soul, are interwoven in it, animate my actions, and form my taste: certain qualities are calculated to call forth my sympathies, and make me all I am capable of being. The governing affection gives its stamp to the rest — because I am capable of loving one, I have that kind of charity to all my fellow-creatures which is not easily provoked. Milton has asserted, That earthly love is the scale by which to heavenly we may ascend."[1]

She went on with eagerness. "My opinions on some subjects are not wavering; my pursuit through life has ever been the same: in solitude were my sentiments formed; they are indelible, and nothing can efface them but death — No, death itself cannot efface them, or my soul must be created afresh, and not improved. Yet a little while am I parted from my Ann — I could not exist without the hope of seeing her again — I could not bear to think that time could wear away an affection that was founded on what is not liable to perish; you might as well attempt to per-

---

1   In a passage that may indicate Milton's indebtedness to the doctrine of accommodation in Neoplatonic philosophy (and to which Wollstonecraft's future son-in-law, Percy Bysshe Shelley [1792-1822], would refer throughout his *oeuvre*), the angel Raphael explains to Adam in Book VIII of *Paradise Lost*,

   "... love refines
   The thoughts, and heart enlarges, hath his seat
   In reason, and is judicious, is the scale
   By which to heavenly love thou mayst ascend." (ll. 589-92)
   Wollstonecraft would revisit this comparison between earthly and heavenly love in *A Vindication of the Rights of Men* (1790), in which she judges "that Plato and Milton were grossly mistaken in asserting that human love led to heavenly, and was only an exaltation of the same affection" (114).

suade me that my soul is matter, and that its feelings arose from certain modifications of it."[1]

"Dear enthusiastic creature," whispered Henry, "how you steal into my soul." She still continued. "The same turn of mind which leads me to adore the Author of all Perfection — which leads me to conclude that he only can fill my soul; forces me to admire the faint image — the shadows of his attributes here below;[2] and my imagination gives still bolder strokes to them. I knew I am in some degree under the influence of a delusion — but does not this strong delusion prove that I myself 'am of subtiler essence than the trodden clod:'[3] these flights of the imagination

---

1 Certainly a reference to David Hartley's (1705-57) associationist theory, first presented in *Observations on Man* (1749). Joseph Johnson published Joseph Priestley's (1733-1804) text on Hartley's associationism—*Hartley's Theory of the Human Mind, on the Principle of the Association of Ideas*—in 1775. In his description of Hartley's psychological theory of what he calls "vibratiuncles," or the faint after-effect of the vibration of the medullary substance in the nerves that form mental associations, Priestley writes,

> It will stagger some persons, that so much of the business of thinking should be made to depend upon mere matter, as the doctrine of vibrations supposes. For, ... *immateriality*, as far as it has been supposed to belong to man, would be excluded altogether. But I do not know that this supposition need give any concern, except to those who maintain that a future life depends upon the immateriality of the human soul. (xix)

Nor was Hartley the first to emphasize the physical basis of the human mind, often conflated with the "soul" in the eighteenth century: Priestley notes that Locke also attributed thinking to mere matter (xxiii). In this passage, Wollstonecraft may also gesture to Voltaire's (1694-1778) exploration of the nature of the soul in the *Philosophical Dictionary* (1752): "The opinion which, unquestionably, we should embrace, is that the soul is an immaterial being; but as certainly you do not conceive what this immaterial being is.... What then do you call your soul? What idea have you of it? All you can of yourself, without a revelation, allow to be in yourself, is a power unknown to you of feeling and thinking" (335-36).

2 In Neoplatonic theory, as founded by Plotinus, the doctrine of accommodation postulates that the things of this material, fallen world are shadows of the empyrean, eternal realm. These ideas were taken up in medieval Christian philosophy to explain how God reveals himself to man.

3 From Young's *Night-Thoughts*: "Of subtler Essence than the trodden Clod" (I, l. 100).

point to futurity; I cannot banish them. Every cause in nature produces an effect; and am I an exception to the general rule? have I desires implanted in me only to make me miserable? will they never be gratified? shall I never be happy? My feelings do not accord with the notion of solitary happiness. In a state of bliss, it will be the society of beings we can love, without the alloy that earthly infirmities mix with our best affections, that will constitute great part of our happiness.

"With these notions can I conform to the maxims of worldly wisdom? can I listen to the cold dictates of worldly prudence, and bid my tumultuous passions cease to vex me, be still, find content in grovelling pursuits, and the admiration of the misjudging crowd, when it is only one I wish to please — one who could be all the world to me. Argue not with me, I am bound by human ties; but did my spirit ever promise to love, or could I consider when forced to bind myself — to take a vow, that at the awful day of judgment I must give an account of. My conscience does not smite me, and that Being who is greater than the internal monitor, may approve of what the world condemns; sensible that in Him I live, could I brave His presence, or hope in solitude to find peace, if I acted contrary to conviction, that the world might approve of my conduct — what could the world give to compensate for my own esteem? it is ever hostile and armed against the feeling heart!

"Riches and honours await me, and the cold moralist might desire me to sit down and enjoy them — I cannot conquer my feelings, and till I do, what are these baubles to me? you may tell me I follow a fleeting good, an *ignis fatuus*;[1] but this chase, these struggles prepare me for eternity — when I no longer see through a glass darkly I shall not reason about, but *feel* in what happiness consists."

Henry had not attempted to interrupt her; he saw she was determined, and that these sentiments were not the effusion of the moment, but well digested ones, the result of strong affections, a high sense of honour, and respect for the source of all virtue and truth. He was startled, if not entirely convinced by her arguments; indeed her voice, her gestures were all persuasive.

---

1 Latin for "foolish fire." The phrase refers to a fond hope that is unlikely to be realized, as well as denoting a "will o' the wisp," or the phosphorescent light over swampy ground, viewed at night, which may be caused by the release of gasses emitted by rotting organic matter.

Some one now entered the room; he looked an answer to her long harangue; it was fortunate for him, or he might have been led to say what in a cooler moment he had determined to conceal; but were words necessary to reveal it? He wished not to influence her conduct — vain precaution; she knew she was beloved; and could she forget that such a man loved her, or rest satisfied with any inferior gratification. When passion first enters the heart, it is only a return of affection that is sought after, and every other remembrance and wish is blotted out.

## CHAP. XIX.

TWO days passed away without any particular conversation; Henry, trying to be indifferent, or to appear so, was more assiduous than ever. The conflict was too violent for his present state of health; the spirit was willing, but the body suffered; he lost his appetite, and looked wretchedly; his spirits were calmly low — the world seemed to fade away — what was that world to him that Mary did not inhabit; she lived not for him.

He was mistaken; his affection was her only support; without this dear prop she had sunk into the grave of her lost — long-loved friend; — his attention snatched her from despair. Inscrutable are the ways of Heaven!

The third day Mary was desired to prepare herself; for if the wind continued in the same point, they should set sail the next evening. She tried to prepare her mind, and her efforts were not useless; she appeared less agitated than could have been expected, and talked of her voyage with composure. On great occasions she was generally calm and collected, her resolution would brace her unstrung nerves; but after the victory she had no triumph; she would sink into a state of moping melancholy, and feel ten-fold misery when the heroic enthusiasm was over.

The morning of the day fixed on for her departure she was alone with Henry only a few moments, and an awkward kind of formality made them slip away without their having said much to each other. Henry was afraid to discover his passion, or give any other name to his regard but friendship; yet his anxious solicitude for her welfare was ever breaking out — while she as artlessly expressed again and again, her fears with respect to his declining health.

"We shall soon meet," said he, with a faint smile; Mary smiled too; she caught the sickly beam; it was still fainter by being reflected, and not knowing what she wished to do, started up and left the room. When she was alone she regretted she had left him so precipitately. "The few precious moments I have thus thrown away may never return," she thought — the reflection led to misery.

She waited for, nay, almost wished for the summons to depart. She could not avoid spending the intermediate time with the ladies and Henry; and the trivial conversations she was obliged to bear a part in harassed her more than can be well conceived.

The summons came, and the whole party attended her to the vessel. For a while the remembrance of Ann banished her regret at parting with Henry, though his pale figure pressed on her sight; it may seem a paradox, but he was more present to her when she sailed; her tears then were all his own.

"My poor Ann!" thought Mary, "along this road we came, and near this spot you called me your guardian angel — and now I leave thee here! ah! no, I do not — thy spirit is not confined to its mouldering tenement! Tell me, thou soul of her I love, tell me, ah! whither art thou fled?" Ann occupied her until they reached the ship.

The anchor was weighed. Nothing can be more irksome than waiting to say farewel. As the day was serene, they accompanied her a little way, and then got into the boat; Henry was the last; he pressed her hand, it had not any life in it; she leaned over the side of the ship without looking at the boat, till it was so far distant, that she could not see the countenances of those that were in it: a mist spread itself over her sight — she longed to exchange one look — tried to recollect the last; — the universe contained no being but Henry! — The grief of parting with him had swept all others clean away. Her eyes followed the keel of the boat, and when she could no longer perceive its traces: she looked round on the wide waste of waters, thought of the precious moments which had been stolen from the waste of murdered time.

She then descended into the cabin, regardless of the surrounding beauties of nature, and throwing herself on her bed in the little hole which was called the state-room[1] — she wished to forget her existence. On this bed she remained two days, listening to the dashing waves, unable to close her eyes. A small taper made the darkness visible; and the third night, by its glimmering light, she wrote the following fragment.

---

1  Apparently Mary's room is a superior first-class cabin—or "state room"—in name only, not quality.

"Poor solitary wretch that I am; here alone do I listen to the whistling winds and dashing waves; — on no human support can I rest — when not lost to hope I found pleasure in the society of those rough beings; but now they appear not like my fellow creatures; no social ties draw me to them. How long, how dreary has this day been; yet I scarcely wish it over — for what will to-morrow bring — to-morrow, and to-morrow will only be marked with unvaried characters of wretchedness. —Yet surely, I am not alone!"

Her moistened eyes were lifted up to heaven; a crowd of thoughts darted into her mind, and pressing her hand against her forehead, as if to bear the intellectual weight, she tried, but tried in vain, to arrange them. "Father of Mercies, compose this troubled spirit: do I indeed wish it to be composed — to forget my Henry?" [Through] the *my*, the pen[1] was directly drawn across in an agony.

## CHAP. XX.

THE mate of the ship, who heard her stir, came to offer her some refreshment; and she, who formerly received every offer of kindness or civility with pleasure, now shrunk away disgusted: peevishly she desired him not to disturb her; but the words were hardly articulated when her heart smote her, she called him back, and requested something to drink. After drinking it, fatigued by her mental exertions, she fell into a death-like slumber, which lasted some hours; but did not refresh her, on the contrary, she awoke languid and stupid.

The wind still continued contrary; a week, a dismal week, had she struggled with her sorrows; and the struggle brought on a slow fever, which sometimes gave her false spirits.[2]

---

1   This passage is not the first to include odd phrasing, most instances of which I leave as they appear in the source text, but I wish to emend this one because it is potentially confusing: to mark the beginning of a new sentence and make the phrase logical, a capitalized word such as "Through" should appear before the phrase "the *my*."

2   This theory of "false spirits" was particular to Wollstonecraft's own medical theorizing, I believe, as I cannot find the phrase in other eighteenth-century medical texts on nerves. However, the following passage, from an anonymous novel of sensibility called *Emma; or, The Unfortunate Attachment* (1787), may well be the source for her ideas, as it certainly seems to be the source for her phraseology: one character, Sutton, advises another, Walpole, "'Be advised by me, and do not vainly attempt to forget your discontents by calling up false spirits: they will leave you more depressed after a few hours, than they found you'" (184).

The winds then became very tempestuous, the Great Deep was troubled, and all the passengers appalled. Mary then left her bed, and went on deck, to survey the contending elements: the scene accorded with the present state of her soul; she thought in a few hours I may go home; the prisoner may be released. The vessel rose on a wave and descended into a yawning gulph — Not slower did her mounting soul return to earth, for — Ah! her treasure and her heart was there. The squalls rattled amongst the sails, which were quickly taken down; the wind would then die away, and the wild undirected waves rushed on every side with a tremendous roar. In a little vessel in the midst of such a storm she was not dismayed; she felt herself independent.

Just then one of the crew perceived a signal of distress; by the help of a glass he could plainly discover a small vessel dismasted, drifted about, for the rudder had been broken by the violence of the storm. Mary's thoughts were now all engrossed by the crew on the brink of destruction. They bore down to the wreck; they reached it, and hailed the trembling wretches: at the sound of the friendly greeting, loud cries of tumultuous joy were mixed with the roaring of the waves, and with ecstatic transport they leaped on the shattered deck, launched their boat in a moment, and committed themselves to the mercy of the sea. Stowed between two casks, and leaning on a sail, she watched the boat, and when a wave intercepted it from her view — she ceased to breathe, or rather held her breath until it rose again.

At last the boat arrived safe along-side the ship, and Mary caught the poor trembling wretches as they stumbled into it, and joined them in thanking that gracious Being, who though He had not thought fit to still the raging of the sea, had afforded them unexpected succour.

Amongst the wretched crew was one poor woman, who fainted when she was hauled on board: Mary undressed her, and when she had recovered, and soothed her, left her to enjoy the rest she required to recruit her strength, which fear had quite exhausted. She returned again to view the angry deep; and when she gazed on its perturbed state, she thought of the Being who rode on the wings of the wind, and stilled the noise of the sea, and the madness of the people — He only could speak peace to her troubled spirit! she grew more calm; the late transaction had gratified her benevolence, and stole her out of herself.

One of the sailors, happening to say to another, "that he believed the world was going to be at an end;" this observation led her into a new train of thoughts: some of Handel's sublime compositions occurred to her, and she sung them to the grand accompaniment. The Lord God Omnipotent reigned, and would reign for ever, and ever![1] — Why then did she fear the sorrows that were passing away, when she knew that He would bind up the broken-hearted, and receive those who came out of great tribulation. She retired to her cabin; and wrote in the little book that was now her only confident. It was after midnight.

"At this solemn hour, the great day of judgment fills my thoughts; the day of retribution, when the secrets of all hearts will be revealed; when all worldly distinctions will fade away, and be no more seen. I have not words to express the sublime images which the bare contemplation of this awful day raises in my mind. Then, indeed, the Lord Omnipotent will reign, and He will wipe the tearful eye, and support the trembling heart — yet a little while He hideth his face, and the dun shades of sorrow, and the thick clouds of folly separate us from our God; but when the glad dawn of an eternal day breaks, we shall know even as we are known. Here we walk by faith, and not by sight; and we have this alternative, either to enjoy the pleasures of life, which are but for a season, or look forward to the prize of our high calling, and with fortitude, and that wisdom which is from above, endeavour to bear the warfare of life. We know that many run the race; but he that striveth obtaineth the crown of victory. Our race is an arduous one! How many are betrayed by traitors lodged in their own breasts, who wear the garb of Virtue, and are so near akin; we sigh to think they should ever lead into folly, and slide imperceptibly into vice. Surely any thing like happiness is madness! Shall probationers of an hour presume to pluck the fruit of

---

1   Georg Friederich Händel (later semi-anglicized to George Frideric Handel) (1685-1759) became an English citizen in 1726 and wrote many "sublime" pieces for the English royalty, such as the Water Music (1717), the Music for the Royal Fireworks (1749), and the four majestic Coronation anthems (1727). This sentence reveals that Mary sings "The Hallelujah Chorus" from Handel's "Messiah," which begins with the following lyrics:
    Hallelujah! Hallelujah! Hallelujah! Hallelujah! Hallelujah!
    For the Lord God Omnipotent reigneth.

    . . . . . . . . . . . . . . . . . . . . . . . . . . . . . . .
    The kingdom of this world
    Is become the kingdom of our Lord,
    And of His Christ, and of His Christ;
    And He shall reign for ever and ever,
    For ever and ever, forever and ever.

immortality, before they have conquered death? it is guarded, when the great day, to which I allude, arrives, the way will again be opened. Ye dear delusions, gay deceits, farewel! and yet I cannot banish ye for ever; still does my panting soul push forward, and live in futurity, in the deep shades o'er which darkness hangs. — I try to pierce the gloom, and find a resting-place, where my thirst of knowledge will be gratified, and my ardent affections find an object to fix them. Every thing material must change; happiness and this fluctuating[1] principle is not compatible. Eternity, immateriality, and happiness, — what are ye? How shall I grasp the mighty and fleeting conceptions ye create?"

After writing, serenely she delivered her soul into the hands of the Father of Spirits; and slept in peace.

## CHAP. XXI.

MARY rose early, refreshed by the seasonable rest, and went to visit the poor woman, whom she found quite recovered: and, on enquiry, heard that she had lately buried her husband, a common sailor; and that her only surviving child had been washed overboard the day before. Full of her own danger, she scarcely thought of her child till that was over; and then she gave way to boisterous emotions.

Mary endeavoured to calm her at first, by sympathizing with her; and she tried to point out the only solid source of comfort; but in doing this she encountered many difficulties; she found her grossly ignorant, yet she did not despair: and as the poor creature could not receive comfort from the operations of her own mind, she laboured to beguile the hours, which grief made heavy, by adapting her conversation to her capacity.[2]

There are many minds that only receive impressions through the medium of the senses: to them did Mary address herself; she made her some presents, and promised to assist her when they should arrive in England. This employment roused her out of her late stupor, and again set the faculties of her soul in motion;

---

1 Fluctuating.
2 Another surprisingly classist remark, but a valuable one, since it reveals Wollstonecraft's philosophy regarding the purpose of human thought and intelligence. She echoes this sentiment in a letter to Reverend Henry Dyson Gabell from 1787: "Why have we implanted in us an irresistible desire to think — if thinking is not in some measure necessary to make us wise unto salvation" (*Letters* 120).

made the understanding contend with the imagination, and the heart throbbed not so irregularly during the contention. How short-lived was the calm! when the English coast was descried, her sorrows returned with redoubled vigor. — She was to visit and comfort the mother of her lost friend — And where then should she take up her residence? These thoughts suspended the exertions of her understanding; abstracted reflections gave way to alarming apprehensions; and tenderness undermined fortitude.

## CHAP. XXII.

IN England then landed the forlorn wanderer. She looked round for some few moments — her affections were not attracted to any particular part of the Island. She knew none of the inhabitants of the vast city to which she was going: the mass of buildings appeared to her a huge body without an informing soul. As she passed through the streets in an hackney-coach, disgust and horror alternately filled her mind. She met some women drunk; and the manners of those who attacked the sailors, made her shrink into herself, and exclaim, are these my fellow creatures!

Detained by a number of carts near the water-side, for she came up the river in the vessel, not having reason to hasten on shore, she saw vulgarity, dirt, and vice — her soul sickened; this was the first time such complicated misery obtruded itself on her sight. — Forgetting her own griefs, she gave the world a much indebted tear; mourned for a world in ruins. She then perceived, that great part of her comfort must arise from viewing the smiling face of nature, and be reflected from the view of innocent enjoyments: she was fond of seeing animals play, and could not bear to see her own species sink below them.

In a little dwelling in one of the villages near London, lived the mother of Ann; two of her children still remained with her; but they did not resemble Ann. To her house Mary directed the coach, and told the unfortunate mother of her loss. The poor woman, oppressed by it, and her many other cares, after an inundation of tears, began to enumerate all her past misfortunes, and present cares. The heavy tale lasted until midnight, and the impression it made on Mary's mind was so strong, that it banished sleep till towards morning; when tired nature sought forgetfulness, and the soul ceased to ruminate about many things.

She sent for the poor woman they took up at sea, provided her a lodging, and relieved her present necessities. A few days were spent in a kind of listless way; then the mother of Ann began to enquire when she thought of returning home. She had hitherto treated her with the greatest respect, and concealed her wonder at Mary's choosing a remote room in the house near the garden, and ordering some alterations to be made, as if she intended living in it.

Mary did not choose to explain herself; had Ann lived, it is probable she would never have loved Henry so fondly; but if she had, she could not have talked of her passion to any human creature. She deliberated, and at last informed the family, that she had a reason for not living with her husband, which must some time remain a secret — they stared — Not live with him! how will you live then? This was a question she could not answer; she had only about eighty pounds remaining, of the money she took with her to Lisbon; when it was exhausted where could she get more? I will work, she cried, do any thing rather than be a slave.[1]

## CHAP. XXIII.

UNHAPPY, she wandered about the village, and relieved the poor; it was the only employment that eased her aching heart; she became more intimate with misery — the misery that rises from poverty and the want of education. She was in the vicinity of a great city; the vicious poor in and about it must ever grieve a benevolent contemplative mind.

One evening a man who stood weeping in a little lane, near the house she resided in, caught her eye. She accosted him; in a confused manner, he informed her, that his wife was dying, and his children crying for the bread he could not earn. Mary desired to be conducted to his habitation; it was not very distant, and was the upper room in an old mansion-house, which had been once the abode of luxury. Some tattered shreds of rich hangings still remained, covered with cobwebs and filth; round the ceiling, through which the rain drop'd, was a beautiful cornice moulder-

---

1 Wollstonecraft allies herself with a strong coterie of English abolitionists by using the word "slave," which she would also use dozens of times throughout *Rights of Woman*, the most relevant instance being, perhaps, when she calls wives "house slave[s]" (213). William Murray, Lord Mansfield (1705-93) had worked to abolish slavery in England in 1772. However, the slave-trade was still alive and well in the English colonies and would not be outlawed until 1808, when the government finally bowed to the pressure of the many tracts, poems, and protests written in favour of total abolition, in addition to other circumstances.

ing; and a spacious gallery was rendered dark by the broken windows being blocked up; through the apertures the wind forced its way in hollow sounds, and reverberated along the former scene of festivity.

It was crowded with inhabitants: som[1] were scolding, others swearing, or singing indecent songs. What a sight for Mary! Her blood ran cold; yet she had sufficient resolution to mount to the top of the house. On the floor, in one corner of a very small room, lay an emaciated figure of a woman; a window over her head scarcely admitted any light, for the broken panes were stuffed with dirty rags. Near her were five children, all young, and covered with dirt; their sallow cheeks, and languid eyes, exhibited none of the charms of childhood. Some were fighting, and others crying for food; their yells were mixed with their mother's groans, and the wind which rushed through the passage. Mary was petrified; but soon assuming more courage, approached the bed, and, regardless of the surrounding nastiness, knelt down by the poor wretch, and breathed the most poisonous air; for the unfortunate creature was dying of a putrid fever, the consequence of dirt and want.[2]

Their state did not require much explanation. Mary sent the husband for a poor neighbour, whom she hired to nurse the woman, and take care of the children; and then went herself to buy them some necessaries at a shop not far distant. Her knowledge of physic had enabled her to prescribe for the woman; and she left the house, with a mixture of horror and satisfaction.

She visited them every day, and procured them every comfort; contrary to her expectation, the woman began to recover; cleanliness and wholesome food had a wonderful effect; and Mary saw her rising as it were from the grave. Not aware of the danger she ran into, she did not think of it till she perceived she had caught the fever. It made such an alarming progress, that she was prevailed on to send for a physician; but the disorder was so violent, that for some days it baffled his skill; and Mary felt not her danger, as she was delirious. After the crisis, the symptoms were more favourable, and she slowly recovered, without regaining

---

1 This typographical error for "some" is in the source text.
2 Typhus fever. According to the *OED*, "typhus" and other "putrid fevers" were associated with the living conditions wrought by poverty, such as a lack of cleanliness and cramped, crowded quarters, which spread the contagion; for the same reasons, typhus was also called "hospital fever" or "prison fever" (*OED*).

much strength or spirits; indeed they were intolerably low: she wanted a tender nurse.

For some time she had observed, that she was not treated with the same respect as formerly; her favors were forgotten when no more were expected. This ingratitude hurt her, as did a similar instance in the woman who came out of the ship. Mary had hitherto supported her; as her finances were growing low, she hinted to her, that she ought to try to earn her own subsistence: the woman in return loaded her with abuse.

Two months were elapsed; she had not seen, or heard from Henry. He was sick — nay, perhaps had forgotten her; all the world was dreary, and all the people ungrateful.

She sunk into apathy, and endeavouring to rouse herself out of it, she wrote in her book another fragment:

"Surely life is a dream, a frightful one! and after those rude, disjointed images are fled, will light ever break in? Shall I ever feel joy? Do all suffer like me; or am I framed so as to be particularly susceptible of misery? It is true, I have experienced the most rapturous emotions — short-lived delight! — ethereal beam, which only serves to shew my present misery — yet lie still, my throbbing heart, or burst; and my brain — why dost thou whirl about at such a terrifying rate? why do thoughts so rapidly rush into my mind, and yet when they disappear leave such deep traces? I could almost wish for the madman's happiness, and in a strong imagination lose a sense of woe.

"Oh! reason, thou boasted guide, why desert me, like the world, when I most need thy assistance! Canst thou not calm this internal tumult, and drive away the death-like sadness which presses so sorely on me, — a sadness surely very nearly allied to despair. I am now the prey of apathy — I could wish for the former storms! a ray of hope sometimes illumined my path; I had a pursuit; but now *it visits not my haunts forlorn*.[1] Too well have I loved my fellow creatures! I have been wounded by ingratitude; from every one it has something of the serpent's tooth.[2]

---

1  From Charlotte Turner Smith's (1749-1806) "To Hope" in *Elegiac Sonnets* (1784): "Oh, Hope! thou soother sweet of human woes! / How shall I lure thee to my haunts forlorn?" (ll. 1-2).

2  The phrase "serpent's tooth" is from Shakespeare's *The Tragedy of King Lear* (1605-06), in which Lear invokes nature to curse his daughter, Goneril, with maternal torment to repay her for her ingratitude:
     Dry up in her the organs of increase,
     And from her derogate body never spring         (*continued*)

"When overwhelmed by sorrow, I have met unkindness; I looked for some one to have pity on me; but found none! — The healing balm of sympathy is denied; I weep, a solitary wretch, and the hot tears scald my cheeks. I have not the medicine of life, the dear chimera I have so often chased, a friend. Shade of my loved Ann! dost thou ever visit thy poor Mary? Refined spirit, thou wouldst weep, could angels weep, to see her struggling with passions she cannot subdue; and feelings which corrode her small portion of comfort!"

She could not write any more; she wished herself far distant from all human society; a thick gloom spread itself over her mind: but did not make her forget the very beings she wished to fly from. She sent for the poor woman she found in the garret; gave her money to clothe herself and children, and buy some furniture for a little hut, in a large garden, the master of which agreed to employ her husband, who had been bred a gardener. Mary promised to visit the family, and see their new abode when she was able to go out.

## CHAP. XXIV.

MARY still continued weak and low, though it was spring, and all nature began to look gay; with more than usual brightness the sun shone, and a little robin which she had cherished during the winter sung one of his best songs. The family were particularly civil this fine morning, and tried to prevail on her to walk out. Any thing like kindness melted her; she consented.

Softer emotions banished her melancholy, and she directed her steps to the habitation she had rendered comfortable.

Emerging out of a dreary chamber, all nature looked cheerful; when she had last walked out, snow covered the ground, and bleak winds pierced her through and through: now the hedges were green, the blossoms adorned the trees, and the birds sung.

---

A babe to honour her: if she must teem,
Create her child of spleen, that it may live
And be a thwart disnatured torment to her:
Let it stamp wrinkles in her brow of youth;
With cadent tears fret channels in her cheeks,
Turn all her mother's pains and benefits
To laughter and contempt, that she may feel
How sharper than a serpent's tooth it is
To have a thankless child! (I, iv, 227-37)

She reached the dwelling, without being much exhausted; and while she rested there, observed the children sporting on the grass, with improved complexions. The mother with tears thanked her deliverer, and pointed out her comforts. Mary's tears flowed not only from sympathy, but a complication of feelings and recollections; the affections which bound her to her fellow creatures began again to play, and reanimated nature. She observed the change in herself, tried to account for it, and wrote with her pencil a rhapsody on sensibility.

"Sensibility is the most exquisite feeling of which the human soul is susceptible: when it pervades us, we feel happy; and could it last unmixed, we might form some conjecture of the bliss of those paradisiacal days, when the obedient passions were under the dominion of reason, and the impulses of the heart did not need correction.

"It is this quickness, this delicacy of feeling, which enables us to relish the sublime touches of the poet, and the painter; it is this, which expands the soul, gives an enthusiastic greatness, mixed with tenderness, when we view the magnificent objects of nature; or hear of a good action. The same effect we experience in the spring, when we hail the returning sun, and the consequent renovation of nature; when the flowers unfold themselves, and exhale their sweets, and the voice of music is heard in the land. Softened by tenderness; the soul is disposed to be virtuous. Is any sensual gratification to be compared to that of feeling the eyes moistened after having comforted the unfortunate?

"Sensibility is indeed the foundation of all our happiness; but these raptures are unknown to the depraved sensualist, who is only moved by what strikes his gross senses; the delicate embellishments of nature escape his notice; as do the gentle and interesting affections. — But it is only to be felt; it escapes discussion."

She then returned home, and partook of the family meal, which was rendered more cheerful by the presence of a man, past the meridian of life, of polished manners, and dazzling wit. He endeavoured to draw Mary out, and succeeded; she entered into conversation, and some of her artless flights of genius struck him with surprise; he found she had a capacious mind, and that her reason was as profound as her imagination was lively. She glanced from earth to heaven, and caught the light of truth. Her expressive countenance shewed what passed in her mind, and her tongue was ever the faithful interpreter of her heart; duplicity never threw a shade over her words or actions. Mary found him a man of learning; and the exercise of her understanding would frequently make her forget her griefs, when nothing else could, except benevolence.

This man had known the mistress of the house in her youth; good nature induced him to visit her; but when he saw Mary he had another inducement. Her appearance, and above all, her genius, and cultivation of mind, roused his curiosity; but her dignified manners had such an effect on him, he was obliged to suppress it. He knew men, as well as books; his conversation was entertaining and improving. In Mary's company he doubted whether heaven was peopled with spirits masculine;[1] and almost forgot that he had called the sex "the pretty play things that render life tolerable."

He had been the slave of beauty,[2] the captive of sense; love he ne'er had felt; the mind never rivetted the chain, nor had the purity of it made the body appear lovely in his eyes. He was humane, despised meanness; but was vain of his abilities, and by no means a useful member of society. He talked often of the beauty of virtue; but not having any solid foundation to build the practice on, he was only a shining, or rather a sparkling character: and though his fortune enabled him to hunt down pleasure, he was discontented.

Mary observed his character, and wrote down a train of reflections, which these observations led her to make; these reflections received a tinge from her mind; the present state of it, was that kind of painful quietness which arises from reason clouded by disgust; she had not yet learned to be resigned; vague hopes agitated her.

"There are some subjects that are so enveloped in clouds, as you dissipate one, another overspreads it. Of this kind are our reasonings concerning happiness, till we are obliged to cry out with the Apostle, *That it hath not entered into the heart of man to conceive in what it could consist,*[3] or how satiety could be pre-

---

1   A possible reference to the widely noted fact that all of the angels in Milton's *Paradise Lost* are male, such as Michael and Raphael.

2   By calling this man a "slave of beauty," Wollstonecraft introduces two of the major themes that she would develop in *Rights of Woman*—slavery and the evils of beauty—to show how men, too, are negatively affected by these evils. For more information on this topic, see p. 131, note 1.

3   Reference to the apostle St. Paul's first letter to the Corinthians: "But as it is written, Eye hath not seen, nor ear heard, neither have entered into the heart of man, the things which God hath prepared for them that love him" (2:9).

vented. Man seems formed for action, though the passions are seldom properly managed; they are either so languid as not to serve as a spur, or else so violent, as to overleap all bounds.

"Every individual has its own peculiar trials; and anguish, in one shape or other, visits every heart. Sensibility produces flights of virtue; and not curbed by reason, is on the brink of vice talking, and even thinking of virtue.

"Christianity can only afford just principles to govern the wayward feelings and impulses of the heart: every good disposition runs wild, if not transplanted into this soil; but how hard is it to keep the heart diligently, though convinced that the issues of life depend on it.

"It is very difficult to discipline the mind of a thinker, or reconcile him to the weakness, the inconsistency of his understanding; and a still more laborious task for him to conquer his passions, and learn to seek content, instead of happiness. Good dispositions, and virtuous propensities, without the light of the Gospel, produce eccentric characters: comet-like, they are always in extremes; while revelation resembles the laws of attraction, and produces uniformity; but too often is the attraction feeble; and the light so obscured by passion, as to force the bewildered soul to fly into void space, and wander in confusion."

## CHAP. XXV.

A FEW mornings after, as Mary was sitting ruminating, harassed by perplexing thoughts, and fears, a letter was delivered to her: the servant waited for an answer. Her heart palpitated; it was from Henry; she held it some time in her hand, then tore it open; it was not a long one; and only contained an account of a relapse, which prevented his sailing in the first packet, as he had intended. Some tender enquiries were added, concerning her health, and state of mind; but they were expressed in rather a formal style: it vexed her, and the more so, as it stopped the current of affection, which the account of his arrival and illness had made flow to her heart — it ceased to beat for a moment — she read the passage over again; but could not tell what she was hurt by — only that it did not answer the expectations of her affection. She wrote a laconic, incoherent note in return, allowing him to call on her the next day — he had requested permission at the conclusion of his letter.

Her mind was then painfully active; she could not read or walk; she tried to fly from herself, to forget the long hours that were yet to run before to-morrow could arrive: she knew not what time he would come; certainly in the morning, she concluded; the morning then was anxiously wished for; and every wish produced a sigh, that arose from expectation on the stretch, damped by fear and vain regret.

To beguile the tedious time, Henry's favorite tunes were sung; the books they read together turned over; and the short epistle read at least a hundred times. — Any one who had seen her, would have supposed that she was trying to decypher Chinese characters.

After a sleepless night, she hailed the tardy day, watched the rising sun, and then listened for every footstep, and started if she heard the street door opened. At last he came, and she who had been counting the hours, and doubting whether the earth moved, would gladly have escaped the approaching interview.

With an unequal, irresolute pace, she went to meet him; but when she beheld his emaciated countenance, all the tenderness, which the formality of his letter had damped, returned, and a mournful presentiment stilled the internal conflict. She caught his hand, and looking wistfully at him, exclaimed, "Indeed, you are not well!"

"I am very far from well; but it matters not," added he with a smile of resignation; "my native air may work wonders, and besides, my mother is a tender nurse, and I shall sometimes see thee."

Mary felt for the first time in her life, envy; she wished involuntarily, that all the comfort he received should be from her. She enquired about the symptoms of his disorder; and heard that he had been very ill; she hastily drove away the fears, that former dear bought experience suggested: and again and again did she repeat, that she was sure he would soon recover. She would then look in his face, to see if he assented, and ask more questions to the same purport. She tried to avoid speaking of herself, and Henry left her, with, a promise of visiting her the next day.

Her mind was now engrossed by one fear — yet she would not allow herself to think that she feared an event she could not name. She still saw his pale face; the sound of his voice still vibrated on her ears; she tried to retain it; she listened, looked round, wept, and prayed.

Henry had enlightened the desolate scene: was this charm of life to fade away, and, like the baseless fabric of a vision, leave not a wreck behind?[1] These thoughts disturbed her reason, she shook her head, as if to drive them out of it; a weight, a heavy one, was on her heart; all was not well there.

Out of this reverie she was soon woke to keener anguish, by the arrival of a letter from her husband; it came to Lisbon after her departure: Henry had forwarded it to her, but did not choose to deliver it himself, for a very obvious reason; it might have produced a conversation he wished for some time to avoid; and his precaution took its rise almost equally from benevolence and love.

She could not muster up sufficient resolution to break the seal: her fears were not prophetic, for the contents gave her comfort. He informed her that he intended prolonging his tour, as he was now his own master, and wished to remain some time on the continent, and in particular to visit Italy without any restraint: but his reasons for it appeared childish; it was not to cultivate his taste, or tread on classic ground, where poets and philosophers caught their lore; but to join in the masquerades, and such burlesque amusements.

These instances of folly relieved Mary, in some degree reconciled her to herself, added fuel to the devouring flame — and silenced something like a pang, which reason and conscience made her feel, when she reflected, that it is the office of Religion to reconcile us to the seemingly hard dispensations of providence; and that no inclination, however strong, should oblige us to desert the post assigned us, or force us to forget that virtue should be an active principle; and that the most desirable station, is the one that exercises our faculties, refines our affections, and enables us to be useful.

---

1 Slightly misquoted from Prospero's speech in Shakespeare's *The Tempest* (1611):
Our revels now are ended. These our actors,
As I foretold you, were all spirits and
Are melted into air, into thin air,
And, like the baseless fabric of this vision,
The cloud-capped towers, the gorgeous palaces,
The solemn temples, the great globe itself,
Yea, all which it inherit, shall dissolve,
And, like this insubstantial pageant faded,
Leave not a rack behind. We are such stuff
As dreams are made on; and our little life
Is rounded with a sleep. (IV, i, 161-71)

One reflection continually wounded her repose; she feared not poverty; her wants were few; but in giving up a fortune, she gave up the power of comforting the miserable, and making the sad heart sing for joy.

Heaven had endowed her with uncommon humanity, to render her one of His benevolent agents, a messenger of peace; and should she attend to her own inclinations?

These suggestions, though they could not subdue a violent passion, increased her misery. One moment she was a heroine, half determined to bear whatever fate should inflict; the next, her mind would recoil — and tenderness possessed her whole soul. Some instances of Henry's affection, his worth and genius, were remembered: and the earth was only a vale of tears,[1] because he was not to sojourn with her.

## CHAP. XXVI.

HENRY came the next day, and once or twice in the course of the following week; but still Mary kept up some little formality, a certain consciousness restrained her; and Henry did not enter on the subject which he found she wished to avoid. In the course of conversation, however, she mentioned to him, that she earnestly desired to obtain a place in one of the public offices for Ann's brother, as the family were again in a declining way.

Henry attended, made a few enquiries, and dropped the subject; but the following week, she heard him enter with unusual haste; it was to inform her, that he had made interest with a

---

1  Psalm 84:6: "Who passing through the valley of Baca make it a well; the rain also filleth the pools." The phrase "valley of Baca" is sometimes translated as "vale of tears" or "valley of weeping" in other versions of the Bible. I use the King James Bible, since it has been the standard Bible for England since 1611. Wollstonecraft may have used a different Bible, or she may simply have been referring to a common interpretation of this passage. Intriguingly for literary scholars, she may have used Christopher Smart's (1722-71) translation of the Hebrew text, *A Translation of the Psalms of David, Attempted in the Spirit of Christianity, and Adapted to the Divine Service* (1765). In this self-published work, Smart translates line 25 of Psalm 84 ("As thro' this vale of tears he goes") and Psalm 23:44-7 as follows:
    Yea, tho' from hence my journey lies
    Down thro' the vale of tears and sighs,
        And up the steep of pain,
    No terror shall my course withstand.

person of some consequence, whom he had once obliged in a very disagreeable exigency, in a foreign country; and that he had procured a place for her friend, which would infallibly lead to something better, if he behaved with propriety. Mary could not speak to thank him; emotions of gratitude and love suffused her face; her blood eloquently spoke. She delighted to receive benefits through the medium of her fellow creatures; but to receive them from Henry was exquisite pleasure.

As the summer advanced, Henry grew worse; the closeness of the air, in the metropolis, affected his breath; and his mother insisted on his fixing on some place in the country, where she would accompany him. He could not think of going far off, but chose a little village on the banks of the Thames, near Mary's dwelling: he then introduced her to his mother.

They frequently went down the river in a boat; Henry would take his violin, and Mary would sometimes sing, or read, to them. She pleased his mother; she inchanted him. It was an advantage to Mary that friendship first possessed her heart; it opened it to all the softer sentiments of humanity: — and when this first affection was torn away, a similar one sprung up, with a still tenderer sentiment added to it.

The last evening they were on the water, the clouds grew suddenly black, and broke in violent showers, which interrupted the solemn stillness that had prevailed previous to it. The thunder roared; and the oars plying quickly, in order to reach the shore, occasioned a not unpleasing sound. Mary drew still nearer Henry; she wished to have sought with him a watry grave; to have escaped the horror of surviving him.[1] — She spoke not, but Henry saw the workings of her mind — he felt them; threw his arm round her waist — and they enjoyed the luxury of wretchedness. — As they touched the shore, Mary perceived that Henry was wet; with eager anxiety she cried, What shall I do! — this day will kill thee, and I shall not die with thee!

This accident put a stop to their pleasurable excursions; it had injured him, and brought on the spitting of blood he was subject to — perhaps it was not the cold that he caught, that occasioned it. In vain did Mary try to shut her eyes; her fate pursued her! Henry every day grew worse and worse.

---

1  Wollstonecraft would have a similar wish some years later: to drown with her and Imlay's infant daughter, Fanny. In 1795, she wrote to Imlay, "I have looked at the sea, and at my child, hardly daring to own to myself the secret wish, that it might become our tomb" (*Letters* 297).

## CHAP. XXVII.

OPPRESSED by her foreboding fears, her sore mind was hurt by new instances of ingratitude: disgusted with the family, whose misfortunes had often disturbed her repose, and lost in anticipated sorrow, she rambled she knew not where; when turning down a shady walk, she discovered her feet had taken the path they delighted to tread. She saw Henry sitting in his garden alone; he quickly opened the garden-gate, and she sat down by him.

"I did not," said he, "expect to see thee this evening, my dearest Mary; but I was thinking of thee. Heaven has endowed thee with an uncommon portion of fortitude, to support one of the most affectionate hearts in the world. This is not a time for disguise; I know I am dear to thee — and my affection for thee is twisted with every fibre of my heart. — I loved thee ever since I have been acquainted with thine: thou art the being my fancy has delighted to form; but which I imagined existed only there! In a little while the shades of death will encompass me — ill-fated love perhaps added strength to my disease, and smoothed the rugged path. Try, my love, to fulfil thy destined course — try to add to thy other virtues patience. I could have wished, for thy sake, that we could have died together — or that I could live to shield thee from the assaults of an unfeeling world! Could I but offer thee an asylum in these arms — a faithful bosom, in which thou couldst repose all thy griefs —" He pressed her to it, and she returned the pressure — he felt her throbbing heart. A mournful silence ensued! when he resumed the conversation. "I wished to prepare thee for the blow — too surely do I feel that it will not be long delayed! The passion I have nursed is so pure, that death cannot extinguish it — or tear away the impression thy virtues have made on my soul. I would fain comfort thee —"

"Talk not of comfort," interrupted Mary, "it will be in heaven with thee and Ann — while I shall remain on earth the veriest wretch!" — She grasped his hand.

"There we shall meet, my love, my Mary, in our Father's —" His voice faultered; he could not finish the sentence; he was almost suffocated — they both wept, their tears relieved them; they walked slowly to the garden-gate (Mary would not go into the house); they could not say farewel when they reached it — and Mary hurried down the lane, to spare Henry the pain of witnessing her emotions.

When she lost sight of the house she sat down on the ground, till it grew late, thinking of all that had passed. Full of these thoughts, she crept along, regardless of the descending rain; when lifting up her eyes to heaven, and then turning them wildly on the prospects around, without marking them; she only felt that the scene accorded with her present state of mind. It was the last glimmering of twilight, with a full moon, over which clouds continually flitted. Where am I wandering, God of Mercy! she thought; she alluded to the wanderings of her mind. In what a labyrinth am I lost! What miseries have I already encountered — and what a number lie still before me.

Her thoughts flew rapidly to something. I could be happy listening to him, soothing his cares. — Would he not smile upon me — call me his own Mary? I am not his — said she with fierceness — I am a wretch! and she heaved a sigh that almost broke her heart, while the big tears rolled down her burning cheeks; but still her exercised mind, accustomed to think, began to observe its operation, though the barrier of reason was almost carried away, and all the faculties not restrained by her, were running into confusion. Wherefore am I made thus? Vain are my efforts — I cannot live without loving — and love leads to madness. — Yet I will not weep; and her eyes were now fixed by despair, dry and motionless; and then quickly whirled about with a look of distraction.

She looked for hope; but found none — all was troubled waters. — No where could she find rest. I have already paced to and fro in the earth; it is not my abiding place — may I not too go home! Ah! no. Is this complying with my Henry's request, could a spirit thus disengaged expect to associate with his? Tears of tenderness strayed down her relaxed countenance, and her softened heart heaved more regularly. She felt the rain, and turned to her solitary home.

Fatigued by the tumultuous emotions she had endured, when she entered the house she ran to her own room, sunk on the bed, and exhausted nature soon closed her eyes; but active fancy was still awake, and a thousand fearful dreams interrupted her slumbers.

Feverish and languid, she opened her eyes, and saw the unwelcome sun dart his rays through a window, the curtains of which she had forgotten to draw. The dew hung on the adjacent trees, and added to the lustre; the little robin began his song, and distant birds joined. She looked; her countenance was still vacant — her sensibility was absorbed by one object.

Did I ever admire the rising sun, she slightly thought, turning from the window, and shutting her eyes: she recalled to view the last night's scene. His faltering voice, lingering step, and the look of tender woe, were all graven on her heart; as were the words "Could these arms shield thee from sorrow — afford thee an asylum from an unfeeling world." The pressure to his bosom was not forgot. For a moment she was happy; but in a long-drawn sigh every delightful sensation evaporated. Soon — yes, very soon, will the grave again receive all I love! and the remnant of my days — she could not proceed — Were there then days to come after that?

## CHAP. XXVIII.

JUST as she was going to quit her room, to visit Henry, his mother called on her.

"My son is worse to-day," said she. "I come to request you to spend not only this day, but a week or two with me. — Why should I conceal any thing from you? Last night my child made his mother his confident, and, in the anguish of his heart, requested me to be thy friend — when I shall be childless. I will not attempt to describe what I felt when he talked thus to me. If I am to lose the support of my age, and be again a widow — may I call her Child whom my Henry wishes me to adopt?"[1]

This new instance of Henry's disinterested affection, Mary felt most forcibly; and striving to restrain the complicated emotions, and sooth the wretched mother, she almost fainted: when the unhappy parent forced tears from her, by saying, "I deserve this blow; my partial fondness ma[d]e[2] me neglect him, when most he wanted a mother's care; this neglect, perhaps, first injured his constitution: righteous Heaven has made my crime its own punishment; and now I am indeed a mother, I shall lose my child — my only child!"

When they were a little more composed they hastened to the invalide; but during the short ride, the mother related several

---

1 It is unclear how losing her son would make Henry's mother a "widow." This passage adds to the number of odd familial relationships that appear throughout the novella. For example, the next phrase suggests that Mary would become a bereaved sister to Henry, to whom she is romantically attached—and their relationship is already complicated by his comment in Chapter XVI (p. 117) that he wishes to be as a tender father to her.

2 The source edition contains a typographical error: "mae."

instances of Henry's goodness of heart. Mary's tears were not those of unmixed anguish; the display of his virtues gave her extreme delight — yet human nature prevailed; she trembled to think they would soon unfold themselves in a more genial clime.

## CHAP. XXIX.

SHE found Henry very ill. The physician had some weeks before declared he never knew a person with a similar pulse recover. Henry was certain he could not live long; all the rest he could obtain, was procured by opiates. Mary now enjoyed the melancholy pleasure of nursing him, and softened by her tenderness the pains she could not remove. Every sigh did she stifle, every tear restrain, when he could see or hear them. She would boast of her resignation — yet catch eagerly at the least ray of hope. While he slept she would support his pillow, and rest her head where she could feel his breath. She loved him better than herself — she could not pray for his recovery; she could only say, The will of Heaven be done.[1]

While she was in this state, she labored to acquire fortitude; but one tender look destroyed it all — she rather labored, indeed, to make him believe she was resigned, than really to be so.

She wished to receive the sacrament with him, as a bond of union which was to extend beyond the grave. She did so, and received comfort from it; she rose above her misery.

His end was now approaching. Mary sat on the side of the bed. His eyes appeared fixed — no longer agitated by passion, he only felt that it was a fearful thing to die. The soul retired to the citadel; but it was not now solely filled by the image of her who in silent despair watched for his last breath. Collected, a frightful calmness stilled every turbulent emotion.

The mother's grief was more audible. Henry had for some time only attended to Mary — Mary pitied the parent, whose stings of conscience increased her sorrow; she whispered him, "Thy mother weeps, disregarded by thee; oh! comfort her! — My mother, thy son blesses thee. —" The oppressed parent left the room. And Mary *waited* to see him die.

---

1  An exact echo of Abergavenny from Shakespeare's *The Life of King Henry the Eighth* (1613): "The will of heaven be done, and the king's pleasure / By me obeyed" (I, i, 252-53). The phrase is also strongly reminiscent of the Lord's Prayer, from the Sermon on the Mount: "Thy kingdom come. Thy will be done in earth, as *it is* in heaven" (St. Matthew 6:10).

She pressed with trembling eagerness his parched lips — he opened his eyes again; the spreading film retired, and love returned them — he gave a look — it was never forgotten. My Mary, will you be comforted?

Yes, yes, she exclaimed in a firm voice; you go to be happy — I am not a complete wretch! The words almost choked her.

He was a long time silent; the opiate produced a kind of stupor. At last, in an agony, he cried, It is dark; I cannot see thee; raise me up. Where is Mary? did she not say she delighted to support me? let me die in her arms.

Her arms were opened to receive him; they trembled not. Again he was obliged to lie down, resting on her: as the agonies increased he leaned towards her: the soul seemed flying to her, as it escaped out of its prison. The breathing was interrupted; she heard distinctly the last sigh — and lifting up to Heaven her eyes, Father, receive his spirit, she calmly cried.[1]

The attendants gathered round; she moved not, nor heard the clamor; the hand seemed yet to press hers; it still was warm. A ray of light from an opened window discovered the pale face.

She left the room, and retired to one very near it; and sitting down on the floor, fixed her eyes on the door of the apartment which contained the body. Every event of her life rushed across her mind with wonderful rapidity — yet all was still — fate had given the finishing stroke. She sat till midnight. — Then rose in a phrensy, went into the apartment, and desired those who watched the body to retire.

She knelt by the bed side; — an enthusiastic devotion overcame the dictates of despair. — She prayed most ardently to be supported, and dedicated herself to the service of that Being into whose hands, she had committed the spirit she almost adored — again — and again, — she prayed wildly — and fervently — but attempting to touch the lifeless hand — her head swum — she sunk —

---

1 This phrase recalls Jesus' words before he died, as reported by St. Luke: "Father, into thy hands I commend my spirit" (24:4). Despite verbs that clearly indicate the presence of speech in this paragraph and the next two, such as "she exclaimed" and "he cried," the source edition does not include quotation marks.

# CHAP. XXX.

THREE months after, her only friend, the mother of her lost Henry began to be alarmed, at observing her altered appearance; and made her own health a pretext for travelling. These complaints roused Mary out of her torpid state; she imagined a new duty now forced her to exert herself — a duty love made sacred! —

They went to Bath, from that to Bristol; but the latter place they quickly left; the sight of the sick that resort there, they neither of them could bear. From Bristol they flew to Southampton. The road was pleasant — yet Mary shut her eyes; — or if they were open, green fields and commons, passed in quick succession, and left no more traces behind than if they had been waves of the sea.

Some time after they were settled at Southampton, they met the man who took so much notice of Mary, soon after her return to England. He renewed his acquaintance; he was really interested in her fate, as he had heard her uncommon story; besides, he knew her husband; knew him to be a good-natured, weak man. He saw him soon after his arrival in his native country, and prevented his hastening to enquire into the reasons of Mary's strange conduct. He desired him not to be too precipitate, if he ever wished to possess an invaluable treasure. He was guided by him, and allowed him to follow Mary to Southampton, and speak first to her friend.

This friend determined to trust to her native strength of mind, and informed her of the circumstance; but she overrated it: Mary was not able, for a few days after the intelligence, to fix on the mode of conduct she ought now to pursue. But at last she conquered her disgust, and wrote her *husband* an account of what had passed since she had dropped his correspondence.

He came in person to answer the letter. Mary fainted when he approached her unexpectedly. Her disgust returned with additional force, in spite of previous reasonings, whenever he appeared; yet she was prevailed on to promise to live with him, if he would permit her to pass one year, travelling from place to place; he was not to accompany her.

The time too quickly elapsed, and she gave him her hand — the struggle was almost more than she could endure. She tried to appear calm; time mellowed her grief, and mitigated her torments; but when her husband would take her hand, or mention any thing like love, she would instantly feel a sickness, a faintness at her heart, and wish, involuntarily, that the earth would open and swallow her.

## CHAP. XXXI.

MARY visited the continent, and sought health in different climates; but her nerves were not to be restored to their former state. She then retired to her house in the country, established manufactories, threw the estate into small farms; and continually employed herself this way to dissipate care, and banish unavailing regret. She visited the sick, supported the old, and educated the young.

These occupations engrossed her mind; but there were hours when all her former woes would return and haunt her. — Whenever she did, or said, any thing she thought Henry would have approved of — she could not avoid thinking with anguish, of the rapture his approbation ever conveyed to her heart — a heart in which there was a void, that even benevolence and religion could not fill. The latter taught her to struggle for resignation; and the former rendered life supportable.

Her delicate state of health did not promise long life. In moments of solitary sadness, a gleam of joy would dart across her mind — She thought she was hastening to that world *where there is neither marrying*, nor giving in marriage.[1]

## END.

---

1  A suggestive reworking of Jesus' words regarding the condition of people in heaven: "For when they shall rise from the dead, they neither marry, nor are given in marriage; but are as the angels which are in heaven" (St. Mark 12:25). St. Luke 20:35 and St. Matthew 22:30 report almost identical words, and none of these biblical passages use the word "giving" instead of "given," as Wollstonecraft does—for sound grammatical reasons, but this change may also suggest myriad interpretations about a character who appears to live only for others.

THE WRONGS OF WOMAN:

OR,

MARIA.

A FRAGMENT.

IN TWO VOLUMES.

------------------------

VOL. I.

POSTHUMOUS WORKS

OF THE

AUTHOR

OF *A*

*VINDICATION OF THE RIGHTS OF WOMAN.*

IN FOUR VOLUMES.

----------------------

VOL. I.

----------------------

*LONDON*:
PRINTED FOR J. JOHNSON, NO. 72, ST. PAUL'S
CHURCH-YARD; AND G. G. AND J. ROBINSON,
PATERNOSTER-ROW.
1798.

POSTHUMOUS WORKS

OF

MARY WOLLSTONECRAFT GODWIN.

VOL. I.

# PREFACE.

THE public are here presented with the last literary attempt of an author, whose fame has been uncommonly extensive, and whose talents have probably been most admired, by the persons by whom talents are estimated with the greatest accuracy and discrimination. There are few, to whom her writings could in any case have given pleasure, that would have wished that this fragment should have been suppressed, because it is a fragment. There is a sentiment, very dear to minds of taste and imagination, that finds a melancholy delight in contemplating these unfinished productions of genius, these sketches of what, if they had been filled up in a manner adequate to the writer's conception, would perhaps have given a new impulse to the manners of a world.

The purpose and structure of the following work, had long formed a favourite subject of meditation with its author, and she judged them capable of producing an important effect.[1] The composition had been in progress for a period of twelve months. She was anxious to do justice to her conception, and recommenced and revised the manuscript several different times. So much of it as is here given to the public, she was far from considering as finished, and, in a letter to a friend directly written on this subject, she says, "I am perfectly aware that some of the incidents ought to be transposed, and heightened by more harmonious shading; and I wished in some degree to avail myself of criticism, before I began to adjust my events into a story, the outline of which I had sketched in my mind."[2] The only friends to whom

---

1 By "purpose and structure," Godwin, the writer of this preface (see p. 156, note 2 for more information on him), may refer to Wollstonecraft's literary purpose of reforming her audience's ideas about marriage, women's status in society, and the ways in which novels of sensibility contribute to this inequality. By "structure," Godwin may refer to the hybrid form of the novel as both a Gothic novel and a fictionalization of her polemical prose work, *Rights of Woman*, a form that Godwin employed when he fictionalized *Enquiry Concerning the Principles of Political Justice* (1793) in *Things as They Are; or, The Adventures of Caleb Williams* (1794). Gary Kelly dubs this narrative form "the Jacobin novel" in his seminal work, *The English Jacobin Novel, 1780-1805*.

2 A more copious extract of this letter is subjoined to the author's preface. [Godwin's note]

the author communicated her manuscript, were Mr. Dyson, the translator of *the Sorcerer*, and the present editor; and it was impossible for the most inexperienced author to display a stronger desire of profiting by the censures and sentiments that might be suggested.[1]

In revising these sheets for the press, it was necessary for the editor, in some places, to connect the more finished parts with the pages of an older copy, and a line or two in addition sometimes appeared requisite for that purpose. Wherever such a liberty has been taken, the additional phrases will be found inclosed in brackets; it being the editor's most earnest desire, to intrude nothing of himself into the work, but to give to the public the words, as well as ideas, of the real author.

What follows in the ensuing pages, is not a preface regularly drawn out by the author, but merely hints for a preface, which, though never filled up in the manner the writer intended, appeared to be worth preserving.

W. GODWIN.[2]

---

1 The part communicated consisted of the first fourteen chapters. [Godwin's note] George Dyson (d. 1822) was a writer and painter. He translated a novel by Georg P.L.L. Wächter (1762-1837, penname Veit Weber) called *The Sorcerer*, which was published in 1795 by Joseph Johnson (Todd, *Letters* 385).

2 Godwin, influential writer, Wollstonecraft's husband, and father of their child, Mary, presumably published the "posthumous works" of the woman whom he called "the object dearest to my heart that the universe contained" (*Memoirs* 180) to honour her and, as this preface indicates, from his belief that her work was of a calibre that demanded publication.

# AUTHOR's PREFACE.

------------------------

The Wrongs of Woman, like the wrongs of the oppressed part of mankind, may be deemed necessary by their oppressors:[1] but surely there are a few, who will dare to advance before the improvement of the age, and grant that my sketches are not the abortion of a distempered fancy, or the strong delineations of a wounded heart.

In writing this novel, I have rather endeavoured to pourtray passions than manners.

In many instances I could have made the incidents more dramatic, would I have sacrificed my main object, the desire of exhibiting the misery and oppression, peculiar to women, that arise out of the partial laws and customs of society.[2]

In the invention of the story, this view restrained my fancy; and the history ought rather to be considered, as of woman, than of an individual.[3]

The sentiments I have embodied.

In many works of this species, the hero is allowed to be mortal, and to become wise and virtuous as well as happy, by a train of

---

1 See p. 131, note 1 for more information on Wollstonecraft's frequent comparison of women to slaves (here present in the phrase "the oppressed part of mankind") in both her fiction and polemical prose. Of interest in this instance is Wollstonecraft's reference to the notion of "the white man's burden," or English colonists' self-aggrandizing belief that colonization—or, here, slavery—was a means of generously spreading Christianity and English law and order, rather than a selfish way to augment their own wealth.

2 By "partial laws," Wollstonecraft refers to the marriage laws of her time, in which women were considered to be the property of their husbands, as were any assets they owned before entering the marriage. As such, married women were not legally recognized as autonomous individuals and therefore had no personal rights. Moreover, men could file for divorce on the grounds of adultery, but women could not; they had to prove that they were in physical danger or abandoned to secure a divorce, which was only granted to them in the rarest of cases. Divorced husbands always won custody of children, too.

3 By using the singular "woman" to refer to womankind, Wollstonecraft underlines the connection between this novella and *Rights of Woman*, as well as Thomas Paine's *The Rights of Man* (1791), both of which well-known polemical tracts on human rights establish this novella as having a purpose far beyond entertainment.

events and circumstances. The heroines, on the contrary, are to be born immaculate, and to act like goddesses of wisdom, just come forth highly finished Minervas from the head of Jove.[1]

------------------------

[The following is an extract of a letter from the author to a friend, to whom she communicated her manuscript.][2]

------------------------

For my part, I cannot suppose any situation more distressing, than for a woman of sensibility, with an improving mind, to be bound to such a man as I have described for life; obliged to renounce all the humanizing affections, and to avoid cultivating her taste, lest her perception of grace and refinement of sentiment, should sharpen to agony the pangs of disappointment. Love, in which the imagination mingles its bewitching colouring, must be fostered by delicacy. I should despise, or rather call her an ordinary woman,[3] who could endure such a husband as I have sketched.

---

1 In Roman myth, Minerva is the equivalent of the Greek goddess Athena, the "goddess of wisdom," while Jove is identified with the Greek God Zeus. As Wollstonecraft suggests, the goddess leapt fully formed (and dressed!) from her father's head. Here Wollstonecraft uses the myth of the birth of Minerva to protest that female characters in "works of this species," or novels, are "flat," to use E.M. Forster's terminology from *Aspects of the Novel* (1927); like Minerva, they do not grow or have faults, but are presented as wise and perfect throughout the narrative. In short, they do not seem human. Wollstonecraft attempts to redress this fault in her representation of women in this novel.

2 Godwin's note. Godwin takes the final two paragraphs of the "Author's Preface" from Wollstonecraft's letter to George Dyson; as Todd points out in the *Letters*, the letter is undated, but she gives the postmark as 16 May 1797 (411).

3 In her focus on the personality and mind of her protagonist in these paragraphs, coupled with her statement that she "should ... call her an ordinary woman, who could endure such a husband as I have sketched," Wollstonecraft hints that her goal in *The Wrongs of Woman* is, in at least one way, the same as in *Mary*, as she outlines it in the Epigraph of *Mary*: she sketches the development of female "genius"—a woman who is of exceptional intelligence.

These appear to me (matrimonial despotism of heart and conduct) to be the peculiar Wrongs of Woman, because they degrade the mind. What are termed great misfortunes, may more forcibly impress the mind of common readers; they have more of what may justly be termed *stage-effect*; but it is the delineation of finer sensations, which, in my opinion, constitutes the merit of our best novels. This is what I have in view; and to show the wrongs of different classes of women, equally oppressive, though, from the difference of education, necessarily various.[1]

---

1 Below the "Author's Preface," Godwin includes the textual errata; I have listed them in notes to the relevant passages in the novella.

# WRONGS

# OF

# WOMAN.

------------------------

## CHAP. I.

ABODES of horror have frequently been described, and castles, filled with spectres and chimeras, conjured up by the magic spell of genius to harrow the soul, and absorb the wondering mind. But, formed of such stuff as dreams are made of,[1] what were they to the mansion of despair, in one corner of which Maria sat, endeavouring to recall her scattered thoughts!

Surprise, astonishment, that bordered on distraction, seemed to have suspended her faculties, till, waking by degrees to a keen sense of anguish, a whirlwind of rage and indignation roused her torpid pulse. One recollection with frightful velocity following another, threatened to fire her brain, and make her a fit companion for the terrific[2] inhabitants, whose groans and shrieks were no unsubstantial sounds of whistling winds, or startled birds, modulated by a romantic fancy, which amuse while they affright; but such tones of misery as carry a dreadful certainty directly to the

---

1  As in *Mary*, Chapter XXV, Wollstonecraft echoes Prospero's famous speech in Shakespeare's *The Tempest* ("We are such stuff / As dreams are made on" [IV, i, 169-70]); see p. 139, note 1 for a longer quotation of Shakespeare's text). Wollstonecraft's paragraph suggests a multiplicity of literary forms, even as it undercuts them: through the Shakespearean quotation, Wollstonecraft invokes the dramatic genre; her reference to "abodes of horror ... and castles, filled with spectres and chimeras" suggests the Gothic form of the novel; and her method of introducing the action of this novella *in medias res* (Latin for "in the middle of affairs") recalls the epic form. By invoking these diverse forms in close succession, Wollstonecraft undercuts the primacy of each, thereby fulfilling her promise in the preface, as cobbled together by Godwin, to provide a new kind of work that challenges audience expectations of literature.

2  Although today we frequently use the word "terrific" to mean "wonderful" or some similarly positive adjective, Wollstonecraft uses the word here in its original sense (and in accordance with the primary definition of it in the *OED*): "Causing terror, terrifying; fitted to terrify; dreadful, terrible, frightful."

heart. What effect must they then have produced on one, true to the touch of sympathy, and tortured by maternal apprehension!

Her infant's image was continually floating on Maria's sight, and the first smile of intelligence remembered, as none but a mother, an unhappy mother, can conceive. She heard her half speaking half cooing,[1] and felt the little twinkling fingers on her burning bosom — a bosom bursting with the nutriment for which this cherished child might now be pining in vain. From a stranger she could indeed receive the maternal aliment,[2] Maria was grieved at the thought — but who would watch her with a mother's tenderness, a mother's self-denial?

The retreating shadows of former sorrows rushed back in a gloomy train, and seemed to be pictured on the walls of her prison, magnified by the state of mind in which they were viewed — Still she mourned for her child, lamented she was a daughter, and anticipated the aggravated ills of life that her sex rendered almost inevitable,[3] even while dreading she was no more. To think that she was blotted out of existence was agony, when the imagination had been long employed to expand her faculties; yet to suppose her turned adrift on an unknown sea, was scarcely less afflicting.

After being two days the prey of impetuous, varying emotions, Maria began to reflect more calmly on her present situation, for she had actually been rendered incapable of sober

---

1 The errata listed in the front matter of the volume directs the removal of the second "half" in this sentence, but the emended phrase "She heard her half speaking cooing" makes little sense.

2 The issue of breastfeeding was a loaded and political one in the 1790s. Commonly, aristocratic women hired wet-nurses to breastfeed their children, as it was thought *gauche* to do it oneself. Radical writers in England (and French Revolutionary advisors) warned against this practice, frequently with the argument that breastfeeding was an important means of bonding between children and mothers, which thereby strengthened society as a whole. In *Rights of Woman*, Wollstonecraft contends, moreover, that the sexual ideal of weakness in women contributed to the breakdown of society by hindering mothers from breastfeeding: "Women becoming ... weaker, in mind and body, than they ought to be, were one of the grand ends of their being taken into account, that of bearing and nursing children, have not sufficient strength to discharge the first duty of a mother; and sacrificing to lasciviousness the parental affection ... either destroy the embryo in the womb, or cast it off when born" (316).

3 In 1794, Wollstonecraft wrote to Imlay of their baby daughter, "I lament that my little darling, fondly as I doat on her, is a girl" (*Letters* 276).

reflection, by the discovery of the act of atrocity of which she was the victim. She could not have imagined, that, in all the fermentation of civilized depravity, a similar plot could have entered a human mind. She had been stunned by an unexpected blow; yet life, however joyless, was not to be indolently resigned, or misery endured without exertion, and proudly termed patience. She had hitherto meditated only to point the dart of anguish, and suppressed the heart heavings of indignant nature merely by the force of contempt. Now she endeavoured to brace her mind to fortitude, and to ask herself what was to be her employment in her dreary cell? Was it not to effect her escape, to fly to the succour of her child, and to baffle the selfish schemes of her tyrant — her husband?

These thoughts roused her sleeping spirit, and the self-possession returned, that seemed to have abandoned her in the infernal solitude into which she had been precipitated. The first emotions of overwhelming impatience began to subside, and resentment gave place to tenderness, and more tranquil meditation; though anger once more stopt the calm current of reflection, when she attempted to move her manacled arms.[1] But this

---

1 Maria's "manacled arms" emphasize her humiliating lack of freedom and represent powerfully women's bondage on many levels. Moreover, this image may also function to identify women as members of a victimized and misjudged group in need of humanitarian concern, like the mad in asylums at the turn of the nineteenth century, who, their champions argued, were not subhumans whose existences were defined by their bodies alone, contrary to popular belief. The revolution in the treatment for the insane coincided roughly with the French Revolution. In October 1793, Philippe Pinel (1745-1826) freed the patients at Bicêtre, the hospital for the insane in Paris, an act that "heralded a new attitude to the insane," as Pinel "abolished brutal repression" and "replaced it by a humanitarian medical approach" that advocated freeing patients of physical restraints and emphasizing their abilities to monitor their own behaviour, while re-educating them about social mores and expectations; this approach was commonly called "moral management" or "moral treatment" (Hunter 603). Although Pinel's methods were already being used by the Quakers William (1732-1822) and Samuel (1784-1857) Tuke— the first of whom established, in 1796, The Retreat, an asylum at York that employed moral management practices, and the second of whom wrote about that successful asylum in his celebrated study, *A Description of the Retreat* (1813)—the French physician's approach to madness officially entered English history when his text, *A Treatise on Insanity*, was translated into English in 1806 by D.D. Davis.

was an outrage that could only excite momentary feelings of scorn, which evaporated in a faint smile; for Maria was far from thinking a personal insult the most difficult to endure with magnanimous indifference.

She approached the small grated window of her chamber, and for a considerable time only regarded the blue expanse; though it commanded a view of a desolate garden, and of part of a huge pile of buildings, that, after having been suffered, for half a century, to fall to decay, had undergone some clumsy repairs, merely to render it habitable. The ivy had been torn off the turrets, and the stones not wanted to patch up the breaches of time, and exclude the warring elements, left in heaps in the disordered court. Maria contemplated this scene she knew not how long; or rather gazed on the walls, and pondered on her situation. To the master of this most horrid of prisons, she had, soon after her entrance, raved of injustice, in accents that would have justified his treatment, had not a malignant smile, when she appealed to his judgment, with a dreadful conviction stifled her remonstrating complaints. By force, or openly, what could be done? But surely some expedient might occur to an active mind, without any other employment, and possessed of sufficient resolution to put the risk of life into the balance with the chance of freedom.

A woman entered in the midst of these reflections, with a firm, deliberate step, strongly marked features, and large black eyes, which she fixed steadily on Maria's, as if she designed to intimidate her, saying at the same time — "You had better sit down and eat your dinner, than look at the clouds."

"I have no appetite," replied Maria, who had previously determined to speak mildly; "why then should I eat?"

"But, in spite of that, you must and shall eat something. I have had many ladies under my care, who have resolved to starve themselves; but, soon or late, they gave up their intent, as they recovered their senses."

"Do you really think me mad?" asked Maria, meeting the searching glance of her eye.

"Not just now. But what does that prove? — only that you must be the more carefully watched, for appearing at times so reasonable.[1] You have not touched a morsel since you entered the

---

1 Here Wollstonecraft introduces the notion of what was called "lucid intervals," or momentary bouts of sanity, as expressed in such texts as James Carkesse's (fl. 1679) "Lucida Intervella" (1679). She also hints at the idea, common in psychological texts of the period, that the insane

house." — Maria sighed intelligibly. — "Could any thing but madness produce such a disgust for food?"

"Yes, grief; you would not ask the question if you knew what it was." The attendant shook her head; and a ghastly smile of desperate fortitude served as a forcible reply, and made Maria pause, before she added — "Yet I will take some refreshment: I mean not to die. — No; I will preserve my senses; and convince even you, sooner than you are aware of, that my intellects have never been disturbed, though the exertion of them may have been suspended by some infernal drug."

Doubt gathered still thicker on the brow of her guard, as she attempted to convict her of mistake.

"Have patience!" exclaimed Maria, with a solemnity that inspired awe. "My God! how have I been schooled into the practice!" A suffocation of voice betrayed the agonizing emotions she was labouring to keep down; and conquering a qualm of disgust, she calmly endeavoured to eat enough to prove her docility, perpetually turning to the suspicious female, whose observation she courted, while she was making the bed and adjusting the room.

"Come to me often," said Maria, with a tone of persuasion, in consequence of a vague plan that she had hastily adopted, when, after surveying this woman's form and features, she felt convinced that she had an understanding above the common standard;[1]

---

were cunning and intent on deceiving their asylum keepers about their madness. As Allan Ingram reports, quoting William Pargeter's (1760-1810) influential text, *Observations on Maniacal Disorders* (1792), the insane were viewed as "manipulative, witty, subversive and.... 'extremely subdolous'" (6).

1 By noting that Maria believes she can judge the intellect of her keeper by "surveying this woman's form and [facial] features," Wollstonecraft indicates her character's belief in the Romantic-era psychological approach of physiognomy, devised by Johann Caspar Lavater, which studied the bodily expression of the psychological and spiritual aspects of the subject. As Godwin notes in *Memoirs*, Wollstonecraft created (but did not publish) an abridgement of a French version of Lavater's *Physiognomische Fragmente* (1775). She also includes references to physiognomy in "Cave of Fancy" (1787; see the excerpt from it in Appendix A2 to this volume). Moreover, in the first section of *The Female Reader* (1789), called "Select Desultory Thoughts," she included several aphorisms by Lavater—none of which, however, are physiognomical or even scientific. The following is a typical example: "Modesty is silent when it would not be improper to speak: the humble, without being called upon, never recollects to say any thing of herself" (11).

"and believe me mad, till you are obliged to acknowledge the contrary." The woman was no fool, that is, she was superior to her class; nor had misery quite petrified the life's-blood of humanity, to which reflections on our own misfortunes only give a more orderly course. The manner, rather than the expostulations, of Maria made a slight suspicion dart into her mind with corresponding sympathy, which various other avocations, and the habit of banishing compunction, prevented her, for the present, from examining more minutely.

But when she was told that no person, excepting the physician appointed by her family, was to be permitted to see the lady at the end of the gallery, she opened her keen eyes still wider, and uttered a — "hem!" before she enquired — "Why?" She was briefly told, in reply, that the malady was hereditary, and the fits not occurring but at very long and irregular intervals, she must be carefully watched; for the length of these lucid periods only rendered her more mischievous, when any vexation or caprice brought on the paroxysm of phrensy.

Had her master trusted her, it is probable that neither pity nor curiosity would have made her swerve from the straight line of her interest; for she had suffered too much in her intercourse with mankind, not to determine to look for support, rather to humouring their passions, than courting their approbation by the integrity of her conduct. A deadly blight had met her at the very threshold of existence; and the wretchedness of her mother seemed a heavy weight fastened on her innocent neck, to drag her down to perdition. She could not heroically determine to succour an unfortunate; but, offended at the bare supposition that she could be deceived with the same ease as a common servant, she no longer curbed her curiosity; and, though she never seriously fathomed her own intentions, she would sit, every moment she could steal from observation, listening to the tale, which Maria was eager to relate with all the persuasive eloquence of grief.

It is so cheering to see a human face, even if little of the divinity of virtue beam in it, that Maria anxiously expected the return of the attendant, as of a gleam of light to break the gloom of idleness. Indulged sorrow, she perceived, must blunt or sharpen the faculties to the two opposite extremes; producing stupidity, the moping melancholy of indolence; or the restless activity of a disturbed imagination. She sunk into one state, after being fatigued by the other: till the want of occupation became even more painful than the actual pressure or apprehension of sorrow; and the confinement that froze her into a nook of existence, with an unvaried prospect before her, the most insupportable of evils. The lamp of life seemed to be spending itself to chase the vapours of a dungeon which no art could dissipate. — And to what purpose did she rally all her energy? — Was not the world a vast prison, and women born slaves?

Though she failed immediately to rouse a lively sense of injustice in the mind of her guard, because it had been sophisticated into misanthropy, she touched her heart. Jemima (she had only a claim to a Christian name, which had not procured her any Christian privileges)[1] could patiently hear of Maria's confinement on false pretences; she had felt the crushing hand of power, hardened by the exercise of injustice, and ceased to wonder at the perversions of the understanding, which systematize oppression; but, when told that her child, only four months old, had been torn from her, even while she was discharging the tenderest maternal office, the woman awoke in a bosom long estranged from feminine emotions, and Jemima determined to alleviate all in her power, without hazarding the loss of her place, the sufferings of a wretched mother, apparently injured, and certainly unhappy. A sense of right seems to result from the simplest act of reason, and to preside over the faculties of the mind, like the master-sense of feeling, to rectify the rest; but (for the comparison may be carried still farther) how often is the exquisite sensibility of both weakened or destroyed by the vulgar occupations, and ignoble pleasures of life?

The preserving her situation was, indeed, an important object to Jemima, who had been hunted from hole to hole, as if she had been a beast of prey, or infected with a moral plague. The wages she received, the greater part of which she hoarded, as her only chance for independence, were much more considerable than she could reckon on obtaining any where else, were it possible that she, an outcast from society, could be permitted to earn a subsistence in a reputable family. Hearing Maria perpetually complain of listlessness, and the not being able to beguile grief by resuming her customary pursuits, she was easily prevailed on, by compassion, and that involuntary respect for abilities, which those who possess them can never eradicate, to bring her some books and implements for writing. Maria's conversation had amused and interested her, and the natural consequence was a desire,

---

1  In his endnote to this passage, Kelly points out that Jemima cannot claim her father's surname because she is a bastard (*Wrongs* 188, endnote 73).

scarcely observed by herself, of obtaining the esteem of a person she admired. The remembrance of better days was rendered more lively; and the sentiments then acquired appearing less romantic than they had for a long period, a spark of hope roused her mind to new activity.

How grateful was her attention to Maria! Oppressed by a dead weight of existence, or preyed on by the gnawing worm of discontent, with what eagerness did she endeavour to shorten the long days, which left no traces behind! She seemed to be sailing on the vast ocean of life, without seeing any land-mark to indicate the progress of time; to find employment was then to find variety, the animating principle of nature.

## CHAP. II.

EARNESTLY as Maria endeavoured to soothe, by reading, the anguish of her wounded mind, her thoughts would often wander from the subject she was led to discuss, and tears of maternal tenderness obscured the reasoning page. She descanted on "the ills which flesh is heir to,"[1] with bitterness, when the recollection of her babe was revived by a tale of fictitious woe, that bore any resemblance to her own; and her imagination was continually employed, to conjure up and embody the various phantoms of misery, which folly and vice had let loose on the world. The loss of her babe was the tender string; against other cruel remembrances she laboured to steel her bosom; and even a ray of hope, in the midst of her gloomy reveries, would sometimes gleam on the dark horizon of futurity, while persuading herself that she ought to cease to hope, since happiness was no where to be found. — But of her child, debilitated by the grief with which its mother had been assailed before it saw the light, she could not think without an impatient struggle.

---

1 Misquoted from Hamlet's famous soliloquy in Shakespeare's play:
To be, or not to be, that is the question:
Whether 'tis nobler in the mind to suffer
The slings and arrows of outrageous fortune,
Or to take arms against a sea of troubles,
And by opposing end them? To die, to sleep —
No more — and by a sleep to say we end
The heartache and the thousand natural shocks
That flesh is heir to: 'tis a consummation
Devoutly to be wished. (III, i, 62-70)

"I, alone, by my active tenderness, could have saved," she would exclaim, "from an early blight, this sweet blossom; and, cherishing it, I should have had something still to love."

In proportion as other expectations were torn from her, this tender one had been fondly clung to, and knit into her heart.

The books she had obtained, were soon devoured, by one who had no other resource to escape from sorrow, and the feverish dreams of ideal wretchedness or felicity, which equally weaken the intoxicated sensibility. Writing was then the only alternative, and she wrote some rhapsodies[1] descriptive of the state of her mind; but the events of her past life pressing on her, she resolved circumstantially to relate them, with the sentiments that experience, and more matured reason, would naturally suggest. They might perhaps instruct her daughter, and shield her from the misery, the tyranny, her mother knew not how to avoid.

This thought gave life to her diction, her soul flowed into it, and she soon found the task of recollecting almost obliterated impressions very interesting. She lived again in the revived emotions of youth, and forgot her present in the retrospect of sorrows that had assumed an unalterable character.

Though this employment lightened the weight of time, yet, never losing sight of her main object, Maria did not allow any opportunity to slip of winning on the affections of Jemima; for she discovered in her a strength of mind, that excited her esteem, clouded as it was by the misanthropy of despair.

An insulated being, from the misfortune of her birth, she despised and preyed on the society by which she had been oppressed, and loved not her fellow-creatures, because she had never been beloved. No mother had ever fondled her, no father or brother had protected her from outrage; and the man who had plunged her into infamy, and deserted her when she stood in greatest need of support, deigned not to smooth with kindness the road to ruin. Thus degraded, was she let loose on the world; and virtue, never nurtured by affection, assumed the stern aspect of selfish independence.

This general view of her life, Maria gathered from her exclamations and dry remarks. Jemima indeed displayed a strange mixture of interest and suspicion; for she would listen to her with earnestness, and then suddenly interrupt the conversation, as if

---

1 The OED defines "rhapsody" in the following way: "2. a. A literary work consisting of miscellaneous or disconnected pieces; a written composition having no fixed form or plan. Sometimes depreciative. Obs."

afraid of resigning, by giving way to her sympathy, her dear-bought knowledge of the world.

Maria alluded to the possibility of an escape, and mentioned a compensation, or reward; but the style in which she was repulsed made her cautious, and determine not to renew the subject, till she knew more of the character she had to work on. Jemima's countenance, and dark hints, seemed to say, "You are an extraordinary woman; but let me consider, this may only be one of your lucid intervals." Nay, the very energy of Maria's character, made her suspect that the extraordinary animation she perceived might be the effect of madness. "Should her husband then substantiate his charge, and get possession of her estate, from whence would come the promised annuity, or more desired protection? Besides, might not a woman, anxious to escape, conceal some of the circumstances which made against her? Was truth to be expected from one who had been entrapped, kidnapped, in the most fraudulent manner?"

In this train Jemima continued to argue, the moment after compassion and respect seemed to make her swerve; and she still resolved not to be wrought on to do more than soften the rigour of confinement, till she could advance on surer ground.

Maria was not permitted to walk in the garden; but sometimes, from her window, she turned her eyes from the gloomy walls, in which she pined life away, on the poor wretches who strayed along the walks, and contemplated the most terrific of ruins — that of a human soul.[1] What is the view of the fallen column, the mouldering arch, of the most exquisite workmanship, when compared with this living memento of the fragility, the instability, of reason, and the wild luxuriancy of noxious passions? Enthusiasm turned adrift, like some rich stream overflowing its banks, rushes forward with destructive velocity, inspiring a sublime concentration of thought. Thus thought Maria — These are the ravages over which humanity must ever mournfully ponder, with a degree of anguish not excited by crumbling marble, or cankering brass, unfaithful to the trust of monumental fame. It is not over the decaying productions of the mind,

---

1 Here Wollstonecraft uses the popular Gothic image of architectural ruins to represent another great Gothic theme, the ruined mind, or madness. Her identification of the mind with the "soul" was a common one in the period. As G.S. Rousseau remarks in "Nerves, Spirits, and Fibres: Towards Defining the Origins of Sensibility" (1976), the brain was regarded as the seat of the soul throughout the eighteenth century.

embodied with the happiest art, we grieve most bitterly. The view of what has been done by man, produces a melancholy, yet aggrandizing, sense of what remains to be achieved by human intellect; but a mental convulsion, which, like the devastation of an earthquake, throws all the elements of thought and imagination into confusion, makes contemplation giddy, and we fearfully ask on what ground we ourselves stand.

Melancholy and imbecility marked the features of the wretches allowed to breathe at large; for the frantic, those who in a strong imagination had lost a sense of woe, were closely confined. The playful tricks and mischievous devices of their disturbed fancy, that suddenly broke out, could not be guarded against, when they were permitted to enjoy any portion of freedom; for, so active was their imagination, that every new object which accidentally struck their senses, awoke to phrenzy their restless passions; as Maria learned from the burden of their incessant ravings.

Sometimes, with a strict injunction of silence, Jemima would allow Maria, at the close of evening, to stray along the narrow avenues that separated the dungeon-like apartments, leaning on her arm. What a change of scene! Maria wished to pass the threshold of her prison, yet, when by chance she met the eye of rage glaring on her, yet unfaithful to its office, she shrunk back with more horror and affright, than if she had stumbled over a mangled corpse. Her busy fancy pictured the misery of a fond heart, watching over a friend thus estranged, absent, though present — over a poor wretch lost to reason and the social joys of existence; and losing all consciousness of misery in its excess. What a task, to watch the light of reason quivering in the eye, or with agonizing expectation to catch the beam of recollection; tantalized by hope, only to feel despair more keenly, at finding a much loved face or voice, suddenly remembered, or pathetically implored, only to be immediately forgotten, or viewed with indifference or abhorrence!

The heart-rending sigh of melancholy sunk into her soul; and when she retired to rest, the petrified figures she had encountered, the only human forms she was doomed to observe, haunting her dreams with tales of mysterious wrongs, made her wish to sleep to dream no more.[1]

---

1 Maria's fantasies about the "mysterious wrongs" that may have been perpetrated by her fellow inmates suggest that she subscribes to the belief, common in the eighteenth century, that insanity    (*continued*)

Day after day rolled away, and tedious as the present moment appeared, they passed in such an unvaried tenor, Maria was surprised to find that she had already been six weeks buried alive,[1] and yet had such faint hopes of effecting her enlargement. She was, earnestly as she had sought for employment, now angry with herself for having been amused by writing her narrative; and grieved to think that she had for an instant thought of any thing, but contriving to escape.

Jemima had evidently pleasure in her society: still, though she often left her with a glow of kindness, she returned with the same chilling air; and, when her heart appeared for a moment to open, some suggestion of reason forcibly closed it, before she could give utterance to the confidence Maria's conversation inspired.

Discouraged by these changes, Maria relapsed into despondency, when she was cheered by the alacrity with which Jemima brought her a fresh parcel of books; assuring her, that she had taken some pains to obtain them from one of the keepers, who attended a gentleman confined in the opposite corner of the gallery.

Maria took up the books with emotion. "They come," said she, "perhaps, from a wretch condemned, like me, to reason on the nature of madness, by having wrecked minds continually under his eye; and almost to wish himself — as I do — mad, to escape from the contemplation of it." Her heart throbbed with

---

was a punishment for immorality. By the turn of the nineteenth century, this view of madness was being replaced by a more sympathetic account of its causes, partly because of the insanity of King George III, who was popularly regarded as having had a fine upbringing and strong moral values. This sentence also echoes, again, the passage from Shakespeare's *Hamlet* as quoted in part in the first note of this chapter, p. 168: "...To die, to sleep — / No more ... / ...To die, to sleep: / To sleep, perchance to dream: ay, there's the rub" (III, i, 66-67, 70-71).

1 At this time, insane asylums were, indeed, regarded as tombs for the living and madness as a kind of living death. By 1838, though, Robert Gardiner Hill (1811-78) could write with shock at this attitude towards the insane in Britain:

neither medical men, nor the public at large, had any hope of a cure of the insane.... And to what period, think you, does this description apply? It is scarcely twenty years since nearly every word of it might be said with truth of the receptacles of the insane in Britain! It was only at that period that a better spirit spread abroad on the subject of Insanity. Asylums began to be regarded as places for the cure, not for the living burial, of Lunatics. (*Total Abolition of Personal Restraint in the Treatment of the Insane* [1838], 10-11) sympathetic alarm; and she turned over the leaves with awe, as if they had become sacred from passing through the hands of an unfortunate being, oppressed by a similar fate.

Dryden's *Fables*, Milton's *Paradise Lost*,[1] with several modern productions, composed the collection. It was a mine of treasure. Some marginal notes, in Dryden's *Fables*, caught her attention: they were written with force and taste; and, in one of the modern pamphlets, there was a fragment left, containing various observations on the present state of society and government, with a comparative view of the politics of Europe and America. These remarks were written with a degree of generous warmth, when alluding to the enslaved state of the labouring majority, perfectly in unison with Maria's mode of thinking.

She read them over and over again; and fancy, treacherous fancy, began to sketch a character, congenial with her own, from these shadowy outlines. — "Was he mad?" She re-perused the marginal notes, and they seemed the production of an animated, but not of a disturbed imagination. Confined to this speculation, every time she re-read them, some fresh refinement of sentiment, or accuteness[2] of thought impressed her, which she was astonished at herself for not having before observed.

What a creative power has an affectionate heart! There are beings who cannot live without loving, as poets love; and who feel the electric spark of genius, wherever it awakens sentiment or grace. Maria had often thought, when disciplining her wayward heart, "that to charm, was to be virtuous." "They who make me wish to appear the most amiable and good in their eyes, must possess in a degree," she would exclaim, "the graces and virtues they call into action."

She took up a book on the powers of the human mind; but, her attention strayed from cold arguments on the nature of what she felt, while she was feeling, and she snapt the chain of the theory to read Dryden's "Guiscard and Sigismunda."[3]

---

1   John Dryden's (1631-1700) *Fables Ancient and Modern* (1700) and John Milton's *Paradise Lost*. This reading list suggests the mysterious inmate's good taste and even his reason, since these eminent works would be lost on a truly insane person.

2   Wollstonecraft's spelling.

3   A reference to "Sigismonda and Guiscardo," Dryden's translation of Boccaccio's tale in the *Fables*. Finding scientific texts about the mind too "cold," or logical, Maria turns to stories about love. Her preference illustrates her irrationality, emotionalism, and, thus, indulgence in the kind of sensibility to which Wollstonecraft objects in this fiction.

Maria, in the course of the ensuing day, returned some of the books, with the hope of getting others — and more marginal notes. Thus shut out from human intercourse, and compelled to view nothing but the prison of vexed spirits, to meet a wretch in the same situation, was more surely to find a friend, than to imagine a countryman one, in a strange land, where the human voice conveys no information to the eager ear.

"Did you ever see the unfortunate being to whom these books belong?" asked Maria, when Jemima brought her supper. "Yes. He sometimes walks out, between five and six, before the family is stirring, in the morning, with two keepers; but even then his hands are confined."

"What! is he so unruly?" enquired Maria, with an accent of disappointment.

"No, not that I perceive," replied Jemima; "but he has an untamed look, a vehemence of eye, that excites apprehension. Were his hands free, he looks as if he could soon manage both his guards: yet he appears tranquil."

"If he be so strong, he must be young," observed Maria.

"Three or four and thirty, I suppose; but there is no judging of a person in his situation."

"Are you sure that he is mad?" interrupted Maria with eagerness. Jemima quitted the room, without replying.

"No, no, he certainly is not!" exclaimed Maria, answering herself; "the man who could write those observations was not disordered in his intellects."

She sat musing, gazing at the moon, and watching its motion as it seemed to glide under the clouds. Then, preparing for bed, she thought, "Of what use could I be to him, or he to me, if it be true that he is unjustly confined? — Could he aid me to escape, who is himself more closely watched? — Still I should like to see him." She went to bed, dreamed of her child, yet woke exactly at half after five o'clock, and starting up, only wrapped a gown around her, and ran to the window. The morning was chill, it was the latter end of September; yet she did not retire to warm herself and think in bed, till the sound of the servants, moving about the house, convinced her that the unknown would not walk in the garden that morning. She was ashamed at feeling disappointed; and began to reflect, as an excuse to herself, on the little objects which attract attention when there is nothing to divert the mind; and how difficult it was for women to avoid growing romantic, who have no active duties or pursuits.[1]

At breakfast, Jemima enquired whether she understood French? for, unless she did, the stranger's stock of books was exhausted. Maria replied in the affirmative; but forbore to ask any more questions respecting the person to whom they belonged. And Jemima gave her a new subject for contemplation, by describing the person of a lovely maniac, just brought into an adjoining chamber. She was singing the pathetic ballad of old Rob[2] with the most heart-melting falls and pauses. Jemima had half-opened the door, when she distinguished her voice, and Maria stood close to it, scarcely daring to respire, lest a modulation should escape her, so exquisitely sweet, so passionately wild.

---

1 Wollstonecraft develops a similar idea throughout *Rights of Woman*. She claims that, by treating women as sex-objects and denying them serious, rational pursuits, society relegates them to a lifetime of plotting romances and attracting men; for example, she writes, "only taught to please, ... with true heroic ardour [women] endeavour to gain hearts merely to resign, or spurn them" (120).

2 In the source edition, several spaces appear between "Rob" and "with"; an unknown hand has written "in Gray" in the intervening spaces, so that, when the typed and written letters are read together, they spell "Old Robin Gray." "Auld Robin Gray" is a Scottish ballad written by Lady Anne Lindsay (1750-1825) in 1773 (552). It tells the story of a young woman whose lover, Jamie, is thought to be lost at sea. When her parents become too old and infirm to work and old Robin Gray proposes marriage to her, she accepts his offer out of filial duty (she desires to support her parents). However, the two are not married more than a month before Jamie returns, leaving the young wife (and speaker of the ballad) "like a ghaist" in her shock and disappointment (l. 33). As revealed in the following lines, the ballad's theme of a young woman ruined by love and imprisoned in marriage echoes that of *The Wrongs of Woman*, as well as the story of the young madwoman who sings the ballad in Maria's asylum:

   O sair, sair did we greet, and muckle did we say;
   We took but ae kiss, and we tore ourselves away:
   I wish that I were dead, but I'm no like to dee;
   And why was I born to say, Wae is me! (29-32)

   The ballad appears to have been immensely popular, for it was published in several volumes in the eighteenth century, and an anonymous balladeer wrote a reply to it in a broadside called *Jamie's Complaint, or, The Answer to Auld Robin Gray* (1795?).

She began with sympathy to pourtray to herself another victim, when the lovely warbler flew, as it were, from the spray, and a torrent of unconnected exclamations and questions burst from her, interrupted by fits of laughter, so horrid, that Maria shut the door, and, turning her eyes up to heaven, exclaimed — "Gracious God!"

Several minutes elapsed before Maria could enquire respecting the rumour of the house (for this poor wretch was obviously not confined without a cause); and then Jemima could only tell her, that it was said, "she had been married, against her inclination, to a rich old man, extremely jealous (no wonder, for she was a charming creature); and that, in consequence of his treatment, or something which hung on her mind, she had, during her first lying-in, lost her senses."[1]

What a subject of meditation — even to the very confines of madness.

"Woman, fragile flower! why were you suffered to adorn a world exposed to the inroad of such stormy elements?" thought Maria, while the poor maniac's strain was still breathing on her ear, and sinking into her very soul.

Towards the evening, Jemima brought her Rousseau's *Heloïse*;[2] and she sat reading with eyes and heart, till the return of her guard to extinguish the light. One instance of her kindness was, the permitting Maria to have one, till her own hour of retiring to rest. She had read this work long since; but now it seemed to open a new world to her — the only one worth inhabiting. Sleep was not to be wooed; yet, far from being fatigued by the restless

---

1  "Lying-in" refers to childbirth. Considered in conjunction with the inmate's subsequent insanity, this passage suggests that she suffers from severe post-partum depression. Wollstonecraft's sister, Eliza, experienced a serious depression in 1783 after the birth of her baby. Wollstonecraft took Eliza away from her home and husband, Meredith Bishop, whom she (with Eliza and their sister Everina) thought was destroying Eliza's mental stability. Soon thereafter, Wollstonecraft reports in a letter to Everina, "I was afraid in the coach she was going to have one of her flights for she bit her *wedding ring* to pieces" (Wollstonecraft's emphasis; *Letters* 43).

2  Although Wollstonecraft was disgusted by Rousseau's portrayal of women and female education in *Émile*, she admired his representation of female desire and emotion in *Julie, ou, La Nouvelle Héloïse*. (See the note reference to the epigraph of *Mary* and p. 75, note 2 for more information).

rotation of thought, she rose and opened her window, just as the thin watery clouds of twilight made the long silent shadows visible. The air swept across her face with a voluptuous freshness that thrilled to her heart, awakening indefinable emotions; and the sound of a waving branch, or the twittering of a startled bird, alone broke the stillness of reposing nature. Absorbed by the sublime sensibility which renders the consciousness of existence felicity, Maria was happy, till an autumnal scent, wafted by the breeze of morn from the fallen leaves of the adjacent wood, made her recollect that the season had changed since her confinement; yet life afforded no variety to solace an afflicted heart. She returned dispirited to her couch, and thought of her child till the broad glare of day again invited her to the window. She looked not for the unknown, still how great was her vexation at perceiving the back of a man, certainly he, with his two attendants, as he turned into a side-path which led to the house! A confused recollection of having seen somebody who resembled him, immediately occurred, to puzzle and torment her with endless conjectures. Five minutes sooner, and she should have seen his face, and been out of suspense — was ever any thing so unlucky! His steady, bold step, and the whole air of his person, bursting as it were from a cloud, pleased her, and gave an outline to the imagination to sketch the individual form she wished to recognize.

Feeling the disappointment more severely than she was willing to believe, she flew to Rousseau, as her only refuge from the idea of him, who might prove a friend, could she but find a way to interest him in her fate; still the personification of Saint Preux, or of an ideal lover far superior, was after this imperfect model, of which merely a glance had been caught, even to the minutiae of the coat and hat of the stranger.[1] But if she lent St. Preux, or the demi-god of her fancy, his form, she richly repaid him by the donation of all St. Preux's sentiments and feelings, culled to gratify her own, to which he seemed to have an undoubted right, when she read on the margin of an impassioned letter, written in the well-known hand — "Rousseau alone, the true Prometheus of sentiment, possessed the fire of genius necessary to pourtray the passion, the truth of which goes so directly to the heart."[2]

---

1 Saint Preux is Julie's lover in Rousseau's *Julie*.
2 In Greek mythology, Prometheus becomes the benefactor to mankind by bringing us fire stolen from Zeus, for which he was eternally punished. The idea of a "Prometheus of sentiment" suggests that sentiment is divine and that its purveyors have super-human access to this realm.

Maria was again true to the hour, yet had finished Rousseau, and begun to transcribe some selected passages; unable to quit either the author or the window, before she had a glimpse of the countenance she daily longed to see; and, when seen, it conveyed no distinct idea to her mind where she had seen it before. He must have been a transient acquaintance; but to discover an acquaintance was fortunate, could she contrive to attract his attention, and excite his sympathy.

Every glance afforded colouring for the picture she was delineating on her heart; and once, when the window was half open, the sound of his voice reached her. Conviction flashed on her; she had certainly, in a moment of distress, heard the same accents. They were manly, and characteristic of a noble mind; nay, even sweet — or sweet they seemed to her attentive ear.

She started back, trembling, alarmed at the emotion a strange coincidence of circumstances inspired, and wondering why she thought so much of a stranger, obliged as she had been by his timely interference; [for she recollected, by degrees all the circumstances of their former meeting.][1] She found however that she could think of nothing else; or, if she thought of her daughter, it was to wish that she had a father whom her mother could respect and love.

## CHAP. III.

WHEN perusing the first parcel of books, Maria had, with her pencil, written in one of them a few exclamations, expressive of compassion and sympathy, which she scarcely remembered, till turning over the leaves of one of the volumes, lately brought to her, a slip of paper dropped out, which Jemima hastily snatched up.

"Let me see it," demanded Maria impatiently, "You surely are not afraid of trusting me with the effusions of a madman?" "I must consider," replied Jemima; and withdrew, with the paper in her hand.

In a life of such seclusion, the passions gain undue force; Maria therefore felt a great degree of resentment and vexation, which she had not time to subdue, before Jemima, returning, delivered the paper.

---

1 These brackets are in the source text.

"Whoever you are, who partake of my fate, accept my sincere commiseration — I would have said protection; but the privilege of man is denied me.

"My own situation forces a dreadful suspicion on my mind — I may not always languish in vain for freedom — say are you — I cannot ask the question; yet I will remember you when my remembrance can be of any use. I will enquire, *why* you are so mysteriously detained — and I *will* have an answer.["][1]

                                    "HENRY DARNFORD."

By the most pressing intreaties, Maria prevailed on Jemima to permit her to write a reply to this note. Another and another succeeded, in which explanations were not allowed relative to their present situation; but Maria, with sufficient explicitness, alluded to a former obligation; and they insensibly entered on an interchange of sentiments on the most important subjects. To write these letters was the business of the day, and to receive them the moment of sunshine. By some means, Darnford having discovered Maria's window, when she next appeared at it, he made her, behind his keepers, a profound bow of respect and recognition.

Two or three weeks glided away in this kind of intercourse, during which period Jemima, to whom Maria had given the necessary information respecting her family, had evidently gained some intelligence, which increased her desire of pleasing her charge, though she could not yet determine to liberate her. Maria took advantage of this favourable charge,[2] without too minutely enquiring into the cause; and such was her eagerness to hold human converse, and to see her former protector, still a stranger to her, that she incessantly requested her guard to gratify her more than curiosity.

Writing to Darnford, she was led from the sad objects before her, and frequently rendered insensible to the horrid noises around her, which previously had continually employed her feverish fancy. Thinking it selfish to dwell on her own sufferings, when in the midst of wretches, who had not only lost all that endears life, but their very selves, her imagination was occupied with melancholy earnestness to trace the mazes of misery, through which so many wretches must have passed to this gloomy receptacle of disjointed souls, to the grand source of human corruption. Often at midnight was she waked by the dismal shrieks of demoniac rage, or of excruciating despair,

---

1 The closing quotation mark is my own.
2 Probably a typographical error for "change."

uttered in such wild tones of indescribable anguish as proved the total absence of reason, and roused phantoms of horror in her mind, far more terrific than all that dreaming superstition ever drew. Besides, there was frequently something so inconceivably picturesque in the varying gestures of unrestrained passion, so irresistibly comic in their sallies, or so heart-piercingly pathetic in the little airs they would sing, frequently bursting out after an awful silence, as to fascinate the attention, and amuse the fancy, while torturing the soul. It was the uproar of the passions which she was compelled to observe; and to mark the lucid beam of reason, like a light trembling in a socket, or like the flash which divides the threatening clouds of angry heaven only to display the horrors which darkness shrouded.

Jemima would labour to beguile the tedious evenings, by describing the persons and manners of the unfortunate beings, whose figures or voices awoke sympathetic sorrow in Maria's bosom; and the stories she told were the more interesting, for perpetually leaving room to conjecture something extraordinary. Still Maria, accustomed to generalize her observations, was led to conclude from all she heard, that it was a vulgar error to suppose that people of abilities were the most apt to lose the command of reason.[1] On the contrary, from most of the instances she could investigate, she thought it resulted, that the passions only appeared strong and disproportioned, because the judgment was weak and unexercised; and that they gained strength by the decay of reason, as the shadows lengthen during the sun's decline.

Maria impatiently wished to see her fellow-sufferer; but Darnford was still more earnest to obtain an interview. Accustomed to submit to every impulse of passion, and never taught, like women, to restrain the most natural, and acquire, instead of the bewitching frankness of nature, a factitious propriety of behaviour, every desire became a torrent that bore down all opposition.

His travelling trunk, which contained the books lent to Maria, had been sent to him, and with a part of its contents he bribed his principal keeper; who, after receiving the most solemn promise that he would return to his apartment without attempting to explore any part of the house, conducted him, in the dusk of the evening, to Maria's room.

---

1  Wollstonecraft refers to the ancient association between genius and madness, which, according to Frederick Burwick in *Poetic Madness and the Romantic Imagination* (1996), may be traced to Seneca (ca. 4-65 CE) and Aristotle (22).

Jemima had apprized her charge of the visit, and she expected with trembling impatience, inspired by a vague hope that he might again prove her deliverer, to see a man who had before rescued her from oppression.[1] He entered with an animation of countenance, formed to captivate an enthusiast; and, hastily turned his eyes from her to the apartment, which he surveyed with apparent emotions of compassionate indignation. Sympathy illuminated his eye, and, taking her hand, he respectfully bowed on it, exclaiming — "This is extraordinary! — again to meet you, and in such circumstances!" Still, impressive as was the coincidence of events which brought them once more together, their full hearts did not overflow. —[2]

------------------------

[And though, after this first visit, they were permitted frequently to repeat their interviews, they were for some time employed in] a reserved conversation, to which all the world might have listened; excepting, when discussing some literary subject, flashes of sentiment, inforced by each relaxing feature, seemed to remind them that their minds were already acquainted.

[By degrees, Darnford entered into the particulars of his story.] In a few words, he informed her that he had been a thoughtless, extravagant young man; yet, as he described his faults, they appeared to be the generous luxuriancy of a noble mind. Nothing like meanness tarnished the lustre of his youth, nor had the worm of selfishness lurked in the unfolding bud, even while he had been the dupe of others. Yet he tardily acquired the experience necessary to guard him against future imposition.

"I shall weary you," continued he, "by my egotism; and did not powerful emotions draw me to you," — his eyes glistened as he spoke, and a trembling seemed to run through his manly

------------------------

1 The surprising implication in this passage that Mary and Darnford had a previous relationship may be attributed to the unfinished nature of the novella. Presumably, Wollstonecraft would have developed this thread of the narrative, had she not died in childbirth before it was finished. See p. 185, note 1 for Godwin's commentary on this subject.

2 The copy which had received the author's last corrections, breaks off in this place, and the pages which follow, to the end of Chap. IV, are printed from a copy in a less finished state. [Godwin's note] The square brackets that appear in the following passages are in the source text.

frame, — "I would not waste these precious moments in talking of myself.

"My father and mother were people of fashion; married by their parents. He was fond of the turf, she of the card-table. I, and two or three other children since dead, were kept at home till we became intolerable. My father and mother had a visible dislike to each other, continually displayed[;][1] the servants were of the depraved kind usually found in the houses of people of fortune. My brothers and parents all dying, I was left to the care of guardians, and sent to Eton.[2] I never knew the sweets of domestic affection, but I felt the want of indulgence and frivolous respect at school. I will not disgust you with a recital of the vices of my youth, which can scarcely be comprehended by female delicacy. I was taught to love by a creature I am ashamed to mention; and the other women with whom I afterwards became intimate, were of a class of which you can have no knowledge. I formed my acquaintance with them at the theaters; and, when vivacity danced in their eyes, I was not easily disgusted by the vulgarity which flowed from their lips. Having spent, a few years after I was of age, [the whole of] a considerable patrimony, excepting a few hundreds, I had no resource but to purchase a commission in a new-raised regiment, destined to subjugate America. The regret I felt to renounce a life of pleasure, was counter-balanced by the curiosity I had to see America,[3] or rather to travel; [nor had any of those circumstances occurred to my youth, which might have been calculated] to bind my country to my heart. I shall not trouble you with the details of a military life. My blood was still kept in motion; till, towards the close of the contest, I was wounded and taken prisoner.

---

1 I have inserted a semi-colon here, but it is unclear from the source edition what the punctuation mark should be because part of it has been obliterated, leaving only a dot at about the middle height of the letters. I replace the dot with a semi-colon because the top of a semi-colon in the font used in the source text appears at that height, and it also makes grammatical sense to use one here.

2 Eton remains an exclusive private school for the sons of rich and well-connected English families. Darnford reveals his class by mentioning his education there.

3 Darnford's fascination with America indicates his untraditional political, and possibly even revolutionary, leanings in his youth; America asserted its independence from British rule in the eighteenth century through the American Revolution.

"Confined to my bed, or chair, by a lingering cure, my only refuge from the preying activity of my mind, was books, which I read with great avidity, profiting by the conversation of my host, a man of sound understanding. My political sentiments now underwent a total change; and, dazzled by the hospitality of the Americans, I determined to take up my abode with freedom. I, therefore, with my usual impetuosity, sold my commission, and travelled into the interior parts of the country, to lay out my money to advantage. Added to this, I did not much like the puritanical manners of the large towns. Inequality of condition was there most disgustingly galling. The only pleasure wealth afforded, was to make an ostentatious display of it; for the cultivation of the fine arts, or literature, had not introduced into the first circles that polish of manners which renders the rich so essentially superior to the poor in Europe. Added to this, an influx of vices had been let in by the Revolution, and the most rigid principles of religion shaken to the centre, before the understanding could be gradually emancipated from the prejudices which led their ancestors undauntedly to seek an inhospitable clime and unbroken soil. The resolution, that led them, in pursuit of independence, to embark on rivers like seas, to search for unknown shores, and to sleep under the hovering mists of endless forests, whose baleful damps agued their limbs, was now turned into commercial speculations, till the national character exhibited a phenomenon in the history of the human mind — a head enthusiastically enterprising, with cold selfishness of heart. And woman, lovely woman! — they charm everywhere — still there is a degree of prudery, and a want of taste and ease in the manners of the American women, that renders them, in spite of their roses and lilies, far inferior to our European charmers. In the country, they have often a bewitching simplicity of character; but, in the cities, they have all the airs and ignorance of the ladies who give the tone to the circles of the large trading towns in England. They are fond of their ornaments, merely because they are good, and not because they embellish their persons; and are more gratified to inspire the women with jealousy of these exterior advantages, than the men with love. All the frivolity which often (excuse me, Madam) renders the society of modest women so stupid in England, here seemed to throw still more leaden fetters on their charms. Not being an adept in gallantry, I found that I could only keep myself awake in their company by making downright love to them.

"But, not to intrude on your patience, I retired to the track of land which I had purchased in the country, and my time passed pleasantly enough while I cut down the trees, built my house, and planted my different crops. But winter and idleness came, and I longed for more elegant society, to hear what was passing in the world, and to do something better than vegetate with the animals that made a very considerable part of my household. Consequently, I determined to travel. Motion was a substitute for variety of objects; and, passing over immense tracks of country, I exhausted my exuberant spirits, without obtaining much experience. I every where saw industry the fore-runner and not the consequence, of luxury; but this country, every thing being on an ample scale, did not afford those picturesque views, which a certain degree of cultivation is necessary gradually to produce. The eye wandered without an object to fix upon over immeasureable plains, and lakes that seemed replenished by the ocean, whilst eternal forests of small clustering trees, obstructed the circulation of air, and embarrassed the path, without gratifying the eye of taste. No cottage smiling in the waste, no travellers hailed us, to give life to silent nature; or, if perchance we saw the print of a footstep in our path, it was a dreadful warning to turn aside; and the head ached as if assailed by the scalping knife. The Indians who hovered on the skirts of the European settlements had only learned of their neighbours to plunder, and they stole their guns from them to do it with more safety.

"From the woods and back settlements, I returned to the towns, and learned to eat and drink most valiantly; but without entering into commerce (and I detested commerce) I found I could not live there; and, growing heartily weary of the land of liberty and vulgar aristocracy, seated on her bags of dollars, I resolved once more to visit Europe. I wrote to a distant relation in England, with whom I had been educated, mentioning the vessel in which I intended to sail. Arriving in London, my senses were intoxicated. I ran from street to street, from theatre to theatre, and the women of the town (again I must beg pardon for my habitual frankness) appeared to me like angels.

"A week was spent in this thoughtless manner, when, returning very late to the hotel in which I had lodged ever since my arrival, I was knocked down in a private street, and hurried, in a state of insensibility, into a coach, which brought me hither, and I only recovered my senses to be treated like one who had lost them. My keepers are deaf to my remonstrances and enquiries, yet assure me that my confinement shall not last long. Still I cannot guess, though I weary myself with conjectures, why I am confined, or in what part of England this house is situated. I imagine sometimes that I hear the sea roar, and wished myself again on the Atlantic, till I had a glimpse of you."[1]

A few moments were only allowed to Maria to comment on this narrative, when Darnford left her to her own thoughts, to the "never ending, still beginning,"[2] task of weighing his words, recollecting his tones of voice, and feeling them reverberate on her heart.

## CHAP. IV.

PITY, and the forlorn seriousness of adversity, have both been considered as dispositions favourable to love, while satirical writers have attributed the propensity to the relaxing effect of idleness; what chance then had Maria of escaping, when pity, sorrow, and solitude all conspired to soften her mind, and nourish romantic wishes, and, from a natural progress, romantic expectations?

Maria was six-and-twenty. But, such was the native soundness of her constitution, that time had only given to her countenance the character of her mind. Revolving thought, and exercised affections had banished some of the playful graces of innocence, producing insensibly that irregularity of features which the struggles of the understanding to trace or govern the strong emotions of the heart, are wont to imprint on the yielding mass.[3] Grief and

---

1 The introduction of Darnford as the deliverer of Maria in a former instance, appears to have been an after-thought of the author. This has occasioned the omission of any allusion to that circumstance in the preceding narration. EDITOR. [Godwin's note]

2 Besides showing her familiarity with Dryden's work, this passage may be further evidence of Wollstonecraft's appreciation of the music of Handel (1685-1759), as does the protagonist's performance of the "Hallelujah Chorus" from *Messiah* in Chapter XX of *Mary*. Notably, it contains a quotation from John Dryden's poem, *Alexander's Feast: or, The Power of Musick. An Ode, Written by Mr. Dryden. Set to Musick by Mr. Handel* (1739):

War, he sung, is Toil and Trouble;
Honour but an empty Bubble,
Never ending, still beginning,
Fighting still, and still destroying,
If the World be worth thy winning,
Think, O think, it worth enjoying. (ll. 81-86)

3 By suggesting that Maria's physical features are shaped by her emotions, Wollstonecraft invokes, again, the Romantic-era theory of physiognomy; see p. 165, note 1 for more information on this topic.

care had mellowed, without obscuring, the bright tints of youth, and the thoughtfulness which resided on her brow did not take from the feminine softness of her features; nay, such was the sensibility which often mantled over it, that she frequently appeared, like a large proportion of her sex, only born to feel; and the activity of her well-proportioned, and even almost voluptuous figure, inspired the idea of strength of mind, rather than of body. There was a simplicity sometimes indeed in her manner, which bordered on infantine ingenuousness, that led people of common discernment to underrate her talents, and smile at the flights of her imagination. But those who could not comprehend the delicacy of her sentiments, were attached by her unfailing sympathy, so that she was very generally beloved by characters of very different descriptions; still, she was too much under the influence of an ardent imagination to adhere to common rules.

There are mistakes of conduct which at five-and-twenty prove the strength of the mind, that, ten or fifteen years after, would demonstrate its weakness, its incapacity to acquire a sane judgment. The youths who are satisfied with the ordinary pleasures of life, and do not sigh after ideal phantoms of love and friendship, will never arrive at great maturity of understanding; but if these reveries are cherished, as is too frequently the case with women,[1] when experience ought to have taught them in what human happiness consists, they become as useless as they are wretched. Besides, their pains and pleasures are so dependent on outward circumstances, on the objects of their affections, that they seldom act from the impulse of a nerved mind, able to choose its own pursuit.

Having had to struggle incessantly with the vices of mankind, Maria's imagination found repose in pourtraying the possible virtues the world might contain. Pygmalion[2] formed an ivory maid, and longed for an informing soul. She, on the contrary,

---

1  Wollstonecraft herself was never "satisfied with the ordinary pleasures of life" and held "ideal phantoms of love and friendship," as a letter to a friend, Jane Arden, from 1774—more than two decades earlier—illustrates: "I have formed romantic notions of friendship.... I am a little singular in my thoughts of love and friendship; I must have the first place or none.—I own your behaviour is more according to the opinion of the world, but I would break such narrow bounds" (*Letters* 13).
2  The Greek myth of Pygmalion describes a sculptor who falls in love with his ivory statue of a beautiful woman, which Aphrodite endows with life in response to Pygmalion's prayer.

combined all the qualities of a hero's mind, and fate presented a statue in which she might enshrine them.

We mean not to trace the progress of this passion, or recount how often Darnford and Maria were obliged to part in the midst of an interesting conversation. Jemima ever watched on the tip-toe of fear, and frequently separated them on a false alarm, when they would have given worlds to remain a little longer together.

A magic lamp now seemed to be suspended in Maria's prison, and fairy landscapes flitted round the gloomy walls, late so blank. Rushing from the depth of despair, on the seraph wing of hope, she found herself happy. — She was beloved, and every emotion was rapturous.

To Darnford she had not shown a decided affection; the fear of outrunning his, a sure proof of love, made her often assume a coldness and indifference foreign from her character; and, even when giving way to the playful emotions of a heart just loosened from the frozen bond of grief, there was a delicacy in her manner of expressing her sensibility, which made him doubt whether it was the effect of love.

One evening, when Jemima left them, to listen to the sound of a distant footstep, which seemed cautiously to approach, he seized Maria's hand — it was not withdrawn. They conversed with earnestness of their situation; and, during the conversation, he once or twice gently drew her towards him. He felt the fragrance of her breath, and longed, yet feared, to touch the lips from which it issued; spirits of purity seemed to guard them, while all the enchanting graces of love sported on her cheeks, and languished in her eyes.

Jemima entering, he reflected on his diffidence with poignant regret, and, she once more taking alarm, he ventured, as Maria stood near his chair, to approach her lips with a declaration of love. She drew back with solemnity, he hung down his head abashed; but lifting his eyes timidly, they met her's; she had determined, during that instant, and suffered their rays to mingle. He took, with more ardour, reassured, a half-consenting, half-reluctant kiss, reluctant only from modesty; and there was a sacredness in her dignified manner of reclining her glowing face on his shoulder, that powerfully impressed him. Desire was lost in more ineffable emotions, and to protect her from insult and sorrow — to make her happy, seemed not only the first wish of his heart, but the most noble duty of his life. Such angelic confidence demanded the fidelity of honour; but could he, feeling her in every pulsation, could he ever change, could he be a villain? The emotion with which she, for a moment, allowed herself to be pressed to his bosom, the tear of rapturous sympathy, mingled with a soft melancholy sentiment of recollected disappointment, said — more of truth and faithfulness, than the tongue could have given utterance to in hours! They were silent — yet discoursed, how eloquently? till, after a moment's reflection, Maria drew her chair by the side of his, and, with a composed sweetness of voice, and supernatural benignity of countenance, said, "I must open my whole heart to you; you must be told who I am, why I am here, and why, telling you I am a wife, I blush not to" — the blush spoke the rest.

Jemima was again at her elbow, and the restraint of her presence did not prevent an animated conversation, in which love, sly urchin, was ever at bo-peep.

So much of heaven did they enjoy, that paradise bloomed around them; or they, by a powerful spell, had been transported into Armida's garden. Love, the grand enchanter, "lapt them in Elysium," and every sense was harmonized to joy and social extacy.[1] So animated, indeed, were their accents of tenderness, in discussing what, in other circumstances, would have been commonplace subjects, that Jemima felt, with surprise, a tear of pleasure trickling down her rugged cheeks. She wiped it away, half ashamed; and when Maria kindly enquired the cause, with all the eager solicitude of a happy being wishing to impart to all nature its overflowing felicity, Jemima owned that it was the first tear that social enjoyment had ever drawn from her. She seemed indeed to breathe more freely; the cloud of suspicion cleared

---

1 In *Rinaldo* (1562), a verse narrative by the Italian poet Torquato Tasso (1544-95), the sorceress Armida is sent by Satan to tempt the Christian crusaders, including Rinaldo, whom she transports to and seduces in her magical garden. The phrase "lapt them in Elysium" echoes a line from Milton's *Comus* (1634), spoken by the title character:

> Amidst the flowery-kirtled Naiades,
> Culling their potent herbs, and baleful drugs,
> Who as they sung, would take the prisoned soul,
> And lap it in Elysium. (ll. 254-57)

In ancient Greek mythology, Elysium is the paradise of the underworld. Again, Wollstonecraft's literary reference implies that romance is dangerous.

away from her brow; she felt herself, for once in her life, treated like a fellow-creature.

Imagination! who can paint thy power; or reflect the evanescent tints of hope fostered by thee? A despondent gloom had long obscured Maria's horizon — now the sun broke forth, the rainbow appeared, and every prospect was fair. Horror still reigned in the darkened cells, suspicion lurked in the passages, and whispered along the walls. The yells of men possessed, sometimes, made them pause, and wonder that they felt so happy, in a tomb of living death. They even chid themselves for such apparent insensibility; still the world contained not three happier beings. And Jemima, after again patrolling the passage, was so softened by the air of confidence which breathed around her, that she voluntarily began an account of herself.

## CHAP. V.

"MY father," said Jemima, "seduced my mother, a pretty girl, with whom he lived fellow-servant; and she no sooner perceived the natural, the dreaded consequence, than the terrible conviction flashed on her — that she was ruined. Honesty, and a regard for her reputation, had been the only principles inculcated by her mother; and they had been so forcibly impressed, that she feared shame, more than the poverty to which it would lead. Her incessant importunities to prevail upon my father to screen her from reproach by marrying her, as he had promised in the fervour of seduction, estranged him from her so completely, that her very person became distasteful to him; and he began to hate, as well as despise me, before I was born.

"My mother, grieved to the soul by his neglect, and unkind treatment, actually resolved to famish herself; and injured her health by the attempt; though she had not sufficient resolution to adhere to her project, or renounce it entirely. Death came not at her call; yet sorrow, and the methods she adopted to conceal her condition, still doing the work of a house-maid, had such an effect on her constitution, that she died in the wretched garret, where her virtuous mistress had forced her to take refuge in the very pangs of labour, though my father, after a slight reproof, was allowed to remain in his place — allowed by the mother of six children, who, scarcely permitting a footstep to be heard, during her month's indulgence, felt no sympathy for the poor wretch, denied every comfort required by her situation.

"The day my mother died, the ninth after my birth,[1] I was consigned to the care of the cheapest nurse my father could find; who suckled her own child at the same time, and lodged as many more as she could get, in two cellar-like apartments.

"Poverty, and the habit of seeing children die off her hands, had so hardened her heart, that the office of a mother did not awaken the tenderness of a woman; nor were the feminine caresses which seem a part of the rearing of a child, ever bestowed on me. The chicken has a wing to shelter under; but I had no bosom to nestle in, no kindred warmth to foster me. Left in dirt, to cry with cold and hunger till I was weary, and sleep without ever being prepared by exercise, or lulled by kindness to rest; could I be expected to become any thing but a weak and rickety babe? Still, in spite of neglect, I continued to exist, to learn to curse existence,"[2] her countenance grew ferocious as she spoke, "and the treatment that rendered me miserable, seemed to sharpen my wits. Confined then in a damp hovel, to rock the cradle of the succeeding tribe, I looked like a little old woman, or a hag shrivelling into nothing. The furrows of reflection and care contracted the youthful cheek, and gave a sort of supernatural wildness to the ever watchful eye. During this period, my father had married another fellow-servant, who loved him less, and knew better how to manage his passion, than my mother. She likewise proving with child, they agreed to keep a shop: my step-mother, if, being an illegitimate offspring, I may venture thus to characterize her, having obtained a sum of a rich relation, for that purpose.

"Soon after her lying-in, she prevailed on my father to take me home, to save the expense of maintaining me, and of hiring a girl to assist her in the care of the child. I was young, it was true, but appeared a knowing little thing, and might be made handy. Accordingly I was brought to her house; but not to a home — for

---

1 Wollstonecraft would die eleven days after giving birth to her second daughter, Mary.

2 The errata directs that square brackets around the phrase "her countenance grew ferocious as she spoke" should be replaced with inverted quotation marks to indicate a pause in Jemima's spoken words; I have made the suggested changes in the text. In a related matter—and in keeping with my editorial policy of minimal intrusion—I replicate the punctuation practice in the source text by omitting closing quotation marks at the ends of paragraphs that are followed by words uttered by the same speaker.

a home I never knew. Of this child, a daughter, she was extravagantly fond; and it was a part of my employment, to assist to spoil her, by humouring all her whims, and bearing all her caprices. Feeling her own consequence, before she could speak, she had learned the art of tormenting me, and if I ever dared to resist, I received blows, laid on with no compunctious hand, or was sent to bed dinnerless, as well as supperless. I said that it was a part of my daily labour to attend this child, with the servility of a slave; still it was but a part. I was sent out in all seasons, and from place to place, to carry burdens far above my strength, without being allowed to draw near the fire, or ever being cheered by encouragement or kindness. No wonder then, treated like a creature of another species, that I began to envy, and at length to hate, the darling of the house. Yet, I perfectly remember, that it was the caresses, and kind expressions of my step-mother, which first excited my jealous discontent. Once, I cannot forget it, when she was calling in vain her wayward child to kiss her, I ran to her, saying, 'I will kiss you, ma'am!' and how did my heart, which was in my mouth, sink, what was my debasement of soul, when pushed away with — 'I do not want you, pert thing!' Another day, when a new gown had excited the highest good humour, and she uttered the appropriate *dear*, addressed unexpectedly to me, I thought I could never do enough to please her; I was all alacrity, and rose proportionably in my own estimation.

"As her daughter grew up, she was pampered with cakes and fruit, while I was, literally speaking, fed with the refuse of the table, with her leavings. A liquorish tooth is, I believe, common to children, and I used to steal any thing sweet, that I could catch up with a chance of concealment. When detected, she was not content to chastize me herself at the moment, but, on my father's return in the evening (he was a shopman), the principal discourse was to recount my faults, and attribute them to the wicked disposition which I had brought into the world with me, inherited from my mother. He did not fail to leave the marks of his resentment on my body, and then solaced himself by playing with my sister. — I could have murdered her at those moments. To save myself from these unmerciful corrections, I resorted to falshood, and the untruths which I sturdily maintained, were brought in judgment against me, to support my tyrant's inhuman charge of my natural propensity to vice. Seeing me treated with contempt, and always being fed and dressed better, my sister conceived a contemptuous opinion of me, that proved an obstacle to all affection; and my father, hearing continually of my faults, began to consider me as a curse entailed on him for his sins: he was therefore easily prevailed on to bind me apprentice to one of my stepmother's friends, who kept a slop-shop in Wapping.[1] I was represented (as it was said) in my true colours; but she, 'warranted,' snapping her fingers, 'that she should break my spirit or heart.'

"My mother replied, with a whine, 'that if any body could make me better, it was such a clever woman as herself; though, for her own part, she had tried in vain; but good-nature was her fault.'

"I shudder with horror, when I recollect the treatment I had now to endure. Not only under the lash of my task-mistress, but the drudge of the maid, apprentices and children, I never had a taste of human kindness to soften the rigour of perpetual labour. I had been introduced as an object of abhorrence into the family; as a creature of whom my step-mother, though she had been kind enough to let me live in the house with her own child, could make nothing. I was described as a wretch, whose nose must be kept to the grinding stone — and it was held there with an iron grasp. It seemed indeed the privilege of their superior nature to kick me about, like the dog or cat. If I were attentive, I was called fawning, if refractory, an obstinate mule, and like a mule I received their censure on my loaded back. Often has my mistress, for some instance of forgetfulness, thrown me from one side of the kitchen to the other, knocked my head against the wall, spit in my face, with various refinements on barbarity that I forbear to enumerate, though they were all acted over again by the servant, with additional insults, to which the appellation of *bastard*, was commonly added, with taunts or sneers. But I will not attempt to give you an adequate idea of my situation, lest you, who probably have never been drenched with the dregs of human misery, should think I exaggerate.

"I stole now, from absolute necessity, — bread; yet whatever else was taken, which I had it not in my power to take, was ascribed to me. I was the filching cat, the ravenous dog, the dumb brute, who must bear all; for if I endeavoured to exculpate

1 According to the *OED*, a "slop-shop" is a store where "slop" clothing is sold; the fifth definition of "slop" in the *OED* seems the most relevant to this case: "pl. Ready-made clothing and other furnishings supplied to seamen from the ship's stores; hence, ready-made, cheap, or inferior garments generally." The slop-shop in Jemima's narrative is appropriately situated, since Wapping is a London borough, lying east of the City of London and on the north bank of the Thames, with strong maritime ties.

myself, I was silenced, without any enquiries being made, with 'Hold your tongue, you never tell truth.' Even the very air I breathed was tainted with scorn; for I was sent to the neighbouring shops with Glutton, Liar, or Thief, written on my forehead. This was, at first, the most bitter punishment; but sullen pride, or a kind of stupid desperation, made me, at length, almost regardless of the contempt, which had wrung from me so many solitary tears at the only moments when I was allowed to rest.

"Thus was I the mark of cruelty till my sixteenth year; and then I have only to point out a change of misery; for a period I never knew. Allow me first to make one observation. Now I look back, I cannot help attributing the greater part of my misery, to the misfortune of having been thrown into the world without the grand support of life — a mother's affection. I had no one to love me; or to make me respected, to enable me to acquire respect. I was an egg dropped on the sand; a pauper by nature, hunted from family to family, who belonged to nobody — and nobody cared for me. I was despised from my birth, and denied the chance of obtaining a footing for myself in society. Yes; I had not even the chance of being considered as a fellow-creature — yet all the people with whom I lived, brutalized as they were by the low cunning of trade, and the despicable shifts of poverty, were not without bowels,[1] though they never yearned for me. I was, in fact, born a slave, and chained by infamy to slavery during the whole of existence, without having any companions to alleviate it by sympathy, or teach me how to rise above it by their example. But, to resume the thread of my tale. —

"At sixteen, I suddenly grew tall, and something like comeliness appeared on a Sunday, when I had time to wash my face, and put on clean clothes. My master had once or twice caught hold of me in the passage; but I instinctively avoided his disgusting caresses. One day however, when the family were at a methodist meeting, he contrived to be alone in the house with me, and by blows — yes; blows and menaces, compelled me to submit to his ferocious desire; and, to avoid my mistress's fury, I was obliged in future to comply, and skulk to my loft at his command, in spite of increasing loathing.

---

1 An archaic use of the word "bowel" to signify one's interior organs and, figuratively, one's inner feelings. The third definition of "bowel" in the *OED* is as follows: "(Considered as the seat of the tender and sympathetic emotions, hence): Pity, compassion, feeling, 'heart.' Chiefly pl., and now somewhat arch[aic]."

"The anguish which was now pent up in my bosom, seemed to open a new world to me: I began to extend my thoughts beyond myself, and grieve for human misery, till I discovered, with horror — ah! what horror! — that I was with child. I know not why I felt a mixed sensation of despair and tenderness, excepting that, ever called a bastard, a bastard appeared to me an object of the greatest compassion in creation.[1]

"I communicated this dreadful circumstance to my master, who was almost equally alarmed at the intelligence; for he feared his wife, and public censure at the meeting.[2] After some weeks of deliberation had elapsed, I in continual fear that my altered shape would be noticed, my master gave me a medicine in a phial, which he desired me to take, telling me, without any circumlocution, for what purpose it was designed. I burst into tears, I thought it was killing myself — yet was such a self as I worth preserving? He cursed me for a fool, and left me to my own reflections. I could not resolve to take this infernal potion; but I wrapped it up in an old gown, and hid it in a corner of my box.

"Nobody yet suspected me, because they had been accustomed to view me as a creature of another species. But the threatening storm at last broke over my devoted head — never shall I forget it! One Sunday evening when I was left, as usual, to take care of the house, my master came home intoxicated, and I became the prey of his brutal appetite. His extreme intoxication made him forget his customary caution, and my mistress entered and found us in a situation that could not have been more hateful to her than me. Her husband was 'pot-valiant,' he feared her not at the moment, nor had he then much reason, for she instantly turned the whole force of her anger another way. She tore off my cap, scratched, kicked, and buffetted me, till she had exhausted her strength, declaring, as she rested her arm, 'that I had wheedled her husband from her. — But, could any thing better be expected from a wretch, whom she had taken into her house out of pure charity?' What a torrent of abuse rushed out? till, almost breathless, she concluded with saying, 'that I was born a strumpet; it ran in my blood, and nothing good could come to those who harboured me.'

---

1  Wollstonecraft's baby with Imlay, Fanny, was born out of wedlock on 14 May 1794.

2  The "meeting" in this sentence refers to the Methodist congregation's gathering, as well as the congregation itself.

"My situation was, of course, discovered, and she declared that I should not stay another night under the same roof with an honest family. I was therefore pushed out of doors, and my trumpery thrown after me, when it had been contemptuously examined in the passage, lest I should have stolen any thing.

"Behold me then in the street, utterly destitute! Whither could I creep for shelter? To my father's roof I had no claim, when not pursued by shame — now I shrunk back as from death, from my mother's cruel reproaches, my father's execrations. I could not endure to hear him curse the day I was born, though life had been a curse to me. Of death I thought, but with a confused emotion of terror, as I stood leaning my head on a post, and start-ing at every footstep, lest it should be my mistress coming to tear my heart out. One of the boys of the shop passing by, heard my tale, and immediately repaired to his master, to give him a description of my situation; and he touched the right key — the scandal it would give rise to, if I were left to repeat my tale to every enquirer. This plea came home to his reason, who had been sobered by his wife's rage, the fury of which fell on him when I was out of her reach, and he sent the boy to me with half-a-guinea, desiring him to conduct me to a house, where beggars, and other wretches, the refuse of society, nightly lodged.

"This night was spent in a state of stupefaction, or despera-tion. I detested mankind, and abhorred myself.

"In the morning I ventured out, to throw myself in my master's way, at his usual hour of going abroad. I approached him, he 'damned me for a b----, declared I had disturbed the peace of the family, and that he had sworn to his wife, never to take any more notice of me.'[1] He left me; but, instantly return-ing, he told me that he should speak to his friend, a parish-officer, to get a nurse for the brat I laid to him; and advised me, if I wished to keep out of the house of correction, not to make free with his name.

"I hurried back to my hole, and, rage giving place to despair, sought for the potion that was to procure abortion, and swal-lowed it, with a wish that it might destroy me, at the same time that it stopped the sensations of new-born life, which I felt with

---

1   The quotation marks enclosing the words "damned" and "me" are in
    the source text, as though what is within them is spoken by Jemima's
    master, but the resultant declaration is somewhat nonsensical. Yet,
    because the author's point is clear enough, I have not altered the text, as
    I do not in similar situations in this edition.

indescribable emotion. My head turned round, my heart grew sick, and in the horrors of approaching dissolution, mental anguish was swallowed up. The effect of the medicine was violent, and I was confined to my bed several days; but, youth and a strong constitution prevailing, I once more crawled out, to ask myself the cruel question, 'Whither I should go?' I had but two shillings left in my pocket, the rest had been expended, by a poor woman who slept in the same room, to pay for my lodging, and purchase the necessaries of which she partook.

"With this wretch I went into the neighbouring streets to beg, and my disconsolate appearance drew a few pence from the idle, enabling me still to command a bed; till, recovering from my illness, and taught to put on my rags to the best advantage, I was accosted from different motives, and yielded to the desire of the brutes I met, with the same detestation that I had felt for my still more brutal master.[1] I have since read in novels of the blandishments of seduction, but I had not even the pleasure of being enticed into vice.

"I shall not," interrupted Jemima, "lead your imagination into all the scenes of wretchedness and depravity, which I was condemned to view; or mark the different stages of my debasing misery. Fate dragged me through the very kennels of society; I was still a slave, a bastard, a common property. Become familiar with vice, for I wish to conceal nothing from you, I picked the pockets of the drunkards who abused me; and proved by my conduct, that I deserved the epithets, with which they loaded me at moments when distrust ought to cease.

"Detesting my nightly occupation, though valuing, if I may so use the word, my independence, which only consisted in choosing the street in which I should wander, or the roof, when I had money, in which I should hide my head, I was some time before I could prevail on myself to accept of a place in a house of ill fame, to which a girl, with whom I had accidentally conversed in

---

1 In *Rights of Woman*, Wollstonecraft details how a lack of proper education and opportunities for gainful employment can force women into Jemima's position, summarizing the situation in two powerful statements: "Necessity never makes prostitution the business of men's lives; though numberless are the women who are thus rendered systematically vicious" (156); and "Business of various kinds, [women] ... might likewise pursue, if they were educated in a more orderly manner, which might save many from common and legal prostitution" (338), referring, in the latter case, to marriage.

the street, had recommended me. I had been hunted almost into a fever, by the watchmen of the quarter of the town I frequented; one, whom I had unwittingly offended, giving the word to the whole pack. You can scarcely conceive the tyranny exercised by these wretches: considering themselves as the instruments of the very laws they violate, the pretext which steels their conscience, hardens their heart. Not content with receiving from us, outlaws of society (let other women talk of favours) a brutal gratification gratuitously as a privilege of office, they extort a tithe of prostitution, and harrass with threats the poor creatures whose occupation affords not the means to silence the growl of avarice. To escape from this persecution, I once more entered into servitude.

"A life of comparative regularity restored my health; and — do not start — my manners were improved, in a situation where vice sought to render itself alluring, and taste was cultivated to fashion the person, if not to refine the mind. Besides, the common civility of speech, contrasted with the gross vulgarity to which I had been accustomed, was something like the polish of civilization. I was not shut out from all intercourse of humanity. Still I was galled by the yoke of service, and my mistress often flying into violent fits of passion, made me dread a sudden dismission, which I understood was always the case. I was therefore prevailed on, though I felt a horror of men, to accept the offer of a gentleman, rather in the decline of years, to keep his house, pleasantly situated in a little village near Hampstead.

"He was a man of great talents, and of brilliant wit; but, a worn-out votary of voluptuousness, his desires became fastidious in proportion as they grew weak, and the native tenderness of his heart was undermined by a vitiated imagination. A thoughtless career of libertinism and social enjoyment, had injured his health to such a degree, that, whatever pleasure his conversation afforded me (and my esteem was ensured by proofs of the generous humanity of his disposition), the being his mistress was purchasing it at a very dear rate. With such a keen perception of the delicacies of sentiment, with an imagination invigorated by the exercise of genius, how could he sink into the grossness of sensuality!

"But, to pass over a subject which I recollect with pain, I must remark to you, as an answer to your often-repeated question, 'Why my sentiments and language were superior to my station?' that I now began to read, to beguile the tediousness of solitude, and to gratify an inquisitive, active mind. I had often, in my childhood, followed a ballad-singer, to hear the sequel of a dismal story, though sure of being severely punished for delaying to return with whatever I was sent to purchase. I could just spell and put a sentence together, and I listened to the various arguments, though often mingled with obscenity, which occurred at the table where I was allowed to preside: for a literary friend or two frequently came home with my master, to dine and pass the night. Having lost the privileged respect of my sex, my presence, instead of restraining, perhaps gave the reins to their tongues; still I had the advantage of hearing discussions, from which, in the common course of life, women are excluded.

"You may easily imagine, that it was only by degrees that I could comprehend some of the subjects they investigated, or acquire from their reasoning what might be termed a moral sense. But my fondness of reading increasing, and my master occasionally shutting himself up in this retreat, for weeks together, to write, I had many opportunities of improvement. At first, considering money (I was right!" exclaimed Jemima, altering her tone of voice) "as the only means, after my loss of reputation, of obtaining respect, or even the toleration of humanity, I had not the least scruple to secrete a part of the sums intrusted to me, and to screen myself from detection by a system of falshood. But, acquiring new principles, I began to have the ambition of returning to the respectable part of society, and was weak enough to suppose it possible. The attention of my unassuming instructor, who, without being ignorant of his own powers, possessed great simplicity of manners, strengthened the illusion. Having sometimes caught up hints for thought, from my untutored remarks, he often led me to discuss the subjects he was treating, and would read to me his productions, previous to their publication, wishing to profit by the criticism of unsophisticated feeling. The aim of his writings was to touch the simple springs of the heart; for he despised the would-be oracles, the self-elected philosophers, who fright away fancy, while sifting each grain of thought to prove that slowness of comprehension is wisdom.

"I should have distinguished this as a moment of sunshine, a happy period in my life, had not the repugnance the disgusting libertinism of my protector inspired, daily become more painful. — And, indeed, I soon did recollect it as such with agony, when his sudden death (for he had recourse to the most exhilarating cordials to keep up the convivial tone of his spirits) again threw me into the desert of human society. Had he had any time for reflection, I am certain he would have left the little property in his power to me: but, attacked by the fatal apoplexy in town, his heir, a man of rigid morals, brought his wife with him to take possession of the house and effects, before I was even informed of his death, — 'to prevent,' as she took care indirectly to tell me, 'such a creature as she supposed me to be, from purloining any of them, had I been apprized of the event in time.'

"The grief I felt at the sudden shock the information gave me, which at first had nothing selfish in it, was treated with contempt, and I was ordered to pack up my clothes; and a few trinkets and books, given me by the generous deceased, were contested, while they piously hoped, with a reprobating shake of the head, 'that God would have mercy on his sinful soul!' With some difficulty, I obtained my arrears of wages; but asking — such is the spirit-grinding consequence of poverty and infamy — for a character for honesty and economy, which God knows I merited, I was told by this — why must I call her woman? — 'that it would go against her conscience to recommend a kept mistress.' Tears started in my eyes, burning tears; for there are situations in which a wretch is humbled by the contempt they are conscious they do not deserve.

"I returned to the metropolis; but the solitude of a poor lodging was inconceivably dreary, after the society I had enjoyed. To be cut off from human converse, now I had been taught to relish it, was to wander a ghost among the living. Besides, I foresaw, to aggravate the severity of my fate, that my little pittance would soon melt away. I endeavoured to obtain needle-work; but, not having been taught early, and my hands being rendered clumsy by hard work, I did not sufficiently excel to be employed by the ready-made linen shops, when so many women, better qualified, were suing for it. The want of a character prevented my getting a place; for, irksome as servitude would have been to me, I should have made another trial, had it been feasible. Not that I disliked employment, but the inequality of condition to which I must have submitted. I had acquired a taste for literature, during the five years I had lived with a literary man, occasionally conversing with men of the first abilities of the age; and now to descend to the lowest vulgarity, was a degree of wretchedness not to be imagined unfelt. I had not, it is true, tasted the charms of affection, but I had been familiar with the graces of humanity.

"One of the gentlemen, whom I had frequently dined in company with, while I was treated like a companion, met me in the street, and enquired after my health. I seized the occasion, and began to describe my situation; but he was in haste to join, at dinner, a select party of choice spirits; therefore, without waiting to hear me, he impatiently put a guinea into my hand, saying, 'It was a pity such a sensible woman should be in distress — he wished me well from his soul.'

"To another I wrote, stating my case, and requesting advice. He was an advocate for unequivocal sincerity; and had often, in my presence, descanted on the evils which arise in society from the despotism of rank and riches.

"In reply, I received a long essay on the energy of the human mind, with continual allusions to his own force of character. He added, 'That the woman who could write such a letter as I had sent him, could never be in want of resources, were she to look into herself, and exert her powers; misery was the consequence of indolence, and, as to my being shut out from society, it was the lot of man to submit to certain privations.'

"How often have I heard," said Jemima, interrupting her narrative, "in conversation, and read in books, that every person willing to work may find employment? It is the vague assertion, I believe, of insensible indolence, when it relates to men; but, with respect to women, I am sure of its fallacy, unless they will submit to the most menial bodily labour; and even to be employed at hard labour is out of the reach of many, whose reputation misfortune or folly has tainted.

"How writers, professing to be friends to freedom, and the improvement of morals, can assert that poverty is no evil, I cannot imagine."

"No more can I," interrupted Maria, "yet they even expatiate on the peculiar happiness of indigence, though in what it can consist, excepting in brutal rest, when a man can barely earn a subsistence, I cannot imagine. The mind is necessarily imprisoned in its own little tenement; and, fully occupied by keeping it in repair, has not time to rove abroad for improvement. The book of knowledge is closely clasped, against those who must fulfil their daily task of severe manual labour or die; and curiosity, rarely excited by thought or information, seldom moves on the stagnate lake of ignorance."

"As far as I have been able to observe," replied Jemima, "prejudices, caught up by chance, are obstinately maintained by the poor, to the exclusion of improvement; they have not time to reason or reflect to any extent, or minds sufficiently exercised to adopt the principles of action, which form perhaps the only basis of contentment in every station."[1]

------------------------

"And independence," said Darnford, "they are necessarily strangers to, even the independence of despising their persecutors. If the poor are happy, or can be happy, *things are very well as they are.*[2] And I cannot conceive on what principle those writers contend for a change of system, who support this opinion. The authors on the other side of the question are much more consistent, who grant the fact; yet, insisting that it is the lot of the majority to be oppressed in this life, kindly turn them over to another, to rectify the false weights and measures of this, as the only way to justify the dispensations of Providence. I have not," continued Darnford, "an opinion more firmly fixed by observation in my mind, than that, though riches may fail to produce proportionate happiness, poverty most commonly excludes it, by shutting up all the avenues to improvement."

"And as for the affections," added Maria, with a sigh, "how gross, and even tormenting do they become, unless regulated by an improving mind! The culture of the heart ever, I believe, keeps pace with that of the mind. But pray go on," addressing Jemima, "though your narrative gives rise to the most painful reflections on the present state of society."

"Not to trouble you," continued she, "with a detailed description of all the painful feelings of unavailing exertion, I have only to tell you, that at last I got recommended to wash in a few families, who did me the favour to admit me into their houses, without the most strict enquiry, to wash from one in the morning till eight at night, for eighteen or twenty-pence a day. On the happiness to be enjoyed over a washing-tub I need not comment; yet you will allow me to observe, that this was a wretchedness of situation peculiar to my sex. A man with half my industry, and, I may say, abilities, could have procured a decent livelihood, and discharged some of the duties which knit mankind together;

---

1 The copy which appears to have received the author's last corrections, ends at this place. [Godwin's note]

2 The italicized phrase here is a reference to the novel *Things as They Are; or, The Adventures of Caleb Williams* (1794), by Godwin. See p. 155, note 1 and Appendix C4 for more information about Godwin's novel.

whilst I, who had acquired a taste for the rational, nay, in honest pride let me assert it, the virtuous enjoyments of life, was cast aside as the filth of society. Condemned to labour, like a machine, only to earn bread, and scarcely that, I became melancholy and desperate.

"I have now to mention a circumstance which fills me with remorse, and fear it will entirely deprive me of your esteem. A tradesman became attached to me, and visited me frequently, — and I at last obtained such a power over him, that he offered to take me home to his house. — Consider, dear madam, I was famishing: wonder not that I became a wolf! — The only reason for not taking me home immediately, was the having a girl in the house, with child by him — and this girl — I advised him — yes, I did! would I could forget it! — to turn out of doors: and one night he determined to follow my advice. Poor wretch! She fell upon her knees, reminded him that he had promised to marry her, that her parents were honest! — What did it avail? — She was turned out.

"She approached her father's door, in the skirts of London, — listened at the shutters, — but could not knock. A watchman had observed her go and return several times — Poor wretch! —"The remorse Jemima spoke of, seemed to be stinging her to the soul, as she proceeded.[1]

"She left it, and, approaching a tub where horses were watered, she sat down in it, and, with desperate resolution, remained in that attitude — till resolution was no longer necessary!

"I happened that morning to be going out to wash, anticipating the moment when I should escape from such hard labour. I passed by, just as some men, going to work, drew out the stiff, cold corpse — Let me not recall the horrid moment! — I recognized her pale visage; I listened to the tale told by the spectators, and my heart did not burst. I thought of my own state, and wondered how I could be such a monster! — I worked hard; and, returning home, I was attacked by a fever. I suffered both in body

---

1 The errata directs the square brackets surrounding the phrase "The remorse ... proceeded" to be replaced by inverted quotation marks in order to demarcate the spoken words that surround it; I have taken out both brackets, but I have only replaced the first with inverted quotation marks because the source text already contained quotation marks before "She" in the next paragraph.

and mind. I determined not to live with the wretch. But he did not try me; he left the neighbourhood. I once more returned to the wash-tub.

"Still this state, miserable as it was, admitted of aggravation. Lifting one day a heavy load, a tub fell against my shin, and gave me great pain. I did not pay much attention to the hurt, till it became a serious wound; being obliged to work as usual, or starve. But, finding myself at length unable to stand for any time, I thought of getting into an hospital. Hospitals, it should seem (for they are comfortless abodes for the sick)[1] were expressly endowed for the reception of the friendless; yet I, who had on that plea a right to assistance, wanted the recommendation of the rich and respectable, and was several weeks languishing for admittance; fees were demanded on entering; and, what was still more unreasonable, security for burying me, that expence not coming into the letter of the charity. A guinea was the stipulated sum — I could as soon have raised a million; and I was afraid to apply to the parish for an order, lest they should have passed me, I knew not whither. The poor woman at whose house I lodged, compassionating my state, got me into the hospital; and the family where I received the hurt, sent me five shillings, three and six-pence of which I gave at my admittance — I know not for what.

"My leg grew quickly better; but I was dismissed before my cure was completed, because I could not afford to have my linen washed to appear decently, as the virago of a nurse said, when the gentlemen (the surgeons) came. I cannot give you an adequate idea of the wretchedness of an hospital; every thing is left to the care of people intent on gain. The attendants seem to have lost all feeling of compassion in the bustling discharge of

---

1 Jemima's commentary may function as Wollstonecraft's protest about the terrible condition of charity hospitals for the poor in eighteenth-century England. On this subject, G.S. Rousseau writes, "At first all these charity hospitals were free; but as time passed some form of contribution was necessary," and he adds, "The establishment of hospitals was undoubtedly the most beneficial outcome of the 'Charitable Proposals' of 1715.... Fielding H. Garrison, MD, the great American historian of medicine, has commented that 'Many new hospitals were built in the eighteenth century, but, in respect of cleanliness and administration, these institutions sank to the lowest level known in the history of medicine'" ("Science" 179).

their offices; death is so familiar to them, that they are not anxious to ward it off. Every thing appeared to be conducted for the accommodation of the medical men and their pupils, who came to make experiments on the poor, for the benefit of the rich. One of the physicians, I must not forget to mention, gave me half-a-crown, and ordered me some wine, when I was at the lowest ebb. I thought of making my case known to the lady-like matron; but her forbidding countenance prevented me. She condescended to look on the patients, and make general enquiries, two or three times a week; but the nurses knew the hour when the visit of ceremony would commence, and every thing was as it should be.

"After my dismission, I was more at a loss than ever for a subsistence, and, not to weary you with a repetition of the same unavailing attempts, unable to stand at the washing-tub, I began to consider the rich and poor as natural enemies, and became a thief from principle. I could not now cease to reason, but I hated mankind. I despised myself, yet I justified my conduct. I was taken, tried, and condemned to six months' imprisonment in a house of correction. My soul recoils with horror from the remembrance of the insults I had to endure, till, branded with shame, I was turned loose in the street, pennyless. I wandered from street to street, till, exhausted by hunger and fatigue, I sunk down senseless at a door, where I had vainly demanded a morsel of bread. I was sent by the inhabitant to the work-house, to which he had surlily bid me go, saying, he 'paid enough in conscience to the poor,' when, with parched tongue, I implored his charity. If those well-meaning people who exclaim against beggars, were acquainted with the treatment the poor receive in many of these wretched asylums, they would not stifle so easily involuntary sympathy, by saying that they have all parishes to go to, or wonder that the poor dread to enter the gloomy walls. What are the common run of workhouses, but prisons, in which many respectable old people, worn out by immoderate labour, sink into the grave in sorrow, to which they are carried like dogs!"

Alarmed by some indistinct noise, Jemima rose hastily to listen, and Maria, turning to Darnford, said, "I have indeed been shocked beyond expression when I have met a pauper's funeral. A coffin carried on the shoulders of three or four ill-looking wretches, whom the imagination might easily convert into a band of assassins, hastening to conceal the corpse, and quarrelling about the prey on their way.[1] I know it is of little consequence how we are consigned to the earth; but I am led by this brutal insensibility, to what even the animal creation appears forcibly to feel, to advert to the wretched, deserted manner in which they died."

"True," rejoined Darnford, "and, till the rich will give more than a part of their wealth, till they will give time and attention to the wants of the distressed, never let them boast of charity. Let them open their hearts, and not their purses, and employ their minds in the service, if they are really actuated by humanity; or charitable institutions will always be the prey of the lowest order of knaves."

Jemima returning, seemed in haste to finish her tale. "The overseer farmed the poor of different parishes, and out of the bowels of poverty was wrung the money with which he purchased this dwelling, as a private receptacle for madness.[2] He had been a keeper at a house of the same description, and conceived that he could make money much more readily in his old occupation. He is a shrewd — shall I say it? — villain. He observed something resolute in my manner, and offered to take me with him, and instruct me how to treat the disturbed minds he meant to intrust to my care. The offer of forty pounds a year, and to quit a work-house, was not to be despised, though the condition of shutting my eyes and hardening my heart was annexed to it.

---

1   The words "assassins" and "prey" in this sentence reveal Maria's suspi-
    cion that the undertakers intend to sell the corpse (probably to an
    anatomy school). This practice became more common in the nineteenth
    century once a law was passed to allocate one corpse (usually a
    beggar's) per year to the schools, an event that increased grave-robbing
    and gave birth to a new term for its practitioners: "resurrection men."
    The famous murder trial of William Burke and William Hare has come
    to represent this historical issue, but it did not occur until 1829.

2   The virtually ungoverned nature of private insane asylums, or "mad-
    houses," gave rise to widespread abuse in eighteenth-century Britain,
    and of the sort that Wollstonecraft describes here: the illegal and unjusti-
    fied incarceration of relatives in exchange for a bribe given to the mad-
    house owner. Partly in response to such issues, the first major parlia-
    mentary inquiries into madhouses were undertaken in 1807 and 1815;
    legislation regarding the incarceration of inmates improved and the
    Asylum Act of 1808 enabled the establishment of the first public and
    government-run lunatic asylums.

"I agreed to accompany him; and four years have I been attendant on many wretches, and" — she lowered her voice, — "the witness of many enormities. In solitude my mind seemed to recover its force, and many of the sentiments which I imbibed in the only tolerable period of my life, returned with their full force. Still what should induce me to be the champion for suffering humanity? — Who ever risked any thing for me? — Whoever acknowledged me to be a fellow-creature?" —

Maria took her hand, and Jemima, more overcome by kindness than she had ever been by cruelty, hastened out of the room to conceal her emotions.

Darnford soon after heard his summons, and, taking leave of him, Maria promised to gratify his curiosity, with respect to herself, the first opportunity.

## CHAP. VI.

ACTIVE as love was in the heart of Maria, the story she had just heard made her thoughts take a wider range. The opening buds of hope closed, as if they had put forth too early, and the[1] happiest day of her life was overcast by the most melancholy reflections. Thinking of Jemima's peculiar fate and her own, she was led to consider the oppressed state of women, and to lament that she had given birth to a daughter.[2] Sleep fled from her eyelids, while she dwelt on the wretchedness of unprotected infancy, till sympathy with Jemima changed to agony, when it seemed probable that her own babe might even now be in the very state she so forcibly described.

Maria thought, and thought again. Jemima's humanity had rather been benumbed than killed, by the keen frost she had to brave at her entrance into life; an appeal then to her feelings, on this tender point, surely would not be fruitless; and Maria began to anticipate the delight it would afford her to gain intelligence of her child. This project was now the only subject of reflection; and she watched impatiently for the dawn of day, with that determinate purpose which generally insures success.

At the usual hour, Jemima brought her breakfast, and a tender note from Darnford. She ran her eye hastily over it, and her heart

---

1 I have omitted an extraneous "the" that appears at this point in the source text.

2 Wollstonecraft repeats the same sentiment in Chapter I of the present novella; see p. 162, note 3 for more information.

calmly hoarded up the rapture a fresh assurance of affection, affection such as she wished to inspire, gave her, without diverting her mind a moment from its design. While Jemima waited to take away the breakfast, Maria alluded to the reflections, that had haunted her during the night to the exclusion of sleep. She spoke with energy of Jemima's unmerited sufferings, and of the fate of a number of deserted females, placed within the sweep of a whirlwind, from which it was next to impossible to escape. Perceiving the effect her conversation produced on the countenance of her guard, she grasped the arm of Jemima with that irresistible warmth which defies repulse, exclaiming — "With your heart, and such dreadful experience, can you lend your aid to deprive my babe of a mother's tenderness, a mother's care? In the name of God, assist me to snatch her from destruction! Let me but give her an education — let me but prepare her body and mind to encounter the ills which await her sex, and I will teach her to consider you as her second mother, and herself as the prop of your age. Yes, Jemima, look at me — observe me closely, and read my very soul; you merit a better fate;" she held out her hand with a firm gesture of assurance; "and I will procure it for you, as a testimony of my esteem, as well as of my gratitude."

Jemima had not power to resist this persuasive torrent; and, owning that the house in which she was confined, was situated on the banks of the Thames,[1] only a few miles from London, and not on the sea-coast, as Darnford had supposed, she promised to invent some excuse for her absence, and go herself to trace the situation, and enquire concerning the health, of this abandoned daughter. Her manner implied an intention to do something more, but she seemed unwilling to impart her design; and Maria, glad to have obtained the main point, thought it best to leave her to the workings of her own mind; convinced that she had the power of interesting her still more in favour of herself and child, by a simple recital of facts.

In the evening, Jemima informed the impatient mother, that on the morrow she should hasten to town before the family hour of rising, and received all the information necessary, as a clue to

---

1 As Michael Donnelly reports in *Managing the Mind* (1983), early nineteenth-century asylums were often built outside or on the borders of city centres for several reasons, such as a lack of land in the city and the citizens' desire to maintain their distance from the noxious, disease-ridden environments of the asylum—where, indeed, typhus often flourished (32).

her search. The "Good night!" Maria uttered was peculiarly solemn and affectionate. Glad expectation sparkled in her eye; and, for the first time since her detention, she pronounced the name of her child with pleasureable fondness; and, with all the garrulity of a nurse, described her first smile when she recognized her mother. Recollecting herself, a still kinder "Adieu!" with a "God bless you!" — that seemed to include a maternal benediction, dismissed Jemima.

The dreary solitude of the ensuing day, lengthened by impatiently dwelling on the same idea, was intolerably wearisome. She listened for the sound of a particular clock, which some directions of the wind allowed her to hear distinctly. She marked the shadow gaining on the wall; and, twilight thickening into darkness, her breath seemed oppressed while she anxiously counted nine. — The last sound was a stroke of despair on her heart; for she expected every moment, without seeing Jemima, to have her light extinguished by the savage female who supplied her place. She was even obliged to prepare for bed, restless as she was, not to disoblige her new attendant. She had been cautioned not to speak too freely to her; but the caution was needless, her countenance would still more emphatically have made her shrink back. Such was the ferocity of manner, conspicuous in every word and gesture of this hag, that Maria was afraid to enquire, why Jemima, who had faithfully promised to see her before her door was shut for the night, came not? — and, when the key turned in the lock, to consign her to a night of suspence, she felt a degree of anguish which the circumstances scarcely justified.

Continually on the watch, the shutting of a door, or the sound of a foot-step, made her start and tremble with apprehension, something like what she felt, when, at her entrance, dragged along the gallery, she began to doubt whether she were not surrounded by demons?

Fatigued by an endless rotation of thought and wild alarms, she looked like a spectre, when Jemima entered in the morning; especially as her eyes darted out of her head, to read in Jemima's countenance, almost as pallid, the intelligence she dared not trust her tongue to demand. Jemima put down the tea-things, and appeared very busy in arranging the table. Maria took up a cup with trembling hand, then forcibly recovering her fortitude, and restraining the convulsive movement which agitated the muscles of her mouth, she said, "Spare yourself the pain of preparing me for your information, I adjure you! — My child is dead!" Jemima solemnly answered, "Yes"; with a look expressive of compassion and angry emotions. "Leave me," added Maria, making a fresh effort to govern her feelings, and hiding her face in her handkerchief, to conceal her anguish — "It is enough — I know that my babe is no more — I will hear the particulars when I am" — *calmer*, she could not utter; and Jemima, without importuning her by idle attempts to console her, left the room.

Plunged in the deepest melancholy, she would not admit Darnford's visits; and such is the force of early associations even on strong minds, that, for a while, she indulged the superstitious notion that she was justly punished by the death of her child, for having for an instant ceased to regret her loss.[1] Two or three letters from Darnford, full of soothing, manly tenderness, only added poignancy to these accusing emotions; yet the passionate style in which he expressed, what he termed the first and fondest wish of his heart, "that his affection might make her some amends for the cruelty and injustice she had endured," inspired a sentiment of gratitude to heaven; and her eyes filled with delicious tears, when, at the conclusion of his letter, wishing to supply the place of her unworthy relations, whose want of principle he execrated, he assured her, calling her his dearest girl, "that it should henceforth be the business of his life to make her happy."

He begged, in a note sent the following morning, to be permitted to see her, when his presence would be no intrusion on her grief; and so earnestly intreated to be allowed, according to promise, to beguile the tedious moments of absence, by dwelling on the events of her past life, that she sent him the memoirs which had been written for her daughter, promising Jemima the perusal as soon as he returned them.

---

1 In the phrase, "such is the force of early associations," Wollstonecraft invokes the Romantic-era psychological approach of associationism. Aside from David Hartley (1705-57), one of the most notable associationists of the Romantic period was Thomas Brown (1778-1820), Professor of Moral Philosophy at Edinburgh University, whose *Lectures on the Philosophy of the Human Mind* (1820) went into nineteen editions by 1851; he summarizes the approach thus: "there is a tendency of ideas to suggest each other, without any renewed perception of the external object which originally excited them, and ... the suggestion is not altogether loose and indefinite, but ... certain ideas have a peculiar tendency to suggest certain other relative ideas in associate trains of thought" (219). See p. 122, note 1 for more information about associationism, as well as the introduction to this edition (p. 46) and Appendix D3.

## CHAP. VII.

"ADDRESSING these memoirs to you, my child, uncertain whether I shall ever have an opportunity of instructing you, many observations will probably flow from my heart, which only a mother — a mother schooled in misery, could make.

"The tenderness of a father who knew the world, might be great; but could it equal that of a mother — of a mother, labouring under a portion of the misery, which the constitution of society seems to have entailed on all her kind? It is, my child, my dearest daughter, only such a mother, who will dare to break through all restraint to provide for your happiness — who will voluntarily brave censure herself, to ward off sorrow from your bosom. From my narrative, my dear girl, you may gather the instruction, the counsel, which is meant rather to exercise than influence your mind. — Death may snatch me from you, before you can weigh my advice, or enter into my reasoning: I would then, with fond anxiety, lead you very early in life to form your grand principle of action, to save you from the vain regret of having, through irresolution, let the spring-tide of existence pass away, unimproved, unenjoyed. — Gain experience — ah! gain it — while experience is worth having, and acquire sufficient fortitude to pursue your own happiness; it includes your utility, by a direct path. What is wisdom too often, but the owl of the goddess,[1] who sits moping in a desolated heart; around me she shrieks, but I would invite all the gay warblers of spring to nestle in your blooming bosom. — Had I not wasted years in deliberating, after I ceased to doubt, how I ought to have acted — I might now be useful and happy. — For my sake, warned by my example, always appear what you are, and you will not pass through existence without enjoying its genuine blessings, love and respect.

"Born in one of the most romantic parts of England, an enthusiastic fondness for the varying charms of nature is the first sentiment I recollect; or rather it was the first consciousness of pleasure that employed and formed my imagination.

"My father had been a captain of a man of war;[2] but, disgusted with the service, on account of the preferment of men

---

1 In Greek mythology, the owl was a symbol of the goddess Athena. See p. 158, note 1 for more information about Athena (Minerva in Roman mythology).

2 A "man of war" is an English battleship.

whose chief merit was their family connections or borough inter-est,[1] he retired into the country; and, not knowing what to do with himself — married. In his family, to regain his lost conse-quence, he determined to keep up the same passive obedience, as in the vessels in which he had commanded. His orders were not to be disputed; and the whole house was expected to fly, at the word of command, as if to man the shrouds, or mount aloft in an elemental strife, big with life or death. He was to be instanta-neously obeyed, especially by my mother, whom he very benevo-lently married for love; but took care to remind her of the obli-gation, when she dared, in the slightest instance, to question his absolute authority. My eldest brother, it is true, as he grew up, was treated with more respect by my father; and became in due form the deputy-tyrant of the house. The representative of my father, a being privileged by nature — a boy, and the darling of my mother, he did not fail to act like an heir apparent. Such indeed was my mother's extravagant partiality, that, in compari-son with her affection for him, she might be said not to love the rest of her children. Yet none of the children seemed to have so little affection for her. Extreme indulgence had rendered him so selfish, that he only thought of himself; and from tormenting insects and animals, he became the despot of his brothers, and still more of his sisters.[2]

---

1   The third definition for "borough" in the *OED* is "A town possessing a municipal corporation and special privileges conferred by royal charter.... Also a town which sends representatives to parliament." "Borough interest" is the political interest of powerful family in their borough. The problem of small numbers of politically powerful people ruling their boroughs like their demesnes was of great concern in Britain and inspired the Reform Acts of 1832, 1867, and 1884, all of which aimed at extending voting rights to disenfranchised citizens. So closely is the issue of "rotten" or "pocket" boroughs identified with the Romantic period that many scholars consider the end of it to coincide with the passing of the first Reform Act in 1832.

2   In this brief psychological sketch of Maria's brother, Wollstonecraft may show her familiarity with such contemporary studies on children's edu-cation and the formation of their characters as *Extract of a Letter on Early Instruction, Particularly that of the Poor* (1792), by Dr. Thomas Beddoes (1760-1808), father of poet and dramatist Thomas Lovell Beddoes (1803-49). Beddoes's tract was published only five years after Wollstonecraft's work on children's education, *Thoughts on the Education of Daughters*. Beddoes states,

    Cruelty to animals is one among the earliest and most pernicious acquisitions of ill-educated children; and yet the same          (*continued*)

"It is perhaps difficult to give you an idea of the petty cares which obscured the morning of my life; continual restraint in the most trivial matters; unconditional submission to orders, which, as a mere child, I soon discovered to be unreasonable, because inconsistent and contradictory. Thus are we destined to experience a mixture of bitterness, with the recollection of our most innocent enjoyments.

"The circumstances which, during my childhood, occurred to fashion my mind, were various; yet, as it would probably afford me more pleasure to revive the fading remembrance of newborn delight, than you, my child, could feel in the perusal, I will not entice you to stray with me into the verdant meadow, to search for the flowers that youthful hopes scatter in every path; though, as I write, I almost scent the fresh green of spring — of that spring which never returns!

"I had two sisters, and one brother, younger than myself; my brother Robert was two years older, and might truly be termed the idol of his parents, and the torment of the rest of the family. Such indeed is the force of prejudice, that what was called spirit and wit in him, was cruelly repressed as forwardness in me.

"My mother had an indolence of character, which prevented her from paying much attention to our education. But the healthy breeze of a neighbouring heath, on which we bounded at pleasure, volatilized the humours that improper food might have generated. And to enjoy open air and freedom, was paradise, after the unnatural restraint of our fire-side, where we were often obliged to sit three or four hours together, without daring to utter a word, when my father was out of humour, from want of employment, or of a variety of boisterous amusement. I had however one advantage, an instructor, the brother of my father, who, intended for the church, had of course received a liberal education. But, becoming attached to a young lady of great beauty and large fortune, and acquiring in the world some opinions not consonant with the profession for which he was designed, he accepted, with the most sanguine expectations of success, the offer of a nobleman to accompany him to India, as his confidential secretary.

---

constitution of their nature, disposes them to acquire the habitual sentiment of compassion for both men and animals; for the cry of distress pierces the bosom of the child, and by exciting a painful sensation, prompts him to attempt the relief of the sufferer! You see then how nature has laid the foundation of virtue in our earliest feelings, and how easy the transition from these feelings to good habits and principles. (6)

"A correspondence was regularly kept up with the object of his affection; and the intricacies of business, peculiarly wearisome to a man of a romantic turn of mind, contributed, with a forced absence, to increase his attachment. Every other passion was lost in this master-one, and only served to swell the torrent. Her relations, such were his waking dreams, who had despised him, would court in their turn his alliance, and all the blandishments of taste would grace the triumph of love. — While he basked in the warm sunshine of love, friendship also promised to shed its dewy freshness; for a friend, whom he loved next to his mistress, was the confident, who forwarded the letters from one to the other, to elude the observation of prying relations. A friend false in similar circumstances, is, my dearest girl, an old tale; yet, let not this example, or the frigid caution of coldblooded moralists, make you endeavour to stifle hopes, which are the buds that naturally unfold themselves during the spring of life! Whilst your own heart is sincere, always expect to meet one glowing with the same sentiments; for to fly from pleasure, is not to avoid pain!

"My uncle realized, by good luck, rather than management, a handsome fortune; and returning on the wings of love, lost in the most enchanting reveries, to England, to share it with his mistress and his friend, he found them — united.

"There were some circumstances, not necessary for me to recite, which aggravated the guilt of the friend beyond measure, and the deception, that had been carried on to the last moment, was so base, it produced the most violent effect on my uncle's health and spirits. His native country, the world! lately a garden of blooming sweets, blasted by treachery, seemed changed into a parched desert, the abode of hissing serpents. Disappointment rankled in his heart; and, brooding over his wrongs, he was attacked by a raging fever, followed by a derangement of mind, which only gave place to habitual melancholy, as he recovered more strength of body.

"Declaring an intention never to marry, his relations were ever clustering about him, paying the grossest adulation to a man, who, disgusted with mankind, received them with scorn, or bitter sarcasms. Something in my countenance pleased him, when I began to prattle. Since his return, he appeared dead to affection; but I soon, by showing him innocent fondness, became a favourite; and endeavouring to enlarge and strengthen my mind, I grew dear to him in proportion as I imbibed his sentiments. He had a forcible manner of speaking, rendered more so by a certain impressive wildness of look and gesture, calculated to engage the attention of a young and ardent mind. It is not then surprising that I quickly adopted his opinions in preference, and reverenced him as one of a superior order of beings. He inculcated, with great warmth, self-respect, and a lofty consciousness of acting right, independent of the censure or applause of the world; nay, he almost taught me to brave, and even despise its censure, when convinced of the rectitude of my own intentions.

"Endeavouring to prove to me that nothing which deserved the name of love or friendship, existed in the world, he drew such animated pictures of his own feelings, rendered permanent by disappointment, as imprinted the sentiments strongly on my heart, and animated my imagination. These remarks are necessary to elucidate some peculiarities in my character, which by the world are indefinitely termed romantic.

"My uncle's increasing affection led him to visit me often. Still, unable to rest in any place, he did not remain long in the country to soften domestic tyranny; but he brought me books, for which I had a passion, and they conspired with his conversation, to make me form an ideal picture of life. I shall pass over the tyranny of my father, much as I suffered from it; but it is necessary to notice, that it undermined my mother's health; and that her temper, continually irritated by domestic bickering, became intolerably peevish.

"My eldest brother was articled to a neighbouring attorney, the shrewdest, and, I may add, the most unprincipled man in that part of the country.[1] As my brother generally came home every Saturday, to astonish my mother by exhibiting his attainments, he gradually assumed a right of directing the whole family, not excepting my father. He seemed to take a peculiar pleasure in tormenting and humbling me; and if I ever ventured to complain of this treatment to either my father or mother, I was rudely rebuffed for presuming to judge of the conduct of my eldest brother.

"About this period a merchant's family came to settle in our neighbourhood. A mansion-house in the village, lately purchased, had been preparing the whole spring, and the sight of the costly furniture, sent from London, had excited my mother's envy, and roused my father's pride. My sensations were very different, and all of a pleasurable kind. I longed to see new characters, to break the tedious monotony of my life; and to find a friend, such as

---

1 Wollstonecraft's own eldest and much-resented brother, Edward (Ned), trained to be a lawyer in London and began practicing law in 1779.

fancy had pourtrayed. I cannot then describe the emotion I felt, the Sunday they made their appearance at church. My eyes were rivetted on the pillar round which I expected first to catch a glimpse of them, and darted forth to meet a servant who hastily preceded a group of ladies, whose white robes and waving plumes, seemed to stream along the gloomy aisle, diffusing the light, by which I contemplated their figures.

"We visited them in form; and I quickly selected the eldest daughter for my friend. The second son, George, paid me particular attention, and finding his attainments and manners superior to those of the young men of the village, I began to imagine him superior to the rest of mankind.[1] Had my home been more comfortable, or my previous acquaintance more numerous, I should not probably have been so eager to open my heart to new affections.

"Mr. Venables, the merchant, had acquired a large fortune by unremitting attention to business; but his health declining rapidly, he was obliged to retire, before his son, George, had acquired sufficient experience, to enable him to conduct their affairs on the same prudential plan, his father had invariably pursued. Indeed, he had laboured to throw off his authority, having despised his narrow plans and cautious speculation. The eldest son could not be prevailed on to enter the firm; and, to oblige his wife, and have peace in the house, Mr. Venables had purchased a commission for him in the guards.

"I am now alluding to circumstances which came to my knowledge long after; but it is necessary, my dearest child, that you should know the character of your father, to prevent your despising your mother; the only parent inclined to discharge a parent's duty. In London, George had acquired habits of libertinism, which he carefully concealed from his father and his commercial connections. The mask he wore, was so complete a covering of his real visage, that the praise his father lavished on his conduct, and, poor mistaken man! on his principles, contrasted with his brother's, rendered the notice he took of me peculiarly flattering. Without any fixed design, as I am now convinced, he continued to single me out at the dance, press my hand at parting, and utter expressions of unmeaning passion, to which I

---

1   Maria's relationship with the Venables echoes strongly Wollstonecraft's relationship with the Bloods, the eldest daughter of whom, Fanny, was her best friend, and who also had a son named George; however, Wollstonecraft does not seem to have fallen in love with George Blood.

gave a meaning naturally suggested by the romantic turn of my thoughts. His stay in the country was short; his manners did not entirely please me; but, when he left us, the colouring of my picture became more vivid — Whither did not my imagination lead me? In short, I fancied myself in love — in love with the disinterestedness, fortitude, generosity, dignity, and humanity, with which I had invested the hero I dubbed. A circumstance which soon after occurred, rendered all these virtues palpable. [The incident is perhaps worth relating on other accounts, and therefore I shall describe it distinctly.][1]

"I had a great affection for my nurse, old Mary, for whom I used often to work, to spare her eyes. Mary had a younger sister, married to a sailor, while she was suckling me; for my mother only suckled my eldest brother, which might be the cause of her extraordinary partiality.[2] Peggy, Mary's sister, lived with her, till her husband, becoming a mate in a West-Indian trader, got a little before-hand in the world. He wrote to his wife from the first port in the Channel,[3] after his most successful voyage, to request her to come to London to meet him; he even wished her to determine on living there for the future, to save him the trouble of coming to her the moment he came on shore; and to turn a penny by keeping a green-stall.[4] It was too much to set out on a journey the moment he had finished a voyage, and fifty miles by land, was worse than a thousand leagues by sea.

"She packed up her alls, and came to London — but did not meet honest Daniel. A common misfortune prevented her, and the poor are bound to suffer for the good of their country — he was pressed in the river — and never came on shore.

"Peggy was miserable in London, not knowing, as she said, 'the face of any living soul.' Besides, her imagination had been employed, anticipating a month or six weeks' happiness with her husband. Daniel was to have gone with her to Sadler's Wells, and

---

1  These square brackets appear in the source text.
2  See p. 162, note 2 for more information about Wollstonecraft's views on, and the politics of, breastfeeding in the Romantic period.
3  The English Channel is the body of water that separates Great Britain from northern France. Peggy's husband worked on a ship trading with the West Indies, a major source of sugar and rum for Britain, as well as a major destination for the English slave trade out of Africa from the seventeenth century until 1807, when England passed the Slave Trade Act to abolish the practice.
4  A vegetable stand.

Westminster Abbey,[1] and to many sights, which he knew she never heard of in the country. Peggy too was thrifty, and how could she manage to put his plan in execution alone? He had acquaintance; but she did not know the very name of their places of abode. His letters were made up of — How do you does, and God bless yous, — information was reserved for the hour of meeting.

"She too had her portion of information, near at heart. Molly and Jacky were grown such little darlings, she was almost angry that daddy did not see their tricks. She had not half the pleasure she should have had from their prattle, could she have recounted to him each night the pretty speeches of the day. Some stories, however, were stored up — and Jacky could say papa with such a sweet voice, it must delight his heart. Yet when she came, and found no Daniel to greet her, when Jacky called papa, she wept, bidding 'God bless his innocent soul, that did not know what sorrow was.' — But more sorrow was in store for Peggy, innocent as she was. — Daniel was killed in the first engagement, and then the *papa* was agony, sounding to the heart. ·

"She had lived sparingly on his wages, while there was any hope of his return; but, that gone, she returned with a breaking heart to the country, to a little market town, nearly three miles from our village. She did not like to go to service, to be snubbed about, after being her own mistress. To put her children out to nurse was impossible: how far would her wages go? and to send them to her husband's parish, a distant one, was to lose her husband twice over.

"I had heard all from Mary, and made my uncle furnish a little cottage for her, to enable her to sell — so sacred was poor Daniel's advice, now he was dead and gone — a little fruit, toys and cakes. The minding of the shop did not require her whole time, nor even the keeping her children clean, and she loved to see them clean; so she took in washing, and altogether made a shift to earn bread for her children, still weeping for Daniel, when Jacky's arch looks made her think of his father. — It was pleasant to work for her children. — 'Yes; from morning till night, could

---

1 Sadler's Wells is a theatre that presented a variety of performances in the eighteenth century, from opera to plays; today it is best known for dance theatre. Westminster Abbey is a medieval-era Gothic cathedral in London that is the burial place of some of the most famous English citizens in history, including kings, politicians, and many literary notables, such as Geoffrey Chaucer and Edmund Spenser.

she have had a kiss from their father, God rest his soul! Yes; had it plased[1] Providence to have let him come back without a leg or an arm, it would have been the same thing to her — for she did not love him because he maintained them — no; she had hands of her own.'

"The country people were honest, and Peggy left her linen out to dry very late. A recruiting party, as she supposed, passing through, made free with a large wash; for it was all swept away, including her own and her children's little stock.

"This was a dreadful blow; two dozen of shirts, stocks and handkerchiefs. She gave the money which she had laid by for half a year's rent, and promised to pay two shillings a week till all was cleared; so she did not lose her employment. This two shillings a week, and the buying a few necessaries for the children, drove her so hard, that she had not a penny to pay her rent with, when a twelvemonth's became due.

"She was now with Mary, and had just told her tale, which Mary instantly repeated — it was intended for my ear. Many houses in this town, producing a borough-interest, were included in the estate purchased by Mr. Venables, and the attorney with whom my brother lived, was appointed his agent, to collect and raise the rents.

"He demanded Peggy's, and, in spite of her intreaties, her poor goods had been seized and sold. So that she had not, and what was worse her children, 'for she had known sorrow enough,' a bed to lie on. She knew that I was good-natured — right charitable, yet not liking to ask for more than needs must, she scorned to petition while people could any how be made to wait. But now, should she be turned out of doors, she must expect nothing less than to lose all her customers, and then she must beg or starve — and what would become of her children? — 'had Daniel not been pressed — but God knows best — all this could not have happened.'

"I had two mattrasses on my bed; what did I want with two, when such a worthy creature must lie on the ground? My mother would be angry, but I could conceal it till my uncle came down; and then I would tell him all the whole truth, and if he absolved me, heaven would.

"I begged the house-maid to come up stairs with me (servants always feel for the distresses of poverty, and so would the rich if

---

1  The source text is missing the e in "pleased," but Wollstonecraft may have omitted it intentionally to replicate Peggy's accent.

they knew what it was). She assisted me to tie up the mattrass; I discovering, at the same time, that one blanket would serve me till winter, could I persuade my sister, who slept with me, to keep my secret. She entering in the midst of the package, I gave her some new feathers, to silence her. We got the mattrass down the back stairs, unperceived, and I helped to carry it, taking with me all the money I had, and what I could borrow from my sister.

"When I got to the cottage, Peggy declared that she would not take what I had brought secretly; but, when, with all the eager eloquence inspired by a decided purpose, I grasped her hand with weeping eyes, assuring her that my uncle would screen me from blame, when he was once more in the country, describing, at the same time, what she would suffer in parting with her children, after keeping them so long from being thrown on the parish, she reluctantly consented.

"My project of usefulness ended not here; I determined to speak to the attorney; he frequently paid me compliments. His character did not intimidate me; but, imagining that Peggy must be mistaken, and that no man could turn a deaf ear to such a tale of complicated distress, I determined to walk to the town with Mary the next morning, and request him to wait for the rent, and keep my secret, till my uncle's return.

"My repose was sweet; and, waking with the first dawn of day, I bounded to Mary's cottage. What charms do not a light heart spread over nature! Every bird that twittered in a bush, every flower that enlivened the hedge, seemed placed there to awaken me to rapture — yes; to rapture. The present moment was full fraught with happiness; and on futurity I bestowed not a thought, excepting to anticipate my success with the attorney.

"This man of the world, with rosy face and simpering features, received me politely, nay kindly; listened with complacency to my remonstrances, though he scarcely heeded Mary's tears. I did not then suspect, that my eloquence was in my complexion, the blush of seventeen, or that, in a world where humanity to women is the characteristic of advancing civilization, the beauty of a young girl was so much more interesting than the distress of an old one. Pressing my hand, he promised to let Peggy remain in the house as long as I wished. — I more than returned the pressure — I was so grateful and so happy. Emboldened by my innocent warmth, he then kissed me — and I did not draw back — I took it for a kiss of charity.

"Gay as a lark, I went to dine at Mr. Venables'. I had previously obtained five shillings from my father, towards re-clothing the poor children of my care, and prevailed on my mother to take one of the girls into the house, whom I determined to teach to work and read.

"After dinner, when the younger part of the circle retired to the music room, I recounted with energy my tale; that is, I mentioned Peggy's distress, without hinting at the steps I had taken to relieve her. Miss Venables gave me half-a-crown; the heir five shillings; but George sat unmoved. I was cruelly distressed by the disappointment — I scarcely could remain on my chair; and, could I have got out of the room unperceived, I should have flown home, as if to run away from myself. After several vain attempts to rise, I leaned my head against the marble chimney-piece, and gazing on the evergreens that filled the fire-place, moralized on the vanity of human expectations; regardless of the company. I was roused by a gentle tap on my shoulder from behind Charlotte's chair. I turned my head, and George slid a guinea into my hand, putting his finger to his mouth, to enjoin me silence.

"What a revolution took place, not only in my train of thoughts, but feelings! I trembled with emotion — now, indeed, I was in love. Such delicacy too, to enhance his benevolence! I felt in my pocket every five minutes, only to feel the guinea; and its magic touch invested my hero with more than mortal beauty. My fancy had found a basis to erect its model of perfection on; and quickly went to work, with all the happy credulity of youth, to consider that heart as devoted to virtue, which had only obeyed a virtuous impulse. The bitter experience was yet to come, that has taught me how very distinct are the principles of virtue, from the casual feelings from which they germinate.

## CHAP. VIII.

"I HAVE perhaps dwelt too long on a circumstance, which is only of importance as it marks the progress of a deception that has been so fatal to my peace; and introduces to your notice a poor girl, whom, intending to serve, I led to ruin.[1] Still it is prob-

---

1 This sentence is mysterious as the novella stands in its fragmentary form. By "poor girl," Wollstonecraft likely refers to Molly, Peggy's daughter, whom she mentions in the previous chapter, and who accompanies Maria to London, according to the first paragraph of the next chapter. These hints, considered in light of the phrase that ends Chapter IX ("what were my feelings at a discovery I made respecting Peggy") and the context in which it occurs, suggest that Venables took sexual advantage of the girl.

able that I was not entirely the victim of mistake; and that your father, gradually fashioned by the world, did not quickly become what I hesitate to call him — out of respect to my daughter.

"But, to hasten to the more busy scenes of my life. Mr. Venables and my mother died the same summer; and, wholly engrossed by my attention to her, I thought of little else. The neglect of her darling, my brother Robert, had a violent effect on her weakened mind; for, though boys may be reckoned the pillars of the house without doors, girls are often the only comfort within. They but too frequently waste their health and spirits attending a dying parent, who leaves them in comparative poverty. After closing, with filial piety, a father's eyes, they are chased from the paternal roof, to make room for the first-born, the son, who is to carry the empty family-name down to posterity; though, occupied with his own pleasures, he scarcely thought of discharging, in the decline of his parent's life, the debt contracted in his childhood. My mother's conduct led me to make these reflections. Great as was the fatigue I endured, and the affection my unceasing solicitude evinced, of which my mother seemed perfectly sensible, still, when my brother, whom I could hardly persuade to remain a quarter of an hour in her chamber, was with her alone, a short time before her death, she gave him a little hoard, which she had been some years accumulating.

"During my mother's illness, I was obliged to manage my father's temper, who, from the lingering nature of her malady, began to imagine that it was merely fancy.[1] At this period, an artful kind of upper servant attracted my father's attention, and the neighbours made many remarks on the finery, not honestly got, exhibited at evening service. But I was too much occupied with my mother to observe any change in her dress or behaviour, or to listen to the whisper of scandal.

"I shall not dwell on the death-bed scene, lively as is the remembrance, or on the emotion produced by the last grasp of my mother's cold hand; when blessing me, she added, 'A little patience, and all will be over!' Ah! my child, how often have those

---

1 In *Mary*, the protagonist's father harbours the same suspicion about her sick mother. Through the repetition of this scenario, Wollstonecraft seems to protest the dismissive response to women's illnesses as imagined or mental, rather than physical.

words rung mournfully in my ears — and I have exclaimed — 'A little more patience, and I too shall be at rest!'[1]

"My father was violently affected by her death, recollected instances of his unkindness, and wept like a child.

"My mother had solemnly recommended my sisters to my care, and bid me be a mother to them. They, indeed, became more dear to me as they became more forlorn; for, during my mother's illness, I discovered the ruined state of my father's circumstances, and that he had only been able to keep up appearances, by the sums which he borrowed of my uncle.

"My[2] father's grief, and consequent tenderness to his children, quickly abated, the house grew still more gloomy or riotous; and my refuge from care was again at Mr. Venables'; the young 'squire having taken his father's place, and allowing, for the present, his sister to preside at his table. George, though dissatisfied with his portion of the fortune, which had till lately been all in trade, visited the family as usual. He was now full of speculations in trade, and his brow became clouded by care. He seemed to relax in his attention to me, when the presence of my uncle gave a new turn to his behaviour. I was too unsuspecting, too disinterested, to trace these changes to their source.

My home every day became more and more disagreeable to me; my liberty was unnecessarily abridged, and my books, on the pretext that they made me idle, taken from me. My father's mistress was with child, and he, doating on her, allowed or overlooked her vulgar manner of tyrannizing over us. I was indignant, especially when I saw her endeavouring to attract, shall I say seduce? my younger brother. By allowing women but one way of rising in the world, the fostering the libertinism of men, society

---

1   In *Memoirs*, Godwin reports, "The last words her [Wollstonecraft's] mother ever uttered were, 'A little patience, and all will be over!' and these words are repeatedly referred to by Mary in the course of her writings" (28). Hauntingly, Wollstonecraft's own last written words may have been very similar; according to Todd in the *Letters*, they were, "I must have a little patience" (437), although Wollstonecraft referred to her anticipation of the safe delivery of her baby, not of death.

2   In the source text, this is the last paragraph that Wollstonecraft introduces with quotation marks, even though Maria's written narrative continues after this paragraph and into the subsequent volume. As in Jemima's narrative, she does not use closing quotation marks after paragraphs that precede words uttered by the same speaker, a practice that I replicate here.

makes monsters of them, and then their ignoble vices are brought forward as a proof of inferiority of intellect.[1]

The wearisomeness of my situation can scarcely be described. Though my life had not passed in the most even tenour with my mother, it was paradise to that I was destined to endure with my father's mistress, jealous of her illegitimate authority. My father's former occasional tenderness, in spite of his violence of temper, had been soothing to me; but now he only met me with reproofs or portentous frowns. The house-keeper, as she was now termed, was the vulgar despot of the family; and assuming the new character of a fine lady, she could never forgive the contempt which was sometimes visible in my countenance, when she uttered with pomposity her bad English, or affected to be well bred.

To my uncle I ventured to open my heart; and he, with his wonted benevolence, began to consider in what manner he could extricate me out of my present irksome situation. In spite of his own disappointment, or, most probably, actuated by the feelings that had been petrified, not cooled, in all their sanguine fervour, like a boiling torrent of lava suddenly dashing into the sea, he thought a marriage of mutual inclination (would envious stars permit it) the only chance for happiness in this disastrous world. George Venables had the reputation of being attentive to business, and my father's example gave great weight to this circumstance; for habits of order in business would, he conceived, extend to the regulation of the affections in domestic life. George seldom spoke in my uncle's company, except to utter a short, judicious question, or to make a pertinent remark, with all due deference to his superior judgment; so that my uncle seldom left his company without observing, that the young man had more in him than people supposed.

In this opinion he was not singular; yet, believe me, and I am not swayed by resentment, these speeches so justly poized, this silent deference, when the animal spirits of other young people were throwing off youthful ebullitions, were not the effect of

---

1   In *Rights of Woman*, Wollstonecraft links female vice with the dearth of women's education and power when she states,

Women ought to endeavour to purify their heart; but can they do so when their uncultivated understandings make them entirely dependent on their senses for employment and amusement, when no noble pursuit sets them above the little vanities of the day, or enables them to curb the wild emotions that agitate a reed over which every passing breeze has power? (54)

thought or humility, but sheer barrenness of mind, and want of imagination. A colt of mettle will curvet and shew his paces. Yes; my dear girl, these prudent young men want all the fire necessary to ferment their faculties, and are characterized as wise, only because they are not foolish. It is true, that George was by no means so great a favourite of mine as during the first year of our acquaintance; still, as he often coincided in opinion with me, and echoed my sentiments; and having myself no other attachment, I heard with pleasure my uncle's proposal; but thought more of obtaining my freedom, than of my lover. But, when George, seemingly anxious for my happiness, pressed me to quit my present painful situation, my heart swelled with gratitude — I knew not that my uncle had promised him five thousand pounds.

Had this truly generous man mentioned his intention to me, I should have insisted on a thousand pounds being settled on each of my sisters; George would have contested; I should have seen his selfish soul; and — gracious God! have been spared the misery of discovering, when too late, that I was united to a heartless, unprincipled wretch. All my schemes of usefulness would not then have been blasted. The tenderness of my heart would not have heated my imagination with visions of the ineffable delight of happy love; nor would the sweet duty of a mother have been so cruelly interrupted.

But I must not suffer the fortitude I have so hardly acquired, to be undermined by unavailing regret. Let me hasten forward to describe the turbid stream in which I had to wade — but let me exultingly declare that it is passed — my soul holds fellowship with him no more. He cut the Gordian knot,[1] which my principles, mistaken ones, respected; he dissolved the tie, the fetters rather, that ate into my very vitals — and I should rejoice, conscious that my mind is freed, though confined in hell itself; the only place that even fancy can imagine more dreadful than my present abode.

These varying emotions will not allow me to proceed. I heave sigh after sigh; yet my heart is still oppressed. For what am I reserved? Why was I not born a man, or why was I born at all?

END OF VOL. I.

---

1   In Phrygian (or modern-day Turkish) legend, the Gordian knot was impossible to untie, but it was overcome when Alexander the Great (356-23 BCE) cut through it with his sword. The phrase "Gordian knot" usually signifies an intricate and unsolvable problem.

THE

WRONGS OF WOMAN:

OR,

MARIA.

A FRAGMENT.

IN TWO VOLUMES.

-----------------------

VOL. II.

POSTHUMOUS WORKS

OF

MARY WOLLSTONECRAFT GODWIN.

VOL. II.

POSTHUMOUS WORKS

OF THE

AUTHOR

OF *A*

*VINDICATION OF THE RIGHTS OF WOMAN.*

IN FOUR VOLUMES.

------------------------

VOL. II.

------------------------

*LONDON:*
PRINTED FOR J. JOHNSON, NO. 72, ST. PAUL'S
CHURCH-YARD; AND G. G. AND J. ROBINSON,
PATERNOSTER-ROW.
1798

*WRONGS*

OF

WOMAN.

------------------------

### CHAP. IX.

"I RESUME my pen to fly from thought. I was married; and we hastened to London. I had purposed taking one of my sisters with me; for a strong motive for marrying, was the desire of having a home at which I could receive them, now their own grew so uncomfortable, as not to deserve the cheering appellation. An objection was made to her accompanying me, that appeared plausible; and I reluctantly acquiesced. I was however willingly allowed to take with me Molly, poor Peggy's daughter. London and preferment, are ideas commonly associated in the country; and, as blooming as May, she bade adieu to Peggy with weeping eyes. I did not even feel hurt at the refusal in relation to my sister, till hearing what my uncle had done for me, I had the simplicity to request, speaking with warmth of their situation, that he would give them a thousand pounds a-piece, which seemed to me but justice. He asked me, giving me a kiss, 'If I had lost my senses?' I started back, as if I had found a wasp in a rose-bush. I expostulated. He sneered; and the demon of discord entered our paradise, to poison with his pestiferous breath every opening joy.

"I had sometimes observed defects in my husband's understanding; but, led astray by a prevailing opinion, that goodness of disposition is of the first importance in the relative situations of life, in proportion as I perceived the narrowness of his understanding, fancy enlarged the boundary of his heart. Fatal error! How quickly is the so much vaunted milkiness of nature turned into gall, by an intercourse with the world, if more generous juices do not sustain the vital source of virtue![1]

---

1 In this sentence, Wollstonecraft develops a theory of personality that mixes colloquial terminology with ancient medical ideas. In her use of the term "milky," she echoes a common eighteenth-century description of a soft, gentle and even weak nature, as the term is defined with reference to personality in the *OED*. "Gall," in the second definition of the first entry of the word in the *OED*, signifies bitterness, a *(continued)*

"One trait in my character was extreme credulity; but, when my eyes were once opened, I saw but too clearly all I had before overlooked. My husband was sunk in my esteem; still there are youthful emotions, which, for a while, fill up the chasm of love and friendship. Besides, it required some time to enable me to see his whole character in a just light, or rather to allow it to become fixed. While circumstances were ripening my faculties, and cultivating my taste, commerce and gross relaxations were shutting his against any possibility of improvement, till, by stifling every spark of virtue in himself, he began to imagine that it no where existed.

"Do not let me lead you astray, my child, I do not mean to assert, that any human being is entirely incapable of feeling the generous emotions, which are the foundation of every true principle of virtue; but they are frequently, I fear, so feeble, that, like the inflammable quality which more or less lurks in all bodies,[1] they often lie for ever dormant; the circumstances never occurring, necessary to call them into action.

"I discovered however by chance, that, in consequence of some losses in trade, the natural effect of his gambling desire to start suddenly into riches, the five thousand pounds given me by my uncle, had been paid very opportunely. This discovery, strange as you may think the assertion, gave me pleasure; my

---

figurative use of the word that refers to the bitter substance secreted by the liver; yet, "gall" is also another word for "bile," two kinds of which—yellow and black—are "humours" in the ancient medical theory of personality and physical constitution. See p. 96, note 1 for more information about the humours. Wollstonecraft extends this figurative and medical meditation on the bodily liquids that constitute human nature by considering the "more generous juices" that might "sustain the vital source of virtue," as if virtue were itself the product of the body's moisture balance.

1  In the phrase, "the inflammable quality which more or less lurks in all bodies," Wollstonecraft establishes her knowledge about one of the most cutting-edge scientific endeavours of her time: experimentation with gases, such as hydrogen (often called "inflammable air" in the late eighteenth century) and oxygen. Her probable source for this knowledge is *Experiments on the Generation of Air from Water; To Which are Prefixed, Experiments Relating to the Decomposition of Dephlogisticated and Inflammable Air* (1793), by Joseph Priestley (1733-1804), who was also the likely source for her ideas about associationism via his influential text, *Hartley's Theory of the Human Mind*. Both texts were published by Wollstonecraft's good friend, colleague, and radical publisher, Joseph Johnson.

husband's embarrassments endeared him to me. I was glad to find an excuse for his conduct to my sisters, and my mind became calmer.

"My uncle introduced me to some literary society; and the theatres were a never-failing source of amusement to me. My delighted eye followed Mrs. Siddons, when, with dignified delicacy, she played Calista; and I involuntarily repeated after her, in the same tone, and with a long-drawn sigh,

'Hearts like our's were pair'd — not match'd.'[1]

"These were, at first, spontaneous emotions, though, becoming acquainted with men of wit and polished manners, I could not sometimes help regretting my early marriage; and that, in my haste to escape from a temporary dependence, and expand my newly fledged wings, in an unknown sky, I had been caught in a trap, and caged for life. Still the novelty of London, and the attentive fondness of my husband, for he had some personal regard for me, made several months glide away. Yet, not forgetting the situation of my sisters, who were still very young, I prevailed on my uncle to settle a thousand pounds on each; and to place them in

---

1 Sarah Siddons (née Kemble) (1755-1831) was one of the most famous British actresses of her day. Born in Wales, she took the English stage by storm, especially with her interpretation of Calista, a figure of female strength and pathos in Thomas Rowe's (1674-1718) *The Fair Penitent* (first performed in 1703). Wollstonecraft's invocation of Calista would doubtlessly have reminded her Romantic-era audience of the character's famous monologue, which resounds with the themes of this novella:

How hard is the condition of our sex,
Thro' ev'ry state of life the slaves of man?
In all the dear delightful days of youth,
A rigid father dictates to our wills,
And deals our pleasures with a scanty hand:
To his the tyrant husband's reign succeeds;
Proud with opinion of superior reason,
He holds domestic bus'ness and devotion
All we are capable to know, and shuts us,
Like cloister'd idiots, from the world's acquaintance,
And all the joys of freedom. Wherefor are we
Born with high souls, but to assert ourselves,
Shake off this vile obedience they exact,
And claim an equal empire o'er the world! (III, i, 40-53)

At the end of this paragraph, Wollstonecraft misquotes Calista's lines, "I tell thee, *Altamont,* / Such hearts as ours were never pair'd above, / Ill-suited to each other; join'd, not match'd" (II, i, 72-74).

a school near town, where I could frequently visit, as well as have them at home with me.

"I now tried to improve my husband's taste, but we had few subjects in common; indeed he soon appeared to have little relish for my society, unless he was hinting to me the use he could make of my uncle's wealth. When we had company, I was disgusted by an ostentatious display of riches, and I have often quitted the room, to avoid listening to exaggerated tales of money obtained by lucky hits.

"With all my attention and affectionate interest, I perceived that I could not become the friend or confident of my husband. Every thing I learned relative to his affairs I gathered up by accident; and I vainly endeavoured to establish, at our fire-side, that social converse, which often renders people of different characters dear to each other. Returning from the theatre, or any amusing party, I frequently began to relate what I had seen and highly relished; but with sullen taciturnity he soon silenced me. I seemed therefore gradually to lose, in his society, the soul, the energies of which had just been in action. To such a degree, in fact, did his cold, reserved manner affect me, that, after spending some days with him alone, I have imagined myself the most stupid creature in the world, till the abilities of some casual visitor convinced me that I had some dormant animation, and sentiments above the dust in which I had been groveling. The very countenance of my husband changed; his complexion became sallow, and all the charms of youth were vanishing with its vivacity.

"I give you one view of the subject; but these experiments and alterations took up the space of five years; during which period, I had most reluctantly extorted several sums from my uncle, to save my husband, to use his own words, from destruction. At first it was to prevent bills being noted, to the injury of his credit; then to bail him; and afterwards to prevent an execution from entering the house. I began at last to conclude, that he would have made more exertions of his own to extricate himself, had he not relied on mine, cruel as was the task he imposed on me; and I firmly determined that I would make use of no more pretexts.

"From the moment I pronounced this determination, indifference on his part was changed into rudeness, or something worse.

"He now seldom dined at home, and continually returned at a late hour, drunk, to bed. I retired to another apartment; I was glad, I own, to escape from his; for personal intimacy without affection, seemed, to me the most degrading, as well as the most painful state in which a woman of any taste, not to speak of the peculiar delicacy of fostered sensibility, could be placed. But my husband's fondness for women was of the grossest kind, and imagination was so wholly out of the question, as to render his indulgences of this sort entirely promiscuous, and of the most brutal nature. My health suffered, before my heart was entirely estranged by the loathsome information; could I then have returned to his sullied arms, but as a victim to the prejudices of mankind, who have made women the property of their husbands?[1] I discovered even, by his conversation, when intoxicated, that his favourites were wantons of the lowest class, who could by their vulgar, indecent mirth, which he called nature, rouse his sluggish spirits. Meretricious ornaments and manners were necessary to attract his attention. He seldom looked twice at a modest woman, and sat silent in their company; and the charms of youth and beauty had not the slightest effect on his senses, unless the possessors were initiated in vice. His intimacy with profligate women, and his habits of thinking, gave him a contempt for female endowments; and he would repeat, when wine had loosed his tongue, most of the common-place sarcasms levelled at them, by men who do not allow them to have minds, because mind would be an impediment to gross enjoyment. Men who are inferior to their fellow men, are always most anxious to establish their superiority over women. But where are these reflections leading me?

"Women who have lost their husband's affection, are justly reproved for neglecting their persons, and not taking the same pains to keep, as to gain a heart; but who thinks of giving the same advice to men, though women are continually stigmatized for being attached to fops; and from the nature of their education, are more susceptible of disgust? Yet why a woman should be expected to endure a sloven, with more patience than a man, and magnanimously to govern herself, I cannot conceive; unless it be

---

1 Sir William Blackstone (1723-80), the most influential commentator on the English legal system in the eighteenth century, summarizes the laws of coverture, which remained in effect until well into the nineteenth century: "By marriage, the husband and wife are one person in law: that is, the very being or legal existence of the woman is suspended during the marriage, or at least is incorporated and consolidated into that of the husband" (77).

supposed arrogant in her to look for respect as well as a maintenance. It is not easy to be pleased, because, after promising to love, in different circumstances, we are told that it is our duty. I cannot, I am sure (though, when attending the sick, I never felt disgust) forget my own sensations, when rising with health and spirit, and after scenting the sweet morning, I have met my husband at the breakfast table. The active attention I had been giving to domestic regulations, which were generally settled before he rose, or a walk, gave a glow to my countenance, that contrasted with his squallid appearance. The squeamishness of stomach alone, produced by the last night's intemperance, which he took no pains to conceal, destroyed my appetite. I think I now see him lolling in an arm-chair, in a dirty powdering gown,[1] soiled linen, ungartered stockings, and tangled hair, yawning and stretching himself. The newspaper was immediately called for, if not brought in on the tea-board, from which he would scarcely lift his eyes while I poured out the tea, excepting to ask for some brandy to put into it, or to declare that he could not eat. In answer to any question, in his best humour, it was a drawling 'What do you say, child?' But if I demanded money for the house expences, which I put off till the last moment, his customary reply, often prefaced with an oath, was, 'Do you think me, madam, made of money?' — The butcher, the baker, must wait; and, what was worse, I was often obliged to witness his surly dismission of tradesmen, who were in want of their money, and whom I sometimes paid with the presents my uncle gave me for my own use.

"At this juncture my father's mistress, by terrifying his conscience, prevailed on him to marry her; he was already become a methodist; and my brother, who now practised for himself, had discovered a flaw in the settlement made on my mother's children, which set it aside, and he allowed my father, whose distress made him submit to any thing, a tithe of his own, or rather our fortune.

"My sisters had left school, but were unable to endure home, which my father's wife rendered as disagreeable as possible, to get rid of girls whom she regarded as spies on her conduct. They were accomplished, yet you can (may you never be reduced to the same destitute state!) scarcely conceive the trouble I had to place them in the situation of governesses, the only one in which even

---

1 A "powdering gown" was a protective cover placed over the clothes while powdering the hair, or wig.

a well-educated woman, with more than ordinary talents, can struggle for a subsistence; and even this is a dependence next to menial.[1] Is it then surprising, that so many forlorn women, with human passions and feelings, take refuge in infamy? Alone in large mansions, I say alone, because they had no companions with whom they could converse on equal terms, or from whom they could expect the endearments of affection, they grew melancholy, and the sound of joy made them sad; and the youngest, having a more delicate frame, fell into a decline. It was with great difficulty that I, who now almost supported the house by loans from my uncle, could prevail on the *master* of it, to allow her a room to die in. I watched her sick bed for some months, and then closed her eyes, gentle spirit! for ever. She was pretty, with very engaging manners; yet had never an opportunity to marry, excepting to a very old man. She had abilities sufficient to have shone in any profession, had there been any professions for women, though she shrunk at the name of milliner or mantua-maker as degrading to a gentlewoman.[2] I would not term this

---

1 In *Thoughts on the Education of Daughters,* Wollstonecraft describes one of the only careers open to middle-class woman in the Romantic period: A governess to young ladies is ... disagreeable. It is ten to one if they meet with a reasonable mother; and if she is not so, she will be continually finding fault to prove she is not ignorant, and be displeased if her pupils do not improve, but angry if the proper methods are taken to make them do so. The children treat them with disrespect, and often with insolence. In the mean time life glides away. (72)
   See p. 81, note 1 for more information on Wollstonecraft's experience as a governess in Ireland.

2 The issue of the scarcity of good jobs available to women was a major theme in Romantic-era feminist writing. Although Maria's sister rejects the very possibility of working as a "milliner or mantua-maker" (that is, a dress-maker) because she thinks these jobs below her class, even they were difficult for women to obtain, as Priscilla Wakefield (1751-1832) laments in *Reflections on the Present Condition of the Female Sex; With Suggestions for its Improvement* (1798):
   it is a subject of great regret, that this inequality [of good jobs for both sexes] should prevail, even where an equal share of skill and application are exerted. Male-stay-makers, mantua-makers, and hairdressers are better paid than female artists of the same professions; but surely it will never be urged as an apology for this disproportion, that women are not as capable of making stays, gowns, dressing hair, and similar arts, as men. (152)

feeling false pride to any one but you, my child, whom I fondly hope to see (yes; I will indulge the hope for a moment!) possessed of that energy of character which gives dignity to any station; and with that clear, firm spirit that will enable you to choose a situation for yourself, or submit to be classed in the lowest, if it be the only one in which you can be the mistress of your own actions.

"Soon after the death of my sister, an incident occurred, to prove to me that the heart of a libertine is dead to natural affection; and to convince me, that the being who has appeared all tenderness, to gratify a selfish passion, is as regardless of the innocent fruit of it, as of the object, when the fit is over. I had casually observed an old, mean-looking woman, who called on my husband every two or three months to receive some money. One day entering the passage of his little counting-house, as she was going out, I heard her say, 'The child is very weak; she cannot live long, she will soon die out of your way, so you need not grudge her a little physic.'

"'So much the better,' he replied, 'and pray mind your own business, good woman.'

"I was struck by his unfeeling, inhuman tone of voice, and drew back, determined when the woman came again, to try to speak to her, not out of curiosity, I had heard enough, but with the hope of being useful to a poor, outcast girl.

"A month or two elapsed before I saw this woman again; and then she had a child in her hand that tottered along, scarcely able to sustain her own weight. They were going away, to return at the hour Mr. Venables was expected; he was now from home. I desired the woman to walk into the parlour. She hesitated, yet obeyed. I assured her that I should not mention to my husband (the word seemed to weigh on my respiration), that I had seen her, or his child. The woman stared at me with astonishment; and I turned my eyes on the squalid object [that accompanied her.][1] She could hardly support herself, her complexion was sallow, and her eyes inflamed, with an indescribable look of cunning, mixed with the wrinkles produced by the peevishness of pain.

"'Poor child!' I exclaimed. 'Ah! you may well say poor child,' replied the woman. 'I brought her here to see whether he would have the heart to look at her, and not get some advice. I do not know what they deserve who nursed her. Why, her legs bent under her like a bow when she came to me, and she has never

---

1 These square brackets appear in the source text.

been well since; but, if they were no better paid than I am, it is not to be wondered at, sure enough.'

"On further enquiry I was informed, that this miserable spectacle was the daughter of a servant, a country girl, who caught Mr. Venables' eye, and whom he seduced. On his marriage he sent her away, her situation being too visible. After her delivery, she was thrown on the town; and died in an hospital within the year. The babe was sent to a parish-nurse, and afterwards to this woman, who did not seem much better; but what was to be expected from such a close bargain? She was only paid three shillings a week for board and washing.

"The woman begged me to give her some old clothes for the child, assuring me, that she was almost afraid to ask master for money to buy even a pair of shoes.

"I grew sick at heart. And, fearing Mr. Venables might enter, and oblige me to express my abhorrence, I hastily enquired where she lived, promised to pay her two shillings a week more, and to call on her in a day or two; putting a trifle into her hand as a proof of my good intention.

"If the state of this child affected me, what were my feelings at a discovery I made respecting Peggy —?[1]

## CHAP. X.

"MY father's situation was now so distressing, that I prevailed on my uncle to accompany me to visit him; and to lend me his assistance, to prevent the whole property of the family from becoming the prey of my brother's rapacity; for, to extricate himself out of present difficulties, my father was totally regardless of futurity. I took down with me some presents for my step-mother; it did not require an effort for me to treat her with civility, or to forget the past.

"This was the first time I had visited my native village, since my marriage. But with what different emotions did I return from the busy world, with a heavy weight of experience benumbing my imagination, to scenes, that whispered recollections of joy and hope most eloquently to my heart! The first scent of the wild flowers from the heath, thrilled through my veins, awakening every sense to pleasure. The icy hand of despair seemed to be

1 The manuscript is imperfect here. An episode seems to have been intended, which was never committed to paper. EDITOR. [Godwin's note]

removed from my bosom; and — forgetting my husband — the nurtured visions of a romantic mind, bursting on me with all their original wildness and gay exuberance, were again hailed as sweet realities. I forgot, with equal facility, that I ever felt sorrow, or knew care in the country; while a transient rainbow stole athwart the cloudy sky of despondency. The picturesque form of several favourite trees, and the porches of rude cottages, with their smiling hedges, were recognized with the gladsome playfulness of childish vivacity. I could have kissed the chickens that pecked on the common; and longed to pat the cows, and frolic with the dogs that sported on it. I gazed with delight on the windmill, and thought it lucky that it should be in motion, at the moment I passed by; and entering the dear green-lane, which led directly to the village, the sound of the well-known rookery gave that sentimental tinge to the varying sensations of my active soul, which only served to heighten the lustre of the luxuriant scenery. But, spying, as I advanced, the spire, peeping over the withered tops of the aged elms that composed the rookery, my thoughts flew immediately to the church-yard, and tears of affection, such was the effect of my imagination, bedewed my mother's grave! Sorrow gave place to devotional feelings. I wandered through the church in fancy, as I used sometimes to do on a Saturday evening. I recollected with what fervour I addressed the God of my youth: and once more with rapturous love looked above my sorrows to the Father of nature. I pause — feeling forcibly all the emotions I am describing; and (reminded, as I register my sorrows, of the sublime calm I have felt, when in some tremendous solitude, my soul rested on itself, and seemed to fill the universe) I insensibly breathe soft, hushing every wayward emotion, as if fearing to sully with a sigh, a contentment so extatic.

"Having settled my fathers affairs, and, by my exertions in his favour, made my brother my sworn foe, I returned to London. My husband's conduct was now changed; I had during my absence, received several affectionate, penitential letters from him; and he seemed on my arrival, to wish by his behaviour to prove his sincerity. I could not then conceive why he acted thus; and, when the suspicion darted into my head, that it might arise from observing my increasing influence with my uncle, I almost despised myself for imagining that such a degree of debasing selfishness could exist.

"He became, unaccountable as was the change, tender and attentive; and, attacking my weak side, made a confession of his follies, and lamented the embarrassments in which I, who merited a far different fate, might be involved. He besought me to aid him with my counsel, praised my understanding, and appealed to the tenderness of my heart.

"This conduct only inspired me with compassion. I wished to be his friend; but love had spread his rosy pinions, and fled far, far away; and had not (like some exquisite perfumes, the fine spirit of which is continually mingling with the air) left a fragrance behind, to mark where he had shook his wings. My husband's renewed caresses then became hateful to me; his brutality was tolerable, compared to his distasteful fondness. Still, compassion, and the fear of insulting his supposed feelings, by a want of sympathy, made me dissemble, and do violence to my delicacy. What a task!

"Those who support a system of what I term false refinement, and will not allow [a][1] great part of love in the female, as well as male breast, to spring in some respects involuntarily, may not admit that charms are as necessary to feed the passion, as virtues to convert the mellowing spirit into friendship. To such observers I have nothing to say, any more than to the moralists, who insist that women ought to, and can love their husbands, because it is their duty. To you, my child, I may add, with a heart tremblingly alive to your future conduct, some observations, dictated by my present feelings, on calmly reviewing this period of my life. When novelists or moralists praise as a virtue, a woman's coldness of constitution, and want of passion; and make her yield to the ardour of her lover out of sheer compassion, or to promote a frigid plan of future comfort, I am disgusted. They may be good women, in the ordinary acceptation of the phrase, and do no harm; but they appear to me not to have those 'finely fashioned nerves,'[2] which render the senses exquisite. They may possess tenderness; but they want that fire of the imagination, which produces *active* sensibility, and *positive* virtue. How does the woman deserve to be characterized, who marries one man, with a heart and imagination devoted to another? Is she not an object of pity or contempt, when thus sacrilegiously violating the purity of her

---

1   I have inserted the indefinite article "a" in brackets here.
2   From Hannah More's (1745-1833) "Sensibility. A Poetic Epistle" (1782):
    Nor is the trembling temper more awake
    To every wound which misery can make,
    Than is the finely-fashion's nerve alive
    To every transport pleasure has to give. (ll. 111-14)

own feelings? Nay, it is as indelicate, when she is indifferent, unless she be constitutionally insensible; then indeed it is a mere affair of barter; and I have nothing to do with the secrets of trade. Yes; eagerly as I wish you to possess true rectitude of mind, and purity of affection, I must insist that a heartless conduct is the contrary of virtuous. Truth is the only basis of virtue; and we cannot, without depraving our minds, endeavour to please a lover or husband, but in proportion as he pleases us. Men, more effectually to enslave us, may inculcate this partial morality, and lose sight of virtue in subdividing it into the duties of particular stations; but let us not blush for nature without a cause!

"After these remarks, I am ashamed to own, that I was pregnant. The greatest sacrifice of my principles in my whole life, was the allowing my husband again to be familiar with my person, though to this cruel act of self-denial, when I wished the earth to open and swallow me, you owe your birth; and I the unutterable pleasure of being a mother. There was something of delicacy in my husband's bridal attentions; but now his tainted breath, pimpled face, and blood-shot eyes, were not more repugnant to my senses, than his gross manners, and loveless familiarity to my taste.

"A man would only be expected to maintain; yes, barely grant a subsistence, to a woman rendered odious by habitual intoxication; but who would expect him, or think it possible to love her? And unless 'youth, and genial years were flown,'[1] it would be thought equally unreasonable to insist, [under penalty of][2] forfeiting almost every thing reckoned valuable in life, that he should not love another: whilst woman, weak in reason, impotent in will, is required to moralize, sentimentalize herself to stone, and pine her life away, labouring to reform her embruted mate.

---

1 From "Song: For Ever Fortune, Wilt Thou Prove" (1750) by James Thomson:

> For ever Fortune wilt thou prove
> An unrelenting foe to love,
> And when we meet a mutual heart,
> Come in between, and bid us part:
>
> Bid us sigh on from day to day,
> And wish, and wish the soul away;
> Till youth and genial years are flown,
> And all the life of life is gone? (ll. 1-8)

2 These square brackets appear in the source text.

He may even spend in dissipation, and intemperance, the very intemperance which renders him so hateful, her property, and by stinting her expences, not permit her to beguile in society, a wearisome, joyless life; for over their mutual fortune she has no power, it must all pass through his hand. And if she be a mother, and in the present state of women, it is a great misfortune to be prevented from discharging the duties, and cultivating the affections of one, what has she not to endure? — But I have suffered the tenderness of one to lead me into reflections that I did not think of making, to interrupt my narrative — yet the full heart will overflow.

"Mr. Venables' embarrassments did not now endear him to me; still, anxious to befriend him, I endeavoured to prevail on him to retrench his expences; but he had always some plausible excuse to give, to justify his not following my advice. Humanity, compassion, and the interest produced by a habit of living together, made me try to relieve, and sympathize with him; but, when I recollected that I was bound to live with such a being for ever — my heart died within me; my desire of improvement became languid, and baleful, corroding melancholy took possession of my soul. Marriage had bastilled me for life.[1] I discovered in myself a capacity for the enjoyment of the various pleasures

---

1 According to the *OED*, the original meaning (since roughly 1340) of "bastille" as a noun is "A tower or bastion of a castle; a fortified tower; a small fortress," but at the time that Wollstonecraft penned this novella, the word would connote, first and foremost, what the *OED* gives as its third definition of the noun: "Name of the prison-fortress built in Paris in the 14th century, and destroyed in 1789." By the eighteenth century, the Bastille had become the symbol of the oppression of the poor and disenfranchised versus the excessive power and cruelty of the rulers of French society because the prison was believed to hold many innocent victims of vengeful aristocrats. On 14 July 1789, the Revolutionaries stormed it to free the inmates (of which there were very few), an act that marked the beginning of the French Revolution and is still celebrated yearly on the same date in France (on "Bastille Day") to recognize the establishment of modern French society. Wollstonecraft's use of the word "bastille" as a verb is not original; the *OED* reports that Edward Young (1683-1765) did the same in his verse *Night-Thoughts* in 1742. However, her usage is more suggestive than Young's because of its unique historical context (the novella was written during the French Revolution), which supports and intensifies the novella's context of marriage and the oppression of women.

existence affords; yet, fettered by the partial laws of society, this fair globe was to me an universal blank.[1]

"When I exhorted my husband to economy, I referred to himself. I was obliged to practise the most rigid, or contract debts, which I had too much reason to fear would never be paid. I despised this paltry privilege of a wife, which can only be of use to the vicious or inconsiderate, and determined not to increase the torrent that was bearing him down. I was then ignorant of the extent of his fraudulent speculations, whom I was bound to honour and obey.

"A woman neglected by her husband, or whose manners form a striking contrast with his, will always have men on the watch to soothe and flatter her. Besides, the forlorn state of a neglected woman, not destitute of personal charms, is particularly interesting, and rouses that species of pity, which is so near akin, it easily slides into love. A man of feeling thinks not of seducing, he is himself seduced by all the noblest emotions of his soul. He figures to himself all the sacrifices a woman of sensibility must make, and every situation in which his imagination places her, touches his heart, and fires his passions. Longing to take to his bosom the shorn lamb, and bid the drooping buds of hope revive, benevolence changes into passion: and should he then discover that he is beloved, honour binds him fast, though foreseeing that he may afterwards be obliged to pay severe damages to the man, who never appeared to value his wife's society, till he found that there was a chance of his being indemnified for the loss of it.

"Such are the partial laws enacted by men; for, only to lay a stress on the dependent state of a woman in the grand question of the comforts arising from the possession of property, she is [even in this article][2] much more injured by the loss of the husband's affection, than he by that of his wife; yet where is she,

---

1   While the phrase "universal blank" comes from Milton's *Paradise Lost*, Book III, l. 48, the sentiment of the sentence as a whole echoes Hamlet's famous speech in Act II, scene ii of Shakespeare's play:

   ... indeed it goes so heavily with my disposition that this goodly frame, the earth, seems to me a sterile promontory, this most excellent canopy, the air, look you, this brave o'erhanging firmament, this majestical roof fretted with golden fire, why, it appears no other thing to me than a foul and pestilent congregation of vapours. What a piece of work is a man! How noble in reason! . . .

   . . . . . . . . . . . . . . . . . . . . . . . . . . . . . . . . . . . . . . . . . . . . . . . . . . . . . . . .

   ... and yet, to me, what is this quintessence of dust? (ll. 280-84; 287)

2   The square brackets appear in the source text.

condemned to the solitude of a deserted home, to look for a compensation from the woman, who seduces him from her? She cannot drive an unfaithful husband from his house, nor separate, or tear, his children from him, however culpable he may be;[1] and he, still the master of his own fate, enjoys the smiles of a world, that would brand her with infamy, did she, seeking consolation, venture to retaliate.

"These remarks are not dictated by experience; but merely by the compassion I feel for many amiable women, the *out-laws* of the world. For myself, never encouraging any of the advances that were made to me, my lovers dropped off like the untimely shoots of spring. I did not even coquet with them; because I found, on examining myself, I could not coquet with a man without loving him a little; and I perceived that I should not be able to stop at the line of what are termed *innocent freedoms*, did I suffer any. My reserve was then the consequence of delicacy. Freedom of conduct has emancipated many women's minds; but my conduct has most rigidly been governed by my principles, till the improvement of my understanding has enabled me to discern the fallacy of prejudices at war with nature and reason.

"Shortly after the change I have mentioned in my husband's conduct, my uncle was compelled by his declining health, to seek the succour of a milder climate, and embark for Lisbon. He left his will in the hands of a friend, an eminent solicitor; he had previously questioned me relative to my situation and state of mind, and declared very freely, that he could place no reliance on the stability of my husband's professions. He had been deceived in the unfolding of his character; he now thought it fixed in a train of actions that would inevitably lead to ruin and disgrace.

"The evening before his departure, which we spent alone together, he folded me to his heart, uttering the endearing appellation of 'child.' — My more than father! why was I not permitted

---

1   Until the Victorian period, English women had almost no rights when it came to divorce (and, even then, divorce laws pertained only to upper-class unions). Husbands could end marriages that were "infertile or otherwise inconvenient," and adultery was a common complaint, but women could not sue for divorce for the same reason because the law was aimed at protecting a man's right to legitimate heirs—and, unlike a wife's adultery, a husband's could not introduce illegitimate heirs into the household. A wife had to complain of cruelty, incest, or some other serious crime to obtain a divorce. From the early 1800s to 1857, the period of parliamentary divorce in England, only four women succeeded in obtaining a divorce through these means (Burton 58).

to perform the last duties of one, and smooth the pillow of death? He seemed by his manner to be convinced that he should never see me more; yet requested me, most earnestly, to come to him, should I be obliged to leave my husband. He had before expressed his sorrow at hearing of my pregnancy, having determined to prevail on me to accompany him, till I informed him of that circumstance. He expressed himself unfeignedly sorry that any new tie should bind me to a man whom he thought so incapable of estimating my value; such was the kind language of affection.

"I must repeat his own words; they made an indelible impression on my mind:

"'[1]The marriage state is certainly that in which women, generally speaking, can be most useful; but I am far from thinking that a woman, once married, ought to consider the engagement as indissoluble (especially if there be no children to reward her for sacrificing her feelings) in case her husband merits neither her love, nor esteem. Esteem will often supply the place of love; and prevent a woman from being wretched, though it may not make her happy. The magnitude of a sacrifice ought always to bear some proportion to the utility in view; and for a woman to live with a man, for whom she can cherish neither affection nor esteem, or even be of any use to him, excepting in the light of a house-keeper, is an abjectness of condition, the enduring of which no concurrence of circumstances can ever make a duty in the sight of God or just men. If indeed she submits to it merely to be maintained in idleness, she has no right to complain bitterly of her fate; or to act, as a person of independent character might, as if she had a title to disregard general rules.

"'[']²But the misfortune is, that many women only submit in appearance, and forfeit their own respect to secure their reputation in the world. The situation of a woman separated from her husband, is undoubtedly very different from that of a man who

---

1 The source text marks off this long passage—Maria's reportage of her uncle's words—with double quotation marks outside of single quotation marks at the start of the passage, and single quotation marks at the start of each line to show that her uncle's words continue. Since the typesetting of the present edition cannot match the original, I have omitted the single quotation marks at the beginning of each line, but I keep all other features of the source text.

2 The source text has only double quotation marks here to mark Maria's words and omits the single quotation marks that mark her uncle's words in the preceding paragraph, even though this passage continues to be composed of them. I have added a single quotation mark in brackets.

has left his wife. He, with lordly dignity, has shaken of[f]¹ a clog; and the allowing her food and raiment, is thought sufficient to secure his reputation from taint. And, should she have been inconsiderate, he will be celebrated for his generosity and forbearance. Such is the respect paid to the master-key of property! A woman, on the contrary, resigning what is termed her natural protector (though he never was so, but in name) is despised and shunned, for asserting the independence of mind distinctive of a rational being, and spurning at slavery.'

"During the remainder of the evening, my uncle's tenderness led him frequently to revert to the subject, and utter, with increasing warmth, sentiments to the same purport. At length it was necessary to say 'Farewell!' — and we parted — gracious God! to meet no more.

## CHAP. XI.

"A GENTLEMAN of large fortune and of polished manners, had lately visited very frequently at our house, and treated me, if possible, with more respect than Mr. Venables paid him; my pregnancy was not yet visible, his society was a great relief to me, as I had for some time past, to avoid expence, confined myself very much at home. I ever disdained unnecessary, perhaps even prudent concealments; and my husband, with great ease, discovered the amount of my uncle's parting present. A copy of a writ² was the stale pretext to extort it from me; and I had soon reason to believe that it was fabricated for the purpose. I acknowledge my folly in thus suffering myself to be continually imposed on. I had adhered to my resolution not to apply to my uncle, on the part of my husband, any more; yet, when I had received a sum sufficient to supply my own wants, and to enable me to pursue a plan I had in view, to settle my younger brother in a respectable employment, I allowed myself to be duped by Mr. Venables' shallow pretences, and hypocritical professions.

"Thus did he pillage me and my family, thus frustrate all my plans of usefulness. Yet this was the man I was bound to respect

---

1 The source text reads "of," but it should be "off."
2 The third definition of the word "writ" in the *OED* explains the term in a legal context: "b. *Law*. A written command, precept, or formal order issued by a court in the name of the sovereign, state, or other competent legal authority, directing or enjoining the person or persons to whom it is addressed to do or refrain from doing some act specified therein."

and esteem: as if respect and esteem depended on an arbitrary will of our own! But a wife being as much a man's property as his horse, or his ass, she has nothing she can call her own. He may use any means to get at what the law considers as his, the moment his wife is in possession of it, even to the forcing of a lock, as Mr. Venables did, to search for notes in my writing-desk — and all this is done with a show of equity, because, forsooth, he is responsible for her maintenance.

"The tender mother cannot *lawfully* snatch from the gripe of the gambling spendthrift, or beastly drunkard, unmindful of his offspring, the fortune which falls to her by chance; or (so flagrant is the injustice) what she earns by her own exertions. No; he can rob her with impunity, even to waste publicly on a courtezan; and the laws of her country — if women have a country[1] — afford her no protection or redress from the oppressor, unless she have the plea of bodily fear; yet how many ways are there of goading the soul almost to madness, equally unmanly, though not so mean? When such laws were framed, should not impartial lawgivers have first decreed, in the style of a great assembly, who recognized the existence of an *être suprême*,[2] to fix the national belief, that the husband should always be wiser and more virtuous than his wife, in order to entitle him, with a show of justice, to keep this idiot, or perpetual minor, for ever in bondage. But I must have done — on this subject, my indignation continually runs away with me.

"The company of the gentleman I have already mentioned, who had a general acquaintance with literature and subjects of taste, was grateful to me; my countenance brightened up as he approached, and I unaffectedly expressed the pleasure I felt. The amusement his conversation afforded me, made it easy to comply with my husband's request, to endeavour to render our house agreeable to him.

---

1   The Declaration of the Rights of Man by the French Revolutionary Assembly extended French citizenship only to men, rendering French women essentially countryless. See p. 34 for more information on Wollstonecraft's references to the new French government, about which she was vastly informed as the author of *An Historical and Moral View of the French Revolution* (1794).

2   Maximilien Robespierre (1758-94), Jacobin leader and the driving force behind the Reign of Terror, established Deism, or the Cult of the Supreme Being (*être suprême*), in 1794 to replace the Cult of Reason as the official religion of the French nation during the Revolution.

"His attentions became more pointed; but, as I was not of the number of women, whose virtue, as it is termed, immediately takes alarm, endeavoured, rather by raillery than serious expostulation, to give a different turn to his conversation. He assumed a new mode of attack, and I was, for a while, the dupe of his pretended friendship.

"I had, merely in the style of *badinage*,[1] boasted of my conquest, and repeated his lover-like compliments to my husband. But he begged me, for God's sake, not to affront his friend, or I should destroy all his projects, and be his ruin. Had I had more affection for my husband, I should have expressed my contempt of this time-serving politeness: now I imagined that I only felt pity; yet it would have puzzled a casuist to point out in what the exact difference consisted.

"This friend began now, in confidence, to discover to me the real state of my husband's affairs. 'Necessity,' said Mr. S——; why should I reveal his name? for he affected to palliate the conduct he could not excuse, 'had led him to take such steps, by accommodation bills,[2] buying goods on credit, to sell them for ready money, and similar transactions, that his character in the commercial world was gone. He was considered,' he added, lowering his voice, 'on 'Change[3] as a swindler.'

"I felt at that moment the first maternal pang. Aware of the evils my sex have to struggle with, I still wished, for my own consolation, to be the mother of a daughter; and I could not bear to think, that the *sins* of her father's entailed disgrace, should be added to the ills to which woman is heir.

"So completely was I deceived by these shows of friendship (nay, I believe, according to his interpretation, Mr. S—— really was my friend) that I began to consult him respecting the best mode of retrieving my husband's character: it is the good name of a woman only that sets to rise no more. I knew not that he had been drawn into a whirlpool, out of which he had not the energy to attempt to escape. He seemed indeed destitute of the power of employing his faculties in any regular pursuit. His principles of

---

1  Playful verbal sparring (French).
2  The eighth definition of "accommodation" in the *OED* contains the phrase "accommodation bill": "a bill not representing or originating in an actual commercial transaction, but for the purpose of raising money on credit."
3  "'Change" is a short form for "the Exchange," a place of commerce, trade, loans, and, indeed, stock exchanges.

action were so loose, and his mind so uncultivated, that every thing like order appeared to him in the shape of restraint; and, like men in the savage state, he required the strong stimulus of hope or fear, produced by wild speculations, in which the interests of others went for nothing, to keep his spirits awake. He one time professed patriotism, but he knew not what it was to feel honest indignation; and pretended to be an advocate for liberty, when, with as little affection for the human race as for individuals, he thought of nothing but his own gratification. He was just such a citizen, as a father. The sums he adroitly obtained by a violation of the laws of his country, as well as those of humanity, he would allow a mistress to squander; though she was, with the same *sang froid*,[1] consigned, as were his children, to poverty, when another proved more attractive.

"On various pretences, his friend continued to visit me; and, observing my want of money, he tried to induce me to accept of pecuniary aid; but this offer I absolutely rejected, though it was made with such delicacy, I could not be displeased.

"One day he came, as I thought accidentally, to dinner. My husband was very much engaged in business, and quitted the room soon after the cloth was removed. We conversed as usual, till confidential advice led again to love. I was extremely mortified. I had a sincere regard for him, and hoped that he had an equal friendship for me. I therefore began mildly to expostulate with him. This gentleness he mistook for coy encouragement; and he would not be diverted from the subject. Perceiving his mistake, I seriously asked him how, using such language to me, he could profess to be my husband's friend? A significant sneer excited[2] my curiosity, and he, supposing this to be my only scruple, took a letter deliberately out of his pocket, saying, 'Your husband's honour is not inflexible. How could you, with your discernment, think it so? Why, he left the room this very day on purpose to give me an opportunity to explain myself; *he* thought me too timid — too tardy.'

---

1 French phrase that literally means "cold blood," but that is used figuratively to signify cool indifference.

2 As the *OED* points out, "In modern use" the word "excite" means "To move to strong emotion, stir to passion; to stir up to eager tumultuous feeling," but this is only the fifth definition of the word. In this passage, Wollstonecraft uses "excite" according to the first definition of it: "To set in motion, stir up. a. fig. To move, stir up, instigate, incite."

"I snatched the letter with indescribable emotion. The purport of it was to invite him to dinner, and to ridicule his chivalrous respect for me. He assured him, 'that every woman had her price, and, with gross indecency, hinted, that he should be glad to have the duty of a husband taken off his hands. These he termed *liberal sentiments*. He advised him not to shock my romantic notions, but to attack my credulous generosity, and weak pity; and concluded with requesting him to lend him five hundred pounds for a month or six weeks.' I read this letter twice over; and the firm purpose it inspired, calmed the rising tumult of my soul. I rose deliberately, requested Mr. S---- to wait a moment, and instantly going into the counting-house, desired Mr. Venables to return with me to the dining-parlour.

"He laid down his pen, and entered with me, without observing any change in my countenance. I shut the door, and, giving him the letter, simply asked, 'whether he wrote it, or was it a forgery?'

"Nothing could equal his confusion. His friend's eye met his, and he muttered something about a joke — But I interrupted him — 'It is sufficient — We part for ever.'

"I continued, with solemnity, 'I have borne with your tyranny and infidelities. I disdain to utter what I have borne with. I thought you unprincipled, but not so decidedly vicious. I formed a tie, in the sight of heaven — I have held it sacred; even when men, more conformable to my taste, have made me feel — I despise all subterfuge! — that I was not dead to love. Neglected by you, I have resolutely stifled the enticing emotions, and respected the plighted faith you outraged. And you dare now to insult me, by selling me to prostitution! — Yes — equally lost to delicacy and principle — you dared sacrilegiously to barter the honour of the mother of your child.'

"Then, turning to Mr. S----, I added, 'I call on you, Sir, to witness,' and I lifted my hands and eyes to heaven, 'that, as solemnly as I took his name, I now abjure it,' I pulled off my ring, and put it on the table; 'and that I mean immediately to quit his house, never to enter it more. I will provide for myself and child. I leave him as free as I am determined to be myself — he shall be answerable for no debts of mine.'

"Astonishment closed their lips, till Mr. Venables, gently pushing his friend, with a forced smile, out of the room, nature for a moment prevailed, and, appearing like himself, he turned round, burning with rage, to me: but there was no terror in the frown, excepting when contrasted with the malignant smile which preceded it. He bade me 'leave the house at my peril; told me he despised my threats; I had no resource; I could not swear the peace against him![1] — I was not afraid of my life! — he had never struck me!'

"He threw the letter in the fire, which I had incautiously left in his hands; and, quitting the room, locked the door on me.

"When left alone, I was a moment or two before I could recollect myself. One scene had succeeded another with such rapidity, I almost doubted whether I was reflecting on a real event. 'Was it possible? Was I, indeed, free?' — Yes; free I termed myself, when I decidedly perceived the conduct I ought to adopt. How had I panted for liberty — liberty, that I would have purchased at any price, but that of my own esteem! I rose, and shook myself; opened the window, and methought the air never smelled so sweet. The face of heaven grew fairer as I viewed it, and the clouds seemed to flit away obedient to my wishes, to give my soul room to expand. I was all soul, and (wild as it may appear) felt as if I could have dissolved in the soft balmy gale that kissed my cheek, or have glided below the horizon on the glowing, descending beams. A seraphic satisfaction animated, without agitating my spirits; and my imagination collected, in visions sublimely terrible, or soothingly beautiful, an immense variety of the endless images, which nature affords, and fancy combines, of the grand and fair. The lustre of these bright picturesque sketches faded with the setting sun; but I was still alive to the calm delight they had diffused through my heart.

"There may be advocates for matrimonial obedience, who, making a distinction between the duty of a wife and of a human being, may blame my conduct. — To them I write not — my feelings are not for them to analyze; and may you, my child, never be able to ascertain, by heart-rending experience, what your mother felt before the present emancipation of her mind!

"I began to write a letter to my father, after closing one to my uncle; not to ask advice, but to signify my determination; when I was interrupted by the entrance of Mr. Venables. His manner was changed. His views on my uncle's fortune made him averse to my quitting his house, or he would, I am convinced, have been glad to have shaken off even the slight restraint my presence imposed

---

1   The *OED* definition of "peace," phrase 5.d, is as follows: "to swear (also pray) the peace against (a person): to swear that one is in bodily fear from (a person), so that he or she may be bound over to keep the peace. Also to swear the peace. Now hist[orical]."

on him; the restraint of showing me some respect. So far from having an affection for me, he really hated me, because he was convinced that I must despise him.

"He told me, that, 'As I now had had time to cool and reflect, he did not doubt but that my prudence, and nice sense of propriety, would lead me to overlook what was passed.'

"'Reflection,' I replied, 'had only confirmed my purpose, and no power on earth could divert me from it.'

"Endeavouring to assume a soothing voice and look, when he would willingly have tortured me, to force me to feel his power, his countenance had an infernal expression, when he desired me, 'Not to expose myself to the servants, by obliging him to confine me in my apartment; if then I would give my promise not to quit the house precipitately, I should be free — and —.' I declared, interrupting him, 'that I would promise nothing. I had no measures to keep with him — I was resolved, and would not condescend to subterfuge.'

"He muttered, 'that I should soon repent of these preposterous airs;' and, ordering tea to be carried into my little study, which had a communication with my bed-chamber, he once more locked the door upon me, and left me to my own meditations. I had passively followed him up stairs, not wishing to fatigue myself with unavailing exertion.

"Nothing calms the mind like a fixed purpose. I felt as if I had heaved a thousand weight[1] from my heart; the atmosphere seemed lightened; and, if I execrated the institutions of society, which thus enable men to tyrannize over women, it was almost a disinterested sentiment. I disregarded present inconveniences, when my mind had done struggling with itself, — when reason and inclination had shaken hands and were at peace. I had no longer the cruel task before me, in endless perspective, aye, during the tedious for ever of life, of labouring to overcome my repugnance — of labouring to extinguish the hopes, the maybes of a lively imagination. Death I had hailed as my only chance for deliverance; but, while existence had still so many charms, and life promised happiness, I shrunk from the icy arms of an unknown tyrant, though far more inviting than those of the man, to whom I supposed myself bound without any other alternative; and was content to linger a little longer, waiting for I knew not

---

1  As defined by the *OED*, the rare word "thousandweight"—spelled as one word in the dictionary—signifies a specific measurement of weight (of a thousand pounds).

what, rather than leave 'the warm precincts of the cheerful day,'[1] and all the unenjoyed affection of my nature.

"My present situation gave a new turn to my reflection; and I wondered (now the film seemed to be withdrawn, that obscured the piercing sight of reason) how I could, previously to the deciding outrage, have considered myself as everlastingly united to vice and folly! 'Had an evil genius cast a spell at my birth; or a demon stalked out of chaos, to perplex my understanding, and enchain my will, with delusive prejudices?'

"I pursued this train of thinking; it led me out of myself, to expatiate on the misery peculiar to my sex. 'Are not,' I thought, 'the despots for ever stigmatized, who, in the wantonness of power, commanded even the most atrocious criminals to be chained to dead bodies? though surely those laws are much more inhuman, which forge adamantine fetters to bind minds together, that never can mingle in social communion! What indeed can equal the wretchedness of that state, in which there is no alternative, but to extinguish the affections, or encounter infamy?'

## CHAP. XII.

"TOWARDS midnight Mr. Venables entered my chamber; and, with calm audacity preparing to go to bed, he bade me make haste, 'for that was the best place for husbands and wives to end their differences.' He had been drinking plentifully to aid his courage.

"I did not at first deign to reply. But perceiving that he affected to take my silence for consent, I told him that, 'If he would not go to another bed, or allow me, I should sit up in my study all night.' He attempted to pull me into the chamber, half joking. But I resisted; and, as he had determined not to give me any reason for saying that he used violence, after a few more efforts, he retired, cursing my obstinacy, to bed.

"I sat musing some time longer; then, throwing my cloak around me, prepared for sleep on a sopha. And, so fortunate seemed my deliverance, so sacred the pleasure of being thus

---

1   From line 87 of Thomas Gray's (1716-71) "Elegy Written in a Country
    Churchyard" (1751):
      For who to dumb Forgetfulness a prey,
      This pleasing anxious being e'er resign'd,
      Left the warm precincts of the cheerful day,
      Nor cast one longing, ling'ring look behind? (ll. 85-88)

wrapped up in myself, that I slept profoundly, and woke with a mind composed to encounter the struggles of the day. Mr. Venables did not wake till some hours after; and then he came to me half-dressed, yawning and stretching, with haggard eyes, as if he scarcely recollected what had passed the preceding evening. He fixed his eyes on me for a moment, then, calling me a fool, asked 'How long I intended to continue this pretty farce? For his part, he was devilish sick of it; but this was the plague of marrying women who pretended to know something.'

"I made no other reply to this harangue, than to say, 'That he ought to be glad to get rid of a woman so unfit to be his companion — and that any change in my conduct would be mean dissimulation; for maturer reflection only gave the sacred seal of reason to my first resolution.'

"He looked as if he could have stamped with impatience, at being obliged to stifle his rage; but, conquering his anger (for weak people, whose passions seem the most ungovernable, restrain them with the greatest ease, when they have a sufficient motive), he exclaimed, 'Very pretty, upon my soul! very pretty, theatrical flourishes! Pray, fair Roxana, stoop from your altitudes, and remember that you are acting a part in real life.'[1]

"He uttered this speech with a self-satisfied air, and went down stairs to dress.

"In about an hour he came to me again; and in the same tone said, 'That he came as my gentleman-usher to hand me down to breakfast.'

"'Of the black rod?' asked I.[2]

"This question, and the tone in which I asked it, a little disconcerted him. To say the truth, I now felt no resentment; my firm resolution to free myself from my ignoble thraldom, had absorbed the various emotions which, during six years, had racked my soul. The duty pointed out by my principles seemed clear; and not one tender feeling intruded to make me swerve.

---

1 Possibly a reference to the titular character of Daniel Defoe's (1661?-1731) *Roxanna: The Fortunate Mistress* (1724), a novel narrated as the autobiography of a woman who enters prostitution for survival and rises to hold a place of power as a high-society courtesan. In this reading, Venables taunts her as low and "putting on airs."

2 A Gentleman Usher of the Black Rod—usually shortened to "Black Rod"—is an official in the House of Lords who brings defendants to trial, amongst other duties, but Wollstonecraft may refer to the staff he bears (and from which he derives his title) to call the House to order.

The dislike which my husband had inspired was strong; but it only led me to wish to avoid, to wish to let him drop out of my memory; there was no misery, no torture that I would not deliberately have chosen, rather than renew my lease of servitude.

"During the breakfast, he attempted to reason with me on the folly of romantic sentiments; for this was the indiscriminate epithet he gave to every mode of conduct or thinking superior to his own. He asserted, 'that all the world were governed by their own interest; those who pretended to be actuated by different motives, were only deeper knaves, or fools crazed by books, who took for gospel all the rodomantade[1] nonsense written by men who knew nothing of the world. For his part, he thanked God, he was no hypocrite; and, if he stretched a point sometimes, it was always with an intention of paying every man his own.'

"He then artfully insinuated, 'that he daily expected a vessel to arrive, a successful speculation, that would make him easy for the present, and that he had several other schemes actually depending, that could not fail. He had no doubt of becoming rich in a few years, though he had been thrown back by some unlucky adventures at the setting out.'

"I mildly replied, 'That I wished he might not involve himself still deeper.'

"He had no notion that I was governed by a decision of judgment, not to be compared with a mere spurt of resentment. He knew not what it was to feel indignation against vice, and often boasted of his placable temper, and readiness to forgive injuries. True; for he only considered the being deceived, as an effort of skill he had not guarded against; and then, with a cant of candour, would observe, 'that he did not know how he might himself have been tempted to act in the same circumstances.' And, as his heart never opened to friendship, it never was wounded by disappointment. Every new acquaintance he protested, it is true, was 'the cleverest fellow in the world;' and he really thought so; till the novelty of his conversation or manners ceased to have any effect on his sluggish spirits. His respect for rank or fortune was more permanent, though he chanced to have no design of availing himself of the influence of either to promote his own views.

---

1 This word is usually spelled "rodomontade," meaning "proud boasting," and is a reference to the character Rodomonte, an arrogant Saracen leader in Ludovico Ariosto's (1474-1533) *Orlando Furioso* (1532).

"After a prefatory conversation, — my blood (I thought it had been cooler) flushed over my whole countenance as he spoke — he alluded to my situation. He desired me to reflect — 'and act like a prudent woman, as the best proof of my superior understanding; for he must own I had sense, did I know how to use it. I was not,' he laid a stress on his words, 'without my passions; and a husband was a convenient cloke. — He was liberal in his way of thinking; and why might not we, like many other married people, who were above vulgar prejudices, tacitly consent to let each other follow their own inclination? — He meant nothing more, in the letter I made the ground of complaint; and the pleasure which I seemed to take in Mr. S.'s company, led him to conclude, that he was not disagreeable to me.'

"A clerk brought in the letters of the day, and I, as I often did, while he was discussing subjects of business, went to the *piano forte*,[1] and began to play a favourite air to restore myself, as it were, to nature, and drive the sophisticated sentiments I had just been obliged to listen to, out of my soul.

"They had excited sensations similar to those I have felt, in viewing the squalid inhabitants of some of the lanes and back streets of the metropolis, mortified at being compelled to consider them as my fellow-creatures, as if an ape had claimed kindred with me.[2] Or, as when surrounded by a mephitical[3] fog, I have wished to have a volley of cannon fired, to clear the incumbered atmosphere, and give me room to breathe and move.

"My spirits were all in arms, and I played a kind of extemporary prelude. The cadence was probably wild and impassioned, while, lost in thought, I made the sounds a kind of echo to my train of thinking.

"Pausing for a moment, I met Mr. Venables' eyes. He was observing me with an air of conceited satisfaction, as much as to say — 'My last insinuation has done the business — she begins to know her own interest.' Then gathering up his letters, he said, 'That he hoped he should hear no more romantic stuff, well

---

1  A piano.
2  James Burnet, Lord Monboddo (1714-99), asserted that humans and primates were close relatives in *Of the Origin and Progress of Language* (6 vols, 1792) (Preece 156).
3  The *OED* definition of "mephitical" establishes it as the archaic equivalent of "mephitic"—itself an "arch[aic] and literary" adjective when used figuratively—which means: "Esp. of a gas or vapour: offensive to the smell, foul-smelling; noxious, poisonous, pestilential."

enough in a miss just come from boarding school;' and went, as was his custom, to the counting-house. I still continued playing; and, turning to a sprightly lesson, I executed it with uncommon vivacity. I heard footsteps approach the door, and was soon convinced that Mr. Venables was listening; the consciousness only gave more animation to my fingers. He went down into the kitchen, and the cook, probably by his desire, came to me, to know what I would please to order for dinner. Mr. Venables came into the parlour again, with apparent carelessness. I perceived that the cunning man was over-reaching himself; and I gave my directions as usual, and left the room.

"While I was making some alteration in my dress, Mr. Venables peeped in, and, begging my pardon for interrupting me, disappeared. I took up some work (I could not read), and two or three messages were sent to me, probably for no other purpose, but to enable Mr. Venables to ascertain what I was about.

"I listened whenever I heard the street-door open; at last I imagined I could distinguish Mr. Venables' step, going out. I laid aside my work; my heart palpitated; still I was afraid hastily to enquire; and I waited a long half hour, before I ventured to ask the boy whether his master was in the counting-house?

"Being answered in the negative, I bade him call me a coach, and collecting a few necessaries hastily together, with a little parcel of letters and papers which I had collected the preceding evening, I hurried into it, desiring the coachman to drive to a distant part of the town.

"I almost feared that the coach would break down before I got out of the street; and, when I turned the corner, I seemed to breathe a freer air. I was ready to imagine that I was rising above the thick atmosphere of earth; or I felt, as wearied souls might be supposed to feel on entering another state of existence.

"I stopped at one or two stands of coaches to elude pursuit, and then drove round the skirts of the town to seek for an obscure lodging, where I wished to remain concealed, till I could avail myself of my uncle's protection. I had resolved to assume my own name immediately, and openly to avow my determination, without any formal vindication, the moment I had found a home, in which I could rest free from the daily alarm of expecting to see Mr. Venables enter.

"I looked at several lodgings; but finding that I could not, without a reference to some acquaintance, who might inform my tyrant, get admittance into a decent apartment — men have not all this trouble — I thought of a woman whom I had assisted to furnish a little haberdasher's shop, and who I knew had a first floor to let.

"I went to her, and though I could not persuade her, that the quarrel between me and Mr. Venables would never be made up, still she agreed to conceal me for the present; yet assuring me at the same time, shaking her head, that, when a woman was once married, she must bear every thing. Her pale face, on which appeared a thousand haggard lines and delving wrinkles, produced by what is emphatically termed fretting, inforced her remark; and I had afterwards an opportunity of observing the treatment she had to endure, which grizzled her into patience. She toiled from morning till night; yet her husband would rob the till, and take away the money reserved for paying bills; and, returning home drunk, he would beat her if she chanced to offend him, though she had a child at the breast.

"These scenes awoke me at night; and, in the morning, I heard her, as usual, talk to her dear Johnny — he, forsooth, was her master; no slave in the West Indies had one more despotic; but fortunately she was of the true Russian breed of wives.[1]

"My mind, during the few past days, seemed, as it were, disengaged from my body; but, now the struggle was over, I felt very forcibly the effect which perturbation of spirits produces on a woman in my situation.

"The apprehension of a miscarriage, obliged me to confine myself to my apartment near a fortnight; but I wrote to my uncle's friend for money, promising 'to call on him, and explain my situation, when I was well enough to go out; mean time I earnestly intreated him, not to mention my place of abode to any one, lest my husband — such the law considered him — should disturb the mind he could not conquer. I mentioned my intention of setting out for Lisbon, to claim my uncle's protection, the moment my health would permit.'

---

1  The shocking final paragraphs of *Rights of Woman* also outline the commonly held view that Russian wives were beaten into habitual submission:

Let woman share the rights and she will emulate the virtues of man; for she must grow more perfect when emancipated, or justify the authority that chains such a weak being to her duty. — If the latter, it will be expedient to open a fresh trade with Russia for whips; a present which a father should always make to his son-in-law on his wedding day, that a husband may keep his whole family in order by the same means. (451)

"The tranquillity however, which I was recovering, was soon interrupted. My landlady came up to me one day, with eyes swollen with weeping, unable to utter what she was commanded to say. She declared, 'That she was never so miserable in her life; that she must appear an ungrateful monster; and that she would readily go down on her knees to me, to intreat me to forgive her, as she had done to her husband to spare her the cruel task.' Sobs prevented her from proceeding, or answering my impatient enquiries, to know what she meant.

"When she became a little more composed, she took a newspaper out of her pocket, declaring, 'that her heart smote her, but what could she do? — she must obey her husband.' I snatched the paper from her. An advertisement quickly met my eye, purporting, that 'Maria Venables had, without any assignable cause, absconded from her husband; and any person harbouring her, was menaced with the utmost severity of the law.'[1]

"Perfectly acquainted with Mr. Venables' meanness of soul, this step did not excite my surprise, and scarcely my contempt. Resentment in my breast, never survived love. I bade the poor woman, in a kind tone, wipe her eyes, and request her husband to come up, and speak to me himself.

"My manner awed him. He respected a lady, though not a woman; and began to mutter out an apology.

"'Mr. Venables was a rich gentleman; he wished to oblige me, but he had suffered enough by the law already, to tremble at the thought; besides, for certain, we should come together again, and then even I should not thank him for being accessary[2] to keeping us asunder. — A husband and wife were, God knows, just as one, — and all would come round at last.' He uttered a drawling 'Hem!' and then with an arch look, added — 'Master might have had his little frolics — but — Lord bless your heart! — men would be men while the world stands.'

"To argue with this privileged first-born of reason, I perceived, would be vain. I therefore only requested him to let me remain

---

1   A similar incident occurs in Godwin's *Caleb Williams*: after Caleb has escaped from wrongful imprisonment and is recovering from an injury under the protection of the captain of a gang of thieves, a member of the gang finds an advertisement offering a substantial reward for his return to the authorities (223).

2   As in similar cases in this edition, this odd spelling appears in the source text. I do not change it because it may be an antiquated spelling, as opposed to a typographical error.

another day at his house, while I sought for a lodging; and not to inform Mr. Venables that I had ever been sheltered there.

"He consented, because he had not the courage to refuse a person for whom he had an habitual respect; but I heard the pent-up choler burst forth in curses, when he met his wife, who was waiting impatiently at the foot of the stairs, to know what effect my expostulations would have on him.

"Without wasting any time in the fruitless indulgence of vexation, I once more set out in search of an abode in which I could hide myself for a few weeks.

"Agreeing to pay an exorbitant price, I hired an apartment, without any reference being required relative to my character: indeed, a glance at my shape seemed to say, that my motive for concealment was sufficiently obvious. Thus was I obliged to shroud my head in infamy.

"To avoid all danger of detection — I use the appropriate word, my child, for I was hunted out like a felon — I determined to take possession of my new lodgings that very evening.

"I did not inform my landlady where I was going. I knew that she had a sincere affection for me, and would willingly have run any risk to show her gratitude; yet I was fully convinced, that a few kind words from Johnny would have found the woman in her, and her dear benefactress, as she termed me in an agony of tears, would have been sacrificed, to recompense her tyrant for condescending to treat her like an equal. He could be kind-hearted, as she expressed it, when he pleased. And this thawed sternness, contrasted with his habitual brutality, was the more acceptable, and could not be purchased at too dear a rate.

"The sight of the advertisement made me desirous of taking refuge with my uncle, let what would be the consequence; and I repaired in a hackney coach (afraid of meeting some person who might chance to know me, had I walked) to the chambers of my uncle's friend.

"He received me with great politeness (my uncle had already prepossessed him in my favour), and listened, with interest, to my explanation of the motives which had induced me to fly from home, and skulk in obscurity, with all the timidity of fear that ought only to be the companion of guilt. He lamented, with rather more gallantry than, in my situation, I thought delicate, that such a woman should be thrown away on a man insensible to the charms of beauty or grace. He seemed at a loss what to advise me to do, to evade my husband's search, without hastening to my uncle, whom, he hesitating said, I might not find alive.

He uttered this intelligence with visible regret; requested me, at least, to wait for the arrival of the next packet; offered me what money I wanted, and promised to visit me.

"He kept his word; still no letter arrived to put an end to my painful state of suspense. I procured some books and music, to beguile the tedious solitary days.

'Come, ever smiling Liberty,
　　And with thee bring thy jocund train:'[1]

I sung — and sung till, saddened by the strain of joy, I bitterly lamented the fate that deprived me of all social pleasure. Comparative liberty indeed I had possessed myself of; but the jocund train lagged far behind!

## CHAP. XIII.

"BY watching my only visitor, my uncle's friend, or by some other means, Mr. Venables discovered my residence, and came to enquire for me. The maid-servant assured him there was no such person in the house. A bustle ensued — I caught the alarm — listened — distinguished his voice, and immediately locked the door. They suddenly grew still; and I waited near a quarter of an hour, before I heard him open the parlour door, and mount the stairs with the mistress of the house, who obsequiously declared that she knew nothing of me.

"Finding my door locked, she requested me to 'open it, and prepare to go home with my husband, poor gentleman! to whom I had already occasioned sufficient vexation.' I made no reply. Mr. Venables then, in an assumed tone of softness, intreated me, 'to consider what he suffered, and my own reputation, and get the better of childish resentment.' He ran on in the same strain, pretending to address me, but evidently adapting his discourse to the capacity of the landlady; who, at every pause, uttered an exclamation of pity; or 'Yes, to be sure — Very true, sir.'

"Sick of the farce, and perceiving that I could not avoid the hated interview, I opened the door, and he entered. Advancing

---

1　From George Frideric Handel's libretto "Judas Maccabaeus" (1746):
　　Come, ever-smiling Liberty,
　　And with thee bring thy jocund Train;
　　For thee we pant, and sigh for thee,
　　With whom eternal Pleasures reign. (quoted in Morell ll. 73-76)

with easy assurance to take my hand, I shrunk from his touch, with an involuntary start, as I should have done from a noisome reptile, with more disgust than terror. His conductress was retiring, to give us, as she said, an opportunity to accommodate matters. But I bade her come in, or I would go out; and curiosity impelled her to obey me.

"Mr. Venables began to expostulate; and this woman, proud of his confidence, to second him. But I calmly silenced her, in the midst of a vulgar harangue, and turning to him, asked, 'Why he vainly tormented me? declaring that no power on earth should force me back to his house.'

"After a long altercation, the particulars of which, it would be to no purpose to repeat, he left the room. Some time was spent in loud conversation in the parlour below, and I discovered that he had brought his friend, an attorney, with him.

******************************
***************************************************************
***************************************************************
***************[1] The tumult on the landing place, brought out a gentleman, who had recently taken apartments in the house; he enquired why I was thus assailed?[2] The voluble attorney instantly repeated the trite tale. The stranger turned to me, observing, with the most soothing politeness and manly interest, that 'my countenance told a very different story.' He added, 'that I should not be insulted, or forced out of the house, by any body.'

"'Not by her husband?' asked the attorney.

"'No, sir, not by her husband.' Mr. Venables advanced towards him — But there was a decision in his attitude, that so well seconded that of his voice,[3]
***************************************************************
***************************************************************

---

1 Almost three rows of asterisks appear in the source text, which I replicate here.

2 The introduction of Darnford as the deliverer of Maria, in an early stage of the history, is already stated (Chap. III.) to have been an afterthought of the author. This has probably caused the imperfectness of the manuscript in the above passage; though, at the same time, it must be acknowledged to be somewhat uncertain, whether Darnford is the stranger intended in this place. It appears from Chap. XVII, that an interference of a more decisive nature was designed to be attributed to him. EDITOR. [Godwin's note]

3 Roughly two and a half lines of asterisks appear at this point in the source text, which I replicate here.

\*\*\*\*\*\*\*\*\*\*\*\*\*\*\*\*\*\*\*\*\*\*\*\*\*\*\*\*\*\*\*\*\*\* They left the house: at the same time protesting, that any one that should dare to protect me, should be prosecuted with the utmost rigour.

"They were scarcely out of the house, when my landlady came up to me again, and begged my pardon, in a very different tone. For, though Mr. Venables had bid her, at her peril, harbour me, he had not attended, I found, to her broad hints, to discharge the lodging. I instantly promised to pay her, and make her a present to compensate for my abrupt departure, if she would procure me another lodging, at a sufficient distance; and she, in return, repeating Mr. Venables' plausible tale, I raised her indignation, and excited her sympathy, by telling her briefly the truth.

"She expressed her commiseration with such honest warmth, that I felt soothed; for I have none of that fastidious sensitiveness, which a vulgar accent or gesture can alarm to the disregard of real kindness. I was ever glad to perceive in others the humane feelings I delighted to exercise; and the recollection of some ridiculous characteristic circumstances, which have occurred in a moment of emotion, has convulsed me with laughter, though at the instant I should have thought it sacrilegious to have smiled. Your improvement, my dearest girl, being ever present to me while I write, I note these feelings, because women, more accustomed to observe manners than actions, are too much alive to ridicule. So much so, that their boasted sensibility is often stifled by false delicacy. True sensibility, the sensibility which is the auxiliary of virtue, and the soul of genius, is in society so occupied with the feelings of others, as scarcely to regard its own sensations. With what reverence have I looked up at my uncle, the dear parent of my mind! when I have seen the sense of his own sufferings, of mind and body, absorbed in a desire to comfort those, whose misfortunes were comparatively trivial. He would have been ashamed of being as indulgent to himself, as he was to others. 'Genuine fortitude,' he would assert, 'consisted in governing our own emotions, and making allowance for the weaknesses in our friends, that we would not tolerate in ourselves.' But where is my fond regret leading me!

"'Women must be submissive,' said my landlady. 'Indeed what could most women do? Who had they to maintain them, but their husbands? Every woman, and especially a lady, could not go through rough and smooth, as she had done, to earn a little bread.'

"She was in a talking mood, and proceeded to inform me how she had been used in the world. 'She knew what it was to have a bad husband, or she did not know who should.' I perceived that she would be very much mortified, were I not to attend to her tale, and I did not attempt to interrupt her, though I wished her, as soon as possible, to go out in search of a new abode for me, where I could once more hide my head.

"She began by telling me, 'That she had saved a little money in service; and was over-persuaded (we must all be in love once in our lives) to marry a likely man, a footman in the family, not worth a groat.[1] My plan,' she continued, 'was to take a house, and let out lodgings; and all went on well, till my husband got acquainted with an impudent slut, who chose to live on other people's means — and then all went to rack and ruin. He ran in debt to buy her fine clothes, such clothes as I never thought of wearing myself, and — would you believe it? — he signed an execution on my very goods, bought with the money I worked so hard to get; and they came and took my bed from under me, before I heard a word of the matter. Aye, madam, these are misfortunes that you gentlefolks know nothing of, — but sorrow is sorrow, let it come which way it will.'

"'I sought for a service again — very hard, after having a house of my own! — but he used to follow me, and kick up such a riot when he was drunk, that I could not keep a place; nay, he even stole my clothes, and pawned them; and when I went to the pawnbroker's, and offered to take my oath that they were not bought with a farthing of his money, they said, 'It was all as one, my husband had a right to whatever I had.'

"'At last he listed for a soldier, and I took a house, making an agreement to pay for the furniture by degrees; and I almost starved myself, till I once more got before-hand in the world.

"'After an absence of six years (God forgive me! I thought he was dead) my husband returned; found me out, and came with such a penitent face, I forgave him, and clothed him from head to foot. But he had not been a week in the house, before some of his creditors arrested him; and, he selling my goods, I found myself once more reduced to beggary; for I was not as well able to work, go to bed late, and rise early, as when I quitted service; and then I thought it hard enough. He was soon tired of me, when there was nothing more to be had, and left me again.

---

1  The *OED* provides the following definition of "groat": "1. Hist[orical]. A denomination of coin" used in the fourteenth century in Europe, and, in a refinement upon that definition, "c. Taken as the type of a very small sum. Obs[olete]."

"[']¹ I will not tell you how I was buffeted about, till, hearing for certain that he had died in an hospital abroad, I once more returned to my old occupation; but have not yet been able to get my head above water: so, madam, you must not be angry if I am afraid to run any risk, when I know so well, that women have always the worst of it, when law is to decide.'

"After uttering a few more complaints, I prevailed on my land-lady to go out in quest of a lodging; and, to be more secure, I condescended to the mean shift of changing my name.

"But why should I dwell on similar incidents! — I was hunted, like an infected beast, from three different apartments, and should not have been allowed to rest in any, had not Mr. Venables, informed of my uncle's dangerous state of health, been inspired with the fear of hurrying me out of the world as I advanced in my pregnancy, by thus tormenting and obliging me to take sudden journeys to avoid him; and then his speculations on my uncle's fortune must prove abortive.

"One day, when he had pursued me to an inn, I fainted, hurrying from him; and, falling down, the sight of my blood alarmed him, and obtained a respite for me. It is strange that he should have retained any hope, after observing my unwavering determination; but, from the mildness of my behaviour, when I found all my endeavours to change his disposition unavailing, he formed an erroneous opinion of my character, imagining that, were we once more together, I should part with the money he could not legally force from me, with the same facility as formerly. My forbearance and occasional sympathy he had mistaken for weakness of character; and, because he perceived that I disliked resistance, he thought my indulgence and compassion mere selfishness, and never discovered that the fear of being unjust, or of unnecessarily wounding the feelings of another, was much more painful to me, than any thing I could have to endure myself. Perhaps it was pride which made me imagine, that I could bear what I dreaded to inflict; and that it was often easier to suffer, than to see the sufferings of others.

"I forgot to mention that, during this persecution, I received a letter from my uncle, informing me, 'that he only found relief from continual change of air; and that he intended to return when the spring was a little more advanced (it was now the

---

1 I have inserted this single opening quotation mark to clarify that the landlady's words continue here.

middle of February), and then we would plan a journey to Italy, leaving the fogs and cares of England far behind.' He approved of my conduct, promised to adopt my child, and seemed to have no doubt of obliging Mr. Venables to hear reason. He wrote to his friend, by the same post, desiring him to call on Mr. Venables in his name; and, in consequence of the remonstrances he dictated, I was permitted to lie-in tranquilly.

"The two or three weeks previous, I had been allowed to rest in peace; but, so accustomed was I to pursuit and alarm, that I seldom closed my eyes without being haunted by Mr. Venables' image, who seemed to assume terrific or hateful forms to torment me, wherever I turned. — Sometimes a wild cat, a roaring bull, or hideous assassin, whom I vainly attempted to fly; at others he was a demon, hurrying me to the brink of a precipice, plunging me into dark waves, or horrid gulfs; and I woke, in violent fits of trembling anxiety, to assure myself that it was all a dream, and to endeavour to lure my waking thoughts to wander to the delightful Italian vales, I hoped soon to visit; or to picture some august ruins, where I reclined in fancy on a mouldering column, and escaped, in the contemplation of the heart-enlarging virtues of antiquity, from the turmoil of cares that had depressed all the daring purposes of my soul. But I was not long allowed to calm my mind by the exercise of my imagination; for the third day after your birth, my child, I was surprised by a visit from my elder brother; who came in the most abrupt manner, to inform me of the death of my uncle. He had left the greater part of his fortune to my child, appointing me its guardian; in short, every step was taken to enable me to be mistress of his fortune, without putting any part of it in Mr. Venables' power. My brother came to vent his rage on me, for having, as he expressed himself, 'deprived him, my uncle's eldest nephew, of his inheritance;' though my uncle's property, the fruit of his own exertion, being all in the funds, or on landed securities, there was not a shadow of justice in the charge.

"As I sincerely loved my uncle, this intelligence brought on a fever, which I struggled to conquer with all the energy of my mind; for, in my desolate state, I had it very much at heart to suckle you, my poor babe. You seemed my only tie to life, a cherub, to whom I wished to be a father, as well as a mother; and the double duty appeared to me to produce a proportionate increase of affection. But the pleasure I felt, while sustaining you, snatched from the wreck of hope, was cruelly damped by melancholy reflections on my widowed state — widowed by the death of my uncle.[1] Of Mr. Venables I thought not, even when I thought of the felicity of loving your father, and how a mother's pleasure might be exalted, and her care softened by a husband's tenderness. — 'Ought to be!' I exclaimed; and I endeavoured to drive away the tenderness that suffocated me; but my spirits were weak, and the unbidden tears would flow. 'Why was I,' I would ask thee, but thou didst not heed me, — 'cut off from the participation of the sweetest pleasure of life?' I imagined with what extacy, after the pains of child-bed, I should have presented my little stranger, whom I had so long wished to view, to a respectable father, and with what maternal fondness I should have pressed them both to my heart! — Now I kissed her with less delight, though with the most endearing compassion, poor helpless one! when I perceived a slight resemblance of him, to whom she owed her existence; or, if any gesture reminded me of him, even in his best days, my heart heaved, and I pressed the innocent to my bosom, as if to purify it — yes, I blushed to think that its purity had been sullied, by allowing such a man to be its father.

"After my recovery, I began to think of taking a house in the country, or of making an excursion on the continent, to avoid Mr. Venables; and to open my heart to new pleasures and affection. The spring was melting into summer, and you, my little companion, began to smile — that smile made hope bud out afresh, assuring me the world was not a desert. Your gestures were ever present to my fancy; and I dwelt on the joy I should feel when you would begin to walk and lisp. Watching your wakening mind, and shielding from every rude blast my tender blossom, I recovered my spirits — I dreamed not of the frost — 'the killing frost,'[2] to

---

1   As in *Mary*, Wollstonecraft mysteriously confounds familial relations here. See p. 144, note 1 for more information.

2   From Cardinal Wolsley's monologue in Shakespeare's *King Henry the Eighth* (1613):

    So farewell to all the little good you bear me.
    Farewell? A long farewell to all my greatness.
    This is the state of man: today he puts forth
    The tender leaves of hope: tomorrow blossoms,
    And bears his blushing honours thick upon him:
    The third day comes a frost, a killing frost,
    And when he thinks, good easy man, full surely
    His greatness is a-ripening, nips his root,
    And then he falls, as I do. (III, ii, 413-21)

which you were destined to be exposed. — But I lose all patience — and execrate the injustice of the world — folly! ignorance! — I should rather call it; but, shut up from a free circulation of thought, and always pondering on the same griefs, I writhe under the torturing apprehensions, which ought to excite only honest indignation, or active compassion; and would, could I view them as the natural consequence of things. But, born a woman — and born to suffer, in endeavouring to repress my own emotions, I feel more acutely the various ills my sex are fated to bear — I feel that the evils they are subject to endure, degrade them so far below their oppressors, as almost to justify their tyranny; leading at the same time superficial reasoners to term that weakness the cause, which is only the consequence of short-sighted despotism.

## CHAP. XIV.

"AS my mind grew calmer, the visions of Italy again returned with their former glow of colouring; and I resolved on quitting the kingdom for a time, in search of the cheerfulness, that naturally results from a change of scene, unless we carry the barbed arrow with us, and only see what we feel.

"During the period necessary to prepare for a long absence, I sent a supply to pay my father's debts, and settled my brothers in eligible situations; but my attention was not wholly engrossed by my family, though I do not think it necessary to enumerate the common exertions of humanity. The manner in which my uncle's property was settled, prevented me from making the addition to the fortune of my surviving sister, that I could have wished; but I had prevailed on him to bequeath her two thousand pounds, and she determined to marry a lover, to whom she had been some time attached. Had it not been for this engagement, I should have invited her to accompany me in my tour; and I might have escaped the pit, so artfully dug in my path, when I was the least aware of danger.

"I had thought of remaining in England, till I weaned my child; but this state of freedom was too peaceful to last, and I had soon reason to wish to hasten my departure. A friend of Mr. Venables, the same attorney who had accompanied him in several excursions to hunt me from my hiding places, waited on me to propose a reconciliation. On my refusal, he indirectly advised me to make over to my husband — for husband he would term him — the greater part of the property I had at command, menacing me with continual persecution unless I complied, and that, as a last resort, he would claim the child. I did not, though intimidated by the last insinuation, scruple to declare, that I would not allow him to squander the money left to me for far different purposes, but offered him five hundred pounds, if he would sign a bond not to torment me any more. My maternal anxiety made me thus appear to waver from my first determination, and probably suggested to him, or his diabolical agent, the infernal plot, which has succeeded but too well.

"The bond was executed; still I was impatient to leave England. Mischief hung in the air when we breathed the same; I wanted seas to divide us, and waters to roll between, till he had forgotten that I had the means of helping him through a new scheme. Disturbed by the late occurrences, I instantly prepared for my departure. My only delay was waiting for a maid-servant, who spoke French fluently, and had been warmly recommended to me. A valet I was advised to hire, when I fixed on my place of residence for any time.

"My God, with what a light heart did I set out for Dover![1] — It was not my country, but my cares, that I was leaving behind. My heart seemed to bound with the wheels, or rather appeared the centre on which they twirled. I clasped you to my bosom, exclaiming 'And you will be safe — quite safe — when — we are once on board the packet. — Would we were there!' I smiled at my idle fears, as the natural effect of continual alarm; and I scarcely owned to myself that I dreaded Mr. Venables's cunning, or was conscious of the horrid delight he would feel, at forming stratagem after stratagem to circumvent me. I was already in the snare — I never reached the packet — I never saw thee more. — I grow breathless. I have scarcely patience to write down the details. The maid — the plausible woman I had hired — put, doubtless, some stupefying potion in what I ate or drank, the morning I left town. All I know is, that she must have quitted the chaise, shameless wretch! and taken (from my breast) my babe with her. How could a creature in a female form see me caress thee, and steal thee from my arms! I must stop, stop to repress a mother's anguish; lest, in bitterness of soul, I imprecate the wrath of heaven on this tiger, who tore my only comfort from me.

"How long I slept I know not; certainly many hours, for I woke at the close of day, in a strange confusion of thought. I was probably roused to recollection by some one thundering at a huge,

---

1  Dover is a channel port and the closest crossing point to France, or mainland Europe.

unwieldy gate. Attempting to ask where I was, my voice died away, and I tried to raise it in vain, as I have done in a dream. I looked for my babe with affright; feared that it had fallen out of my lap, while I had so strangely forgotten her; and, such was the vague intoxication, I can give it no other name, in which I was plunged, I could not recollect when or where I last saw you; but I sighed, as if my heart wanted room to clear my head.

"The gates opened heavily, and the sullen sound of many locks and bolts drawn back, grated on my very soul, before I was appalled by the creaking of the dismal hinges, as they closed after me. The gloomy pile was before me, half in ruins; some of the aged trees of the avenue were cut down, and left to rot where they fell; and as we approached some mouldering steps, a monstrous dog darted forwards to the length of his chain, and barked and growled infernally.

"The door was opened slowly, and a murderous visage peeped out, with a lantern. 'Hush!' he uttered, in a threatning tone, and the affrighted animal stole back to his kennel. The door of the chaise flew back, the stranger put down the lantern, and clasped his dreadful arms around me. It was certainly the effect of the soporific draught, for, instead of exerting my strength, I sunk without motion, though not without sense, on his shoulder, my limbs refusing to obey my will. I was carried up the steps into a close-shut hall. A candle flaring in the socket, scarcely dispersed the darkness, though it displayed to me the ferocious countenance of the wretch who held me.

"He mounted a wide staircase. Large figures painted on the walls seemed to start on me, and glaring eyes to meet me at every turn. Entering a long gallery, a dismal shriek made me spring out of my conductor's arms, with I know not what mysterious emotion of terror; but I fell on the floor, unable to sustain myself.

"A strange-looking female started out of one of the recesses, and observed me with more curiosity than interest; till, sternly bid retire, she flitted back like a shadow. Other faces, strongly marked, or distorted, peeped through the half-opened doors, and I heard some incoherent sounds. I had no distinct idea where I could be — I looked on all sides, and almost doubted whether I was alive or dead.

"Thrown on a bed, I immediately sunk into insensibility again; and next day, gradually recovering the use of reason, I began, starting affrighted from the conviction, to discover where I was confined — I insisted on seeing the master of the mansion — I saw him — and perceived that I was buried alive. —

"Such, my child, are the events of thy mother's life to this dreadful moment — Should she ever escape from the fangs of her enemies, she will add the secrets of her prison-house — and —"

Some lines were here crossed out, and the memoirs broke off abruptly with the names of Jemima and Darnford.

## APPENDIX.

---

## [ADVERTISEMENT.[1]

THE performance, with a fragment of which the reader has now been presented, was designed to consist of three parts. The preceding sheets were considered as constituting one of those parts. Those persons who in the perusal of the chapters, already written and in some degree finished by the author, have felt their hearts awakened, and their curiosity excited as to the sequel of the story, will, of course, gladly accept even of the broken paragraphs and half-finished sentences, which have been found committed to paper, as materials for the remainder. The fastidious and cold-hearted critic may perhaps feel himself repelled by the incoherent form in which they are presented. But an inquisitive temper willingly accepts the most imperfect and mutilated information, where better is not to be had: and readers, who in any degree resemble the author in her quick apprehension of sentiment, and of the pleasures and pains of imagination, will, I believe, find gratification, in contemplating sketches, which were designed in a short time to have received the finishing touches of her genius; but which must now for ever remain a mark to record the triumphs of mortality, over schemes of usefulness, and projects of public interest.]

## CHAP. XV.

DARNFORD returned the memoirs to Maria, with a most affectionate letter, in which he reasoned on "the absurdity of the laws respecting matrimony, which, till divorces could be more easily obtained, was," he declared, "the most insufferable bondage. Ties

---

1 Unlike other editorial comments in the source text, Godwin does not specify that this note is his, but it certainly is. The square brackets surrounding the text are in the original.

of this nature could not bind minds governed by superior principles; and such beings were privileged to act above the dictates of
laws they had no voice in framing, if they had sufficient strength
of mind to endure the natural consequence. In her case, to talk of
duty, was a farce, excepting what was due to herself. Delicacy, as
well as reason, forbade her ever to think of returning to her
husband: was she then to restrain her charming sensibility
through mere prejudice? These arguments were not absolutely
impartial, for he disdained to conceal, that, when he appealed to
her reason, he felt that he had some interest in her heart. — The
conviction was not more transporting, than sacred — a thousand
times a day, he asked himself how he had merited such happiness? — and as often he determined to purify the heart she
deigned to inhabit — He intreated to be again admitted to her
presence."

He was; and the tear which glistened in his eye, when he
respectfully pressed her to his bosom, rendered him peculiarly
dear to the unfortunate mother. Grief had stilled the transports
of love, only to render their mutual tenderness more touching. In
former interviews, Darnford had contrived, by a hundred little
pretexts, to sit near her, to take her hand, or to meet her eyes —
now it was all soothing affection, and esteem seemed to have
rivalled love. He adverted to her narrative, and spoke with
warmth of the oppression she had endured. — His eyes, glowing
with a lambent flame, told her how much he wished to restore her
to liberty and love; but he kissed her hand, as if it had been that
of a saint; and spoke of the loss of her child, as if it had been his
own. — What could have been more flattering to Maria? — Every
instance of self-denial was registered in her heart, and she loved
him, for loving her too well to give way to the transports of
passion.

They met again and again; and Darnford declared, while
passion suffused his cheeks, that he never before knew what it
was to love. —

One morning Jemima informed Maria, that her master
intended to wait on her, and speak to her without witnesses. He
came, and brought a letter with him, pretending that he was ignorant of its contents, though he insisted on having it returned to
him. It was from the attorney already mentioned, who informed
her of the death of her child, and hinted, "that she could not now
have a legitimate heir, and that, would she make over the half of
her fortune during life, she should be conveyed to Dover, and
permitted to pursue her plan of travelling."

Maria answered with warmth, "That she had no terms to make with the murderer of her babe, nor would she purchase liberty at the price of her own respect."

She began to expostulate with her jailor; but he sternly bade her "Be silent — he had not gone so far, not to go further."

Darnford came in the evening. Jemima was obliged to be absent, and she, as usual, locked the door on them, to prevent interruption or discovery. — The lovers were, at first, embarrassed; but fell insensibly into confidential discourse. Darnford represented, "that they might soon be parted," and wished her "to put it out of the power of fate to separate them."

As her husband she now received him, and he solemnly pledged himself as her protector — and eternal friend. —

There was one peculiarity in Maria's mind: she was more anxious not to deceive, than to guard against deception; and had rather trust without sufficient reason, than be for ever the prey of doubt. Besides, what are we, when the mind has, from reflection, a certain kind of elevation, which exalts the contemplation above the little concerns of prudence! We see what we wish, and make a world of our own — and, though reality may sometimes open a door to misery, yet the moments of happiness procured by the imagination, may, without a paradox, be reckoned among the solid comforts of life. Maria now, imagining that she had found a being of celestial mould — was happy, — nor was she deceived. — He was then plastic in her impassioned hand — and reflected all the sentiments which animated and warmed her.

------------------------------------------------------------
------------------------------------------------------------
--------------------------- [1]


## CHAP. XVI.

ONE morning confusion seemed to reign in the house, and Jemima came in terror, to inform Maria, "that her master had left it, with a determination, she was assured (and too many circumstances corroborated the opinion, to leave a doubt of its truth) of never returning. I am prepared then," said Jemima, "to accompany you in your flight."

Maria started up, her eyes darting towards the door, as if afraid that some one should fasten it on her for ever.

---

1  Almost two and a half rows of dashes appear in the source text, which I replicate here.

Jemima continued, "I have perhaps no right now to expect the performance of your promise; but on you it depends to reconcile me with the human race."

"But Darnford!" — exclaimed Maria, mournfully — sitting down again, and crossing her arms — "I have no child to go to, and liberty has lost its sweets."

"I am much mistaken, if Darnford is not the cause of my master's flight — his keepers assure me, that they have promised to confine him two days longer, and then he will be free — you cannot see him; but they will give a letter to him the moment he is free. — In that inform him where he may find you in London; fix on some hotel. Give me your clothes; I will send them out of the house with mine, and we will slip out at the garden-gate. Write your letter while I make these arrangements, but lose no time!"

In an agitation of spirit, not to be calmed, Maria began to write to Darnford. She called him by the sacred name of "husband," and bade him "hasten to her, to share her fortune, or she would return to him." — An hotel in the Adelphi[1] was the place of rendezvous.

The letter was sealed and given in charge; and with light foot-steps, yet terrified at the sound of them, she descended, scarcely breathing, and with an indistinct fear that she should never get out at the garden gate. Jemima went first.

A being, with a visage that would have suited one possessed by a devil, crossed the path, and seized Maria by the arm. Maria had no fear but of being detained — "Who are you? what are you?" for the form was scarcely human. "If you are made of flesh and blood," his ghastly eyes glared on her, "do not stop me!"

"Woman," interrupted a sepulchral voice, "what have I to do with thee?"[2] — Still he grasped her hand, muttering a curse.

---

1 As defined in the *OED*, "Adelphi" is "The name of a group of buildings in London between the Strand and the Thames, laid out by the four brothers, James, John, Robert, and William Adam ... and hence called Adelphi," after the Greek word for "brothers." It was a fashionable area; amongst other notables, the great Shakespearean English actor, David Garrick (1717-79), owned a house there.

2 Oddly, an echo of Jesus' words, as reported in the gospel of St. John:

And the third day there was a marriage in Cana of Galilee; and the mother of Jesus was there:

And both Jesus was called, and his disciples, to the marriage.

And when they wanted wine, the mother of Jesus saith unto him, They have no wine.

Jesus saith unto her, Woman, what have I to do with thee? mine hour is not yet come. (2:1-4)

"No, no; you have nothing to do with me," she exclaimed, "this is a moment of life and death!" —

With supernatural force she broke from him, and, throwing her arms round Jemima, cried, "Save me!" The being, from whose grasp she had loosed herself, took up a stone as they opened the door, and with a kind of hellish sport threw it after them. They were out of his reach.

When Maria arrived in town, she drove to the hotel already fixed on. But she could not sit still — her child was ever before her; and all that had passed during her confinement, appeared to be a dream. She went to the house in the suburbs, where, as she now discovered, her babe had been sent. The moment she entered, her heart grew sick; but she wondered not that it had proved its grave. She made the necessary enquiries, and the church-yard was pointed out, in which it rested under a turf. A little frock which the nurse's child wore (Maria had made it herself) caught her eye. The nurse was glad to sell it for half-a-guinea, and Maria hastened away with the relic, and, re-entering the hackney-coach which waited for her, gazed on it, till she reached her hotel.

She then waited on the attorney who had made her uncle's will, and explained to him her situation. He readily advanced her some of the money which still remained in his hands, and promised to take the whole of the case into consideration. Maria only wished to be permitted to remain in quiet — She found that several bills, apparently with her signature, had been presented to her agent, nor was she for a moment at a loss to guess by whom they had been forged; yet, equally averse to threaten or intreat, she requested her friend [the solicitor][1] to call on Mr. Venables. He was not to be found at home; but at length his agent, the attorney, offered a conditional promise to Maria, to leave her in peace, as long as she behaved with propriety, if she would give up the notes. Maria inconsiderately consented — Darnford was arrived, and she wished to be only alive to love; she wished to forget the anguish she felt whenever she thought of her child.

They took a ready-furnished lodging together, for she was above disguise; Jemima insisting on being considered as her house-keeper, and to receive the customary stipend. On no other terms would she remain with her friend.

Darnford was indefatigable in tracing the mysterious circumstances of his confinement. The cause was simply, that a relation,

---

1 Here, and below, the square brackets appear in the source text.

a very distant one, to whom he was heir, had died intestate, leaving a considerable fortune. On the news of Darnford's arrival in England, a person, intrusted with the management of the property, and who had the writings [in his possession, determining, by one bold stroke, to strip Darnford of the succession,] had planned his confinement; and [as soon as he had taken the measures he judged most conducive to his object, this ruffian, together with his instrument,] the keeper of the private mad-house, left the kingdom. Darnford, who still pursued his enquiries, at last discovered that they had fixed their place of refuge at Paris.

Maria and he determined therefore, with the faithful Jemima, to visit that metropolis, and accordingly were preparing for the journey, when they were informed that Mr. Venables had commenced an action against Darnford for seduction and adultery.[1] The indignation Maria felt cannot be explained; she repented of the forbearance she had exercised in giving up the notes. Darnford could not put off his journey, without risking the loss of his property: Maria therefore furnished him with money for his expedition; and determined to remain in London till the termination of this affair.

She visited some ladies with whom she had formerly been intimate, but was refused admittance; and at the opera, or Ranelagh,[2] they could not recollect her. Among these ladies there were some, not her most intimate acquaintance, who were generally supposed to avail themselves of the cloke of marriage, to conceal a mode of conduct, that would for ever have damned their fame, had they been innocent, seduced girls. These particularly stood aloof. — Had she remained with her husband, practicing insincerity, and neglecting her child to manage an intrigue, she would still have been visited and respected. If, instead of openly living with her lover, she could have condescended to call

---

1  In *Family Law* (2003), Frances Burton describes eighteenth-century legal action regarding adultery thus:
     the method (which was expensive) was to obtain a divorce *a mensa et thoro* [Latin for "from table and bed," signifying a legal separation] from the ecclesiastical courts, then to sue the wife's co-adulterer for "criminal conversation," prior to petitioning and attending the House for cross-examination over whether the petitioner had connived at or colluded with the adultery, or partially or wholly caused it by living apart from his wife. (58)
2  Ranelagh was a public pleasure gardens in London; they closed in 1803 and are now part of the gardens of Chelsea Hospital. I am indebted to Allan Ingram for this information.

into play a thousand arts, which, degrading her own mind, might have allowed the people who were not deceived, to pretend to be so, she would have been caressed and treated like an honourable woman. "And Brutus[1] is an honourable man!" said Mark-Antony with equal sincerity.[2]

With Darnford she did not taste uninterrupted felicity; there was a volatility in his manner which often distressed her; but love gladdened the scene; besides, he was the most tender, sympathizing creature in the world. A fondness for the sex often gives an appearance of humanity to the behaviour of men, who have small pretensions to the reality; and they seem to love others, when they are only pursuing their own gratification. Darnford appeared ever willing to avail himself of her taste and acquirements, while she endeavoured to profit by his decision of character, and to eradicate some of the romantic notions, which had taken root in her mind, while in adversity she had brooded over visions of unattainable bliss.

The real affections of life, when they are allowed to burst forth, are buds pregnant with joy and all the sweet emotions of the soul; yet they branch out with wild ease, unlike the artificial forms of felicity, sketched by an imagination painful alive. The substantial happiness, which enlarges and civilizes the mind, may be compared to the pleasure experienced in roving through nature at large, inhaling the sweet gale natural to the clime; while the reveries of a feverish imagination continually sport themselves in gardens full of aromatic shrubs, which cloy while they delight, and weaken the sense of pleasure they gratify. The heaven

---

1   The name in the manuscript is by mistake written Cæsar. EDITOR. [Godwin's note]

2   From Antony's famous monologue in Shakespeare's *The Tragedy of Julius Caesar* (1599):

> Friends, Romans, countrymen, lend me your ears:
> I come to bury Caesar, not to praise him.
> The evil that men do lives after them:
> The good is oft interréd with their bones.
> So let it be with Caesar. The noble Brutus
> Hath told you Caesar was ambitious:
> If it were so, it was a grievous fault,
> And grievously hath Caesar answered it.
> Here, under leave of Brutus and the rest —
> For Brutus is an honourable man:
> So are they all, all honourable men —
> Come I to speak in Caesar's funeral. (III, ii, 70-81)

of fancy, below or beyond the stars, in this life, or in those ever-smiling regions surrounded by the unmarked ocean of futurity, have an insipid uniformity which palls. Poets have imagined scenes of bliss; but, fencing out sorrow, all the extatic emotions of the soul, and even its grandeur, seem to be equally excluded. We dose over the unruffled lake, and long to scale the rocks which fence the happy valley of contentment,[1] though serpents hiss in the pathless desert, and danger lurks in the unexplored wiles. Maria found herself more indulgent as she was happier, and discovered virtues, in characters she had before disregarded, while chasing the phantoms of elegance and excellence, which sported in the meteors that exhale in the marshes of misfortune. The heart is often shut by romance against social pleasure; and, fostering a sickly sensibility, grows callous to the soft touches of humanity.

To part with Darnford was indeed cruel. — It was to feel most painfully alone; but she rejoiced to think, that she should spare him the care and perplexity of the suit, and meet him again, all his own. Marriage, as at present constituted, she considered as leading to immorality — yet, as the odium of society impedes usefulness, she wished to avow her affection to Darnford, by becoming his wife according to established rules; not to be confounded with women who act from very different motives, though her conduct would be just the same without the ceremony as with it, and her expectations from him not less firm. The being summoned to defend herself from a charge which she was determined to plead guilty to, was still galling, as it roused bitter reflections on the situation of women in society.

## CHAP. XVII.

SUCH was her state of mind when the dogs of law were let loose on her. Maria took the task of conducting Darnford's defence upon herself. She instructed his counsel to plead guilty to the charge of adultery; but to deny that of seduction.

The counsel for the plaintiff opened the cause, by observing, "that his client had ever been an indulgent husband, and had borne with several defects of temper, while he had nothing criminal to lay to the charge of his wife. But that she left his house

---

1 A reference to the "happy valley" of Samuel Johnson's (1709-84) *Rasselas* (1759), the first two chapters of which are dedicated to a description of the place and the discontent of its inhabitant, Rasselas.

without assigning any cause. He could not assert that she was then acquainted with the defendant; yet, when he was once endeavouring to bring her back to her home, this man put the peace-officers to flight, and took her he knew not whither. After the birth of her child, her conduct was so strange, and a melancholy malady having afflicted one of the family,[1] which delicacy forbade the dwelling on, it was necessary to confine her. By some means the defendant enabled her to make her escape, and they had lived together, in despite of all sense of order and decorum. The adultery was allowed, it was not necessary to bring any witnesses to prove it; but the seduction, though highly probable from the circumstances which he had the honour to state, could not be so clearly proved. — It was of the most atrocious kind, as decency was set at defiance, and respect for reputation, which shows internal compunction, utterly disregarded."

A strong sense of injustice had silenced every emotion, which a mixture of true and false delicacy might otherwise have excited in Maria's bosom. She only felt in earnest to insist on the privilege of her nature. The sarcasms of society, and the condemnations of a mistaken world, were nothing to her, compared with acting contrary to those feelings which were the foundation of her

---

1 Wollstonecraft touches on two mental-health issues in this comment: the hereditary nature of insanity and post-partum depression (also known as "the baby blues" in today's popular parlance, or, in medical circles, "puerperal depression"). Both issues touched Wollstonecraft personally, since her sister Eliza experienced what appears to have been puerperal depression; see p. 176, note 1 for more information about Wollstonecraft's experiences with her. As for the reference to hereditary insanity, in *A Revolutionary Life*, Todd claims that Wollstonecraft's other sister, Everina, her brother James, and both parents show "clearly a depressive, even manic depressive, tendency ... in the Wollstonecraft family" (45-46). In addition, Todd maintains not only that Wollstonecraft's brother Henry may have been insane, but also that he may have been the reason for the author's visit to Bethlehem Asylum in 1797 (*Life* 72, 427); she adds that, early in her letters, Wollstonecraft stops mentioning him nearly altogether, whereas she kept scrupulous tabs on the rest of the family, and that the family rather mysteriously moved to Hoxton from Yorkshire—and Hoxton was famous for its high number of mental institutions (*Life* 21). In this belief, Todd joins such critics as Ralph M. Wardle, who, in *Collected Letters of Mary Wollstonecraft*, cites Emily Sunstein: "Sunstein theorizes that there must have been a reason for the family's silence about him — perhaps he suffered a mental breakdown and was confined to an asylum" (417n).

principles. [She therefore eagerly put herself forward, instead of desiring to be absent, on this memorable occasion.][1]

Convinced that the subterfuges of the law were disgraceful, she wrote a paper, which she expressly desired might be read in court:[2]

"Married when scarcely able to distinguish the nature of the engagement, I yet submitted to the rigid laws which enslave women, and obeyed the man whom I could no longer love. Whether the duties of the state are reciprocal, I mean not to discuss; but I can prove repeated infidelities which I overlooked or pardoned. Witnesses are not wanting to establish these facts. I at present maintain the child of a maid servant, sworn to him, and born after our marriage. I am ready to allow, that education and circumstances lead men to think and act with less delicacy, than the preservation of order in society demands from women; but surely I may without assumption declare, that, though I could excuse the birth, I could not the desertion of this unfortunate babe: — and, while I despised the man, it was not easy to venerate the husband. With proper restrictions however, I revere the institution which fraternizes the world. I exclaim against the laws which throw the whole weight of the yoke on the weaker shoulders, and force women, when they claim protectorship as mothers, to sign a contract, which renders them dependent on the caprice of the tyrant, whom chòice or necessity has appointed to reign over them. Various are the cases, in which a woman ought to separate herself from her husband; and mine, I may be allowed emphatically to insist, comes under the description of the most aggravated.

"I will not enlarge on those provocations which only the individual can estimate; but will bring forward such charges only, the truth of which is an insult upon humanity. In order to promote certain destructive speculations, Mr. Venables prevailed on me to borrow certain sums of a wealthy relation; and, when I refused further compliance, he thought of bartering my person; and not

---

1  The square brackets appear in the source text here and after.
2  Again, Wollstonecraft's narrative echoes Godwin's *Caleb Williams* in that the protagonist has her day in court and attempts to persuade her auditors through a reasonable statement of her case. In the endnote to this passage, Kelly reminds us that Mary "could not appear in court in her own behalf, since ... her legal 'personality' was 'covered' by that of her husband" (207, endnote 171). See p. 235, note 1 for more information on the laws of coverture.

only allowed opportunities to, but urged, a friend from whom he borrowed money, to seduce me. On the discovery of this act of atrocity, I determined to leave him, and in the most decided manner, for ever. I consider all obligations as made void by his conduct; and hold, that schisms which proceed from want of principles, can never be healed.

"He received a fortune with me to the amount of five thousand pounds. On the death of my uncle, convinced that I could provide for my child, I destroyed the settlement of that fortune. I required none of my property to be returned to me, nor shall enumerate the sums extorted from me during six years that we lived together.

"After leaving, what the law considers as my home, I was hunted like a criminal from place to place, though I contracted no debts, and demanded no maintenance — yet, as the laws sanction such proceeding, and make women the property of their husbands, I forbear to animadvert. After the birth of my daughter, and the death of my uncle, who left a very considerable property to myself and child, I was exposed to new persecution; and, because I had, before arriving at what is termed years of discretion, pledged my faith, I was treated by the world, as bound for ever to a man whose vices were notorious. Yet what are the vices generally known, to the various miseries that a woman may be subject to, which, though deeply felt, eating into the soul, elude description, and may be glossed over! A false morality is even established, which makes all the virtue of women consist in chastity, submission, and the forgiveness of injuries.

"I pardon my oppressor — bitterly as I lament the loss of my child, torn from me in the most violent manner. But nature revolts, and my soul sickens at the bare supposition, that it could ever be a duty to pretend affection, when a separation is necessary to prevent my feeling hourly aversion.

"To force me to give my fortune, I was imprisoned — yes; in a private mad-house.[1] — There, in the heart of misery, I met the man charged with seducing me. We became attached — I deemed, and ever shall deem, myself free. The death of my babe dissolved the only tie which subsisted between me and my, what is termed, lawful husband.

"To this person, thus encountered, I voluntarily gave myself, never considering myself as any more bound to transgress the

---

1 See p. 205, note 2 for more information on private and government-run insane asylums during the Romantic period.

laws of moral purity, because the will of my husband might be pleaded in my excuse, than to transgress those laws to which [the policy of artificial society has] annexed [positive] punishments. — While no command of a husband can prevent a woman from suffering for certain crimes, she must be allowed to consult her conscience, and regulate her conduct, in some degree, by her own sense of right. The respect I owe to myself, demanded my strict adherence to my determination of never viewing Mr. Venables in the light of a husband, nor could it forbid me from encouraging another. If I am unfortunately united to an unprincipled man, am I for ever to be shut out from fulfilling the duties of a wife and mother? — I wish my country to approve of my conduct; but, if laws exist, made by the strong to oppress the weak, I appeal to my own sense of justice, and declare that I will not live with the individual, who has violated every moral obligation which binds man to man.

"I protest equally against any charge being brought to criminate the man, whom I consider as my husband. I was six-and-twenty when I left Mr. Venables' roof; if ever I am to be supposed to arrive at an age to direct my own actions, I must by that time have arrived at it. — I acted with deliberation. — Mr. Darnford found me a forlorn and oppressed woman, and promised the protection women in the present state of society want. — But the man who now claims me — was he deprived of my society by this conduct? The question is an insult to common sense, considering where Mr. Darnford met me. — Mr. Venables' door was indeed open to me — nay, threats and intreaties were used to induce me to return; but why? Was affection or honour the motive? — I cannot, it is true, dive into the recesses of the human heart — yet I presume to assert, [borne out as I am by a variety of circumstances,] that he was merely influenced by the most rapacious avarice.

"I claim then a divorce, and the liberty of enjoying, free from molestation, the fortune left to me by a relation, who was well aware of the character of the man with whom I had to contend. — I appeal to the justice and humanity of the jury — a body of men, whose private judgment must be allowed to modify laws, that must be unjust, because definite rules can never apply to indefinite circumstances — and I deprecate punishment [upon the man of my choice, freeing him, as I solemnly do, from the charge of seduction.]

"I did not put myself into a situation to justify a charge of adultery, till I had, from conviction, shaken off the fetters which bound me to Mr. Venables. — While I lived with him, I defy the voice of calumny to sully what is termed the fair fame of woman. Neglected by my husband, I never encouraged a lover; and preserved with scrupulous care, what is termed my honour, at the expence of my peace, till he, who should have been its guardian, laid traps to ensnare me. From that moment I believed myself, in the sight of heaven, free — and no power on earth shall force me to renounce my resolution."

The judge, in summing up the evidence, alluded to "the fallacy of letting women plead their feelings, as an excuse for the violation of the marriage-vow. For his part, he had always determined to oppose all innovation, and the new-fangled notions which incroached on the good old rules of conduct. We did not want French principles[1] in public or private life — and, if women were allowed to plead their feelings, as an excuse or palliation of infidelity, it was opening a flood-gate for immorality. What virtuous woman thought of her feelings? — It was her duty to love and obey the man chosen by her parents and relations, who were qualified by their experience to judge better for her, than she could for herself. As to the charges brought against the husband, they were vague, supported by no witnesses, excepting that of imprisonment in a private madhouse. The proofs of an insanity in the family, might render that however a prudent measure; and indeed the conduct of the lady did not appear that of a person of sane mind. Still such a mode of proceeding could not be justified, and might perhaps entitle the lady [in another court] to a sentence of separation from bed and board, during the joint lives of the parties; but he hoped that no Englishman would legalize adultery, by enabling the adulteress to enrich her seducer. Too many restrictions could not be thrown in the way of divorces, if we wished to maintain the sanctity of marriage; and, though they might bear a little hard on a few, very few individuals, it was evidently for the good of the whole."

---

1 Particularly after the French Revolution began (1789), English conservatives commonly invoked the phrase "French principles" to signify radical and immoral ideas that would lead to violent social uprising.

# CONCLUSION,
## BY THE EDITOR.[1]

VERY few hints exist respecting the plan of the remainder of the work. I find only two detached sentences, and some scattered heads for the continuation of the story. I transcribe the whole.

## I.

"Darnford's letters were affectionate; but circumstances occasioned delays, and the miscarriage of some letters rendered the reception of wished-for answers doubtful: his return was necessary to calm Maria's mind."

## II.

"As Darnford had informed her that his business was settled, his delaying to return seemed extraordinary; but love to excess,[2] excludes fear or suspicion."

------------------------

The scattered heads for the continuation of the story, are as follow.[3]

## I.

"Trial for adultery — Maria defends herself — A separation from bed and board is the consequence — Her fortune is thrown into chancery — Darnford obtains a part of his property — Maria goes into the country."

## II.

"A prosecution for adultery commenced — Trial — Darnford sets out for France — Letters — Once more pregnant — He returns — Mysterious behaviour — Visit — Expectation — Discovery — Interview — Consequence."

---

1 This note is by Godwin, as are all of the square brackets in this section. All of Wollstonecraft's words are in quotation marks, as they appear in the source text.

2 A reference to the title of Eliza Haywood's (1693?-1756) novel *Love in Excess; Or, The Fatal Enquiry* (1719-20).

3 To understand these minutes, it is necessary the reader should consider each of them as setting out from the same point in the story, *viz.* the point to which it is brought down in the preceding chapter. [Godwin's note]

### III.

"Sued by her husband — Damages awarded to him — Separation from bed and board — Darnford goes abroad — Maria into the country — Provides for her father — Is shunned — Returns to London — Expects to see her lover — The rack of expectation — Finds herself again with child — Delighted — A discovery — A visit — A miscarriage — Conclusion."

### IV.

"Divorced by her husband — Her lover unfaithful — Pregnancy — Miscarriage — Suicide."

------------------------

[The following passage appears in some respects to deviate from the preceding hints. It is superscribed],

### "THE END.

"She swallowed the laudanum; her soul was calm — the tempest had subsided — and nothing remained but an eager longing to forget herself — to fly from the anguish she endured to escape from thought — from this hell of disappointment.

"Still her eyes closed not — one remembrance with frightful velocity followed another — All the incidents of her life were in arms, embodied to assail her, and prevent her sinking into the sleep of death. — Her murdered child again appeared to her, mourning for the babe of which she was the tomb. — 'And could it have a nobler? — Surely it is better to die with me, than to enter on life without a mother's care! — I cannot live! — but could I have deserted my child the moment it was born? — thrown it on the troubled wave of life, without a hand to support it?' — She looked up; 'What have I not suffered! — may I find a father where I am going! — Her head turned; a stupor ensued; a faintness — 'Have a little patience,' said Maria, holding her swimming head (she thought of her mother),[1] 'this cannot last long; and what is a little bodily pain to the pangs I have endured?'

---

1 See p. 222, note 1 for more information on the echoes in Wollstonecraft's work of her mother's last spoken words, "'A little patience, and all will be over!'" (Godwin, *Memoirs* 28).

"A new vision swam before her. Jemima seemed to enter — leading a little creature, that, with tottering footsteps, approached the bed. The voice of Jemima sounding as at a distance, called her — she tried to listen, to speak, to look!

"'Behold your child!' exclaimed Jemima. Maria started off the bed, and fainted. — Violent vomiting followed.

"When she was restored to life, Jemima addressed her with great solemnity: '----- led me to suspect, that your husband and brother had deceived you, and secreted the child. I would not torment you with doubtful hopes, and I left you (at a fatal moment) to search for the child! — I snatched her from misery — and (now she is alive again) would you leave her alone in the world, to endure what I have endured?'

"Maria gazed wildly at her, her whole frame was convulsed with emotion; when the child, whom Jemima had been tutoring all the journey, uttered the word 'Mamma!' She caught her to her bosom, and burst into a passion of tears — then, resting the child gently on the bed, as if afraid of killing it, — she put her hand to her eyes, to conceal as it were the agonizing struggle of her soul. She remained silent for five minutes, crossing her arms over her bosom, and reclining her head, — then exclaimed: 'The conflict is over! — I will live for my child!'"

-----------------------

A few readers perhaps, in looking over these hints, will wonder how it could have been practicable, without tediousness, or remitting in any degree the interest of the story, to have filled, from these slight sketches, a number of pages, more considerable than those which have been already presented. But, in reality, these hints, simple as they are, are pregnant with passion and distress. It is the refuge of barren authors only, to crowd their fictions with so great a number of events, as to suffer no one of them to sink into the reader's mind. It is the province of true genius to develop events, to discover their capabilities, to ascertain the different passions and sentiments with which they are fraught, and to diversify them with incidents, that give reality to the picture, and take a hold upon the mind of a reader of taste, from which they can never be loosened. It was particularly the design of the author, in the present instance, to make her story subordinate to a great moral purpose, that "of exhibiting the misery and oppression, peculiar to women, that arise out of the partial laws and customs of society. — This view restr[a]ined her fancy[1]." It was necessary for her, to place in a striking point of view, evils that are too frequently overlooked, and to drag into light those details of oppression, of which the grosser and more insensible part of mankind make little account.

### THE END.

---

1   See author's preface. [Godwin's note. The note marker is placed before the punctuation in the source text, as it is here.] The original text is imperfect here: "restrained" reads "restr ined."

# Appendix A: Relevant Texts by and on Mary Wollstonecraft

## 1. From Wollstonecraft, *Thoughts on the Education of Daughters* (1787)

[*Thoughts on the Education of Daughters* is Wollstonecraft's first published work, written while she was a governess for the Kingsboroughs in Ireland. The subject matter demonstrates her early radicalism and introduces topics that she would continue to develop in her more famous texts: she advocates that all mothers nurse their own children at a time when middle- to upper-class women normally hired a lower-class woman to perform the task, and she provides medical and psychological reasons to support her position; she tackles the problem of insufficient career options for middle-class women; she speaks out against the literature of sentiment; and she advocates that everyone should have some knowledge of medicine to maintain their health at a time when too much knowledge, especially biological knowledge, was deemed improper for women. Hester Chapone's (1727-1801) *Letters on the Improvement of the Mind, Addressed to a Young Lady* (1777) was a major influence on this text.]

(Wollstonecraft, Mary. *Thoughts on the Education of Daughters.* London: J. Johnson, 1787. 3-5; 48-51; 69-74; 85-87; 101-02; 104-06.)

The first thing to be attended to, is the laying the foundation of a good constitution. The mother (if there are not very weighty reasons to prevent her) ought to suckle her children. Her milk is their proper nutriment, and for some time is quite sufficient. Were a regular mode of suckling adopted, it would be far from being a laborious task. Children, who are left to the care of ignorant nurses, have their stomachs overloaded with improper food, which turns acid, and renders them very uncomfortable. We should be particularly careful to guard them in their infant state from bodily pain; as their minds can then afford them no amusement to alleviate it. The first years of a child's life are frequently made miserable through negligence or ignorance. Their complaints are mostly in their stomach or bowels; and these complaints generally arise from the quality and quantity of their food.

The suckling of a child also excites the warmest glow of tenderness — Its dependant, helpless state produces an affection, which may properly be termed maternal. I have even felt it, when I have seen a mother perform that office; and am of opinion, that maternal tenderness arises quite as much from habit as instinct. It is possible, I am convinced, to acquire the affection of a parent for an adopted child; it is necessary, therefore, for a mother to perform the office of one, in order to produce in herself a rational affection for her offspring.

[...]

## Reading.

It is an old, but a very true observation, that the human mind must ever be employed. A relish for reading, or any of the fine arts, should be cultivated very early in life; and those who reflect can tell, of what importance it is for the mind to have some resource in itself, and not to be entirely dependant on the senses for employment and amusement. If it unfortunately is so, it must submit to meanness, and often to vice, in order to gratify them. The wisest and best are too much under their influence; and the endeavouring to conquer them, when reason and virtue will not give their sanction, constitutes great part of the warfare of life. What support, then, have they who are all senses, and who are full of schemes, which terminate in temporal objects?

Reading is the most rational employment, if people seek food for the understanding, and do not read merely to remember words; or with a view to quote celebrated authors, and retail sentiments they do not understand or feel. Judicious books enlarge the mind and improve the heart, though some, by them, "are made coxcombs whom nature meant for fools."[1]

Those productions which give a wrong account of the human passions, and the various accidents of life, ought not to be read before the judgment is formed, or at least exercised. Such accounts are one great cause of the affectation of young women. Sensibility is described and praised, and the effects of it represented in a way so different from nature, that those who imitate it must make themselves very ridiculous. A false taste is acquired, and sensible books appear dull and insipid after those superficial performances, which obtain their full end if they can keep the mind in a continual ferment. Gallantry is made the only interesting subject with the novelist; reading, therefore, will often co-operate to make his fair admirers insignificant.

[...]

---

1  From Alexander Pope's "An Essay on Criticism" (1711), line 27.

## Unfortunate Situation of Females, Fashionably Educated, and Left Without a Fortune.

I have hitherto only spoken of those females, who will have a provision made for them by their parents. But many who have been well, or at least fashionably educated, are left without a fortune, and if they are not entirely devoid of delicacy, they must frequently remain single.

Few are the modes of earning a subsistence, and those very humiliating. Perhaps to be an humble companion to some rich old cousin, or what is still worse, to live with strangers, who are so intolerably tyrannical, that none of their own relations can bear to live with them, though they should even expect a fortune in reversion. It is impossible to enumerate the many hours of anguish such a person must spend. Above the servants, yet considered by them as a spy, and ever reminded of her inferiority when in conversation with the superiors. If she cannot condescend to mean flattery, she has not a chance of being a favorite; and should any of the visitors take notice of her, and she for a moment forget her subordinate state, she is sure to be reminded of it.

Painfully sensible of unkindness, she is alive to every thing, and many sarcasms reach her, which were perhaps directed another way. She is alone, shut out from equality and confidence, and the concealed anxiety impairs her constitution; for she must wear a cheerful face, or be dismissed. The being dependant on the caprice of a fellow-creature, though certainly very necessary in this state of discipline, is yet a very bitter corrective, which we would fain shrink from.

A teacher at a school is only a kind of upper servant, who has more work than the menial ones.

A governess to young ladies is equally disagreeable. It is ten to one if they meet with a reasonable mother; and if she is not so, she will be continually finding fault to prove she is not ignorant, and be displeased if her pupils do not improve, but angry if the proper methods are taken to make them do so. The children treat them with disrespect, and often with insolence. In the mean time life glides away, and the spirits with it; "and when youth and genial years are flown,"[1] they have nothing to subsist on; or, perhaps, on some extraordinary occasion, some small allowance may be made for them, which is thought a great charity.

The few trades which are left, are now gradually falling into the hands of the men, and certainly they are not very respectable.

---

1  Misquoted from James Thomson's "Song" (1750): "Till youth and genial years are flown" (l. 7). See p. 242, note 1 for more information on this reference.

It is hard for a person who has a relish for polished society, to herd with the vulgar, or to condescend to mix with her former equals when she is considered in a different light. What unwelcome heart-breaking knowledge is then poured in on her! I mean a view of the selfishness and depravity of the world; for every other acquirement is a source of pleasure, though they may occasion temporary inconveniences. How cutting is the contempt she meets with! — A young mind looks round for love and friendship; but love and friendship fly from poverty: expect them not if you are poor!

[...]

It is too universal a maxim with novelists, that love is felt but once; though it appears to me, that the heart which is capable of receiving an impression at all, and can distinguish, will turn to a new object when the first is found unworthy. I am convinced it is practicable, when a respect for goodness has the first place in the mind, and notions of perfection are not affixed to constancy. Many ladies are delicately miserable, and imagine that they are lamenting the loss of a lover, when they are full of self-applause, and reflections on their own superior refinement. Painful feelings are prolonged beyond their natural course, to gratify our desire of appearing heroines, and we deceive ourselves as well as others. When any sudden stroke of fate deprives us of those we love, we may not readily get the better of the blow; but when we find we have been led astray by our passions, and that it was our own imaginations which gave the high colouring to the picture, we may be certain time will drive it out of our minds.

[...]

In a comfortable situation, a cultivated mind is necessary to render a woman contented; and in a miserable one, it is her only consolation. A sensible, delicate woman, who by some strange accident, or mistake, is joined to a fool or a brute, must be wretched beyond all names of wretchedness, if her views are confined to the present scene.[1] Of what

---

1 A decade later (16 May 1797), Wollstonecraft would express a similar sentiment in a letter to George Dyson with reference to *Maria*: "For my part I cannot suppose any situation more distressing than for a woman of sensibility with an improving mind to be bound, to such a man as I have described, for life — obliged to renounce all the humanizing affections, and to avoid cultivating her taste lest her perception of grace, and refinement of sentiment should sharpen to agony the pangs of disappointment" (412).

importance, then, is intellectual improvement, when our comfort here, and happiness hereafter, depends upon it.

[...]

The ignorant imagine there is something very mysterious in the practice of physic. They expect a medicine to work like a charm, and know nothing of the progress and crisis of disorders. The keeping of the patient low appears cruel, all kind of regimen is disregarded, and though the fever rages, they cannot be persuaded not to give them inflammatory food. "How (say they) can a person get well without nourishment?"

The mind, too, should be soothed at the same time; and indeed, whenever it sinks, soothing is, at first, better than reasoning. The slackened nerves are not to be braced by words. When a mind is worried by care, or oppressed by sorrow, it cannot in a moment grow tranquil, and attend to the voice of reason.

## 2. From Wollstonecraft, "Cave of Fancy" (composed 1787; published 1798)

[Wollstonecraft's "oriental tale," as Godwin calls it in *Memoirs* (63), is a fragment; indeed, she seems not to have attempted to develop it again after 1787. Strongly influenced by Samuel Johnson's *Rasselas* (1759), "Cave of Fancy" is essentially a physiognomical fiction, and was probably inspired by the reading for her translation of the German text *Essays on Physiognomy* by Johann Caspar Lavater (1741-1801), which also remained unfinished.

"Cave of Fancy" is about an old hermit named Sagestus, also called "the sage," who lives in a cave and finds an orphan girl amongst the dead from a shipwreck on a shore near his home. He adopts her and undertakes a course of education for her that, he hopes, will counteract the poor educative and genetic material that is her birthright. As such, this tale reveals to a significant degree Wollstonecraft's struggle to resolve the "nature versus nurture" debate. Lavater's *Essays on Physiognomy* (Appendix D2) illustrate that physiognomists considered human character to be almost entirely established at birth, since one cannot change one's facial features. Ergo, the weak, debased female character—as Wollstonecraft saw it—was innate and could not be significantly altered. In this tale, though, Wollstonecraft contends with physiognomy by exploring whether education can overcome the inborn characteristics that she deemed undesirable for women, a theme that she would continue to explore in *Mary*, which was published in 1788. I propose that her increasing attachment to the notion that education forms, and can reform, human character explains, at least in part, why Wollstonecraft lost interest in her physiognomical projects.

In Chapter II below, Sagestus submits the dead on the beach to physiognomical inquiry and finds the girl's mother sorely wanting. The final selection below provides a definition of "sensibility" that allies it with pain and echoes the "rhapsody on sensibility" in Chapter XXIV of *Mary*.]

("Cave of Fancy. A Tale." *Posthumous Works of the Author of A Vindication of the Rights of Woman*. 4 vols. London: J. Johnson, 1798. Vol. 4. 99-155. 110-11; 122-25; 135-36.)

## Chap. II.

Again Sagestus approached the dead, to view them with a more scrutinizing eye. He was perfectly acquainted with the construction of the human body, knew the traces that virtue or vice leaves on the whole frame; they were now indelibly fixed by death; nay more, he knew by the shape of the solid structure, how far the spirit could range, and saw the barrier beyond which it could not pass: the mazes of fancy he explored, measured the stretch of thought, and, weighing all in an even balance, could tell whom nature had stamped an hero, a poet, or philosopher.

By their appearance, at a transient glance, he knew that the vessel must have contained many passengers, and that some of them were above the vulgar, with respect to fortune and education; he then walked leisurely among the dead, and narrowly observed their pallid features.

[...]

Anxious to observe the mother of his charge, he turned to the lily that had been so rudely snapped, and, carefully observing it, traced every fine line to its source. There was a delicacy in her form, so truly feminine, that an involuntary desire to cherish such a being, made the sage again feel the almost forgotten sensations of his nature. On observing her more closely, he discovered that her natural delicacy had been increased by an improper education, to a degree that took away all vigour from her faculties. And its baneful influence had had such an effect on her mind, that few traces of the exertions of it appeared on her face, though the fine finish of her features, and particularly the form of the forehead, convinced the sage that her understanding might have risen considerably above mediocrity, had the wheels ever been put in motion; but, clogged by prejudices, they never turned quite round, and, whenever she considered a subject, she stopped before she came to a conclusion. Assuming a mask of propriety, she had banished nature; yet its tendency was only to be diverted, not stifled. Some lines, which took from the symmetry of the mouth, not very obvious to a superficial observer, struck Sagestus, and they appeared to him characters of indolent obstinacy. Not having courage to form an opinion of her own, she adhered, with blind partiality, to those she adopted, which she received in the lump, and, as they always remained unopened, of course she only saw the even gloss on the outside. Vestiges of anger were visible on her brow, and the sage concluded, that she had often been offended with, and indeed would scarcely make any allowance for, those who did not coincide with her in opinion, as things always appear self-evident that have never been examined; yet her very weakness gave a charming timidity to her countenance; goodness and tenderness pervaded every lineament, and melted in her dark blue eyes. The compassion that wanted activity, was sincere, though it only embellished her face, or produced casual acts of charity when a moderate alms could relieve present distress. Unacquainted with life, fictitious, unnatural distress drew the tears that were not shed for real misery. In its own shape, human wretchedness excites a little disgust in the mind that has indulged sickly refinement. Perhaps the sage gave way to a little conjecture in drawing the last conclusion; but his conjectures generally arose from distinct ideas, and a dawn of light allowed him to see a great way farther than common mortals.

He was now convinced that the orphan was not very unfortunate in having lost such a mother. The parent that inspires fond affection without respect, is seldom an useful one; and they only are respectable, who consider right and wrong abstracted from local forms and accidental modifications.

Determined to adopt the child, he named it after himself, Sagesta, and retired to the hut where the innocent slept, to think of the best method of educating this child, whom the angry deep had spared.

[...]

Men do not make sufficient distinction, said she, digressing from her story to address Sagestus, between tenderness and sensibility.

To give the shortest definition of sensibility, replied the sage, I should say that it is the result of acute senses, finely fashioned nerves, which vibrate at the slightest touch, and convey such clear intelligence to the brain, that it does not require to be arranged by the judgment. Such persons instantly enter into the characters of others, and instinctively discern what will give pain to every human being; their own feelings are so varied that they seem to contain in themselves, not only all the passions of the species, but their various modifications. Exquisite pain and pleasure is their portion; nature wears for them a different aspect than is displayed to common mortals. One moment it is a paradise; all is beautiful: a cloud arises, an emotion receives a sudden damp; darkness invades the sky, and the world is an unweeded garden; — but go on with your narrative, said Sagestus, recollecting himself.

## 3. From Wollstonecraft, *A Vindication of the Rights of Men* (1790)

[While the title of Wollstonecraft's work echoes that of Edmund Burke's (1729-97) first publication, *A Vindication of Natural Society* (1756),[1] the content engages substantially with his *Reflections on the Revolution in France*, which was published on 1 November 1790. Wollstonecraft published her first foray into political reformism anonymously by 29 November. Of this momentous event, Godwin writes in the *Memoirs*,

> She was in the habit of composing with rapidity, and her
> answer, which was the first of the numerous ones that
> appeared, obtained extraordinary notice. Marked as it is
> with the vehemence and impetuousness of its eloquence, it
> is certainly chargeable with a too contemptuous and intem-
> perate treatment of the great man against whom its attack is
> directed. But this circumstance was not injurious to the
> success of the publication. Burke had been warmly loved by
> the most liberal and enlightened friends of freedom [because
> he supported the American Revolution], and they were pro-
> portionably inflamed and disgusted by the fury of his
> assault, upon what they deemed to be its sacred cause[, the
> French Revolution]. (1st ed.; 75-76).

The second edition, published in mid-December, bore Wollstone-craft's name.

The following selections illustrate that Wollstonecraft's opposition to the language of sentiment was political, not just literary and aesthetic, and that her opposition to contemporary ideals of femininity was bound up with the falsifying weakness of sentiment and its resistance to reason. In the final passage, she introduces the argument on which she would base her next polemical text, *Rights of Woman*, in which her Christian readers are forced to admit to the intellectual

---

1   A prose fiction that parodies political theory.

equality of women or risk blasphemy.]

(Wollstonecraft, Mary. *A Vindication of the Rights of Men, in a Letter to the Right Honourable Edmund Burke; Occasioned by his* Reflections on the Revolution in France. 2nd ed. London: J. Johnson, 1790. 1-2; 64-66; 111-15.)

## A Letter to the Right Honourable Edmund Burke.

Sir,

It is not necessary, with courtly insincerity, to apologise to you for thus intruding on your precious time, not to profess that I think it an honour to discuss an important subject with a man whose literary abilities have raised him to notice in the state. I have not yet learned to twist my periods, nor, in the equivocal idiom of politeness, to disguise my sentiments, and imply what I should be afraid to utter: if, therefore, in the course of this epistle, I chance to express contempt, and even indignation, with some emphasis, I beseech you to believe that it is not a flight of fancy; for truth, in morals, has ever appeared to me the essence of the sublime; and, in taste, simplicity the only criterion of the beautiful.[1] But I war not with an individual when I contend for the *rights of men* and the liberty of reason. You see I do not condescend to cull my words to avoid the invidious phrase, nor shall I be prevented from giving a manly[2] definition of it, by the flimsy ridicule which a lively fancy has interwoven with the present acceptation of the term. Reverencing the rights of humanity, I shall dare to assert them; not intimidated by the horse laugh that you have raised, or waiting till time

---

1  A reference to Burke's famous text on aesthetics, *A Philosophical Enquiry into the Origin of our Ideas of the Sublime and Beautiful* (1757).

2  Throughout *Rights of Men,* Wollstonecraft uses "manly" or "unmanly" (and associated terms) to celebrate powerful, direct writing, or to denigrate disingenuous and weak writing. Her prioritization of masculinity in her use of these gendered terms seems surprising, given that she is the "mother of feminism," but it does not contradict the position she develops throughout her feminist works. After all, her basic argument is constant: current ideals of femininity were pernicious and must be changed. Moreover, she follows a cultural norm in this phrasing, as Macaulay explains in *Letters on Education*: "It must be confessed, that the virtues of the males among the human species, though mixed and blended with a variety of vices and errors, have displayed a bolder and a more consistent picture of excellence than female nature has hitherto done. It is on these reasons that, when we compliment the appearance of a more than ordinary energy in the female mind, we call it masculine" (127-28). See the full passage in Appendix B1 for more information.

has wiped away the compassionate tears which you have elaborately laboured to excite.

[...]

It is a proverbial observation, that a very thin partition divides wit and madness.[1] Poetry therefore naturally addresses the fancy, and the language of passion is with great felicity borrowed from the heightened picture which the imagination draws of sensible objects concentred by impassioned reflection. And, during this "fine phrensy,"[2] reason has no right to rein-in the imagination, unless to prevent the introduction of supernumerary images; if the passion is real, the head will not be ransacked for stale tropes and cold rodomontade. I now speak of the genuine enthusiasm of genius, which, perhaps, seldom appears, but in the infancy of civilization; for as this light becomes more luminous reason clips the wing of fancy — the youth becomes a man.

Whether the glory of Europe is set, I shall not now enquire; but probably the spirit of romance and chivalry is in the wane; and reason will gain by its extinction.[3]

From observing several cold romantic characters I have been led to confine the term romantic to one definition — false, or rather artificial, feelings. Works of genius are read with a prepossession in their favour, and sentiments imitated, because they were fashionable and pretty, and not because they were forcibly felt.

In modern poetry the understanding and memory often fabricate the pretended effusions of the heart, and romance destroys all simplicity; which, in works of taste, is but a synonymous word for truth. This romantic spirit has extended to our prose, and scattered artificial flowers over the most barren heath; or a mixture of verse and prose producing the strangest incongruities. The turgid bombast of some of your periods fully proves these assertions; for when the heart speaks we are seldom shocked by hyperbole, or dry raptures.

---

1  A reference to John Dryden's famous lines in "Absalom and Achitophel": "Great wits are sure to madness near allied, / And thin partitions do their bounds divide" (ll. 163-64).

2  A reference to lines spoken by Theseus in Shakespeare's *A Midsummer Night's Dream*: "The poet's eye, in a fine frenzy rolling, / Doth glance from heaven to earth, from earth to heaven" (V, i, 12-13).

3  A reference to Burke's lament in *Reflections on the Revolution in France*: "the age of chivalry is gone. — That of sophisters, œconomists, and calculators, has succeeded; and the glory of Europe is extinguished forever" (113). See Appendix B2 for a longer extract from the text.

[...]

But without fixed principles even goodness of heart is no security from inconsistency, and mild affectionate sensibility only renders a man more ingeniously cruel, when the pangs of hurt vanity are mistaken for virtuous indignation, and the gall of bitterness for the milk of Christian charity.

Where is the dignity, the infallibility of sensibility, in the fair ladies, whom, if the voice of rumour is to be credited, the captive negroes curse in all the agony of bodily pain, for the unheard of tortures they invent? It is probable that some of them, after the sight of a flagellation, compose their ruffled spirits and exercise their tender feelings by the perusal of the last imported novel.[1] — How true these tears are to nature, I leave you to determine. But these ladies may have read your *Enquiry* concerning the origin of our ideas of the Sublime and Beautiful, and, convinced by your arguments, may have laboured to be pretty, by counterfeiting weakness.[2]

You may have convinced them that *littleness* and *weakness* are the very essence of beauty; and that the Supreme Being, in giving women beauty in the most supereminent degree, seemed to command them, by the powerful voice of Nature, not to cultivate the moral virtues that might chance to excite respect, and interfere with the pleasing sensations they were created to inspire. Thus confining truth, fortitude, and humanity, within the rigid pale of manly morals, they might justly argue, that to be loved, woman's high end and great distinction! they should "learn to lisp, to totter in their walk, and nick-name God's creatures."[3] Never, they might repeat after you, was any man, much less a woman, rendered amiable by the force of those exalted qualities, fortitude, justice, wisdom, and truth; and thus forewarned of the sacrifice they must make to those austere, unnatural virtues, they would be authorized to turn all their attention to their persons,

---

1 Doubtlessly a reference to Rousseau's *Julie, ou, La Nouvelle Héloïse* (1761), but Wollstonecraft may also have in mind *The Sorrows of Young Werther* (*Die Leiden des jungen Werthers*) (1774) by Johann Wolfgang von Goethe. See Appendix C2 for passages from Goethe's sentimental text.

2 See p. 297, note 1.

3 Susan Wolfson notes that the original quotation comes from Shakespeare's *Hamlet*, in which the title character "sneers at poor exploited Ophelia" (166), "You jig, you amble and you lisp, and nickname God's creatures, and make your wantonness your ignorance" (III, i, 143-44). The passage from Burke's *The Sublime and the Beautiful*, to which Wollstonecraft refers more specifically, is the following: women "learn to lisp, to totter in their walk, to counterfeit weakness, and even sickness" (91). Wollstonecraft revisits this phrase on page 9 of *Rights of Woman*; see Appendix A4 for the complete passage.

systematically neglecting morals to secure beauty. — Some rational old woman indeed might chance to stumble at this doctrine, and hint, that in avoiding atheism you had not steered clear of the mussulman's creed;[1] but you could readily exculpate yourself by turning the charge on Nature, who made our idea of beauty independent of reason. Nor would it be necessary for you to recollect, that if virtue has any other foundation than worldly utility, you have clearly proved that one half of the human species, at least, have not souls; and that Nature, by making women *little, smooth, delicate, fair* creatures, never designed that they should exercise their reason to acquire the virtues that produce opposite, if not contradictory, feelings. The affection they excite, to be uniform and perfect, should not be tinctured with the respect which moral virtues inspire, lest pain should be blended with pleasure, and admiration disturb the soft intimacy of love. This laxity of morals in the female world is certainly more captivating to a libertine imagination than the cold arguments of reason, that give no sex to virtue. If beautiful weakness be interwoven in a woman's frame, if the chief business of her life be (as you insinuate) to inspire love, and Nature has made an eternal distinction between the qua[l]ities that dignify a rational being and this animal perfection, her duty and happiness in this life must clash with any preparation for a more exalted state. So that Plato and Milton were grossly mistaken in asserting that human love led to heavenly,[2] and was only an exaltation of the same affection; for the love of the Deity, which is mixed with the most profound reverence, must be love of perfection, and not compassion for weakness.

To say the truth, I not only tremble for the souls of women, but for the good natured man, whom every one loves. The *amiable* weakness of his mind is a strong argument against its immateriality, and seems to prove that beauty relaxes the *solids* of the soul as well as the body.

## 4. From Wollstonecraft, *A Vindication of the Rights of Woman* (1792)

[*A Vindication of the Rights of Woman* is the text for which Wollstonecraft is most renowned. With its appeal to her audience's Christian morality and respect for the powers of reason, the polemical text is a bold statement of the claim to rights for half of the human race. The timing of its publication was perfect: by January 1792, the French Revolution had not yet devolved into a bloodbath and its supporters could still

---

1 It was widely believed in the period that Muslims considered women to be of a lower order of being.
2 See p. 121, note 1 more information on this reference.

champion it as a worthy battle for the noble cause of human equality; moreover, the literary expression of the anti-slavery movement in England had reached a pitch of intensity only a few years before, particularly with Hannah More's "Slavery: A Poem" and William Cowper's "The Negro's Complaint," both published in 1788. Wollstonecraft capitalized on both of these circumstances to emphasize the timeliness of her appeal for women's equality. Indeed, she addresses *Rights of Woman* to M. Talleyrand-Périgord, the influential architect of the new educational curriculum in the French Republic, and she uses the word "slave" and its derivatives dozens of times throughout the work. Wollstonecraft planned to write a second part, but never accomplished it; later in 1792, however, she published a slightly revised second edition of the text.

The passages below detail the following: her argument that improved female education will establish equality between the sexes; her pointed opposition to Jean-Jacques Rousseau's (1712-78) *Émile, ou, de l'Éducation* (1762), particularly in its sentimental construction of the perfect female mate; her presentation of literary sentiment in general as an attack on reason (the guiding principle of the French Revolution, as the *philosophes* presented it); and, finally, her understanding of associationist principles of education.]

(Wollstonecraft, Mary. *A Vindication of the Rights of Woman: with Strictures on Political and Moral Subjects*. London: J. Johnson, 1792. 1-4; 6-9; 134-36; 259-60; 261-64.)

Introduction.

After considering the historic page, and viewing the living world with anxious solicitude, the most melancholy emotions of sorrowful indignation have depressed my spirits, and I have sighed when obliged to confess, that either nature has made a great difference between man and man, or that the civilization which has hitherto taken place in the world has been very partial. I have turned over various books written on the subject of education, and patiently observed the conduct of parents and the management of schools; but what has been the result? — a profound conviction that the neglected education of my fellow-creatures is the grand source of the misery I deplore; and that women, in particular, are rendered weak and wretched by a variety of concurring causes, originating from one hasty conclusion. The conduct and manners of women, in fact, evidently prove that their minds are not in a healthy state; for, like the flowers which are planted in too rich a soil, strength and usefulness are sacrificed to beauty; and the flaunting leaves, after having pleased a fastidious eye, fade, disregarded on the stalk, long before the season when they ought to have arrived at maturity. — One cause of this barren blooming I attribute to a false system of education, gathered from the books written on this subject by men who, considering females rather as women than human creatures, have been more anxious to make them alluring mistresses than rational wives;[1] and the understanding of the sex has been so bubbled by this specious homage, that the civilized women of the present century, with a few exceptions, are only anxious to inspire love, when they ought to cherish a nobler ambition, and by their abilities and virtues exact respect.

In a treatise, therefore, on female rights and manners, the works which have been particularly written for their improvement must not be overlooked; especially when it is asserted, in direct terms, that the minds of women are enfeebled by false refinement; that the books of instruction, written by men of genius, have had the same tendency as more frivolous productions; and that, in the true style of Mahometanism,[2] they are only considered as females, and not as a part of the human species, when improvable reason is allowed to be the dignified distinction which raises men above the brute creation, and puts a natural sceptre in a feeble hand.

Yet, because I am a woman, I would not lead my readers to suppose that I mean violently to agitate the contested question respecting the equality and inferiority of the sex; but as the subject lies in my way, and I cannot pass it over without subjecting the main tendency of my reasoning to misconstruction, I shall stop a moment to deliver, in a few words, my opinion. — In the government of the physical world it is observable that the female, in general, is inferior to the male. The male pursues, the female yields — this is the law of nature; and it does not appear to be suspended or abrogated in favour of woman. This physical superiority cannot be denied — and it is a noble prerogative! But not content with this natural pre-eminence, men endeavour to sink us still lower, merely to render us alluring objects for a moment; and women, intoxicated by the adoration which men, under the influence of their senses, pay them, do not seek to obtain a durable inter-

---

1 This phrase is a direct attack on Jean-Jacques Rousseau's description of the education of the title-character's wife-to-be, Sophie, in *Émile*. Later in this text, Wollstonecraft claims that in *Émile* Rousseau asserts "that woman ought to be weak and passive, because she has less bodily strength than man; and from hence infers, that she was formed to please and to be subject to him; and that it is her duty to render herself *agreeable* to her master — this being the grand end of her existence" (171).
2 See p. 300, note 1 for more information about this criticism of Islam.

est in their hearts, or to become the friends of the fellow creatures who find amusement in their society.

[...]

My own sex, I hope, will excuse me, if I treat them like rational creatures, instead of flattering their *fascinating* graces, and viewing them as if they were in a state of perpetual childhood, unable to stand alone. I earnestly wish to point out in what true dignity and human happiness consists — I wish to persuade women to endeavour to acquire strength, both of mind and body, and to convince them that the soft phrases, susceptibility of heart, delicacy of sentiment, and refinement of taste, are almost synonymous with epithets of weakness, and that those beings who are only the objects of pity and that kind of love, which has been termed its sister, will soon become objects of contempt.

Dismissing then those pretty feminine phrases, which the men condescendingly use to soften our slavish dependence, and despising that weak elegancy of mind, exquisite sensibility, and sweet docility of manners, supposed to be the sexual characteristics of the weaker vessel, I wish to show that elegance is inferior to virtue, that the first object of laudable ambition is to obtain a character as a human being, regardless of the distinction of sex; and that secondary views should be brought to this simple touchstone.

This is a rough sketch of my plan; and should I express my conviction with the energetic emotions that I feel whenever I think of the subject, the dictates of experience and reflection will be felt by some of my readers. Animated by this important object, I shall disdain to cull my phrases or polish my style; — I aim at being useful, and sincerity will render me unaffected; for wishing rather to persuade by the force of my arguments, than dazzle by the elegance of my language, I shall not waste my time in rounding periods, nor in fabricating the turgid bombast of artificial feelings, which, coming from the head, never reach the heart.[1] — I shall be employed about things, not words! — and, anxious to render my sex more respectable members of society, I shall try to avoid that flowery diction which has glided from essays into novels, and from novels into familiar letters and conversation.

These pretty nothings — these caricatures of the real beauty of sensibility, dropping glibly from the tongue, vitiate the taste, and create a kind of sickly delicacy that turns away from simple unadorned truth;

---

1 Compare this sentence with the opening paragraph of *Rights of Men* in Appendix A3, in which Wollstonecraft writes that she disdains to "condescend to cull my words to avoid the invidious phrase."

and a deluge of false sentiments and over-stretched feelings, stifling the natural emotions of the heart, render the domestic pleasures insipid, that ought to sweeten the exercise of those severe duties, which educate a rational and immortal being for a nobler field of action.

The education of women has, of late, been more attended to than formerly; yet they áre still reckoned a frivolous sex, and ridiculed or pitied by the writers who endeavour by satire or instruction to improve them. It is acknowledged that they spend many of the first years of their lives in acquiring a smattering of accomplishments: meanwhile, strength of body and mind are sacrificed to libertine notions of beauty, to the desire of establishing themselves, — the only way women can rise in the world, — by marriage. And this desire making mere animals of them, when they marry they act as such children may be expected to act: — they dress; they paint, and nickname God's creatures. — Surely these weak beings are only fit for the seraglio! Can they govern a family, or take care of the poor babes whom they bring into the world?

[...]

Ignorance is a frail base for virtue! Yet, that it is the condition for which woman was organized, has been insisted upon by the writers who have most vehemently argued in favour of the superiority of man; a superiority not in degree, but essence; though, to soften the argument, they have laboured to prove, with chivalrous generosity, that the sexes ought not to be compared; man was made to reason, woman to feel: and that together, flesh and spirit, they make the most perfect whole, by blending happily reason and sensibility into one character.

And what is sensibility? "Quickness of sensation; quickness of perception; delicacy." Thus is it defined by Dr. Johnson; and the definition gives me no other idea than of the most exquisitely polished instinct. I discern not a trace of the image of God in either sensation or matter. Refined seventy times seven,[1] they are still material; intellect dwells not there; nor will fire ever make lead gold!

I come round to my old argument; if woman be allowed to have an immortal soul, she must have as the employment of life, an understanding to improve. And when, to render the present state more complete, though every thing proves it to be but a fraction of a mighty sum, she is incited by present gratification to forget her grand desti-

---

1  A reference to the Book of Matthew in the New Testament: "Then came Peter to him, and said, Lord, how oft shall my brother sin against me, and I forgive him? till seven times? / Jesus saith unto him, I say not unto thee, Until seven times: but, Until seventy times seven" (St. Matthew 18: 21-22).

nation, Nature is counteracted, or she was born only to procreate and rot. Or, granting brutes, of every description, a soul, though not a reasonable one, the exercise of instinct and sensibility may be the step, which they are to take, in this life, towards the attainment of reason in the next; so that through all eternity they will lag behind man, who, why we cannot tell, had the power given him of attaining reason in his first mode of existence.

[...]

## The Effect which an Early Association of Ideas has upon the Character.

Educated in the enervating style recommended by the writers on whom I have been animadverting; and not having a chance, from their subordinate state in society, to recover their lost ground, is it surprising that women every where appear a defect in nature? Is it surprising, when we consider what a determinate effect an early association of ideas has on the character, that they neglect their understandings, and turn all their attention to their persons?

The great advantages which naturally result from storing the mind with knowledge, are obvious from the following considerations. The association of our ideas[1] is either habitual or instantaneous; and the latter mode seems rather to depend on the original temperature of the mind than on the will. When the ideas, and matters of fact, are once taken in, they lie by for use, till some fortuitous circumstance makes the information dart into the mind with illustrative force, that has been received at very different periods of our lives. Like the lightning's flash are many recollections; one idea assimilating and explaining another, with astonishing rapidity.

[...]

Education thus only supplies the man of genius with knowledge to give variety and contrast to his associations; but there is an habitual association of ideas, that grows "with our growth," which has a great effect on the moral character of mankind; and by which a turn is given to the mind that commonly remains throughout life. So ductile is the understanding, and yet so stubborn, that the associations which depend on adventitious circumstances, during the period that the body takes to arrive at maturity, can seldom be disentangled by

---

1  See the Introduction to this edition (p. 46) and Appendix D3 for more on David Hartley's psychological theory of associationism.

reason. One idea calls up another, its old associate, and memory, faithful to the first impressions, particularly when the intellectual powers are not employed to cool our sensations, retraces them with mechanical exactness.

This habitual slavery, to first impressions, has a more baneful effect on the female than the male character, because business and other dry employments of the understanding, tend to deaden the feelings and break associations that do violence to reason. But females, who are made women of when they are mere children, and brought back to childhood when they ought to leave the go-cart forever, have not sufficient strength of mind to efface the superinductions of art that have smothered nature.

Every thing that they see or hear serves to fix impressions, call forth emotions, and associate ideas, that give a sexual character to the mind. False notions of beauty and delicacy stop the growth of their limbs and produce a sickly soreness, rather than delicacy of organs; and thus weakened by being employed in unfolding instead of examining the first associations, forced on them by every surrounding object, how can they attain the vigour necessary to enable them to throw off their factitious character? — where find strength to recur to reason and rise superior to a system of oppression, that blasts the fair promises of spring? This cruel association of ideas, which every thing conspires to twist into all their habits of thinking, or, to speak with more precision, of feeling, receives new force when they begin to act a little for themselves; for they then perceive, that it is only through their address to excite emotions in men, that pleasure and power are to be obtained. Besides, all the books professedly written for their instruction, which make the first impression on their minds, all inculcate the same opinions. Educated in worse than Egyptian bondage, it is unreasonable, as well as cruel, to upbraid them with faults that can scarcely be avoided, unless a degree of native vigour be supposed, that falls to the lot of very few amongst mankind.

## 5. William Godwin, "Preface" to the Letters in *Posthumous Works* (1798)

[After Wollstonecraft's death in 1798, Godwin published the *Posthumous Works* to formally collect her papers, such as fragmentary works like *Maria*, and her letters, his "Preface" to which I reproduce here. The letters constitute the entire third volume of the *Posthumous Works* and include her promises to Imlay to commit suicide. Godwin has been lambasted in modern criticism for distributing such personal and damaging information, on one hand, and, on the other, for characterizing Wollstonecraft as a sentimental heroine and her suicide as an aesthetic event by comparing her to Johann Wolfgang von Goethe's title character in *The Sorrows of Young Werther* (*Die Leiden des jungen Werthers*) (1774). See Appendix A6 for more evidence of Godwin's "Wertherization" of Wollstonecraft.]

(Godwin, William. Preface to the Letters. Po*sthumous Works of the Author of A Vindication of the Rights of Woman*. 4 vols. London: J. Johnson, 1798. Vol. 3. unpag. 3 pages.)

Preface.

The following Letters may possibly be found to contain the finest examples of the language of sentiment and passion ever presented to the world. They bear a striking resemblance to the celebrated romance of Werter, though the incidents to which they relate are of a very different cast. Probably the readers to whom Werter is incapable of affording pleasure, will receive no delight from the present publication. The editor apprehends in the judgment of those best qualified to decide upon the comparison, these Letters will be admitted to have the superiority over the fiction of Goethe. They are the offspring of a glowing imagination, and a heart penetrated with the passion it essays to describe.

To the series of letters constituting the principle article in these two volumes, are added various pieces, none of which, it is hoped, will be found discreditable to the talents of the author. The slight fragment of Letters on the Management of Infants, may be thought a trifle; but it seems to have some value, as presenting to us with vividness the intention of the writer on this important subject.

## 6. From William Godwin, *Memoirs* of Wollstonecraft (1798)

[Godwin published the *Memoirs of the Author of A Vindication of the Rights of Woman*, the first biography about Wollstonecraft, in the year of her death. The work was instantly controversial for its revelations about Wollstonecraft's suicide attempts and liberal lifestyle (she had never married Imlay, with whom she had a child, and she also became pregnant out of wedlock with Godwin's child). Wollstonecraft's poor reputation throughout the nineteenth century is widely attributed to the *Memoirs*. Contemporary feminist readers marvel that Godwin characterizes her as a weak and pitiable woman of sensibility and a female Werther in this text. See Appendix A5 for more evidence of Godwin's "Wertherization" of Wollstonecraft.]

(Godwin, William. *Memoirs of the Author of A Vindication of the Rights of Woman*. 2nd ed., corrected. London: Johnson, 1798. 80-84; 114-15.)

The work is certainly a very bold and original production. The strength and firmness with which the author repels the opinions of Rousseau, Dr. Gregory, and Dr. James Fordyce, respecting the condition of women, cannot but make a strong impression upon every ingenuous reader. The public at large formed very different opinions respecting the character of the performance. Many of the sentiments are undoubtedly of a rather masculine description. The spirited and decisive way in which the author explodes the system of gallantry, and the species of homage with which the sex is usually treated, shocked the majority. Novelty produced a sentiment in their mind, which they mistook for a sense of injustice. The pretty, soft creatures that are so often to be found in the female sex, and that class of men who believe they could not exist without such pretty, soft creatures to resort to, were in arms against the author of so heretical and blasphemous a doctrine. There are also, it must be confessed, occasional passages of a stern and rugged feature, incompatible with the writer's essential character. But, if they did not belong to her fixed and permanent character, they belonged to her character of the moment; and what she thought, she scorned to qualify.

Yet, along with this rigid, and somewhat amazonian temper, which characterised some parts of the book, it is impossible not to remark a luxuriance of imagination, and a trembling delicacy of sentiment, which would have done honour to a poet, burning with all the visions of an Armida and a Dido.[1]

The preconceived ideas of the public were not less erroneous as to the person of the author, than those they had formed of the temper of the book. In the champion of her sex, who was described as endeavouring to invest them with all the rights of man, those whom curiosity led to seek an opportunity of seeing her, expected to find a rude, pedantic, dictatorial virago; and they were not a little surprised when, instead of all this, they found a woman, lovely in her person, and, in the best and most engaging sense, feminine in her manners.

The *Vindication of the Rights of Woman* is a very unequal performance, and eminently deficient in method and arrangement. When tried by the hoary and long-established laws of literary composition, it can

---

1  Armida is a sorceress from the Italian poet Torquato Tasso's (1544-95) verse narrative *Rinaldo* (1562). See p. 188, note 1 for more on Tasso's Armida. Dido was the Queen of Carthage (today's Tunisia) who, in Virgil's *Aeneid*, commits suicide after Aeneas betrays her. Both literary figures represent abandoned women.

scarcely maintain its claim to be placed in the class of finished productions. But, when we consider the importance of its doctrines, and the eminence of genius it displays, it seems not very improbable that it will be read as long as the English language endures. The publication of this book forms an epocha in the subject to which it belongs; and Mary Wollstonecraft will perhaps hereafter be found to have performed more substantial service for the cause of her sex, than all the other writers, male or female, that ever felt themselves animated by the contemplation of their oppressed and injured state.

The censure of the liberal critic as to the defects of this performance, will be changed into astonishment, when I tell him, that a work of this inestimable moment, was begun, carried on, and finished in the state in which it now appears, in a period of no more than six weeks.

[...]

Some persons may be inclined to observe, that the evils here enumerated, are not among the heaviest in the catalogue of human calamities. But evils take their rank less from their own nature, than from the temper of the mind that suffers them. Upon a man of a hard and insensible disposition, the shafts of misfortune often fall pointless and impotent. There are persons, by no means hard and insensible, who, from an elastic and sanguine turn of mind, are continually prompted to look on the fair side of things, and, having suffered one fall, immediately rise again, to pursue their course with the same eagerness, the same hope and gaiety, as before. On the other hand, we not unfrequently meet with persons, endowed with the most exquisite and refined sensibility, whose minds seem almost of too delicate a texture to encounter the vicissitudes of human affairs, to whom pleasure is transport, and disappointment is agony indescribable. This character is finely pourtrayed by the author of the *Sorrows of Werter*. Mary was in this respect a female Werter.

# Appendix B: The Political Context: Education, Human Rights, and the French Revolution

## 1. From Catharine Macaulay, *Letters on Education* (1790)

[Catharine Macaulay (1731-91) was one of the most radical women writers in eighteenth-century England. Long before she wrote about female education, she established her reputation as a polemical writer with the controversial, eight-volume *History of England from the Accession of James I to that of the Brunswick Line* (1763-83), which defended Cromwell's regicidal government and demonstrated "generally antimonarchal Whig sympathies" (Wolfson, "Catherine" 319). Wollstonecraft admired Macaulay for these views, as did George Washington, Benjamin Franklin, and John Adams, all of whom Macaulay met during a trip to America in 1785. Edmund Burke, however, called her a "republican Virago." When, at age 57, she married William Graham, age 21, her enemies were delighted to add the unusual marriage to the list of supposed crimes that earned her this lasting reputation. Writing in 1803, Mary Hays touches on the genuine reason for Macaulay's illfame: "A female historian, by its singularity, could not fail to excite attention: she seemed to have stepped out of the province of her sex; curiosity was sharpened, and malevolence provoked. The author was attacked by petty and personal scurrilities, to which it was believed her sex would render her vulnerable" (292).

Wollstonecraft describes Macaulay in glowing terms in *Rights of Woman*: "Catharine Macaulay was an example of intellectual acquirements supposed to be incompatible with the weakness of her sex. In her style of writing, indeed, no sex appears, for it is like the sense it conveys, strong and clear.... [S]he writes with sober energy and argumentative closeness" (235). Poignantly, she adds, "When I first thought of writing these strictures I anticipated Mrs. Macaulay's approbation, with ... sanguine ardour ...; but soon heard with the sickly qualm of disappointed hope; and the still seriousness of regret — that she was no more!" (236). In a fascinating development, critic Bridget Hill has discovered that Wollstonecraft not only admired Macaulay across the distance of her published statements, but that the women were correspondents and *mutual* admirers. Hill states that, until the discovery of their correspondence, there was "no proof that they were acquainted" and "no evidence that the admiration was reciprocated or that Macaulay had read any of Wollstonecraft's works"

(179). Yet, Macaulay's letter to Wollstonecraft reveals her familiarity with *A Vindication of the Rights of Men*, as well as her esteem for the younger woman's writing: "I was pleased ... that this publication which I have so greatly admired from its pathos & sentiment should have been written by a woman and thus to see my opinion of the powers and talents of the sex in your pen so early verified" (quoted in Hill 178). Wollstonecraft had therefore good reason to anticipate Macaulay's approbation of *Rights of Woman*, in which she quotes pages of Macaulay's work at length (312; 132-33 of Macaulay's *Letters*). Her review of Macaulay's *Letters on Education* in the November 1790 edition of the *Analytical Review* anticipated the positive comments on Macaulay's work that appear in *Rights of Woman*. Macaulay's basic argument in the *Letters*—that the only difference between the sexes is physical—echoes throughout Wollstonecraft's work, as does her focus on associationist psychology, her lambasting of Rousseau's theory of female intellect, and her opposition to the degrading ideal of femininity promoted by the culture of nerves and sensibility.]

(Macaulay Graham, Catharine. *Letters on Education. With Observations on Religious and Metaphysical Subjects.* Dublin: H. Chamberlaine and Rice, 1790. v-vi; 127-31.)

Of all the arts of life, that of giving useful instruction to the human mind, and of rendering it the master of its affections, is the most important. Several very distinguished persons in the rank of literature have acknowledged this truth, by exerting the power of genius in forming rules of discipline for taming the untractable mind of man, and bringing it into a proper subjection to the dictates of virtue. Indeed we have learned as much from our ancestors on this subject, as mere practical experience could suggest. But it is to the modern metaphysicians we owe those lights into the operations of the mind, which can alone afford us a reasonable prospect of success.

For without adequate knowledge of the power of association, by which a single impression calls up a host of ideas, which, arising in imperceptible succession, form a close and almost inseparable combination, it will be impracticable for a tutor to fashion the mind of his pupil according to any particular idea he may frame of excellence.[1] Nor can his instructions be adequate to any such management of the mental faculties as shall invariably produce volitions agreeable to the laws of virtue and prudence.

---

1 See the Introduction to this edition (p. 46) and Appendix D3 for more on David Hartley's psychological theory of associationism.

If the partizans of liberty and necessity would lay aside their subtile investigations, which can never tend to real improvement, and would unite in acknowledging the power of those principles which govern the mind, we might then hope to see the education of youth assigned to men, whose learning, knowledge, and talents, place them at the head of the republic of letters. The culture of that artificial being, a social man, is in its nature so complex, there are so many evils to be avoided, so many important ends to be pursued; there is such a delicate machine to work upon, and so much to be apprehended from external causes, that the invention of the learned may be employed for ages, before such a system of education can be framed as will admit of no improvement.

[...]

## Letter XXII. No Characteristic Difference in Sex.

The great difference that is observable in the characters of the sexes, Hortensia,[1] as they display themselves in the scenes of social life, has given rise to much false speculation on the natural qualities of the female mind. — For though the doctrine of innate ideas, and innate affections, are in a great measure exploded by the learned, yet few persons reason so closely and so accurately on abstract subjects as, through a long chain of deductions, to bring forth a conclusion which in no respect militates with their premises.

It is a long time before the crowd give up opinions they have been taught to look upon with respect; and I know many persons who will follow you willingly through the course of your argument, till they perceive it tends to the overthrow of some fond prejudice; and then they will either sound a retreat, or begin a contest in which the contender for truth, though he cannot be overcome, is effectually silenced, from the mere weariness of answering positive assertions, reiterated without end. It is from such causes that the notion of a sexual difference in the human character has, with a very few exceptions, universally prevailed from the earliest times, and the pride of one sex, and the ignorance and vanity of the other, have helped to support an opinion which a close observation of Nature, and a more accurate way of reasoning, would disprove.

It must be confessed, that the virtues of the males among the human species, though mixed and blended with a variety of vices and errors, have displayed a bolder and a more consistent picture of excellence

---

1 Macaulay's fictional addressee.

than female nature has hitherto done. It is on these reasons that, when we compliment the appearance of a more than ordinary energy in the female mind, we call it masculine; and hence it is, that Pope has elegantly said *a perfect woman's but a softer man*.[1] And if we take in the consideration, that there can be but one rule of moral excellence for beings made of the same materials, organized after the same manner, and subjected to similar laws of Nature, we must either agree with Mr. Pope, or we must reverse the proposition, and say, that *a perfect man is a woman formed after a coarser mold*. The difference that actually does subsist between the two sexes, is too flattering for men to be willingly imputed to accident; for what accident occasions, wisdom might correct; and it is better, says Pride, to give up the advantages we might derive from the perfection of our fellow associates, than to own that Nature has been just in the equal distribution of her favours. These are the sentiments of the men; but mark how readily they are yielded to by the women; not from humility I assure you, but merely to preserve with character those fond vanities on which they set their hearts. No; suffer them to idolize their persons, to throw away their life in the pursuit of trifles, and to indulge in the gratification of the meaner passions, and they will heartily join in the sentence of their degradation.

Among the most strenuous asserters of sexual difference in character, Rousseau is the most conspicuous, both on account of that warmth of sentiment which distinguishes all his writings, and the eloquence of his compositions: but never did enthusiasm and the love of paradox, those enemies to philosophical disquisition, appear in more strong opposition to plain sense than in Rousseau's definition of this difference. He sets out with a supposition, that Nature intended the subjection of the one sex to the other; that consequently there must be an inferiority of intellect in the subjected party; but as man is a very imperfect being, and apt to play the capricious tyrant, Nature, to bring things nearer to an equality, bestowed on the woman such attractive graces, and such an insinuating address, as to turn the balance on the other scale. Thus Nature, in a giddy mood, recedes from her purposes, and subjects prerogative to an influence which must produce confusion and disorder in the system of human affairs. Rousseau saw this objection; and in order to obviate it, he has made up a moral person

---

1  Macaulay paraphrases the following lines from Alexander Pope's second *Moral Essay* (1735), "Of the Characters of Women," a verse epistle supposed to be written to Pope's life-long friend, Martha Blount:
   And yet believe me, good as well as ill,
   Woman's at best a contradiction still.
   Heaven, when it strives to polish all it can
   Its last best work, but forms a softer man. (ll. 269-72)

of the union of the two sexes, which, for contradiction and absurdity, outdoes every metaphysical riddle that was ever formed in the schools. In short, it is not reason, it is not wit; it is pride and sensuality that speak in Rousseau, and, in this instance, has lowered the man of genius to the licentious pedant.[1]

But whatever might be the wise purpose intended by Providence in such a disposition of things, certain it is, that some degree of inferiority, in point of corporal strength, seems always to have existed between the two sexes; and this advantage, in the barbarous ages of mankind, was abused to such a degree, as to destroy all the natural rights of the female species, and reduce them to a state of abject slavery. What accidents have contributed in Europe to better their condition, would not be to my purpose to relate; for I do not intend to give you a history of women; I mean only to trace the sources of their peculiar foibles and vices; and these I firmly believe to originate in situation and education only: for so little did a wise and just Providence intend to make the condition of slavery an unalterable law of female nature, that in the same proportion as the male sex have consulted the interest of their own happiness, they have relaxed in their tyranny over women; and such is their use in the system of mundane creation, and such their natural influence over the male mind, that were these advantages properly exerted, they might carry every point of any importance to their honour and happiness. However, till that period arrives in which women will act wisely, we will amuse ourselves in talking of their follies.

The situation and education of women, Hortensia, is precisely that which must necessarily tend to corrupt and debilitate both the powers of mind and body. From a false notion of beauty and delicacy, their system of nerves is depraved before they come out of their nursery; and this kind of depravity has more influence over the mind, and consequently over morals, than is commonly apprehended. But it would be well if such causes only acted towards the debasement of the sex; their moral education is, if possible, more absurd than their physical. The principles and nature of virtue, which is never properly explained to boys, is kept quite a mystery to girls. They are told indeed, that they must abstain from those vices which are contrary to their personal happiness, or they will be regarded as criminals, both by God and man; but all the higher parts of rectitude, every thing that ennobles our being, and that renders us both innoxious and useful, is either not taught, or is taught in such a manner as to leave no proper impression

---

1  An echo of Wollstonecraft's many complaints about the description of woman's place in Jean-Jacques Rousseau's *Émile*. See, for example, p. 302, note 1.

on the mind. This is so obvious a truth, that the defects of female education have ever been a fruitful topic of declamation for the moralist; but not one of this class of writers have laid down any judicious rules for amendment. Whilst we still retain the absurd notion of a sexual excellence, it will militate against the perfecting a plan of education for either sex. The judicious Addison[1] animadverts on the absurdity of bringing a young lady up with no higher idea of the end of education than to make her agreeable to a husband, and confining the necessary excellence for this happy acquisition to the mere graces of her person.

Every parent and tutor may not express himself in the same manner as is marked out by Addison; yet certain it is, that the admiration of the other sex is held out to women as the highest honour they can attain; and whilst this is considered as their *summum bonum*,[2] and the beauty of their persons the chief *desideratum*[3] of men, Vanity, and its companion, Envy, must taint, in their characters, every native and every acquired excellence. Nor can you, Hortensia, deny, that these qualities, when united to ignorance, are fully equal to the engendering and rivetting all those vices and foibles which are peculiar to the female sex; vices and foibles which have caused them to be considered, in ancient times, as beneath cultivation, and in modern days have subjected them to the censure and ridicule of writers of all descriptions, from the deep thinking philosophers to the man of ton and gallantry, who, by the bye, sometimes distinguishes himself by qualities which are not greatly superior to those he despises in women. Nor can I better illustrate the truth of this observation than by the following picture, to be found in the polite and gallant Chesterfield. "Women," says his Lordship, "are only children of a larger growth. They have an entertaining tattle, sometimes wit; but for solid reasoning, and good sense, I never in my life knew one that had it, or who acted or reasoned in consequence of it for four and twenty hours together. A man of sense only trifles with them, plays with them, humours and flatters them, as he does an engaging child; but he neither consults them, nor trusts them in serious matters."[4]

---

1 Joseph Addison (1672-1719), English poet and essayist, was a co-founder of *The Spectator* magazine (with Richard Steele [1672-1729], an Irish writer and politician).
2 "The chief or supreme good" (*OED*).
3 "Something for which a desire or longing is felt; something wanting and required or desired" (*OED*).
4 According to Roger Coxon in *Chesterfield and his Critics* (1977), Lord Chesterfield wrote these words in a letter to his son on 5 September 1748 (162).

## 2. From Edmund Burke, *Reflections on the French Revolution* (1790)

[Burke's text inspired an avalanche of responses from pro-French Revolutionary—sometimes termed "Jacobin"—writers in England, including Wollstonecraft's first polemical text, *Vindication of the Rights of Men* (1790), which was published only one month after Burke's text appeared, and even before the more famous response, Thomas Paine's *The Rights of Man* (1791).[1] Burke's conservative argument that monarchy must be maintained to provide the "decent drapery of life" (114) inflamed the ire of pro-democracy writers, particularly because they had believed him to be one of their own, given his early support of the American Revolution. Edmund Burke (1729-97) served the Whig party, to be sure, but he developed the conservative side of Whig politics. As such, today he is regarded as the founder of both modern conservatism and classical liberalism, or early libertarianism—diverse political factions, indeed.

The selections below embody aspects of the text that Wollstonecraft lambasted in *Rights of Men*, particularly as represented in Appendix A3. Burke's famously sentimental—or what Wollstonecraft would also call his effeminate—description of Marie Antoinette amounts to goddess-worship, which illustrates well his basic contention that the aristocracy should command the rest of society because they are exceptional beings and far superior to the plebeians they rule, thereby undermining any notion of natural human rights based on the equality of all people. These passages also demonstrate his veneration of chivalry, the *politesse* without which "the glory of Europe is extinguished forever," he claimed (113). Wollstonecraft would answer this passage in *Rights of Men* by asserting that "romance and chivalry is in the wane; and reason will gain by its extinction" (65), while Godwin would develop a narrative fiction around the idea that chivalry is a pernicious law that destroys the power of private judgment in *Caleb Williams* (1793).]

(Burke, Edmund. *Reflections on the Revolution in France, and On the Proceedings in Certain Societies in London Relative to that Event. In a Letter Intended to have been Sent to a Gentleman in Paris.* London: J. Dodsley, 1790. 111-16.)

---

1 See Appendix B3.

I hear, and I rejoice to hear, that the great lady,[1] the other object of the triumph,[2] has borne that day (one is interested that beings made for suffering should suffer well), and that she bears all the succeeding days, that she bears the imprisonment of her husband, and her own captivity, and the exile of her friends, and the insulting adulation of addresses, and the whole weight of her accumulated wrongs, with a serene patience, in a manner suited to her rank and race, and becoming the offspring of a sovereign distinguished for her piety and her courage; that, like her, she has lofty sentiments; that she feels with the dignity of a Roman matron; that in the last extremity she will save herself from the last disgrace; and that, if she must fall, she will fall by no ignoble hand.

It is now sixteen or seventeen years since I saw the queen of France, then the dauphiness, at Versailles; and surely never lighted on this orb, which she hardly seemed to touch, a more delightful vision. I saw her just above the horizon, decorating and cheering the elevated sphere she just began to move in, — glittering like the morning-star, full of life, and splendor, and joy. Oh! what a revolution! and what an heart must I have to contemplate without emotion that elevation and that fall! Little did I dream that, when she added titles of veneration to those of enthusiastic, distant, respectful love, that she should ever be obliged to carry the sharp antidote against disgrace concealed in that bosom; little did I dream that I should have lived to see such disasters fallen upon her in a nation of gallant men, in a nation of men of honour and of cavaliers. I thought ten thousand swords must have leaped from their scabbards to avenge even a look that threatened her with insult. — But the age of chivalry is gone. — That of sophisters, œconomists, and calculators, has succeeded; and the glory of Europe is extinguished forever. Never, never more, shall we behold that gen-

---

1  Marie Antoinette (1755-93), wife of Louis XVI, Queen of France (1774-93). She, like her husband, would be guillotined by the French Revolutionaries three years after Burke's text was published. He refers here to the arrest of the royals at Versailles on 5 October 1789, and their conveyance by the National Guard to the Tuileries Palace, where they were kept under house arrest.

2  At this point in the text, Burke has just described how well Louis XVI comported himself in the hour of his arrest at Versailles. Amazingly, Wollstonecraft agreed with him; in a letter from Paris to Joseph Johnson, dated 26 December 1792, she confessed, "About nine o'clock this morning, the king passed by my window, moving silently along ... through empty streets, surrounded by the national guards, who, clustering round the carriage, seemed to deserve their name.... I can scarcely tell you why, but an association of ideas made the tears flow insensibly from my eyes, when I saw Louis sitting, with more dignity than I expected from his character, in a hackney coach, going to meet death" (216).

erous loyalty to rank and sex, that proud submission, that dignified obedience, that subordination of the heart, which kept alive, even in servitude itself, the spirit of an exalted freedom. The unbought grace of life, the cheap defence of nations, the nurse of manly sentiment and heroic enterprize is gone! It is gone, that sensibility of principle, that chastity of honour, which felt a stain like a wound, which inspired courage whilst it mitigated ferocity, which ennobled whatever it touched, and under which vice itself lost half its evil, by losing all its grossness.

This mixed system of opinion and sentiment had its origin in the antient chivalry; and the principle, though varied in its appearance by the varying state of human affairs, subsisted and influenced through a long succession of generations, even to the time we live in. If it should ever be totally extinguished, the loss I fear will be great. It is this which has given its character to modern Europe. It is this which has distinguished it under all its forms of government, and distinguished it to its advantage, from the states of Asia, and possibly from those states which flourished in the most brilliant periods of the antique world. It was this, which, without confounding ranks, had produced a noble equality, and handed it down through all the gradations of social life. It was this opinion which mitigated kings into companions, and raised private men to be fellows with kings. Without force, or opposition, it subdued the fierceness of pride and power; it obliged sovereigns to submit to the soft collar of social esteem, compelled stern authority to submit to elegance, and gave a domination vanquisher of laws, to be subdued by manners.

But now all is to be changed. All the pleasing illusions, which made power gentle, and obedience liberal, which harmonized the different shades of life, and which, by a bland assimilation, incorporated into politics the sentiments which beautify and soften private society, are to be dissolved by this new conquering empire of light and reason. All the decent drapery of life is to be rudely torn off. All the superadded ideas, furnished from the wardrobe of a moral imagination, which the heart owns, and the understanding ratifies, as necessary to cover the defects of our naked, shivering nature, and to raise it to dignity in our own estimation, are to be exploded as a ridiculous, absurd, and antiquated fashion.

On this scheme of things, a king is but a man; a queen is but a woman; a woman is but an animal; and an animal not of the highest order. All homage paid to the sex in general as such, and without distinct views, is to be regarded as romance and folly. Regicide, and parricide, and sacrilege, are but fictions of superstition, corrupting jurisprudence by destroying its simplicity. The murder of a king, or a queen, or a bishop, or a father, are only common homicide; and if the people are by any chance, or in any way gainers by it, a sort of homicide much the most pardonable, and into which we ought not to make too severe a scrutiny.

On the scheme of this barbarous philosophy, which is the offspring of cold hearts and muddy understandings, and which is as void of solid wisdom, as it is destitute of all taste and elegance, laws are to be supported only by their own terrors, and by the concern which each individual may find in them, from his own private speculations, or can spare to them from his own private interests. In the groves of *their* academy, at the end of every visto,[1] you see nothing but the gallows. Nothing is left which engages the affections on the part of the commonwealth. On the principles of this mechanic philosophy, our institutions can never be embodied, if I may use the expression, in persons; so as to create in us love, veneration, admiration, or attachment. But that sort of reason which banishes the affections is incapable of filling their place. These public affections, combined with manners, are required sometimes as supplements, sometimes as correctives, always as aids to law. The precept given by a wise man, as well as a great critic, for the construction of poems, is equally true as to states. *Non satis est pulchra esse poemata, dulcia sunto.*[2] There ought to be a system of manners in every nation which a well-formed mind would be disposed to relish. To make us love our country, our country ought to be lovely.

### 3. From Thomas Paine, *Rights of Man* (1791)

[Thomas Paine (1737-1809), an English pamphleteer who lived for some time in America, is best known for penning *Common Sense* (1776), the most influential statement in favour of American Independence from British rule. When he wrote *Rights of Man* (1791) in response to Burke's *Reflections on the French Revolution*, it was widely received as the most powerful—and remains the most famous—defence of the French Revolution.

In the passages below, Paine, like Wollstonecraft before him, attacks Burke for his devotion to chivalry by characterizing it as revealing his opposition to reason, the idol of eighteenth-century Enlightenment thinkers. In his comparison of Burke to Don Quixote, Paine goes so

---

1  "Visto" was a common spelling for "vista" until well into the nineteenth century.

2  From Horace's *Ars Poetica*: "It is not enough that poetry is agreeable, it should also be interesting" (99).

far as to accuse his opponent of insanity, a point that he also reiterates more directly. The comparison to Don Quixote underlines Paine's depiction of Burke as so caught up in his sentimental rhetoric and unrealistic, fictionalized view of the world that he believes himself a hero of the monarchy, truly a knight-errant of 1790s English society. In this way, Paine's polemic echoes the argument that Wollstonecraft develops throughout her *oeuvre*: the language of sentiment is far from a facilitator of pleasant and harmless escapism; rather, it is politically dangerous because it encourages political negligence and incapacity.]

(Paine, Thomas. *Rights of Man. Being an Answer to Mr. Burke's Attack on the French Revolution.* 4th ed. London: J.S. Jordan, 1791. 24-27.)

As to the tragic paintings by which Mr. Burke has outraged his own imagination, and seeks to work upon that of his readers, they are very well calculated for theatrical representation, where facts are manufactured for the sake of show, and accommodated to produce, through the weakness of sympathy, a weeping effect. But Mr. Burke should recollect that he is writing History, and not *Plays*; and that his readers will expect truth, and not the spouting rant of high-toned exclamation.

When we see a man dramatically lamenting in a publication intended to be believed, that, "*The age of chivalry is gone!* that *The glory of Europe is extinguished for ever!* that *The unbought grace of life* (if anyone knows what it is), *the cheap defence of nations, the nurse of manly sentiment and heroic enterprize is gone!*" and all this because the Quixote age of chivalry nonsense is gone.[1] What opinion can we form of his judgment, or what regard can we pay to his facts? In the rhapsody of his imagination, he has discovered a world of wind-mills, and his sorrows are, that there are no Quixotes to attack them. But if the age of aristocracy, like that of chivalry, should fall, and they had originally some connection, Mr. Burke, the trumpeter of the Order, may con-

---

1   A reference to Spanish author Miguel de Cervantes' comedic novel, *The Ingenious Gentleman Don Quixote of La Mancha*, published in two volumes in 1605 and 1615. Perhaps the best-known edition of the work in English in the eighteenth century was by Tobias Smollett: *The History and Adventures of the Renowned Don Quixote. Translated from the Spanish of Miguel de Cervantes Saavedra, To which is Prefixed, Some Account of the Author's Life* (1755). The delusional protagonist, Don Quixote, believes that he is a knight-errant on a noble quest to find adventure (involving, famously, windmills-as-foes); to battle for the love of a pure damsel (who is the neighbouring farmgirl); and, of course, to uphold the principles of chivalry.

tinue his parody to the end, and finish with exclaiming, "*Othello's occupation's gone!*"[1]

Notwithstanding Mr. Burke's horrid paintings, when the French Revolution is compared with that of other countries, the astonishment will be, that it is marked with so few sacrifices;[2] but this astonishment will cease when we reflect that *principles*, and not *persons*, were the meditated objects of destruction. The mind of the nation was acted upon by a higher stimulus than what the consideration of persons could inspire, and sought a higher conquest than could be produced by the downfal[3] of an enemy. Among the few who fell, there do not appear to be any that were intentionally singled out. They all of them had their fate in the circumstances of the moment, and were not pursued with that long, cold-blooded, unabated revenge which pursued the unfortunate Scotch in the affair of 1745.[4]

Through the whole of Mr. Burke's book I do not observe that the Bastille is mentioned more than once, and that with a kind of implication as if he were sorry it was pulled down, and wished it were built up again. "We have rebuilt Newgate (says he), and tenanted the mansion; and we have prisons almost as strong as the Bastille for those who dare to libel the Queens of France"[.... C]ertain it is that Mr. Burke, who does not call himself a madman, whatever other people may do, has libelled, in the most unprovoked manner, and in the grossest style of the most vulgar abuse, the whole representative authority of France; and yet Mr. Burke takes his seat in the British House of Commons! From his violence and his grief, his silence on some points, and his excess on others, it is difficult not to believe that Mr. Burke is sorry, extremely sorry, that arbitrary power, the power of the Pope, and the Bastille, are pulled down.

Not one glance of compassion, not one commiserating reflection, that I can find throughout his book, has he bestowed on those who lingered out the most wretched of lives, a life without hope, in the most

---

1 From Shakespeare's *The Tragedy of Othello, The Moor of Venice* (III, iii, 395). Although he has forged his identity as a great war-hero and military leader through many years of hard experience, Othello states that he cannot rule an army with the belief—suggested to him by the conniving Iago—that his wife, Desdemona, has been unfaithful.

2 Paine could truthfully claim as much in 1791, but he could not do so after, for example, the September Massacres of 1792, or the Reign of Terror, which began in 1793.

3 Spelling in original.

4 According to Robert DeMaria, Jr., Paine refers to "The last attempt by Jacobites to restore the House of Stuart to power, crushed at Culloden (1746) and severely recriminated thereafter" (849).

miserable of prisons. It is painful to behold a man employing his talents to corrupt himself. Nature has been kinder to Mr. Burke than he is to her. He is not affected by the reality of distress touching his heart, but by the showy resemblance of it striking his imagination. He pities the plumage, but forgets the dying bird.[1] Accustomed to kiss the aristocratical hand that hath purloined him from himself, he degenerates into a composition of art, and the genuine soul of nature forsakes him. His hero or his heroine must be a tragedy-victim expiring in show, and not the real prisoner of misery, sliding into death in the silence of a dungeon.

## 4. From William Godwin, *Enquiry Concerning Political Justice* (1793)

[Godwin wrote the *Enquiry* as a response to Burke's *Reflections* and Paine's *Rights of Man*, but he does not discuss the present historical and political situation as they do. Rather, he discusses political principles and theory, a focus that, incidentally, Burke derided years before in his first publication, *Vindication of Natural Society* (1756). Godwin develops his famous theory of human perfectibility in "Chapter VI. Human Inventions capable of perpetual improvement," where he asserts that the potential for infinite advancement in science establishes the possibility of infinite advancement in human morals. This contention demonstrates his devotion to science as the ultimate representative of reason and its importance to radical politics, as, indeed, Wollstonecraft's and Macaulay's works also reveal. The second of the sections from *Enquiry* that is provided below shows Godwin's confidence in Hartley's scientific theory of associationism, which "cannot be too highly applauded," he claims (296). In the first of the sections below, Godwin describes the importance of literature to political and rational disquisition; this passage delineates why he eventually wrote the novel *Caleb Williams* (1794) to fictionalize the principles that he develops in *Enquiry*, a pattern that Wollstonecraft would repeat when she wrote *Maria* to fictionalize the principles of *Rights of Woman*.]

(Godwin, William. *Enquiry Concerning Political Justice, and its Influence on General Virtue and Happiness*. 2 vols. Dublin: Luke White, 1793. Vol. 1. 20-22; 295-96.)

Few engines can be more powerful, and at the same time more salutary in their tendency, than literature. Without enquiring for the present into the cause of this phenomenon, it is sufficiently evident in

---

1   The most famous phrase from Paine's tract.

fact, that the human mind is strongly infected with prejudice and mistake. The various opinions prevailing in different countries and among different classes of men upon the same subject, are almost innumerable; and yet of all these opinions only one can be true. Now the effectual way for extirpating these prejudices and mistakes seems to be literature.

Literature has reconciled the whole thinking world respecting the great principles of the system of the universe, and extirpated upon this subject the dreams of romance and the dogmas of superstition. Literature has unfolded the nature of the human mind, and Locke and others have established certain maxims respecting man, as Newton has done respecting matter, that are generally admitted for unquestionable....

Indeed, if there be such a thing as truth, it must infallibly be struck out by the collision of mind with mind. The restless activity of intellect will for a time be fertile in paradox and error; but these will be only diurnals, while the truths that occasionally spring up, like sturdy plants, will defy the rigour of season and climate. In proportion as one reasoner compares his deductions with those of another, the weak places of his argument will be detected, the principles he too hastily adopted will be overthrown, and the judgments, in which his mind was exposed to no sinister influence, will be confirmed.[1] All that is requisite in these discussions is unlimited speculation, and a sufficient variety of systems and opinions. While we only dispute about the best way of doing a thing in itself wrong, we shall indeed make but a trifling progress; but, when we are once persuaded that nothing is too sacred to be brought to the touchstone of examination, science will advance with rapid strides. Men, who turn their attention to the boundless field of enquiry, and still more who recollect the innumerable errors and caprices of mind, are apt to imagine that the labour is without benefit and endless. But this cannot be the case, if truth at last have any real existence. Errors will, during the whole period of their reign, combat each other; prejudices that have passed unsuspected for ages, will have their era of detection; but, if in any science we discover one solitary truth, it cannot be overthrown.

Such are the arguments that may be adduced in favour of literature.

[...]

---

1  Compare Godwin's confidence in the power of truth to destroy baseless convictions in the human mind with Macaulay's far less cheery view of people's willingness to admit to ideas, however true, that differ from their own "fond prejudices" in Appendix B1.

# Chapter VII.
## Of the Mechanism of the Human Mind.

[W]e may conceive the human body to be so constituted as to be susceptible of vibrations, in the same manner as the strings of a musical instrument are susceptible of vibrations. These vibrations, having begun upon the surface of the body, are conveyed to the brain; and, in a manner that is equally the result of construction, produce a second set of vibrations beginning in the brain, and conveyed to the different organs or members of the body. Thus it may be supposed, that a piece of iron considerably heated is applied to the body of an infant, and that the report of this uneasiness, or irritation and separation of parts being conveyed to the brain, vents itself again in a shrill and piercing cry. It is in this manner that we are apt to imagine certain convulsive and spasmodic affections to take place in the body. The case, as here described, is similar to that of the bag of a pair of bagpipes, which, being pressed in a certain manner, utters a groan, without anything more being necessary to account for this phenomenon, than the known laws of matter and motion. Let us add to these vibrations a system of associations to be carried on by traces to be made upon the medullary substance of the brain, by means of which past and present impressions are connected according to certain laws, as the traces happen to approach or run into each other; and we have then a complete scheme for accounting in a certain way for all the phenomena of human action. It is to be observed, that, according to this system, mind or perception is altogether unnecessary to explain the appearances. It might for other reasons be desirable or wise, in the author of the universe for example, to introduce a thinking substance or a power of perception as a spectator of the process. But this percipient power is altogether neutral, having apparently no concern either as a medium or otherwise in producing the events.

# Appendix C: The Novel of Sentiment, the Woman of Sensibility, and the Gothic

## 1. From Jean-Jacques Rousseau, *Émile, ou, de l'Éducation* (1762)

[Jean-Jacques Rousseau's (1712-78) *Émile*, published a year after his novel *Julie, ou, La Nouvelle Héloïse* (1761), was one of the most influential sentimental and educational texts of the eighteenth century. As one of the great *philosophes* of Enlightenment France, the Genevan writer's prominence meant that his proclamations on male and female education, as well as his construction of sentimental literature, were powerful and reifying forces—which made the sexist elements of it all the more threatening for writers like Wollstonecraft and Macaulay.[1] Today, Rousseau is best known for his belief that humankind is most authentic and morally superior in nature, which, he argued, stands in glorious opposition to the perverting, man-made structures of the class-system and religion. Fellow *philosophes* such as Voltaire (1694-1778) and Denis Diderot (1713-84) believed, on the contrary, that man would not find his best self in an emotional identification with nature, but in the perfection of his reason; this disagreement was the source of the falling out between these erstwhile friends about which Rousseau complains so bitterly in *Confessions* (1783; first English translation) and it also describes well Wollstonecraft's own inner conflict about the value of sensibility versus reason. This ambivalence characterized Wollstonecraft's attitude towards Rousseau as a man and writer, too. While she deeply resented his characterization of the perfect woman as one who is only educated enough to render her the charming mate of a more intellectual husband in *Émile* (*Rights of Woman* 51), she also admired the emotional beauty of his writing. Indeed, in a letter to Imlay from 1794, she goes so far as to state about Rousseau, "I have always been half in love with him" (*Posthumous Works* vol. 3, 59).

The passages below represent the aspects of the text that so enraged Wollstonecraft and Macaulay, such as Rousseau's declaration that women's weaker body is a reflection of her innately weaker intellect,

---

1 See, for example, p. 73, note 1 for more information about Wollstonecraft's reaction to Rousseau.

and that women's charm lies in their weakness, even of the intellectual sort, and therefore they should not be educated like men are.]

(Rousseau, J.J. *Emilius and Sophia: or, A New System of Education*. 2nd ed. 4 vols. London: T. Becket and P.A. De Hondt, 1763. vol. 4. 2-4; 7-8; 16-18.)

Sophia should be such a woman, as Emilius is a man; that is, she should possess every thing requisite in the constitution of her species and sex, to fill her place in the physical and moral order of things. To know whether she be so qualified, we shall enter first on an examination in the various instances of conformity and difference between her sex and ours.

In every thing which does not regard the sex, woman is the same as man; she has the same organs, the same necessities, the same faculties: the corporeal machine is constructed in the same manner, its component parts are alike, their operation the same, and the figure similar in both; in whatever light we regard them, they differ from each other only in degree.

On the other hand, in every thing immediately respecting sex, the woman differs entirely from the man; the difficulty of comparing them together, lying in our inability to determine what are those particulars in the constitution of each that immediately relate to the sex. From their comparative anatomy, and even from simple inspection, we perceive some general distinctions between them, that do not appear to relate to sex; and yet there can be no doubt that they do, although we are not capable of tracing their modes of relation. Indeed we know not how far the difference of sex may extend. All that we know, of a certainty, is that whatever is common to both is only characteristic of their species; and that every thing in which they differ, is distinctive of their sex. Under this two-fold consideration, we find so much resemblance and dissimilitude that it appears even miraculous, that nature should form two beings so much alike, and, at the same time, so very different.

This difference and similitude must necessarily have an influence over their moral character: such an influence is, indeed, obvious, and perfectly agreeable to experience; clearly demonstrating the vanity of the disputes that have been held concerning the superiority or equality of the sexes; as if, in answering the different ends for which nature designed them, both were not more perfect than they would be in more nearly resembling each other. In those particulars which are common to both, they are equal; and as to those wherein they differ, no comparison is to be made between them. A perfect man and a complete woman should no more resemble each other in mind than in feature; nor is their perfection reducible to any common standard.

In the union of the sexes, both pursue one common object, but not in the same manner. From their diversity in this particular, arises the first determinate difference between the moral relations of each. The one should be active and strong, the other passive and weak: it is necessary the one should have both the power and the will, and that the other should make little resistance.

This principle being established, it follows that woman is expressly formed to please the man: if the obligation be reciprocal also, and the man ought to please in his turn, it is not so immediately necessary: his great merit lies in his power, and he pleases merely because he is strong. This, I must confess, is not one of the refined maxims of love; it is, however, one of the laws of nature, prior to love itself.

If woman be formed to please and to be subjected to man, it is her place doubtless to render herself agreeable to him, instead of challenging his passion. The violence of his desires depends on her charms; it is by means of these she should urge him to the exertion of those powers which nature hath given him. The most successful method of exciting them is, to render such exertion necessary by her resistance; as in that case, self-love is added to desire, and the one triumphs in the victory which the other obliged him to acquire. Hence arise the various modes of attack and defence between the sexes, the boldness of one sex and the timidity of the other; and, in a word, that bashfulness and modesty with which nature hath armed the weak, in order to subdue the strong.

[...]

Hence we deduce a third consequence from the different constitutions of the sexes; which is, that the strongest should be master in appearance, and be dependent in fact on the weakest; and that not from any frivolous practice of gallantry, or vanity of protectorship, but from an invariable law of nature, which, furnishing woman with a greater facility to excite desires than she has given man to satisfy them, makes the latter dependent on the good pleasure of the former, and compels him to endeavour to please in his turn, in order to obtain her consent that he should be strongest. On these occasions, the most delightful circumstance a man finds in his victory is, to doubt whether it was the woman's weakness that yielded to his superior strength, or whether her inclinations spoke in his favour: the females are also generally artful enough to leave this matter in doubt. The understanding of women answers, in this respect, perfectly to their constitution: so far from being ashamed of their weakness, they glory in it; their tender muscles make no resistance; they affect to be incapable of lifting the smallest burthens, and would blush to be thought robust and strong. To what purpose is all this? Not merely for the sake of appearing delicate, but through an artful precaution: it is thus they provide an excuse beforehand, and a right to be feeble when they think it expedient.

[...]

The women, again, on their part, are constantly crying out, that we educate them to be vain and coquettish; that we constantly entertain them with puerilities, in order to maintain our authority over them; and attribute to us the failing for which we reproach them. What a ridiculous accusation! How long is it that the men have troubled themselves about the education of women? What hinders mothers from bringing up their daughters just as they please? There are, to be sure, no colleges and academies for girls: a sad misfortune truly! Would to God there were none also for boys; they would be more sensibly and virtuously educated than they are. Who, ye mothers, compels your daughters to throw away their time in trifles? to spend half their lives, after your example, at the toilette? Who hinders you from instructing, or causing them to be instructed in the manner you chuse? Is it our fault that they charm us when they are pretty, that we are seduced by their affected airs, that the arts they learn of you attract and flatter us, that we love to see them becomingly dressed, and that we permit them to prepare at leisure those arms with which they subdue us at their pleasure? Educate them, if you think proper, like the men; we shall readily consent to it. The more they resemble our sex, the less power will they have over us; and when they once become like ourselves, we shall then be truly their masters.

The qualities common to both sexes are not equally allotted to each; though taken all together they are equal in both: the woman is more perfect as a woman, and less as a man. In every case where she makes use of her own privileges, she has the advantage over us; but where she would usurp ours, she becomes inferior. The only reply to be made to this general truth, is by bringing exceptions into it; the method of argumentation constantly used by the superficial partizans of the fair sex.

To cultivate in women, therefore, the qualifications of the men, and neglect those which are peculiar to the sex, would be acting to their prejudice: they see this very well, and are too artful to become the dupes of such conduct: they endeavour, indeed, to usurp our advantages, but they take care not to give up their own. By these means, however, it happens that, not being capable of both, because they are incompatible, they fail of obtaining the perfection of their own sex, as well as of ours, and lose half their merit. Let not the sensible mother, then, think of educating her daughter as a man, in contradiction to nature; but as a virtuous woman; and she may be assured it will be much better both for her child and herself.

It does not hence follow, however, that she ought to be educated in perfect ignorance, and confined merely to domestic concerns. Would a man make a servant of his companion, and deprive himself of the greatest pleasure of society? To make her the more submissive, would he prevent her from acquiring the least judgment or knowledge? would he reduce her to a mere automaton? Surely not! Nature hath dictated otherwise, in giving the sex such refined and agreeable talents: on the contrary, she hath formed them for thought, for judgment, for love, and knowledge. They should bestow as much care on their understandings, therefore, as to their persons, and add the charms of the one to the other, in order to supply their own want of strength, and to direct ours. They should doubtless learn many things, but only those which it is proper for them to know.

## 2. From Johann Wolfgang von Goethe, *The Sorrows of Young Werther* (1774)

[Johann Wolfgang von Goethe's (1749-1832) epistolary novel about frustrated love is a sentimental classic and inspired numerous imitations, both in literature—Wollstonecraft's *Mary* is one example—and in the living flesh: myriad young men modelled themselves after Werther by adopting his dress, his passionate emotionalism, and, so the critical myth goes, even his final act of suicide.[1] This real-life manifestation of the effects of sentimental literature underscores the legitimacy of Wollstonecraft's concern that women are formed by such reading (*VRW* 8).

The passages below illustrate how extreme sensibility is closely allied to insanity. Even though *Mary* is uncritical of similar histrionics, Wollstonecraft seems to recognize the madness of intense sensibility—or, at least, its opposition to reason—by the time she wrote *Maria*; after all, she presented her protagonist as imprisoned in a madhouse as a result of her sentimental ideas about love and her view of herself and Darnford as heroes in a fiction.]

---

1 Godwin seems to want to expand the possibilities of life mirroring art when he writes in the *Memoirs* that Wollstonecraft was a "female Werter" (115); see Appendix A6 for more information. In my commentary about Goethe's protagonist, I spell the name "Werther" because this is the most common spelling, even though Godwin and this edition of the text spell it without an h.

(Goethe, Johann Wolfgang von. *The Sorrows of Werter: A German Story.*
2 vols. Dublin: C. Jackson, 1780. Vol. 2. 80-81; 83-84; 94-96; 118.)

I feel, as those wretches must have felt who were formerly supposed to
be possessed by devils. Sometimes I am seized with strange starts and
motions; — it is not agony, it is not passion, it is an interior secret rage
which tears my bosom, and seems to seize my throat — Wretch that I
am! — Then I run, and wander amidst the dark and gloomy scenes
which this unfriendly season exhibits. Last night I felt thus constrained
to go out of the town. I had been told that the river, and all the brooks
in the neighbourhood, had overflown their banks, and that my
favourite valley was under water. I ran thither at past eleven o'clock; it
was a gloomy and aweful[1] sight! the moon was behind a cloud, but by
means of a few scattered rays I could perceive the foaming waves
rolling over the fields and meadows, and beating against the bushes;
the whole valley was as a stormy sea, tossed by furious winds. The
moon then appeared again, and rested on a dark cloud; the splendor
of her light encreased the disorder of nature. The echoes repeated and
redoubled the roarings of the wind and the waters. I drew near to the
precipice; I wished and shuddered; I stretched out my arms, I leaned
over, I sighed, and lost myself in the happy thought of burying all my
sufferings, all my torments, in that abyss, and tossing amidst the
waves. Why were my feet rooted to the earth? why could I not thus
have put an end to my misery? — But I feel it, my dear friend, my hour
is not yet come. With what delight should I have changed my nature,
and have incorporated with the whirlwinds to rend the clouds and
disturb the waters! Perhaps I may one day quit my prison, and taste
these pleasures.

[...]

I know not how it is, my dear friend, my imagination is full of terror!
Is not my love for her the purest and the most sacred? Is it not the love
of a brother for his sister? Did ever my heart form a wish that was
criminal? — I will make no vows. — And now a dream — Oh! they
were much in the right who attributed contending passions to powers
that are foreign to us! — This very night — I tremble as I write it —
this very night I held her in my arms, I pressed her to my bosom,
devoured her trembling lips with kisses. The most melting softness was
in her eyes, in mine equal extasy. — When I now at this moment recal
these transports with delight, am I guilty of a crime? — Oh! Charlotte!
Charlotte! 'tis all over; — my senses are disordered, and for these

---

1   All odd spellings appear in the source text.

seven days I have not been myself; — my eyes are full of tears; — all places are alike to me; in none am I at peace; — I desire nothing, I ask nothing. — Ah! 'twere better far that I should depart!

[...]

[Monday morning, the 21st of December, he (Werter) wrote the following letter, which was found sealed on his bureau after his death, and given to Charlotte. I shall insert it in fragments, as it appears by several circumstances to have been written.][1]

— It is all over. — Charlotte, I am resolved to die; I tell it you deliberately and coolly, without any romantic passion. The morning of that day on which I am to see you for the last time; at the very moment when you read these lines, Oh! best of women! a cold grave holds the inanimate remains of that agitated unhappy man, who in the last moments of his life knew no pleasure so great as that of conversing with you. I have passed a dreadful night — or rather let me call it a propitious one: for it has determined me, it has fixed my purpose; I am resolved to die. When I tore myself from you yesterday, my senses were in the greatest tumult and disorder; my heart was oppressed; hope and every ray of pleasure were fled for ever from me; and a petrifying cold seemed to surround my wretched being. — I could scarcely reach my room — I threw myself on my knees. — Heaven for the last time granted me the consolation of shedding tears. My troubled soul was agitated by a thousand ideas, a thousand different schemes! at length one thought took possession of me, and is now fixed in my heart — I will die. — It is not despair, it is conviction that I have filled up the measure of my sufferings, that I have reached the terms, and that I sacrifice myself for you. Yes, Charlotte, why should I not say it? It is necessary for one of us three[2] to depart — It shall be Werter. — Oh! my dear Charlotte! this heart, governed by rage and fury, has often conceived the horrid idea of murdering your husband — you — myself — I must then depart. — When in the fine evenings of summer, you walk towards the mountains, think of me; recollect the times you have so often seen me come up from the valley; raise your eyes to the church-yard which contains my grave; and by the light of the departing sun, see how the evening-breeze waves the high grass which grows over me!

---

1 This bracketed section is marked as a note from the "editor to the reader"; the opening bracket is on the previous page, but I transpose it here to distinguish these words from the narrative proper.
2 Albert, Charlotte's husband, is the third.

— I was calm when I began my letter; but the recollection of these scenes makes me cry like a child.

[...]

Charlotte! I do not shudder now that I hold in my hand the fatal instrument of my death. You present it to me, and I do not draw back. All, all is now finished; — this is the accomplishment of all my hopes; thus all my vows are fulfilled!

Why had I not the satisfaction to die for you, Charlotte? to sacrifice myself for you? — And could I restore peace and happiness to your bosom, with what resolution, with what pleasure should I meet my fate! But to a chosen few only it is given to shed their blood for those who are dear to them, and augment their happiness by the sacrifice.

## 3. Anna Lætitia Barbauld, "To a Lady, With Some Painted Flowers" (1792)

[Anna Lætitia Barbauld (1743-1825) was a prolific and widely admired poet in the Romantic period. She was a member of the Blue-stockings, a group of literary women who are often associated with feminism today. However, in the context of Wollstonecraft's and Macaulay's far more radical and contemporary brand of feminism, Barbauld scarcely seems to deserve the label. For example, she was less than supportive of the cause of female education. In response to Elizabeth Montagu's proposal to set up a literary school for girls, Barbauld responded, "'Young ladies ... ought only to have a general tincture of knowledge as to make them agreeable companions to a man of sense.... [T]he thefts of knowledge in our sex are only connived at while carefully concealed, and if displayed, punished with disgrace'" (Egers 171). Nonetheless, Barbauld contributed to other aspects of the radical cause through her poetry; indeed, "Epistle to William Wilberforce" (1791) was one of the best-known and most influential poems written for the cause of abolition.

Wollstonecraft seems to have admired Barbauld as a fellow intellectual, but she was particularly hard on her in *Rights of Woman*, singling out one of the elder writer's poems for special mockery. Introducing "To a Lady, With Some Painted Flowers" as an "ignoble comparison," Wollstonecraft quotes almost the entire poem as a shameful example of how the literature of sentiment constructs women as identifiable "with the smiling flowers that only adorn the land. This has ever been the language of men, and the fear of departing from a supposed sexual character, has made even women of superiour sense adopt the same sentiments" (112-13). Given that the book of poetry in which the poem appeared was published by Joseph Johnson, Wollstonecraft's publisher and close friend, Barbauld must have been shocked at this public criticism from one whom she might have considered a colleague. Her poetic repartee, "The Rights of Woman," is a scathing—if illogical and therefore ineffectual—indication of her personal reaction.]

(Barbauld, Anna Lætitia. "To a Lady, With Some Painted Flowers." *Poems*. London: Joseph Johnson, 1792. pp. 96-97.)

Flowers to the fair: To you these flowers I bring,
And strive to greet you with an earlier spring.
Flowers sweet, and gay, and delicate like you;
Emblems of innocence, and beauty too.
With flowers the Graces bind their yellow hair,
And flowery wreaths consenting lovers wear.
Flowers, the sole luxury which nature knew,
In Eden's pure and guiltless garden grew.
    To loftier forms are rougher tasks assign'd;
The sheltering oak resists the stormy wind,
The tougher yew repels invading foes,
And the tall pine for future navies grows;
But this soft family, to cares unknown,
Were born for pleasure and delight alone.
Gay without toil, and lovely without art,
They spring to cheer the sense, and glad the heart.
Nor blush, my fair, to own you copy these;
Your best, your sweetest empire is — to please.

## 4. From William Godwin, *Caleb Williams* (1794)

[William Godwin (1756-1836), Wollstonecraft's husband and father of her second child (the future author of *Frankenstein*, Mary Shelley), is remembered today as the father of philosophical anarchism because of his proclamations about the corrupt nature of all political systems and laws in *Enquiry Concerning Political Justice* (1793). Despite the success of the work, Godwin asserted that the fictionalization of its philosophical principles in *Things as They Are; or, The Adventures of Caleb Williams* might be more effective in realizing social change. In the preface to the "Standard Novels" edition (1832), Godwin notes, "I said to myself a thousand times, 'I will write a tale, that shall constitute an epoch in the mind of the reader, that no one, after he has read it, shall ever be exactly the same man that he was before'"

(McCracken 338).[1] He hit his mark. William Hazlitt—writer of the *The Spirit of the Age* (1825)—declared, "No one ever began *Caleb Williams* that did not read it through: no one that ever read it could possibly forget it, or speak of it after any length of time but with an impression as if the events and feelings had been personal to himself" (quoted in McCracken vii).

In the first selection below, the titular character expresses a sentiment about the inhumane nature of imprisonment, from which he has recently fled, and how freedom makes us fully human, the political import of which establishes clearly the argumentative link between Godwin's *Enquiry* and the novel. In the second passage, Caleb conveys his desire to crush tyranny by "unfold[ing] a tale" (269)—the same motive that resulted in this novel, as well as the novella it inspired, Wollstonecraft's *Maria*. Also like Wollstonecraft's novella, *Caleb Williams* illustrates that excess of passion, as is evident in Caleb's declaration here, constitutes the kinship between the novel of sentiment and the Gothic literary forms.]

(Godwin, William. *Things as They Are; or, The Adventures of Caleb Williams*. 3 vols. London: B. Crosby, 1794. Vol. 3. 8-12; 267-70.)

Having quitted my retreat, I at first advanced with weak and tottering steps; but, as I proceeded, increased my pace. The barren heath which reached to the edge of the town was at least on this side without a path; but the stars shone, and guiding myself by them I determined to steer as far as possible from the hateful scene where I had been so long confined. The line I pursued was of irregular surface, sometimes obliging me to climb a steep ascent, and at others to go down into a dark and impenetrable dell. I was often compelled by the dangerousness of the way to deviate considerably from the direction I wished to pursue. In the mean time I advanced with as much rapidity, as these and similar obstacles would permit me to do. The swiftness of the motion and the thinness of the air restored to me my alacrity. I forgot the inconveniences under which I laboured, and my mind became lively, spirited and enthusiastic.

I had now reached the border of the heath and entered upon what is usually termed the forest. Strange as it may seem, it is nevertheless true, that, exhausted as I was with hunger, destitute of all provision for the future, and surrounded with the most alarming dangers, my mind suddenly became glowing, animated and chearful. I thought that by this time the most formidable difficulties of my undertaking were surmounted; and I could not believe that, after having effected so much,

---

1 Quoted from Appendix II of the Oxford edition of the novel.

I should find any thing invincible in what remained to be done. I recollected the confinement I had undergone and the fate that had impended over me with horror. Never did man feel more vividly than I felt at that moment the sweets of liberty. Never did man more strenuously prefer poverty with independence to the artificial allurements of a life of slavery. I stretched forth my arms with rapture, I clapped my hands one upon the other, and exclaimed, Ah, this is indeed to be a man! These wrists were lately galled with fetters; all my motions, whether I rose up or sat down, were echoed to with the clanking of chains; I was tied down like a wild beast, and could not move but in a circle of a few feet in circumference. Now I can run, fleet as a greyhound; and leap like a young roe upon the mountains. Oh, God! (if God there be, that condescends to record the lonely beatings of an anxious heart) thou only canst tell with what delight a prisoner, just broke forth from his dungeon, hugs the blessings of new-found liberty! Sacred and indescribable moment, when man regains his rights! But lately I held my life in jeopardy, because one man was unprincipled enough to assert what he knew to be false; I was destined to suffer an early and inexorable death from the hands of others, because none of them had penetration enough to distinguish from falsehood what I uttered with the entire conviction of a full-fraught heart! Strange, that men from age to age should consent to hold their lives at the breath of another, merely that each in his turn may have a power of acting the tyrant according to law! Oh, God! give me poverty! shower upon me all the imaginary hardships of human life! I will receive them all with thankfulness. Turn me a prey to the wild beasts of the desert, so I be never again the victim of man dressed in the gore-dripping robes of authority! Suffer me at least to call life and the pursuits of life my own! Let me hold it at the mercy of elements, of the hunger of beasts or the revenge of barbarians, but not of the cold-blooded prudence of monopolists and kings! — How enviable was the enthusiasm which could thus furnish me with energy, in the midst of hunger, poverty, and universal desertion!

[...]

My thoughts wander from one idea of horror to another with incredible rapidity. I have had no sleep. I have scarcely remained in one posture for a minute together. It has been with the utmost difficulty that I have been able to command myself far enough to add a few pages to my story. But, uncertain as I am of the events of each succeeding hour, I thought it right to force myself to the performance of this task. All is not right within me. How it will terminate God knows. I sometimes fear that I shall be wholly deserted of my reason.

What — dark, mysterious, unfeeling, unrelenting tyrant! — is it come to this? When Nero and Caligula swayed the Roman sceptre, it was a fearful thing to offend these bloody rulers. The empire had already spread itself from climate to climate, and from sea to sea. If their unhappy victim fled to the rising of the sun, where the luminary of day seems to us first to ascend from the waves of the ocean, the power of the tyrant was still behind him. If he withdrew to the west, to Hesperian darkness, and the shores of barbarian Thule, still he was not safe from his gore-drenched foe. — Falkland! art thou the offspring in whom the lineaments of these tyrants are faithfully preserved? Was the world with all its climates made in vain for thy helpless unoffending victim?

Tremble!

Tyrants have trembled, surrounded with whole armies of their Janissaries! What should make thee inaccessible to my fury? — No, I will use no daggers! I will unfold a tale — ! I will show thee for what thou art to the world, and all the men that live shall confess my truth! — Didst thou imagine that I was altogether passive, a mere worm, organised to feel sensations of pain, but no emotion of resentment? Didst thou imagine that there was no danger in inflicting on me pains however great, miseries however dreadful? Didst thou believe me impotent, imbecil,[1] and idiot-like, with no understanding to contrive thy ruin, and no energy to perpetrate it?

I will tell a tale — ! The justice of the country shall hear me! The elements of nature in universal uproar shall not interrupt me! I will speak with a voice more fearful than thunder! — Why should I be supposed to speak from any dishonourable motive? I am under no prosecution now! I shall not now appear to be endeavouring to remove a criminal indictment from myself, by throwing it back on its author! — Shall I regret the ruin that will overwhelm thee! Too long have I been tender-hearted and forbearing! What benefit has ever resulted from my mistaken clemency? There is no evil thou hast scrupled to accumulate upon me! Neither will I be more scrupulous! Thou hast shown no mercy; and thou shalt receive none! — I must be calm! Bold as a lion, yet collected!

### 5. From William Beckford, *Elegant Enthusiast* (1796)

[William Beckford (1760-1844) was an eccentric writer, best known for his Gothic novel, *Vathek* (1786), and his neo-Gothic castle, Fonthill Abbey, which featured a newly built crumbling tower. *The Elegant Enthusiast*, which Beckford attributed to an aristocratic lady on

---

1 Spelling in source text.

the title page, is notable for being a mockery of novels of sensibility and thus challenging the popular form—much as both of Wollstonecraft's novellas do—and for appearing on Wollstonecraft's reading list: in a letter to Mary Hays, dated 15 September 1796, Wollstonecraft wrote, "If you are not reading the *Elegant Enthusiast* send it by Mary [Wollstonecraft's servant], and I shall soon return it" (*Letters* 364).

The passages below mock novels of sensibility for many of the features that Wollstonecraft despised in them: their obsession with romantic love, their unlikely plot developments and characterization, their ridiculously melodramatic tragic elements and their absurd tear-jerking attempts. This passage also outlines some real-life problems in the culture of sensibility that Wollstonecraft bemoaned, such as the lazy habits of "elegant" women, whose main occupation in life was to play cards and fall in love, as well as the (perhaps causal, she implies) connection between nervous debility and the ideal of the woman of sensibility (Beckford's Lucinda dies almost instantly of a nervous collapse brought on by the mere sight of stern men).]

(Beckford, William. *Modern Novel Writing, or The Elegant Enthusiast; and Interesting Emotions of Arabella Bloomville. A Rhapsodical Romance; Interspersed with Poetry. By the Right Hon. Lady Harriet Marlow.* 2 vols. London: G.G. and J. Robinson, 1796. Vol. 2. 103-08.)

As the elegant Lucinda was one morning walking upon the terrace of Lady Fairville's garden, ruminating upon her sad and hopeless destiny, she observed a youth sleeping on a bank of daiseys, fashionably attired. She stared at the sight and faintly screamed, while he, at the sound of her angelic voice sprang towards her, and folding his fond arms around her, professed himself the eternal slave of her beauty and attraction. "O!" exclaimed he with the most wild and energetic passion, "O thou mirror of superhuman excellence, thou soft sustainer of all earthly good, to every zone I will declare the ardor of that flame which now consumes my heart, thou are a divinity of the first order, a lambent fire of exquisite delight that plays upon the wings of fancy, and settles both the judgment and the wish! How beautifully fall those luxuriant tresses in soft profusion on a neck of snow, which seems as it were just tinged by the last weak blush of evening. Ha! those lips, how inconceivably tempting, those eyes how penetrating, how brilliant, how expressive — chin, nose, mouth, teeth, arms, elbows, breast and shape, how beyond all conception captivating and enchanting!" She now reclined her head upon his burning bosom, while many a dewy drop moistened her glowing cheek. Her sensibility yielded to the impression of so much tenderness and truth, she clasped him tenderly in a soft embrace and almost fainted.

There happened to be a hermitage at no great distance from the scene of action — it was made of moss, and in it was a couch for Lady Fairville to repose herself, after the fatigues of company and cards. Thither the gallant handsome youth bore the yielding Lucinda "nothing loth,"[1] and there, if we may use the words of Shakespeare, he

"Robbed her of that which naught enriched him,
And made her poor indeed."[2]

The two lovers passed several hours in this heavenly retreat, vowing eternal fidelity to each other, "And mingling soft discourse with kisses sweet."[3]

As at length, however, it became necessary for them to put a period to so interesting a tete-a-tete. Lucinda, with her accustomed prudence, reminded him that it was time to depart, and he instantly obeyed her command, but not till she had given him one balmy parting salute, and had promised to marry him the first opportunity. To which, the enamoured youth being overcome by the fineness of his sensations, could make no reply.

As Lucinda was tripping across the lawn towards the house, she unfortunately met Mr. Squares and Mr. Gifford, who were taking an *abusive* walk,

"As is their custom in an afternoon."[4]

She was shocked at the sight of these two cynics, and though she was somewhat relieved to find that Sam Slybore was not with them, yet the severity of their aspect had such an effect upon her delicate nerves, that she immediately fell sick with a bilious fever, and notwithstanding all the care of the Satirist, and the pious prayers of the Parson, before twelve o'clock on the next day, she was as dead as Julius Caesar. The following beautiful epitaph upon her was written by a learned and

---

1   From the scene in which Adam leads a similarly willing Eve to a verdurous bed in John Milton's *Paradise Lost*, Book IX, line 1039: "He led her nothing loath; flowers were the couch."

2   From Shakespeare's *Othello*, spoken by Iago about one who ruins another man's reputation: he "Robs me of that which not enriches him / And makes me poor indeed" (III, iii, 181-82).

3   From James Hammond's "Elegy XIII" (1743): "To mingle sweet Discourse with Kisses sweet" (l. 27).

4   From Shakespeare's *Hamlet* regarding the secret murder of Hamlet's father, who was poisoned, his ghost tells Hamlet, while "... Sleeping within my orchard, / My custom always in the afternoon" (I, v, 64-65).

ingenious schoolmaster of Dedham in Essex; it was composed in less than eight months, and is engraved upon her tombstone in Banbury church-yard.

### The Epitaph.

"Here lies the body of Lucinda Howard,
Who neither ugly was, nor false, nor froward;
But good and pretty, as this verse declares,
And sav'd from drowning by his Reverence Squares.
But small the 'vantage, for she scarce was *dried*,
Before she made a sad *faux pas* — and DIED.

# Appendix D: Education versus Nature: Phrenology, Associationism, and Nerve Theory

## 1. From William Perfect, *Cases of Insanity* (1785)

[William Perfect (1737-1809) represents a late-eighteenth century medical type, as his story was played out by many of the best-known doctors of his time: he took his medical training in Scotland, came to the study of nerve theory after beginning his career in other medical fields (he was a trained as a man-midwife), and he followed the early lead of George Cheyne, whose best-selling text, *The English Malady: or, A Treatise of Nervous Diseases of All Kinds, as Spleen, Vapours, Lowness of Spirits, Hypochondriacal, and Hysterical Distempers &c.* (1733), established nerve theory as the dominant approach to human health, replacing the earlier humoural system. Indeed, like Cheyne, Perfect believed bad nerves were the result of overindulgence in luxuries like rich food and excessive idleness. Yet, Perfect also revealed himself to be something of a radical in his approach to nerve theory: by classifying nervous illness as a kind of insanity—a diagnosis that Cheyne strongly repudiated—Perfect posits the disease as undesirable and demonstrates his refusal to hone his diagnoses to praise rich patients. In this way, Perfect, like Wollstonecraft, shows his opposition to the aristocratic and literary culture of sensibility associated with Cheyne in the eighteenth century.

In this volume, Perfect takes the mystery out of psychology by elucidating his methods of treatment. The fact that *Cases of Insanity* went on to be republished as *Select Cases in the Different Species of Insanity, Lunacy, or Madness, with the Modes of Practice as Adopted in the Treatment of Each* in 1787—and was later complemented by *A Remarkable Case of Madness, With the Diet and Medicines, Used in the Cure* in 1791—suggests that the volume sold so well that its audience could not have been limited to medical practitioners, a democratic approach to understanding the human body and mind that Wollstonecraft applauded in *Rights of Woman*. In the passages below, Perfect describes postpartum depression, which struck Wollstonecraft's sister Eliza; the young, beautiful, new inmate in *Maria* who sings movingly in Chapter II; and Maria herself, according to Venables' counsel in Chapter XVII (he claims that "After the birth of her child, her conduct was so strange, and a melancholy malady having afflicted one of the family, which delicacy forbade the dwelling on, it was necessary to confine her").

The text's focus on "nervous disorders," "hypochondriacal affection," and "hysteric passion," moreover, make it important to an understanding of how women's physical and mental health was defined in the period. By the late eighteenth century, the word "hypochondriacal," which formerly referred to a kind of stomach ailment accompanied by depression, began to acquire the modern signification of "hyphochondria." In *Observations on the Nature, Kinds, Causes, and Prevention of Insanity, Lunacy, or Madness* (1782-86), Thomas Arnold asserts, "In Hypochondriacal Insanity the patient is for ever in distress about his own state of health, has a variety of disagreeable, and sometimes painful feelings, to which he is ever anxiously attentive, and from which he can rarely divert his thoughts" (220). Women were more likely to be labelled "hysterical" if they showed these tendencies, however. In *Mary*, the protagonist's father seems to harbour the suspicion that her sick mother is hysterical, in the eighteenth-century use of the word: "As her mother grew imperceptibly worse and worse, her father, who did not understand such a lingering complaint, imagined his wife was only grown still more whimsical, and that if she could be prevailed on to exert herself, her health would soon be re-established" (85).]

(Perfect, William. *Cases of Insanity, the Epilepsy, Hypochondriacal Affection, Hysteric Passion, and Nervous Disorders, Successfully Treated.* Rochester: T. Fisher, [1785?]. 25-29; 73-75.)

## Case IV.

A Lady, in the 37th year of her age, of a delicate constitution, in lying-in of her second child, and about a month after her delivery, was seized with a shivering fit, succeeded by a fever, delirium, inflammation of the eyes, and watching. She was attended by Gentlemen, eminent in the medical art; by whose assistance, in about the space of three weeks, she was so far recovered as to be able to walk across the room; when, on a sudden, from a mistaken apprehension of her husband's conduct, she became anxious, irresolute, incoherently talkative, turbulent, and so mischievous, that her attendants were obliged to confine her; raving, foaming at the mouth, involuntary laughter, or loud lamentation ensued; from a pleasing, open, chearful countenance, her face was contracted to a rigidly emaciated and truly maniacal appearance; and, from a decent and delicate choice of words, her expressions bordered upon blasphemy, or vented the rankest obscenity. The general methods had been referred to, under the direction and care of a most eminent physician, by whose advice she had been four times bled, within the space of three months; blisters had been prescribed for the occiput,[1] back, and legs; a seton[2] had been fixed in her neck; to lenient purges cathartics had succeeded[3]; the gums, and fetid anti-hysterics,[4] had been administered in abundance; vomits often prescribed, and cold-bathing not omitted. All painful applications, and every method, hitherto used, had rather aggravated than lessened her complaint; and, in a state of Insanity, little short of raving, she was committed to my care in May 1773; she had then a blister[5] open on her back, and an issue in her arm; but as no good effect had ever accrued from muscular irritation, they were both suffered to dry up, and in a few days there was no discharge from either. I lodged her in a quiet, retired, darkened room, gave her magnesia, to occasionally relax the bowels; and, for the heat and quickness of pulse, two spoonsful of a neutral mixture every five or six hours, with an addition in the evening of a few drops of the paregoric elixir. In ten days the spasms abated, the febrile heats were allayed — the pulse, from near a hundred, was, at times, reduced to below eighty; when a decoction of the bark,[6] with nitre, was made use of. The intervals, from a few hours at first, were, in three weeks time, prolonged to a day, and sometimes to two; from a week to a fortnight, three weeks; and, at length, till the frenzy entirely subsided. During the continuance of this course, I suffered no one to visit or converse with her but myself and one female attendant, the relations and acquaintance being strictly enjoined from the first not to come near her. By means of the above practice, retirement, and a regimen properly adapted to her case, in November of the same year, I had happiness to restore this Lady to her worthy partner and family, and the chearful reception of a large circle of genteel acquaintance, who has experienced many anxious feelings on her deplorable situation.

[...]

---

1  "The back or posterior part of the head" (*OED*).
2  "A thread, piece of tape, or the like, drawn through a fold of skin so as to maintain an issue or opening for discharges, or drawn through a sinus or cavity to keep this from healing up" (*OED*).
3  The sense of this oddly phrased sentence seems to be: "cathartics had been prescribed to effect mild purges."
4  The *OED* defines "fetid gum" as "a pill containing Asafœtida."
5  Like setons, medical practitioners intentionally created blisters on the skin in order to encourage the expulsion of bodily fluids that they understood to be partly responsible for the patient's symptoms.
6  Peruvian bark, of which Perfect discusses his use on page 41, 42, and 100 of this text.

The Hysteric Passion; "A Disorder peculiar to the Fair Sex, differing in most cases very essentially from the Hypochondriac Affection, both in Cause and Situation."

The fits accompanying this complaint are, in general, very uncertain; in some, they will return weekly, or monthly; in others, four, five, or six times in a year, or oftener, upon any sudden commotion of the mind, or disturbance of the spirits; by fear, grief, anger, or disappointment; wind, and acrid humours, vellicating[1] the nerves of the stomach and intestines, will frequently produce the fits in women of a delicate habit, whose nervous system is naturally weak and irritable. The symptoms preceding the fits, are different in different persons; those attending them, are well known, to be a difficult respiration, and sometimes weak and easy, as if the patient was asleep, convulsed agonies of the whole body, involuntary laughter and crying, paleness of the face, coldness of the extremities, oppression, anxiety, reaching to vomit, a violent rising in the throat, and often a strong intermitting pulse. After the fit is gone off the patient frequently complains of universal soreness, pain in the head, noise in the ears, dimness of sight, the pulse becomes quicker, and more regular, and the patient either relapses into another fit, or falls asleep, and, for that time, recovers. Much more might be added, were it not almost impossible to describe and enumerate the variety of symptoms attendant on either this or the Hypochondriac disorder; for, as the sagacious Sydenham has very wisely observed: "The shapes of Proteus, or the colours of the Camelion, are not more numerous and inconsistent, than the variations of the Hypochondriac or Hysteric disease."[2]

---

1 The *OED* lists "vellicate" as a rare or obscure word, followed by this definition: "Of things: To act upon or affect so as to irritate; esp. to pluck, nip, pinch, or tear (a part of the body) by means of small or sharp points. Chiefly in old medical use with reference to the action of medicaments, sharp or acrid substances, etc., on the tissues of the body. Freq. in the 17th and 18th centuries." Perfect's use of the phrase "acrid humours" reminds us that humoural theory had not completely passed out of medical fashion even by the late eighteenth century — or, for that matter, even in a text on nerve theory, which mostly replaced it.

2 Perfect plagiarizes this passage from Robert Whytt's *Observations on the Nature, Causes, and Cure of those Disorders which have been Commonly called Nervous, Hypochondriac, or Hysteric: To Which are Prefixed Some Remarks on the Sympathy of the Nerves* (1765): "As the sagacious *Sydenham* has justly observed, that the shapes of *Proteus*, or the colours of the *chamæleon* are not more numerous and inconsistent than the variations of the hypochondriac and hysteric disease" (96; Whytt's emphases). Neither Whytt nor Perfect quote

## 2. From Johann Caspar Lavater, *Essays on Physiognomy* (1789)

[Johann Caspar Lavater (1741-1801) was the father of physiognomy, the wildly popular eighteenth-century science of studying the whole body to discover how the psychological and spiritual make-up of the subject expressed itself physically. Physiognomy is sometimes confused with the science that grew out of it, phrenology, devised by Lavater's student, Franz Joseph Gall (1758-1828), and Gall's student Johann Gaspar Spurzheim (1776-1832). However, phrenology differs in being more empirical, and in focussing more specifically on the head and less stringently on the role of the spirit in forming the outer person (Mellor 53). Lavater's science came under severe scrutiny by the turn of the nineteenth century and was almost entirely discredited thereafter.

In the last decades of the eighteenth century, however, the demand for an English translation of Lavater's works was high. In a letter entitled "Physiognomical Fragments" in *Medical and Philosophical Commentaries* (1776), Andrew Duncan writes,

> I hear that a Lady has lately undertaken a translation of it [Lavater's *Essays*]; but, whatever her abilities may be, I am almost sure, that, somehow or other, she will miscarry. There cannot be the least doubt that an English translation would succeed ...; but where is there a person to be found, who, together with sufficient knowledge, possesses both languages to such a degree as to qualify him for the work? (16)

Whoever this precocious "lady" was, she did not succeed in her task. In 1788, the English market still had not been satisfied and, according to Godwin in the *Memoirs*, Wollstonecraft began an abridgment of Lavater's *Essays on Physiognomy* (published in German in 1772) as preparation for a translation of the work from a French edition into English (65-66), a task that informed her physiognomical focus in

---

Sydenham correctly, according to my research; Sydenham writes, "A Day would scarce suffice to reckon up all the Symptoms belonging to Hysterick Diseases; so various are they, and so contrary to one another, that *Proteus* had no more Shapes, nor the *Cameleon* so great Variety of Colours" (307; Sydenham's emphases). Thomas Sydenham (1624-89), sometimes called "the English Hippocrates," was the founder of clinical medicine and epidemiology, as he pioneered the empirical method of studying patients' symptoms closely, rather than treating them on the basis of abstract speculation.

"Cave of Fancy."[1] However, Thomas Holcroft beat her to the finish line: he published a translation of the work from the original German text in 1789.

The passages below clarify a point in Lavater's theory that was particularly crucial in the late eighteenth century, which established the inaugural stages of the nature/nurture debate with respect to female character. Lavater confirms that we are, indeed, "born this way" to a certain extent, which may help to explain why Wollstonecraft seems to have reconsidered her dedication to the validity of physiognomy in the 1790s. Her devotion to the value of education in the formation of the female character reveals her own view that we can change our characters through "industry" to use Lavater's word. The passages below would prognosticate badly for women, as Wollstonecraft portrays them in *Rights of Woman*, for they would suggest that women are innately and somewhat ineluctably non-intellectual, silly, and vain.]

(Lavater, Johann Caspar. *Essays on Physiognomy; For the Promotion of the Knowledge and the Love of Mankind*. Trans. Thomas Holcroft. London: G.G.J. and J. Robinson, 1789. Vol. 1. 166-68.)

XX. On Freedom and Necessity.

My opinion, on this profound and important question, is that man is as free as the bird in the cage; he has a determinate space for action and sensation, beyond which he cannot pass. As each man has a particular circumference of body, so has he likewise a certain sphere of action. One of the unpardonable sins of Helvetius,[2] against reason and experience, is that he has assigned to education the sole power of forming, or deforming, the mind. I doubt if any philosopher of the present century has imposed any doctrine upon the world so insulting to common sense. Can it be denied that certain minds, certain frames, are by nature capable, or incapable, of certain sensation, talents, and actions?

To force a man to think and feel like me is equal to forcing him to have my exact forehead and nose; or to impart unto the eagle the slowness of the snail, and to the snail the swiftness of the eagle: yet this is the philosophy of our modern wits.

Each individual can but what he can, is but what he is. He may arrive at, but cannot exceed, a certain degree of perfection, which

---

1    See Appendix A2 for the physiognomical sections of "Cave of Fancy."
2    Claude-Adrien Helvétius (1715-71), son of the Queen of France's physician, himself a philosopher, philanthropist, and host to the *philosophes*, is best known for his devotion to physical sensation.

scourging, even to death itself, cannot make him surpass. Each man must give his own standard. We must determine what his powers are, and not imagine what the powers of another might effect in a similar situation.

When, oh! Men and brethren, children of common father, when will you begin to judge each other justly? When will you cease to require, to force, from the man of sensibility the abstraction of the cold and phlegmatic; or from the cold and phlegmatic the enthusiasm of the man of sensibility? When cease to require nectarines from an apple tree, or figs from the vine? Man is man, nor can wishes make him angel; and each man is an individual self, with as little ability to become another self as to become an angel.... A certain quantity of power is bestowed on me, which I may use, and, by use, increase by want of use, diminish, and, by misuse, totally lose. But I never can perform, with this quantity of power, what might be performed with a double portion, equally applied. Industry may make near approaches to ingenuity, and ingenuity to genius, wanting exercise, or opportunity of unfolding itself; or, rather, may seem to make these approaches: but never can industry supply total absence of genius or ingenuity. Each must remain what he is, nor can he extend or enlarge himself beyond a certain size.... Truth, physiognomy, and the voice of God, proclaim aloud to man, *Be what thou art, and become what thou canst.*

The character and countenance of every man may suffer astonishing changes; yet, only to a certain extent.

### 3. From Joseph Priestley on Hartley's Associationism (1790)

[Joseph Priestley's (1733-1804) text, *Hartley's Theory of the Human Mind,* first published in 1775, popularized David Hartley's (1705-57) theories as set forth in *Observations on Man* (1749) and made associationism most influential in psychological circles, not to mention literary ones; for example, William Wordsworth weaves associationist theory throughout the manifesto of Romanticism that is the 1800 "Preface" to the *Lyrical Ballads* and his co-author of the volume, Samuel Taylor Coleridge, went so far as to name his son "Hartley." Associationism may be summarized as the theory that all of our ideas, and our very characters, are, through the process of a kind of unconscious education, the result of the early sensations and thoughts that are connected to our original experiences of the ideas and sensations. Hartley theorized that sensation was the result of the vibration of the medullary substance in the nerves—which he thought was an invisible ether, following Sir Isaac Newton—and that memory was the faint after-affect of these vibrations, which he distinguished as "vibratiuncles." However, the "vibratiuncles" part of the theory was disavowed as unempirical even by his devotees and Priestley suppressed most of it. Although John Locke discusses associationist theory as early as 1690 in Chapter XXXIII, "Of the Association of Ideas," in *Essay Concerning Human Understanding*, Priestley's text probably provided most of Wollstonecraft's knowledge of associationism, given that Joseph Johnson published it at the time that she worked closely with him on the *Analytical Review*. Associationism's emphasis on education—the idea that we are the result of acquired experience, not identifiable with our innate characteristics—was important to her developing understanding of human character and, indeed, her hope that womankind could improve itself.]

(Priestley, J. *Hartley's Theory of the Human Mind, on the Principle of the Association of Ideas; With Essays relating to the Subject of It*. 1775. 2nd ed. London: J. Johnson, 1790. vii-ix; xi-xii; xxv-xxvii.)

Since all sensations and ideas are conveyed to the mind by means of the external senses, or more properly by the nerves belonging to them, sensations, as they exist in the brain, must be such things as are capable of being transmitted by the nerves; and since the nerves and the brain are of the same substance, the affection of a nerve during the transmission of a sensation, and the affection of the brain during the perceived presence of it, are probably the same. What sensations, or ideas, are, as they exist in the *mind*, or *sentient principle*,[1] we have no more knowledge of, than we have of the mind or sentient principle itself. And in this ignorance of ourselves, the business of philosophy will be abundantly satisfied, if we be able to point out such a probable affection of the brain, as will correspond to all the variety of sensations and ideas, and the affections of them, of which we are conscious. Ideas themselves, as they exist in the mind, may be as different from what they are in the brain, as that peculiar difference of texture (or rather, as that difference in the rays of light) which occasions difference of colour, is from the colours themselves, as we conceive of them.

Till the time of Sir Isaac Newton,[2] who first, I believe, suggested the doctrine of vibrations, it was generally supposed that an impression at the extremity of a nerve was transmitted to the brain by means of a

---

1 The sentient principle is what animates all living beings, an idea in opposition to the mechanistic view, which held that life was machine-like and required no super-added "spark," if you will, to set it in motion.

2 Sir Isaac Newton (1643-1727), English physicist, is best known for first outlining the law of gravity. He was also an astronomer (he invented the reflecting telescope), mathematician, and one of the greatest scientific minds of all time. In *Opticks: Or, A Treatise of the Reflections, Refractions, Inflections and*

*fluid* with which the nerve was filled; the nerves, for that purpose, being supposed to be tubular. But in what manner this impression was conveyed, whether in succession, by a vibratory motion of the parts of this nervous fluid, or instantaneously, there was no distinct hypothesis formed. The former supposition, however, is more consonant to the prevailing notion of this nervous fluid, as exceedingly subtle, and elastic. Still less had any tolerable hypothesis been advanced concerning the manner in which the brain is affected by this motion of the nervous fluid.

To assist the imagination, indeed, but by no means in any consistency with the notion of a nervous fluid, it had been conceived that ideas resembled characters drawn upon a *tablet;*[1] and the language in which we generally speak of ideas, and their affections, is borrowed from this hypothesis. But neither can any such *tablet* be found in the brain, nor any *style*, by which to make the characters upon it; and though some of the more simple phenomena of ideas, as their being more or less deeply *impressed*, their being *retained* a longer or a shorter time, being capable of being *revived* at pleasure, &c. may be pretty well explained by the hypothesis of such a tablet, and characters upon it, it is wholly inadequate to the explanation of other, and very remarkable phenomena of ideas, especially their mutual *association*. Besides, this hypothesis suggests nothing to explain any of the *mental operations* respecting ideas.

[...]

That sensations are transmitted to the brain in the form of vibrations is rendered very probable from the well-known phenomena of the more perfect senses, as those of seeing and hearing. That the retina is affected with a tremulous motion, in consequence of the action of the rays of light, is evident from the impression continuing some time, and dying away gradually, after the cause of the impression has been removed. It appears to me that no person can keep his eye fixed on a luminous object, and afterwards shut it, and observe how the impression goes off, and imagine that the retina was affected in any other

---

*Colours of Light* (1704), Newton surmises that there may be "Æthereal vibrating Mediums" and that "the Vibrations of one of them constitute Light," but he admits that how they can be suffused through all of the air and not retard other media "is inconceivable" (339).

1 Locke's signature theory of the mind in *An Essay Concerning Human Understanding*, in which he describes it as a *tabula rasa* ("blank slate"), which contains no innate ideas, but records all experiences as memories, like writing upon a "tablet," to use Priestley's term, and is thus formed by them.

manner than with a tremulous or a vibratory motion. And is it most probable, not to say certain, that, since the impression is actually transmitted to the brain, it must be by means of the same kind of motion by which the extremity of the nerve was affected, that is, a vibratory one? And since the *brain* itself is a continuation of the same substance with the nerves, is it not equally evident that the affection of the brain corresponding to a sensation, and consequently to an idea, is a vibratory motion of its parts?

[...]

To show the possibility of Dr. Hartley's theory of the mind, and at the same time to give such an idea of it as may be useful to those who are about to enter upon the study of it, I would observe, that all the phenomena of the mind may be reduced to the faculties of *memory*, *judgment*, the *passions*, and the *will*, to which may be added the power of *muscular motion*.

Supposing the human mind to have acquired a stock of ideas, by means of the external senses, and that these ideas have been variously associated together; so that when one of them is present, it will introduce such others as it has the nearest connection with, and relation to, nothing more seems to be necessary to explain the phenomena [sic] of *memory*. For we have no power of calling up any idea at pleasure, but only recollect such as have a connection, by means of former associations, with those that are at any time present to the mind. Thus the sight, or the idea, of any particular person, generally suggests the idea of his *name*, because they have been frequently associated together. If that fail to introduce the name, we are at a loss, and cannot recollect it at all, till some other associated circumstance help us....

In the wildest flights of *fancy*, it is probable that no single idea occurs to us but such as had a connection with some other impression or idea, previously existing in the mind; and what we call *new thoughts* are only new combinations, of old simple ideas, or decompositions of complex ones.

Judgment is nothing more than the perception of the universal concurrence, or the perfect coincidence of two ideas,.... or transferring the idea of *truth*, by association, from one proposition to another that resembles it....

When we say that any idea or circumstance excites a particular passion, it is explained by observing that certain feelings and emotions have been formerly connected with that particular idea or circumstance, which it has the power of recalling by association.

# Select Bibliography

[This list of non-electronic, English-language, scholarly sources on Wollstonecraft is restricted to the most cited and generalist works, as well as the most pertinent to a study of her fiction. See the Works Cited and Consulted in this edition for additional sources.]

## Primary Sources

Wollstonecraft, Mary. *Mary and The Wrongs of Woman.* Ed. and intro. Gary Kelly. Oxford: Oxford UP, 2007.

———. *The Complete Works of Mary Wollstonecraft.* Ed. Janet Todd and Marilyn Butler. 7 vols. London: William Pickering, 1989.

———. *A Wollstonecraft Anthology.* Ed. Janet Todd. Bloomington: Indiana UP, 1977.

———. "The Wrongs of Woman, or Maria." *Posthumous Works of the Author of A Vindication of the Rights of Woman.* 4 vols. Ed. William Godwin. London: J. Johnson, 1798. Vols. 1 and 2.

———. *A Vindication of the Rights of Woman: With Strictures on Political and Moral Subjects.* London: J. Johnson, 1792.

———. *The Female Reader; or Miscellaneous Pieces in Prose and Verse; Selected from the Best Writers, and Disposed under Proper Heads; for the Improvement of Young Women. By Mr. Cresswick, Teacher of Elocution* [Mary Wollstonecraft]. *To Which is Prefixed A Preface, Containing Some Hints on Female Education.* London: J. Johnson, 1789.

———. *Mary, A Fiction.* London: J. Johnson, 1788.

———. *Thoughts on the Education of Daughters: With Reflections on Female Conduct, in the More Important Duties of Life.* London: J. Johnson, 1787.

Wollstonecraft, Mary and Mary Shelley. *Mary; Maria; Matilda.* Ed. and intro. Janet Todd. New York: Penguin, 1992.

## Criticism

Binhammer, Katherine. "The 'Singular Propensity' of Sensibility's Extremities: Female Same-Sex Desire and the Eroticization of Pain in Late-Eighteenth-Century British Culture." *GLQ: A Journal of Lesbian and Gay Studies* 9.4 (2003): 471-98.

Blakemore, Steven. *Intertextual War: Edmund Burke and the French Revolution in the Writings of Mary Wollstonecraft, Thomas Paine, and James Mackintosh.* Rutherford: Fairleigh Dickinson UP, 1997.

Brock, Marilyn. "Desire and Fear: Feminine Abjection in the Gothic Fiction of Mary Wollstonecraft." *From Wollstonecraft to Stoker: Essays on Gothic and Victorian Sensation Fiction*. Jefferson: McFarland, 2009. 17-29.

Buss, Helen M., David Lorne Macdonald, and Anne Ruth McWhir, eds. *Mary Wollstonecraft and Mary Shelley: Writing Lives*. Waterloo: Wilfrid Laurier UP, 2001.

Butler, Lisa. "The Paradox of Effeminized Masculinity and the Crisis of Authorship." *English Studies in Canada* 31.2-3 (2005): 77-98.

Conger, Syndy McMillen. *Mary Wollstonecraft and the Language of Sensibility*. Rutherford: Fairleigh Dickinson UP, 1994.

Curran, Stuart. "Charlotte Smith, Mary Wollstonecraft, and the Romance of Real Life." *The History of British Women's Writing, 1750-1830*. Ed. and intro. Jacqueline M. Labbe. New York: Palgrave Macmillan, 2010. 194-206.

Eliot, George. "Margaret Fuller and Mary Wollstonecraft." *Enslavement and Emancipation*. Ed. and intro. Harold Bloom. New York: Bloom's Literary Criticism, 2010. 221-28.

Hodson, Jane. *Language and Revolution in Burke, Wollstonecraft, Paine, and Godwin*. Aldershot: Ashgate, 2007.

Hoeveler, Diane Long. "The Construction of the Female Gothic Posture: Wollstonecraft's *Mary* and Gothic Feminism." *Gothic Studies* 6.1 (2004): 30-44.

——. "The Tyranny of Sentimental Form: Wollstonecraft's *Mary* and the Gendering of Anxiety." *Eighteenth-Century Novel* 3 (2003): 217-41.

Johnson, Claudia L. *Equivocal Beings: Politics, Gender, and Sentimentality in the 1790s*. Chicago: U of Chicago P, 1995.

Mallinick, Daniella. "Sublime Heroism and *The Wrongs of Woman*: Passion, Reason, Agency." *European Romantic Review* 18.1 (2007): 1-27.

Manly, Susan. "Mary Wollstonecraft and Her Legacy." *History of Feminist Literary Criticism*. Ed. and intro. Gill Plain and Susan Sellers. Cambridge: Cambridge UP, 2007. 46-65.

Min, Eun Kyung. "The Rights and Wrongs of Woman: A Vindication of Mary Wollstonecraft." *Feminist Studies in English Literature* 14.2 (2006): 125-55.

O'Neill, Daniel I. *The Burke-Wollstonecraft Debate: Savagery, Civilization, and Democracy*. University Park: Penn State UP, 2007.

Peritz, Janice H. "'Necessarily Various': Body Politics and Discursive Ethics in Wollstonecraft's *The Wrongs of Woman*." *European Romantic Review* 21.2 (2010): 251-66.

Poovey, Mary. *The Proper Lady and the Woman Writer: Ideology as Style in the Works of Mary Wollstonecraft, Mary Shelley, and Jane Austen.* Chicago: U of Chicago P, 1984.

Richards, Cynthia. "The Body of Her Work, the Work of Her Body: Accounting for the Life and Death of Mary Wollstonecraft." *Eighteenth-Century Fiction* 21.4 (2009): 565-92.

Sapiro, Virginia. *A Vindication of Political Virtue: The Political Theory of Mary Wollstonecraft.* Chicago: U of Chicago P, 1992.

Swift, Simon. "Mary Wollstonecraft and the 'Reserve of Reason.'" *Studies in Romanticism* 45.1 (2006): 3-24.

Tauchert, Ashley. *Mary Wollstonecraft and the Accent of the Feminine.* New York: Palgrave, 2002.

Taylor, Barbara. *Mary Wollstonecraft and the Feminist Imagination.* Cambridge: Cambridge UP, 2003.

Todd, Janet. *Women's Friendship in Literature.* New York: Columbia UP, 1980.

Waters, Mary A. "'The First of a New Genus': Mary Wollstonecraft as a Literary Critic and Mentor to Mary Hays." *Eighteenth-Century Studies* 37.3 (2004): 415-34.

——. *British Women Writers and the Profession of Literary Criticism, 1789-1832.* Basingstoke: Palgrave Macmillan, 2004.

Weiss, Deborah. "Suffering, Sentiment, and Civilization: Pain and Politics in Mary Wollstonecraft's *Short Residence.*" *Studies in Romanticism* 45.2 (2006): 199-221.

Wilcox, Kirstin R. "Vindicating Paradoxes: Mary Wollstonecraft's 'Woman.'" *Studies in Romanticism* 48.3 (2009): 447-67.

**Biography and Correspondence**

Carlson, Julie Ann. *England's First Family of Writers: Mary Wollstonecraft, William Godwin, Mary Shelley.* Baltimore: Johns Hopkins UP, 2007.

Flexner, Eleanor. *Mary Wollstonecraft: A Biography.* New York: Coward, McCann & Geoghegan, 1972.

George, Margaret. *One Woman's "Situation": A Study of Mary Wollstonecraft.* Champaign: U of Illinois P, 1970.

Gordon, Anthony. *Mary Wollstonecraft: A New Genius.* London: Little, Brown, 2005.

Gordon, Lyndall. *Vindication: A Life of Mary Wollstonecraft.* New York: HarperCollins, 2000.

Ingpen, Roger, ed. *The Love Letters of Mary Wollstonecraft to Gilbert Imlay.* London: Hutchinson & Co., 1908.

Jacobs, Diane. *Her Own Woman: The Life of Mary Wollstonecraft.* New York: Simon & Schuster, 2001.

Jump, Harriet Devine. *Mary Wollstonecraft: Writer*. New York: Harvester Wheatsheaf, 1994.

Kelly, Gary. *Revolutionary Feminism: The Mind and Career of Mary Wollstonecraft*. New York: Palgrave Macmillan, 1996.

Lorch, Jennifer. *Mary Wollstonecraft: The Making of a Radical Feminist*. New York: St. Martin's, 1990.

Nixon, Edna. *Mary Wollstonecraft: Her Life and Times*. London: J.M. Dent, 1971.

St. Clair, William. *The Godwins and the Shelleys: The Biography of a Family*. Baltimore: Johns Hopkins UP, 1991.

Sunstein, Emily. *A Different Face: The Life of Mary Wollstonecraft*. New York: Harper and Row, 1975.

Todd, Janet. *The Collected Letters of Mary Wollstonecraft*. Ed. and intro. Janet Todd. New York: Penguin, 2003.

——. *Mary Wollstonecraft: A Revolutionary Life*. London: Weidenfeld & Nicolson, 2000.

Todd, Janet and Moira Ferguson. *Mary Wollstonecraft*. Boston: Twayne, 1984.

Tomalin, Claire. *The Life and Death of Mary Wollstonecraft*. New York: Harcourt Brace Jovanovich, 1974, 1992.

Wardle, Ralph M., ed. *Collected Letters of Mary Wollstonecraft*. Ithaca: Cornell UP, 1979.

——, ed. *Godwin and Mary: Letters of William Godwin and Mary Wollstonecraft*. London: Constable and Company, 1967.

——. *Mary Wollstonecraft: A Critical Biography*. Lawrence: U of Kansas P, 1951.

## Collections

Craciun, Adriana, ed. *A Routledge Literary Sourcebook on Mary Wollstonecraft's A Vindication of the Rights of Woman*. New York: Routledge, 2002.

Falco, Maria J., ed. *Feminist Interpretations of Mary Wollstonecraft*. University Park: Penn State UP, 1996.

Johnson, Claudia, ed. *The Cambridge Companion to Mary Wollstonecraft*. Cambridge: Cambridge UP, 2002.

## Bibliography

Todd, Janet. *Mary Wollstonecraft: An Annotated Bibliography*. New York: Garland, 1976.